"*Wolf Time* is a fascinating, rich thriller, pushing to the very edge of the genre and beyond."—Roger L. Simon

## FLETCHER SHOULD HAVE BEEN DEAD

He wasn't. The kill should have been clean. But he'd been left a cripple.

Who killed so sloppily, with so little compassion?

Not a hunter. Not a thrill-killer. Not a professional killer. A professional man-hunter would have administered the same sort of *coupe de grace* an animal hunter would have.

An amateur.

A murderous amateur out to kill Hollis Fletcher personally. How did he know? Because only an amateur could maim; only an amateur could be too inept to hunt and kill cleanly.

An amateur would leave a sign, as amateurs always must.

It was the Moon of the Wolf. The season of the hunter. And the hunt had begun.

"A compelling story of real people fueled by strong and honest emotions and an ending that made me gasp."
—Donald E. Westlake

## THE SEVENTH CARRIER SERIES
### by Peter Albano

THE SEVENTH CARRIER                    (2056, $3.95)
The original novel of this exciting, best-selling series. Imprisoned
in a cave of ice since 1941, the great carrier *Yonaga* finally breaks
free in 1983, her maddened crew of samurai determined to carry
out their orders to destroy Pearl Harbor.

THE SECOND VOYAGE OF
THE SEVENTH CARRIER                    (2104, $3.95)
The Red Chinese have launched a particle beam satellite system
into space, knocking out every modern weapons system on earth.
Not a jet or rocket can fly. Now the old carrier *Yonaga* is desperately needed because the Third World nations—with their armed
forces made of old World War II ships and planes—have suddenly become super powers. Terrorism runs rampant. Only the
*Yonaga* can save America and the Free World.

RETURN OF THE SEVENTH CARRIER         (2093, $3.95)
With the war technology of the former superpowers still crippled
by Red China's orbital defense system, a terrorist beast runs
rampant across the planet. Outarmed and outnumbered, the target of crack saboteurs and fanatical assassins, only the *Yonaga*
and its brave samurai crew stand between a Libyan madman and
his fiendish goal of global domination.

QUEST OF THE SEVENTH CARRIER          (2599, $3.95)
Power bases have shifted dramatically. Now a Libyan madman
has the upper hand, planning to crush his western enemies with
an army of millions of Arab fanatics. Only *Yonaga* and her in-
domitable samurai crew can save the besieged free world from the
devastating iron fist of the terrorist maniac. Bravely, the behe-
moth leads a rag tag armada of rusty World War Two warships
against impossible odds on a fiery sea of blood and death!

*Available wherever paperbacks are sold, or order direct from the
Publisher. Send cover price plus 50¢ per copy for mailing and
handling to Zebra Books, Dept. 3095, 475 Park Avenue South,
New York, N.Y. 10016. Residents of New York, New Jersey and
Pennsylvania must include sales tax. DO NOT SEND CASH.*

# JOE GORES

# WOLF TIME

**ZEBRA BOOKS**
**KENSINGTON PUBLISHING CORP.**

*This is a book for*
DORI
*together we pluck*
*the silver apples of the moon*
*the golden apples of the sun*

*and a hunter's farewell for*
MY DAD
*gone gentle into that good night*

Brothers shall fight and fell each other,
And sisters' sons shall kinship stain;
Hard it is on earth, with mighty whoredom;
Ax-time, sword-time, shields are sundered,
Wind-time, wolf-time, ere the world falls;
Nor ever shall men each other spare.

> Destiny speaks to Wotan;
> *Poetic Edda* on the
> ancient Vikings

# I

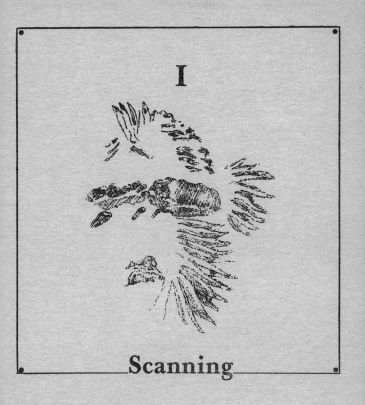

# Scanning

The hunter must know the habits and habitat and the characteristics of each animal. . . . He must know the clues revealing its nearby presence even before he sees it—tracks, calls, feces, smell, the alarm signs given by other animals.

# 1

Hollis Fletcher had thought about his own death for so long that when it came he wasn't ready. Two minutes before his own ultimate moment, he said aloud to himself, "Spooked him." The words came out as puffs of vapor on the cold northern air.

His deep-set brown eyes studied the deer's tracks. The slight drag marks of the big whitetail buck's hooves in the snow told him it had been walking and browsing; then it had scented him, or heard him, and had trotted off into the safety of the marshy squaw grass west of his cabin.

Fletcher straightened slowly from his effortless crouch. He was a rangy man of fifty-six, with a taut nut-brown face his dead wife had delighted in calling Mongol despite his Scots, Welsh, and German blood. Attila the Hun, sweeping down out of the eastern steppe.

"Long gone," he said aloud of the buck, a habit of many men voluntarily alone in an isolated environment.

There was no sun but he was sweating under his parka. When he'd heard the deer's startled whistle he'd started trotting to cut it off; the spoor here showed he'd never had a chance.

Fletcher left the tracks to crunch through the knee-deep snow, away from the leafless yellow birches rimming the marshland into which the buck had run. Vagrant snowflakes drifted down as he wound his familiar way through the raspberry and prickly ash, low brushy undergrowth which had sprung up after a lightning fire had cleared out the white pine and balsam a few years earlier.

He stopped dead, totally surprised. Here his buck had cut back out of the safety of the squaw grass into the open burn again. Not really panicked, since it had been bringing the hind foot down at each step almost exactly into the print left by the front, but stepping right along.

Fletcher looked west, toward the brushy crown of low hills visible beyond the frozen marshland. A hunter moving up there, some last momentary ray of sunlight glinting off a rifle bolt? It would have been enough to spook a buck already spooked by Fletcher. But dusk was only thirty minutes away, and what sort of hunter relished a Minnesota winter night in the open?

Anyway, there would be no surprising this buck tonight. A bow hunter has to make a totally silent upwind stalk to within ten yards of his prey to be sure of a disabling shot, and when just a kid, Fletcher had learned never to leave cripples.

Not leaving cripples was practical as well as honorable when you depended on the bow for your meat. Even now he scored his arrows with the lightning-flash grooves Old Charlie had taught him. Blood from the wounded animal ran down the grooves, dripped on the ground, and made a trackable blood spoor.

As always, he stopped by a fire-blasted spruce a thousand feet down the burn from his cabin to take off his mittens and unstep his bow. The woods, utterly silent under the fitfully drifting snow, had grown somber and still in the few minutes since he'd cut the deer's trail.

He stepped away from the tree and was struck a terrific blow just beneath the left knee. It spun him partway around. He went down on his back. Some cold unshocked center of his brain registered the rifle crack a full second after he'd been hit.

Some damn-fool hunter up there on the crown of the hill, desperate enough for a deer to convince himself Fletcher was it. Had snapped one off, connected, and probably was sighting in again. Fletcher started waving his arms in the air above him.

*"Hey!"* he yelled. *"Don't shoot!"*

His voice wouldn't carry, but those semaphore arms, through the scope, would register as something human that . . .

His left hand was jerked sideways by a hurtling slug. A spray of salty blood splattered across his lips. He rolled desperately toward the bushes, the splintered ends of bone that protruded through his ripped pant leg grating without pain. That wasn't random shooting.

A giant fist shattered his chest. He felt bone and muscle and meat give inward, snap, tear. Blood and bile filled his mouth. Maybe he screamed. He didn't know. He didn't know anything at all.


The killer released his half-breath and let his cheek rest against the stock of the 30.06 Remington as against a lover's thigh. He'd *done* it! Ten minutes earlier, watching a deer trot out into the swamp, he'd known he couldn't pull the trigger when it was a man in his scope. Then it was, and he did.

And 367 yards away, Fletcher lay dead.

As the killer stood up, vomit welled into his throat. He finished wet-eyed and wheezing, rubbed his face red with a mittenful of snow. He kicked groundfall over the mess he'd made.

The scope had shown him the mortal chest shot puff out Fletcher's parka, but even so he fixed the spruce against the fading light before he lit a cigarette with tremoring hands. Had to make sure, like sticking your tongue into the socket where your tooth had been before the dentist got it. He trudged down toward the fire-blackened tree he'd used for sighting in the rifle on a bright fall afternoon two months earlier.

"In the fuckin' infantry you pump your fuckin' carbine dry, sonny, and whadda ya got? A bundle of old clothes fallin' in a fuckin' ditch. But a *sniper,* sonny . . ." The profanity was suddenly gone. "He *sees* his man. The guy's right there,

13

you'd recognize him in a crowd. Only there ain't no crowd. Just that face, right in front of you, the eyes goin' scairt as the chest cavity takes the slug. . . ."

Ex-sergeant Jerzy Hrock, exorcising his memories as a sniper in Korea, shot glass dwarfed by his massive hand.

The killer's mittened hands dropped his cigarette as he tripped over a tussock of dirt and ice-stiffened grass and almost fell. He fumbled out another and stumbled on, now through gray dead timothy and squaw grass beaten by wind and snow into barbed-wire entanglements. It was nearly dark. He was sweating under his new down coat.

The Sarge had sweated while his flat black eyes strained to see the dead faces he could never forget.

"Takes a certain sort of feller to remember them faces afterward, sonny—and still go out and do it all over again."

Once through the squaw-grass entanglements, the killer angled across the burn toward the blackened spruce. He knew he wasn't that sort of feller. Once was all he could take.

More snow here, easier footing, but he crunched loudly through the crust at each step. He stopped. Listened to the forest. Nothing. Nerves. He went on. Spooky here at night, so different from that bright fall afternoon when he'd sighted in the rifle. He hadn't thought he'd ever really do it. Not then. Then, merely an exercise in what-ifs.

His flashlight danced around the dead spruce in sudden panic. No Fletcher. But he'd *used* the spitzer rounds culled from the Sarge's drunken maunderings, and . . .

He grunted aloud in relief at sight of the facedown huddle under a light talcum of fresh snow. Not as bad as imagination had suggested, not if you didn't look too hard at the startling white bone glinting below the left knee. Just Sergeant Hrock's infantryman sprawl of old clothes with a massive dark soaking underneath, an arm thrust out and the face buried in the snow.

The killer turned away, crunching through the snow crust. Only a dead man sprawled with such easy abandon.

The dead man stirred.

Some corner of his dead brain had heard the crunching footsteps, the heavy breathing, had counseled the organism to stillness. Had heard, eventually, the retreat of human sound, had taken from the open receptor ears the normal night noises. Grumpy quill-rattle of porcupine caught out of hibernation by the unexpected early snow. Bright birdlike trill of deer mouse over a treasure of dried berries. Farther off, perhaps in the cedars toward the cabin, the boastful thumping of a snowshoe rabbit.

But no further man sounds sent their alarm signals to that small watchful animal center in the dead brain. And so the dead man stirred and groaned.

Other centers of the brain, fighting through the protective drug of shock, began accepting sensory data again. The head turned slightly from the cup its exhalations had melted in the snow. The eyes opened to the grayness of night. Pain began.

"Holy Jesus," said Fletcher.

But pain meant at least parts of him were still alive. Most of the bleeding, after the first massive outpourings, had stopped. Winter cold to thank for that. He remembered the first shot hitting his leg. His eyes traveled down his sleeve to the abbreviated finger stumps his eyes could pick out even in near-darkness. He remembered that one too.

But not the third. Where had it gone in? Chest, most likely, because that was where a hunter would aim. And because of the amount of blood-soaked snow beneath him.

Had to know. Had studied the field-aid manuals a man living alone in the woods was a fool not to study. He edged his undamaged right arm out from beneath him. Gingerly exploring fingers touched raw meat, then bone. Recoiled. Rats of panic gnawed his brain. Even though the bullet had struck at enough of an angle to glance off rather than penetrate, splintered ends of bone thrust out through the skin meant an open fracture.

He made the gloveless hand keep on exploring. The slug

had glanced away, right enough, but bone splinters could have been driven into . . . He caught his breath — very gently. His probing fingers had slipped off a rib right into the chest cavity that cradled his precious lungs. A cough, a deep breath, almost anything could collapse those lungs by compressing them with air drawn in from outside through the open wound.

How could he make the chest airtight, or reasonably so, without compresses or bandages? Mitten. He'd removed them to unstep the bow, they ought to still be in his pockets. If he could get at one of them, then get his belt off somehow, maybe he could use the belt to cinch the mitten against the wound.

He moved to reach for a mitten, and died again.


Cochrane. Main Street was heaped with the dirty snow of the winter's first storm. Wilmot's General Store already had handmade crepe-paper Christmas cutouts in the windows. Snow wind-splattered against the movie-theater marquee obscured last summer's faded cinematic delights. Two miles beyond town was the airfield, but on impulse the killer jerked over the wheel where Dutch's Tavern spilled gold out across the dirty churned sidewalk snow. He put on his yellow ski glasses before going in.

Seven men studded the bar, two fat farm wives overflowed one of the hardwood booths in the rear. A fishbowl full of hard-boiled eggs with a hand-lettered sign: "2 for 4 bits."

"What'll it be, mister?"

Don't call. They'd remember a call in here. "Bar whiskey," the killer said.

No hunters here, maybe a mistake to come. Only heavy, hard farmers, callused hands holding glasses of draft beer and shots of whiskey as they would hold hymn books on Sunday mornings. Bib overalls, dirty denim jackets washed pale and thin at the elbows, heavy mud- and manure-caked rubbers over their boots.

"Thanks." God, how he'd needed that. "One more,

please."

"Get your deer?"

The killer shifted uncertainly and caught a fragment of himself in the back-bar mirror. Golden glasses, neat goatee, and trim dark mustache. He settled for a wry shrug as an answer.

"Yo, she's slow this year," agreed the thick-bodied bartender, taking the shrug for communication. He dried his hairy-backed hands automatically on his wet-grayed apron. "Bad corn crop 'cause of the drought, so they're hangin' back in them white oaks eatin' acorns."

"Drought, hell!" snapped one of the farmers. Fierce voice, face like a rock garden. "Them bastard deer's the reason the crop's bad in the fust place."

The killer smiled idiotically, mumbled, and headed toward the men's room and pay phone by the rear entrance. Had to keep from panicking, had to avoid conversations, had to remember they couldn't see into his mind. Hold on to the one central fact: Fletcher was dead.


Fletcher coughed. Twisted to his left in the snow and yelled as bone needles stitched his flesh. But the pain had brought him back.

In the manual, neat and orderly as a geographer's terrain report, it said to forcibly exhale, clap on the bandage tightly to make the wound airtight, and cinch in place. Reality: moaning, grunting, pausing when the blackness rose in front of his eyes. But even so, managing one-handed to pull the belt from around his waist with little jerks which overcame inertial friction. Now, the mitt . . .


His dad took off his mitt and went down on one knee to feel some deer tracks just beyond the bobwire fence. He gently blew the drift snow out of the heart-shaped depressions.

17

"Couple days old. Haven't seen a man-track yet, not a fresh one."

"Isn't that good?" asked the boy.

"Not for our kind of hunting. Not enough hunters moving around to stir 'em up and send 'em to us. Stand up on that stump and don't move any more than you have to. I'll go down to the point by the cornfield and swing back through the hardwoods."

With awkward sawing motions, Fletcher got the wide leather belt worked higher and higher up his trunk, until it was around his chest. Then he fumbled the mitten into place over the wound, slid the free end of the belt through the buckle with his right hand, ready to jerk it tight and cinch it in place. He hesitated, like that frozen moment between the strike of the smallmouth bass and your reflexive jerk to set the hook.

Just then the shots started, dull and muffled and far off, like the strokes of a distant hammer. The boy counted thirteen. His father paused halfway through the bobwire fence.

"Got him out in the open away from the trees," he said. "There'll be blood on the snow tonight."

Fletcher exhaled and jerked the belt tight. Coughed blood out onto the snow and fainted.

# 2

Nicole Ross stepped back under the hot shower to wash soap from her left armpit. She absently massaged a breast while soaping under the other arm. A girl in college once had remarked admiringly that she had large soft breasts; only later had Nicole realized it had been an oblique pass. At the time it had just seemed a distressing invasion of privacy.

Eight years and several severe dieting regimes ago. The breasts were firm and shapely now and she meant to keep them that way.

Nicole emerged from the shower dripping and wrapped herself in a huge terry-cloth towel. Steam came with her from the stall to make the mirror image of her heart-shaped, sensual face as ghostly as a double-exposed negative. From the bedroom came the ringing of the phone. As she opened the door, her stepdaughter's preadolescent bellow came up the stairs.

*"Nicole, it's Daddy. He says—"*

*"Tell him I'll get it up here."*

Crossing to the new two-line phone on the walnut nightstand beside the queen-size bed, she left two very distinct wet footprints on the rug, two paler ones, then none.

David's voice on their new unlisted line was slightly accusing. "I called twenty minutes ago, nobody answered."

"You know Robbie's got basketball and that I pick up Katie from ballet on Fridays." Her eyes went to the bedside clock. "Don't tell me you're still at the office."

"Jarvis wanted a list for a personal mailing."

Kent Jarvis, present aide to the governor, perhaps soon-to-be campaign manager. Tonight's gathering might very well decide whether there would be a campaign to manage. She realized that David was still talking.

". . . not even here himself, just called and said he wants a list of key out-of-staters not necessarily active in politics or not even necessarily Democrats, but who the governor's—"

"David, what are you babbling about? We're supposed to be out damn near to Wayzata in under two hours, and this snow—"

"I'll be home as quick as I can."

"Thanks a lot." But he already had hung up. Damn him.

But at least now he owed her one. And she wouldn't have to be picking out his shirt and assuring him, yes, that tie was perfect, just when she was trying to get dressed herself.

She caught sight of herself in the full-length mirror on the back of the door, jerked the floppy transparent shower cap from her head, and shook out golden hair, stylist-fresh, so it gleamed in the glass. She had a short nose and kissable lips and liquid blue intelligent eyes, features that gave her face the beauty of the actress she'd once expected to be, before her excellent mind won out over her insecurities and pushed her away from theater into the mechanics of politics.

She slid down the towel, sucked in her stomach, and cupped her breasts with her hands. Not bad for twenty-nine. In their first year of marriage, David had kissed her breasts each morning before she put on her bra.

Gary, lowering his mouth to her breasts as she lay nude on the motel-room bed . . .

She jerked her hands away abruptly, grabbed up her bra, and began fitting it on. Dressing hurriedly, she felt cold.


The cold made Fletcher's teeth chatter. Each shiver sent a lance of pain through him. Concentrate. Somehow he had to tie the shattered leg to the good one so he could crawl. He ran his good hand lightly over the chest wound. The

— 20

makeshift bandage seemed firmly in place.

Cold. So cold.

So crawl. Cabin. Phone. Survive. How far? A thousand feet? Count 'em. Count your blessings. All the wounds are on the same side of your body, so you *can* crawl. He began groping around in the snow for the bowstring. Could he slip it off the end of the bow so he could tie the legs together, thus using the good one as a splint? His good hand worked at it, sweat starting to pour off him. He could picture all of the activity filling the pleural cavity with bright arterial blood.

Don't think about it.

Think about the squirrel, cussing out the boy from the branch above the stump where he stood. His overshoes already had made the stump-top snow hard-packed and slippery. The squirrel was a gray, jerking his fine bushy tail with each outraged chit.

"You shut up," the boy told him. A big soggy meteor of white fell from a branch and soughed into the groundfall beneath,

jerking Fletcher awake, blowing and spitting, in his terror of smothering.

Lying on his right side, he drew up his good leg and got the other on top of it, positioning the part below the fracture with his hand. He wrapped the bowstring awkwardly around both of them, sobbing with frustration before he finally got it tied.

Courage, man; the hurt cannot be much.

No, 'tis not so deep as a well, nor so wide as a church door. 'Tis but a thousand feet.

Dig with the good elbow, heave with the good shoulder, shove with the good foot. How far? A foot. A thousand such efforts. Dear God.

He raised his head to look around the darkened woods, in case this was his last time to see it. A huge gaunt timber wolf was standing two yards away from him. It had its head slightly lowered, was staring at him with golden eyes. Ears pricked forward. The wolf! *The* wolf! His . . . What? His totem? As the bear had been Old Charlie's?

No wolves in this part of Minnesota. Hallucination? Was he dying? He shook his head and looked again. No wolf.

One . . . two . . . three . . .

Heave. Rest. Heave rest. Heaverest. Heaverestheaverest Shoulder cramping: 122. Elbow numb.

Feet numb. Wriggle the toes. Tap on them with the rifle butt to awaken circulation. A single remote shot cracked the silent cold, a voice hallooed, thin with distance.

The brush right in front of him exploded with a huge buck as he jerked up the gun clawing off the safety pointing jerk jerk jerk, a single flow of unthought motion which nevertheless seemed slow-motion.

"You guys are the picture of slow-motion," bellowed Hodge. Fletch and Gary were both hung-over and hating the boxcar of lumber they had to unload. Slow-motion.

One-ninety-nine . . . 2.0.0 . . . 2 . . 0 . . 1 . . .

After much consideration, Nicole chose the Ted Lapidus wool dress she had bought in a little shop at the Munich Hilton on their European trip last summer. A delicate ecru color, very feminine, fashionable and modest while making the most of her excellent figure. If the governor decided to run, she and David were going to run with him. Going all the way.

She had gone all the way with David on their first date; he was six years older than she and had pleaded like an adolescent.

The phone rang again. She went around the bed and

picked up to hear her husband's voice.

"Katie, tell Nicole that—"

"I'm on the line, David."

She heard her stepdaughter hang up the kitchen extension. David said, "We'd better meet at Olaf's house. By the time I'd get over there to pick you up we'd be so—"

"Can't you get anything right?"

This time she beat him to it, slamming down the phone before he was off. She sat down on the edge of the bed and gave a deep sigh. One little uptight lady tonight, using the same tone with her husband she sometimes used with Katie. But Katie was only nine. She felt a moment of repressed panic. Was *this* the horse she was going to ride to Washington? And she hadn't seen Gary since they'd broken it off, and . . .

Slow down. David had been a damned good account exec, and he was good at his job for the governor. It was just that Jarvis drove everyone too hard out of his own ambition. And when they talked, Gary would carry off their meeting with perfect aplomb, as he did everything. He was a great governor; if he ran and made it, he would be a great president. Washington! A different world. A different *planet*. She felt a slight fluttery tension in her groin, as if she were starting sexual foreplay.

Before they started loving they would turn on a tiny brass lamp with a ten-watt bulb which cast a warm dim golden glow over their bedroom. They liked to see each other, see in the other's face when the moment was at hand, even though Fletcher would have recognized Terry's body among a thousand others by texture alone. The long elegance of thigh and cupped elegance of hip, the unexpected sensuality of flesh beneath finishing-school-taught severity of dress.

Four-twenty-five . . . 426 . . . 427 . . .

Too painful. His face sagged into the snow. He wanted to sleep. Perchance to dream? To weep. Loss. Terry. Blood.

"I . . . must have missed him."

"Buck fever," said his father.

But even so, they pushed through the twisted cover at the foot of the rise.

"Well well well." His father's voice was very soft.

Painfully, turtle-slow, he turned his head to look back at the way he'd crawled. By the newly risen moon he could see the splotches on the snow like the blood clots on the drag trail where the big buck had gone down forty-one years before.

"First blood," said his father in that same soft voice.

The buck lay at the end of the twelve-foot drag trail he'd made going down. His head was wedged up against the bole of a burr oak and his eyes already were glazing. The protruding tongue was flecked with blood. The antlers were shiny scimitars of polished bone, the nose was black and damp and beautiful against the snow.

The most beautiful buck in the world. His buck.

*His* blood spoor. No atheists in foxholes—or on drag trails. So pray. Prey. He was prey. Someone had shot him, had left him a cripple.

He'd once tracked a deer two and a half days because Old Charlie had said real hunters didn't leave cripples. It finally had quit bleeding, had plain outwalked him, might even have found another deeryard in which to shelter. He'd always told himself that it had, and had been able to replenish the heavy expenditure of energy so it hadn't subsequently starved.

He'd come to love that deer more than most of the people he'd known in his lifetime.

Five-fifty-six . . . 557 . . .

Balance lost blood against lost time as strength ebbed and energy expenditure rose. As his beloved deer had done to beat him. As he would do to beat . . . Who?

24

Some stupid hunter who made cripples.

Get to the cabin. Why? Couldn't remember. And why had he dragged the stringless bow along when . . . Latch. Use it to push up the latch. Made to keep out porcupines after salt, but it could keep out a man who had only enough strength to crawl. Last year the porkies had eaten the handle off his ax for the salt.

Six-eighty-nine . . . 690 . . . 691 . . .

If he raised his head, would he see the cabin ahead under the cold moonlight? He raised his head. A few yards ahead of him in the path, facing him, tongue lolling, ears pricked, was his great gray wolf again. Must have been pacing him, stalking beside him as he . . .

No. Not real. He blinked. Cabin ahead? Or just making aimless loops and arabesques under the bushes like a mole under forest leaf mold?

Once when he'd been standing in the forest the leaves had started rustling under his feet. Then they had begun to heave and roil. And suddenly a long black furry blob with little gleaming white pegs in the middle of it had erupted and rolled right over his boots. There it had split in half and scuttled in opposite directions, and he had realized that it had been two moles locked in combat. Blind creatures, fighting blindly. Had they run into each other at the edge of their respective territories? Or was it over a female?

Seven-twenty-five . . . 726 . . .

If he made it, he'd call Victor at home in case he was bleeding inside. Call Victor how? How could he . . .

The bow. Use it to knock the phone off the table. Victor would call an ambulance to meet him at the cabin.

If Fletcher survived as far as the cabin.


As he stepped into the cabin of the Beechcraft from the foothold on the wing, the killer heard the wail of a distant siren. He clamped his safety belt. Beside him, the lanky redheaded pilot pushed the auto-starter. The prop began swishing and the motor chuffed and caught.

The siren. The sheriff had found the body, he was caught.

The engine roared, the plane bumped forward. The killer shut his eyes. When he opened them again, he could look down and see an ambulance racing below them as they banked across the road, gaining altitude for the flight back to Minneapolis. An ambulance, not the police. He leaned back and shut his eyes again. The mild-eyed pilot, who thought the killer was a Minneapolis realtor closing a very confidential off-season recreational land deal in Cochrane, said something into his microphone and adjusted their course.

Ambulance. Going to pick up a woman in labor, perhaps. The killer liked that idea. A life to replace the life he had . . . that had ended. The eternal circle: birth, life, death. He opened his eyes and sat up. It was finished.

"There any coffee?"

"The thermos," said the pilot. "Help yourself."

Suppose they did find Fletcher's body after next spring's thaw, he would be just another statistic of the previous fall's hunting season. So many deer, so many farmers' cows because they were brown like deer, so many hunters because they had forgotten to wear enough red. All part of the hunt.

# 3

At fifty-three, Governor Garrett Westergard was strikingly handsome and knew it. Not with the Kennedy-politician handsomeness which for years had been the measure against which a man's presidential ambitions could be judged; handsome, rather, in the way retired pro quarterbacks who went into sportscasting were handsome. The mood was right for his style in national politics. The public had become wary of charismatic men with chaotic personal lives; his now was exemplary.

"Gentlemen," he said, thrusting his sharp glance at the seventy-five handpicked fat cats shoehorned under the massive oak beams of Olaf Gavle's suburban Minneapolis living room, "you all know me and what I stand for. Voter recognition in Minnesota is not my problem. But outside the farm belt, not many people really know who I am. Unfortunately, outside the farm belt even fewer care."

He paused for the laugh with a sense of timing honed during the quarter-century since he'd won a state-assembly seat while still in law school. The men in this million-dollar house overlooking Lake Minnetonka had known him, or who he was, during most of those years. Yet tonight they'd paid or pledged fifteen hundred dollars apiece to listen to him. Their reactions during the next hour could make or break him on the national political scene.

"You all know the statistics on my reelection for governor three years ago. Sixty-three percent of the vote — a margin of four hundred twenty thousand votes over my

Republican opponent. Proof, I believe, that I can stir the electorate."

He paused for Gavle's carefully rehearsed question. They had been forwards together on the University of Minnesota hockey team in '53 and '54, and in '56 had played on the U.S. Olympic team that had beaten the Russians at Cortina d'Ampezzo.

"We don't doubt your ability to get votes, Mr. Governor. But I think most of us in this room would like to know what sort of timetable we can expect if you decide to run."

"If I'm to be established as a serious contender, then I'm going to have to enter the New Hampshire primary in February as well as the Iowa caucus in January. Which gives us less than three months to prepare."

"Well, Gary, would you plan to win in New Hampshire?"

Another carefully spontaneous question, this from Le-Clerc, state chairman of the Democrat Farmer-Labor party. Fritz Mondale had put LeClerc's organization on the national political map many years before, and he obviously was hoping that Westergard could make the Mondale lightning strike twice in Minnesota.

"Do well in it, Honore. Iowa's a farm state, we can expect a good showing there, but New Hampshire is Yankee — and the first national primary. It will get publicity disproportionate to the delegate votes. There are twenty thousand registered Democrats in that state, and we're going to have to contact ninety-five percent of them to make a good showing."

Gavle fed him the final prepared question. "Isn't that going to take a lot of money and a lot of personal commitment by a great many people, Mr. Governor?"

"That's why we're here tonight, Olaf," said Westergard. "The voters of New Hampshire are blue-collar-conservative and the media have labeled me a 'liberal' due to my progressive programs here in Minnesota. So I'm going to

28

have to appeal to that fabled Yankee independence of mind. Edith and I are going to do a lot of personal campaigning—in stores, in shopping malls, at beano games and beauty parlors and shoe factories."

He leaned toward them, deepening and roughening his voice as if making a summation for a jury. In a sense, he was.

"I can give you dedication. I can give you the physical stamina for a year-long campaign. What I need is money. A television campaign fund to create national voter awareness of what Garrett Westergard will stand for as President of the United States of America. . . ."


Almost the first person Nicole saw when she got to the party was Westergard. It was as if her eyes had pierced the throng like Superman's X-ray vision to pick him out from all the others. He looked solid and devilishly handsome in the midnight-blue three-piece suit that she had picked out for him on a shopping foray his wife had known nothing about.

Just seeing him again after all these months, her heart leapt up. But that was done, gone, ended. She turned away very deliberately—almost into the arms of Edith Westergard, who reminded her, as always, of a plump-breasted chickadee. If chickadees weighed a pound apiece, her father said, they would rule the world. Edith had been a U of M cheerleader in the early fifties, and retained that open-faced sparkle and ruthless energy.

"Nicole! We don't see enough of you since you left the governor's office." She embraced and released Nicole quickly, her head cocked, birdlike. She was a little overweight, just comfortable, with bright eyes and a snub nose and determined mouth. "I suppose David is parking the car . . ."

"I'm meeting him here. Some report for Jarvis."

She was never totally sure Edith Westergard hadn't

29

known about or suspected her onetime affair with Gary; and she also knew that Edith's surface friendliness concealed a will of iron.

"That darn Kent! He pushes everyone so hard! Sometimes I think I'd be glad if Gary decided not to run after all."

No way, lady, thought Nicole as she followed Edith toward the kitchen. You want it as much as he does, maybe more. You'd bleed plenty if he quit.


"It doesn't look like there was much bleeding, doctor."

"He crawled a good ways to the cabin. I'd put the loss from his leg alone at close to a liter, half of it acutely."

It had to have been that big Canuck played center ice for Duluth, thought Fletcher. He'd boarded Fletcher with a really vicious cross-body check, so the third period had been played out with concussion ringing in his ears. Not serious enough to put him here—that padded interior over his head sure was the inside of an ambulance. What went on?

Fletcher tried to sit up to ask, but the lights of an oncoming car swelled and burst against the curved overhead and were gone like soap bubbles; and so was he.

"He's passed out again, doctor. . ."


Nicole was on her second margarita and her third Swedish-meatball canapé, and was thinking that the huge heaps of *crudités* to feed the guests were about as tasteful as the floral arrangements at a gangster's funeral, when she felt a heavy hand on her backside. It curved around her buttock so the fingers could expertly seek the cleft through the thick material of her skirt.

She also caught a whiff of cigar smoke and turned, suppressing her urge to pitch her drink into Jarvis' grinning face. He was stocky and powerful and hairy, with crisp black hair and eyes as blue as her own.

"Practicing up, Kent?" she asked dryly.

"Dreaming the impossible dream."

"Just remember that it is."

"For some but not for all, right, sweetie?"

He grinned and very deliberately patted her bottom again, then slid away into the crowd; he had the wide back and thick neck of a man who spent six hours a week on the Nautilus machine. She watched him transfer his ever-present cigar from one hand to the other so he could slip an arm around the waist of a bosomy blonde with creamy Scandinavian skin.

Probably he'd have the little fool in bed before the night was over; he'd made a pass at Nicole the first time they'd met. She'd never responded to his advances in any way, but a few months later he'd hired David anyway as the governor's head speech writer. Had that perhaps been at Gary's bidding, so that when their affair ended, there would be no recriminations or messiness on her part?

If so, they'd gotten excellent value: David was damned good at what he did. But so was Jarvis. His breezy manner made him an easy man to underestimate. For David's future, she had to remember that Jarvis was as smart and ambitious as they came.

She snagged a soggy Ritz cracker with some sort of meat paste on it from a passing tray and wandered through the crowd, catching snippets of conversation.

"Rigatoni *puttanesca*—whore's pasta. Because it took only a few minutes to make if the girls were busy."

She knew that was not the correct explanation for the name, but in mixed company it was certainly better than the real one. She slipped past the burst of laughter and picked up on the discussion of some artist whose work was appearing in a local downtown gallery.

". . . best modern painter of our generation. Her colors burn your eyes like Gauguin's used to."

Didn't Gauguin's still? she thought, then realized that

31

one could hear either conversation in New York or Los Angeles without changing a word. Was that what moved men like Gary, an urge to harness that energy for change and direct it to the proper channels? Or to what they considered proper channels?

She found herself flanked by two of the governor's aides, pollster Hastings Crandall and media consultant Pete Quarles. Quarles, drink in hand as usual, was a chubby, friendly man of about twenty-five. He sort of dealt with the press on a day-to-day basis, but his main function had become the handing out of eight-by-ten glossies of the governor to the press and other interested parties.

"Hey, Nicole, great to see you again!" he exclaimed. She realized he had—to use his own favorite expression— dipped his beak a few too many times this evening. He had slopped some of his drink on his jacket, and there was a smear of ash on his tie. "Coming back to work for the Guv again?"

"I know when I'm well off." She smiled.

"Why *did* you leave so abruptly?" asked Crandall.

He was a year younger than Quarles, but light-years older than he in intelligence, drive, and ambition. A darkly good-looking man, rather like Montgomery Clift in his younger days, clean-cut, seemingly rather full of himself; but Nicole knew from experience it was foolish to underestimate him on that account. He wore a dark, conservative Brooks Brothers suit, and even in this throng his shoes wore a high gloss as if ready for inspection. His influence with the governor had started to wane with the arrival of Jarvis, and he didn't like it.

"I got tired of answering phones," she said lightly.

"We sure could use you to organize the office. Jarvis is so damned slapdash . . ." The light of inspiration entered his eyes. "Why don't I mention it to the governor? Part-time—"

"One member of the family on staff at a time is

32

enough. And speaking of David . . ."

"Haven't seen him," said Quarles cheerfully. "I know that Jarvis's here, but—"

"Yes, I ran into good old Kent," said Nicole. "Quite literally. If you see David, send him my way, will you?"

She extricated herself and wandered through the crowd. It had been rather a shock to see them, and to realize that she envied them still being in the middle of it. Especially now, when Gary might announce for the presidency at any time.

Then they were face-to-face in the middle of the throng. The very meeting she had wanted to avoid unless she had David at her side—and where was he when she needed him?

"Nicole! How wonderful to see you!"

Westergard embraced her and kissed the air beside her cheek, just as quickly releasing her. He was wearing his politician's face, for which she was grateful, right here in front of God and everybody.

"You too, Gary," she said gravely. "And congratulations on tonight. I heard it went splendidly."

He nodded, his face now warm. He lowered his voice slightly. "It's been so long, Nicole . . ."

"Seven months—"

"Seems like a year."

"—and ten days."

His face changed again; he looked as if he were about to say something she really didn't want to hear. But then the light died in his eyes and the politician's smile appeared again.

"You look wonderful. Wife and mother obviously agrees with you. But we miss you, Nicole." He leaned closer to add in a soft voice, "*I* miss you—Nikki."

"Don't you think you've given up the right to use that name when you . . ." Then, seeing Edith Westergard approaching through the crowd, she broke off to say, "I've got a missing husband *somewhere* around here." In a

33

slightly raised voice she added, "Have you seen David yet, Edith?"

"No, I haven't." Edith hooked her arm proprietarily through that of her husband. "But in this throng . . ."

"I'd better go find him before the boys all start talking politics again."

She smiled at them both and moved away into the anonymity of the crowd. It seemed to her that every sentence they had exchanged had been fraught with hidden perils, but they had negotiated that white water without incident. She realized that she was getting headachy. She had quit smoking yet again, and was being given a nicotine overload from the thick bluish haze.

Damn him, so late she'd had to get the station wagon back out of the garage to come here, and then not here when she needed him to take her mind off the meeting with Gary . . .

David bobbed up beside her, taking her hand and squeezing it hard enough for her to feel the cold pressure of his wedding band against her palm.

"*Damn,* am I glad to see you, honey."

He sounded so actually glad that she forgot momentarily that she was sore at him for not getting home to pick her up. She felt almost grateful, in fact, for having Gary driven from her mind.

"Did you get your report finished?"

"Yeah, and then Jarvis never even got back to the office to see it, can you believe?"

He looked very young and handsome and virile, with his full lips, upturned Irish nose, high forehead, and curly hair. His dark eyes roved the room restlessly.

"Some fanny-bumper, huh? Did Jarvis make it yet?"

"Yes. And it was my fanny he was trying to bump. Last seen wearing a blonde with her brains in her blouse."

David hadn't been listening, as usual. "I'd better get over there to help decide the fate of the nation."

She watched him push through the crowd toward the

picture windows overlooking the lake, where, as she had suspected, Westergard, LeClerc, and Gavle were now holding an impromptu postmortem on the political part of the evening. She saw Jarvis drifting that way, abandoning his blonde for ambition. Crandall and Quarles also were threading their way through the throng toward power and decision.

Motion without movement, men without meaning, she thought, surprising herself with the bitterness of her reaction. Suddenly she was impatient to leave; she would just go, and let David make their good-byes. She had survived her first meeting with Gary since their affair had ended; that was the main thing.

But as she moved toward the foyer to reclaim her coat, she was struck by a very vivid image of Gary making love to her in "their" motel room. She forced her mind back to her husband and his lovemaking. He was conventional and hard-driving in bed, a good lover except that sometimes she had to strain for orgasm so hard she could feel it in her buttocks and the backs of her thighs the next day.

When they got home tonight, perhaps. Yes. That would drive the images of Gary from her consciousness. Deliberately, she summoned sexual images of David, planning their lovemaking with clinical detachment.

# 4

The voice said with clinical detachment, "It carried away the inferior genicular branch of the popliteal artery and vein, the biceps femoris tendon, part of the gastrocnemius muscle, and some of the head of the fibula."

"Will he lose his leg, doctor?"

Lose his leg? Just a damned minute here!

Fletcher tried to rear up on the stretcher to tell them they had it all wrong, the Canuck had high-sticked him in the head, not the leg, but then something solid thunked him below the knee and his leg folded under him and his hands waved in the air and there was a final far rifle crack and . . .

What a headache. That damned Canuck.

Edith appeared in the doorway in a shapeless flannel nightgown with tiny flowers on it, and a green chenille robe that had seen better nights. But she'd grown up in these northern winters and it was now winter again, so even though most houses were no longer winter-cold in Minnesota, seduction could wait for spring.

"Gary, it's after midnight."

Westergard crossed his study quickly to her, moving like a man twenty years younger. He was still dressed in the pants and vest of the conservative blue three-piecer he'd worn to meet the backers. He took her face in both his hands and kissed her on the lips. It was she who finally broke the embrace.

"Sometimes I wonder why you do it, sweetheart."

He began walking up and down the room. "Like Hillary on Everest, maybe—because it's there." He looked over at her. His sleeves were rolled up and his tie was pulled awry. He looked very handsome. "We've got a shot, Edith. A real shot."

"And after?" she asked almost warily.

"Let's worry about before, first. I haven't had the job yet that could kill me. I doubt this one will."


After Edith had gone up to bed, Westergard poured himself a modest snifter of cognac at the sideboard and poked up the fire Lawson had laid while they'd been out. Sparks showered up the chimney. The white-oak logs snapped and crackled. He started pacing the room again.

All right, then, *let's* worry about before.

In his memo of over a year ago, Jarvis had outlined the moves Westergard was going to have to make if he wanted to be president, and Westergard had been making them: trying to establish a national image; reading the New York *Times* and the Washington *Post* daily; developing national files which emphasized the important primary states; selecting someone to devise a complete budget for the campaign; and hiring David Ross as head speech writer early so that Ross would have time to research pertinent issues of the day.

Then, unexpectedly, last April:

Heavy rain falling but the lights not yet lit in the private office with its dark hardwood paneling, a room which once had represented the furthest reach of his ambitions. Westergard was tipped back in the heavy leather swivel chair he would take to Washington with him if he made it, one size-eleven shoe cocked on the edge of his desk. Drink in hand, he was staring out between the drapes at the endless spears of rain. Relishing what that morning's Harris poll had shown.

*Dominant dark-horse position.*

Starting the previous year from nothing, and then, that April morning, *dominant dark-horse position* in the presidential pre-poll. Some mildly celebratory drinks had been drunk, and his tongue and mind had been loosened just enough to say it.

"The presidency. *The presidency of the United States.*" He closed his big right hand into a fist. "Right here. And out there a man who could, if he wanted to . . ." And he had opened his fist and let the presidency slip away through his fingers forever. "Like that."

He'd also let Fletcher's name slip out, though of course not the reason why Fletcher was dangerous—no one would ever know that except him and Fletch, friend of his young manhood—whom, however, he hadn't seen in almost forty years. Not since that drunken night . . .

He thrust the thought away. He'd been uneasy that he had mentioned Fletch's name. It had smacked of Henry Plantagenet's hasty words about *his* boyhood friend, Becket, who had stood in the way of *his* ambitions:

*What a pack of fools and cowards I have nourished in my house, that not one of them will avenge me of this upstart clerk!*

Not that Fletch knowingly stood in his way as Becket had Henry's, but the parallel was close enough so that when he'd been told quietly tonight that Fletcher was dead, he'd had a horrible few moments—Henry, after all, had been obliged by underlings who hadn't understood it was only a voiced wish, not a command.

Thank God Fletch's death had been only a hunting accident, plain and simple; but he'd still been enough of a moral coward to have heaved a secret sigh of relief that Nicole had already left before he could offer his condolences. Odd, now he thought of it, that she'd left the party when she did. Almost right after they'd spoken. But there was no way, really, she could have learned of her father's death. . . .

His mind turned from the unpleasant thoughts to his meeting with Nicole. Somehow he'd been able to control

38

his feelings, or at least the expression of them. Maybe he was becoming a politician, finally, in fact as well as in name.

Westergard carefully poured another thimbleful of cognac. He'd wished her father dead back in April, unthinkingly, and now, in November, dead her father was. He'd known she and Fletch had been pretty well estranged since Terry's death five years before, but even so, after his execrable slip that April day, he'd never again returned to Nicole's bed. Perhaps, in some odd way, that had marked the start of his serious bid for the presidency.

He should be ashamed that tonight, when he'd been assured it had been only an accident, he'd felt only relief untinged with sorrow at Fletcher's death. But he wasn't.


Fletcher, feeling more dead than alive, had one completely lucid moment on the operating table just before the anesthetic started to take effect. The trouble was, he couldn't speak, only listen.

"The bullet was probably tumbling as it went through the clothing, so it struck and exited obliquely." Victor's voice. He felt something icy along his left side. "See? Fragmented the seventh rib, caused intercostal muscle damage and some bleeding. Couple hundred cc's, I'd guess, mostly internal."

"No lung penetration, doctor?"

"None at all. His mitten-bandage was a thing of beauty."


For the first time in his thirty-six years, Kent Jarvis was having some penetration problems of his own. Hell, you knew it happened to other guys, you made locker-room jokes about it, but when it was *you* sitting on the edge of the bed with a limp noodle . . .

Usually just looking at a pair of milkmaid tits like those the blonde was exposing carelessly above the covers would have had him stiff as a ski pole. She turned chilly blue eyes toward him.

"Is this where I'm supposed to say, 'Hey, it's okay, you're tired, you have a lot on your mind'?"

"I'm really sorry, Kristin, what else can I say? It's never happened to me before. I . . ."

She ground out the cigarette and threw back the covers and got out of bed. Rounded hips, strong thighs, a blonde all the way. He'd spotted her in the statehouse typing pool earlier in the week, and had cut her expertly from the herd at Olaf Gavle's house. And then this.

"You sure know how to make a girl feel good, Kent."

"Hey, I didn't mean . . . I'm really sorry . . ."

She pulled pale blue frilly panties up over the blonde pubic redoubt he'd been unable to breach, then drew her dress down over her head and looked at him as she smoothed it over her hips. Her face softened. In a few years she would be heavy and bovine, but right now she was peaches and cream.

"I'm sorry too. I thought this was going to be . . ." She paused and shrugged. "Maybe you *are* just tired." She crossed to the chair and picked up her coat and purse. Her cold gaze made him aware of his impotent nakedness, but he wouldn't give her the satisfaction of getting back under the covers. She turned to him. "I'll get a cab. See you around."

He nodded and lit a cigar as he watched her go out. Cold air rushed in as she shut the door behind her. Shit. He'd have to find a way to get her fired without her knowing it had come from him. He didn't want her talking to the other girls about tonight. But he couldn't really be blamed for this failure, could he? Not after what he'd been through today.

He sighed and stood up and went into the bathroom to urinate before getting dressed and vacating the room himself. At least it was still good for that.

Nicole had brushed her teeth first and was in bed under the covers, listening to David's scrub-splash scrub-splash.

"It's only three days to Thanksgiving," she called.

He appeared in the doorway, toothbrush in hand, wearing the white pajamas with red hearts she had given him as a joke, but which had become his shorthand suggestion that they make love. She'd made sure, when they'd shared a nightcap downstairs before coming up to bed, that the thought was in his mind. She needed his lovemaking right now; Gary was still strong in her memories and emotions.

"So? It's three days to Thanksgiving."

"I was wondering if I should call my father and ask him down for dinner."

He stood there unmoving for a moment, backlit, then shrugged. "Every Thanksgiving, Christmas, and Easter you ask him down. Every Thanksgiving, Christmas, and Easter he says no."

"So, offer anyway and share in the thanks."

He shook his head and turned back into the bathroom, and despite her own sexual needs right then, she thought angrily: That's it for you, buster. But when he got into bed he was trembling, apparently with the cold, and so she let him hold her. Then one thing led to another, until suddenly he was on top of her, holding her down and ramming it into her.

Crude, almost bestial. Sometimes that turned her on, but not tonight. Tonight she had seen Gary. Gary, who was a tender lover, a thoughtful one, sharing the pleasure between them until pleasure became delight became ecstasy became—

And she was going off like a rocket, so suddenly, so vividly, even though unsummoned, had Gary become real for her. In those moments of abandon it was he, not David, who was inside her. For this time, at least, David had ceased to exist for her.

# 5

Fletcher couldn't be sure how many foot-square tiles covered the ceiling of his hospital room, let alone how many little dots there were in each tile. They seemed to shift and change. His mother, when she'd had a fever, always had seen little people walking along the molding around the tops of the sickroom walls. She had found them horrible, but they had never seemed so from her descriptions.

When he was feverish, he remembered forgotten lyrics:

> *It was midnight on the ocean*
> *Not a streetcar was in sight*
> *I stepped into a drugstore*
> *To get myself a light.*

What he found horrible was his tiredness—and his thirst. He craned around the unknown room for something to drink and realized he had an intravenous feed going into the back of his right hand, with a little white mesh tube drawn up over the hand to hold it in place. If it had sequins it would be like the one glove that pop singer wore—Michael Jackson, that was it.

He moved his head again, looking up and to his right, and saw various plastic bags and bottles hung upside down on a metal stand beside the bed, dripping into the I.V. tube. Fifty-six years old and it was the first time he'd ever had an I.V. going into him. Not bad. Only other time in his adult life he'd been in the hospital overnight had been twenty-five years ago in Kisumu, Kenya. Slipped disk. Land-Rover spine; they'd called it there.

He realized, with a wave of what would have been nausea if he hadn't been so tired and thirsty, that where his left hand was supposed to be there was instead a massive oblong of bandage and tape. He sang aloud:

> *"The man behind the counter*
> *Was a woman old and gray,*
> *Who used to peddle shoestrings*
> *On the road to Mandalay."*

The ugly face of Victor Kroonquist, M.D., general practitioner for Cochrane, came into focus beyond the bandage. Fletcher raised what was supposed to be his hand in what was supposed to be a greeting, but Victor took it as a question.

"I was afraid you'd ask that," he said cheerfully.

He unfolded his arms and came erect from the doorframe against which he had been leaning.

"You lost two fingers, the fourth and the fifth counting from the thumb. The cold arrested the bleeding, so mainly we just bandaged them up. Once they heal, we'll oversew with a flap of your own skin and you'll have a couple of cute little movable stumps. You aren't feeling any pain at the moment because we're doing an I.V. morphine drip among a lot of other goodies."

Fourth finger, counting from the thumb, was the ring finger. The plain gold band Terry had put on that finger thirty-one years ago had never been off—until now. He had a sudden quasi-hysterical urge to laugh. The ring wasn't off the finger. The finger was off Fletcher.

He made a very slow and uncoordinated beckoning motion with the bandage that was supposed to be a hand. Victor approached the bed almost cautiously. Fletcher gestured him closer yet. Victor bent to hear the wounded man's first words.

"Christ, you're ugly," Fletcher whispered huskily.

Victor reared back to tower above him, six-six of skinny outraged Scandinavian. "The patient took a turn for the worse," he snorted. "The physician smothered him with a pillow."

He turned and stalked majestically from the room. Out in the hallway he gave a single great bark of laughter, but Fletcher had already gone back to sleep.

But he woke repeatedly through the night, sweating and disoriented, and understood a little of his mother's terror at the diminutive fever-induced men. His hallucinations, morphine-induced, were fragmented, distorted, self-frustrating shards of dreams. There was Terry's dear face — only her nose was broken and flattened against her face so that it seemed to have a bulbous tip, like that of a punch-drunk fighter or like that of the actor who had played Robert Shaw's bodyguard in *The Sting*.

Then it was Rusty, the beloved Irish water spaniel of his youthful duck-hunting days. The dog's head, front, and rear quarters were fine. But his trunk — backbone, belly, and chest — were in the shape of a square-sided U, so the belly and chest, the bottom of the U, were only inches from the ground.

Another dream was of open pages of a book he needed desperately to read, because it was the book of his life. But when he approached to scan the story told there, the letters dissolved into new groups which spelled nothing and which he knew were not in any known language of man. When any of the fragments was long enough to start developing a plot, it immediately turned back upon itself, action canceling action, vista canceling vista, so everything unraveled and became vague and meaningless.

The next morning he asked to be taken off the morphine. Pain was preferable to the sweating nightmare of hallucination.

Fletcher proved to be an ideal convalescent, apart from a sudden and unforeseen pneumonia which nearly killed him.

Two weeks later, he was still alive and knew exactly how many tiles there were in the ceiling. He knew exactly how many tiny perforations there were in each tile. He was working on being able to tell individual tiles apart when the door opened and his daughter Nicole came into the room. Kroonquist towered behind her, his face full of benevolent evil.

"I thought she ought to know, Fletch."

Nicole sat down beside the bed. Light from the window nimbused one side of her head with white light. His hunter's eye cataloged her loveliness, so different from her mother's more austere beauty, as it would note the unbelievable Technicolor flash of a wood duck through somber autumn woods. He was surprised at the thought; all of the trouble after Terry's death should have made seeing Nicole in poetic terms beyond him.

"We almost lost him," said Kroonquist with a dreadful relish. "He developed broncho-pneumonia from exposure, and it was nip and tuck for a while—if you'll pardon the expression. But now . . ." His big bony hand clomp-clomped against Fletcher's mid-thigh cast. He chuckled. "Healthy as a horse."

He nodded to Nicole and drifted silently from the room, a gaunt gray wolf melting into snow-splattered winter timber. Nicole was holding her hands in her lap like a schoolgirl, knees primly together. Again, it should have irritated him to see Terry's posture on his daughter, who was anything but demure and had been pure hell in those first few years after her mother's death; but he found himself genuinely moved by her visit.

He surprised himself further by saying, "I didn't know you were a blonde."

"This year. David likes it."

"How is David?"

"Working too hard now that the governor's announced." Her mind didn't seem to be on David. "Why didn't you let us know?"

He waved an arm. "All creature comforts cared for."

"And paid for?" When he had come to Cochrane, he had put the Minneapolis house into Nicole's name, so whenever she got the chance she liked to fuss about his finances.

"I'll poach Victor a deer a year for life. Hunting and trapping *are* what I do, and barter still prevails in Cochrane."

Nicole fiddled with her purse. She was wearing a full-length quilted down coat with a turn-up collar that probably was the latest fashion.

"Dad, what happened? Really?"

"It was late, the light was failing, some deer hunter could shoot better than he could see. That's all there is to it."

She was almost frowning with the intensity of her attention. "Will there be . . ." She paused. "Will you be . . ."

"Victor hasn't seen fit to enlighten me yet." Before she could respond, he added, "How are Katie the Kat and Robbie?"

"They wanted to come along when Victor called this morning." Anger thickened her voice. "Almost two weeks after it happened . . ."

She came around to the head of the bed to kiss him gravely on the forehead, as she had done as a child on her way to bed. He felt again that unexpected rush of warmth for her. He closed his eyes so she would not see the tears rise up in them.

"Dad, if there's anything . . ."

He shook his head quickly. "I'll be out in another week."

"Then you'll come down for Christmas. Stay a few days." She took a card from her purse and scribbled on the back of it. "Here's our new unlisted number—the kids always have the other one tied up, and David wants to be able to reach me when he calls from the office now that the governor's in the race. . . ."

"I can't be sure," he said evasively. She stuck the card between the pages of his current book, the recent definitive collection of Hemingway's short stories. "The doctor—"

"Will say anything you want him to say."

"He called you when I didn't want him to."

She laughed suddenly, darkly. " 'I am all the daughters of

46

my father's house, And all the brothers too,' Victor remembered that even if you didn't."

Until her third year in college, when she had abruptly switched into political science, Nicole had planned to be an actress, still did a lot of little theater, and had a quote for every occasion.

"You know what I mean. Driving up here . . ."

"I keep wishing I hadn't let David talk me out of asking you down for Thanksgiving. I wouldn't have gotten you, and would have called the hospital, and would have known."

"No harm done."

After she had kissed him again and departed, without the promise of a Christmas visit, Victor trotted back into the room a little sideways, like a wary fox. He went to the window and peered out into the cold sunshine. The light glinted coldly off the stethoscope calipered around his neck.

"Full moon in ten days," Fletcher told him. "Want to go out poaching rabbits if we have the snow?"

"Christmas in ten days and she's expecting you there for it, Fletch." Fletcher didn't respond, so Victor turned from the window to stare at him shrewdly. "You're not going to be up to all-night hedgerow-hopping for quite a while."

Fletcher pushed himself to a more upright position with his arms and good leg. The nurse had to rub lotion daily on the points of his shoulder blades to prevent friction burns from the sheets.

"It's that time, is it?"

Victor nodded. Light at his back, thought Fletcher, so his face won't give anything away.

"There's some good news and some bad news, Fletch. The good news is that you don't have a tipped uterus. The bad news is that some unmannerly bugger shot you three times. The fingers you know about. Since it wasn't thumb and forefinger, that problem is more cosmetic than medical. Slight loss of dexterity, of course — and they will take several months to heal totally."

Fletcher nodded. "What else?"

"We've been removing the drain in your leg gradually as

47

the tissue knits and the possibility of infection lessens. It all was set back ten days by your pneumonia. Because the head of the bone was fractured, we've had to insert the tendon just below the damaged area. Once the cast comes off, you can control the speed of recovery to some extent by how hard you're willing to work at it. But . . ."

He hesitated. Fletcher gestured impatiently with his good hand.

"You'll walk with a limp. No way around it, even when you're totally healed. You've got to live with that."

"Okay," said Fletcher, "let's have Big Casino."

"The chest wound. It healed clean, no infection. No penetration of the lung. You ever hear of the phenomenon called 'splinting'?"

"No."

"The inability to take a really good deep breath because of pain in the chest wall." He took an unconsciously deep breath, released it. "You won't be running down any more deer, Fletch. Not now, not ever."

Fletcher did not immediately respond; he was staring straight ahead. Victor was fidgeting like a lanky-legged heron dithering about the upwind approach of a canoe it could see but couldn't scent. Fletcher finally turned his head slightly to stare at his friend.

"If I'd been shot down in Minneapolis," he said, "there might have been a doctor around to treat me."

Victor grinned his beautifully ugly grin. "But you've got to admit you can't beat the price." He sobered again. "One other thing, Fletch."

Fletcher waited. They'd been friends almost from the day he'd arrived in Cochrane, bought the acreage a few miles north of town accessible only by a logging road and not even that after heavy winter snows or spring-melt floods, and had sliced his calf with his ax while starting to build his cabin.

"Why haven't you wanted me to notify the sheriff of the shooting?"

"Because it was a hunting accident."

"Three shots. That's a man persistent in his error."

After Victor had departed, Fletcher thought: What else was there to believe? That someone had deliberately tried to kill him? That made no sense at all. Most of his adult life had been spent as an engineer, building bridges and roads in remote areas of the world—now considered as more curse than blessing by the environmentalists, but still, not anything to be killed for. Besides, it had been over five years since his last professional engineering contract.

Gone three months, six months, a year at a time, homing back to Terry between jobs . . . She'd been buried a week when they finally got word to him that she was dead. He'd come back to an empty house and an angry daughter. She wouldn't speak to him for almost two years because she blamed him for not being there at the end.

He hadn't spent a whole lot of time with Terry down through the years, yet on her death had discovered how deeply rooted his sense of life and future had been in her existence. In a very real way his life had ended with the accident which had taken hers. He no longer found much to live for, but because he'd seen so many living things fight too hard to stay alive, blindly, against incredible pain, he somehow could not choose to die by his own hand.

Nevertheless, guilt over her death had made it impossible to continue in his profession. But flat-out retirement in his early fifties had been equally impossible. He'd gone with his lifetime distaste for, or at least indifference to, mankind in general, and had taken up professionally the amateur avocation of his youth: hunting and trapping for a sketchy living.

For five years it had been enough. And it meant that he now was a man of few friends and no enemies, not any at all. Just not a man to anger anyone, be in anyone's way, threaten anyone. Not a man anyone could conceivably want dead.

How about someone who just wanted to shoot somebody? It made sense in a way. Up here in the woods, thrill-kill

49

someone, his body was found, it was just a hunting accident. He'd survived, but no use to tell the sheriff about it. The sheriff could never find out who did it anyway.

Fletcher's trouble with that reconstruction was that he'd been shot because he'd ignored the big buck's warning signs about someone in . . . His mind strained to recover facts, once known about the shooting, now gone with the protective haze of shock. Someone up . . . Hell, it was truly gone.

But he *had* ignored that uneasiness, and because he'd ignored it, he now was a cripple, with a limp and splinting when he took a deep breath. Why hadn't the assailant, after checking out his kill, made sure with a final bullet to the brain? Because the killer was squeamish? Because that would have given the shooting away as deliberate murder?

But wouldn't a thrill-killer have just wandered around, pretending to hunt deer, until he chanced upon a lone hunter? Sure. Then just blow him away and walk away. End of story.

But this killer had lain in ambush four hundred yards away as if sure his prey would pass that way. Something turned over in Fletcher's mind, like the flash of silver when a big northern swirls lazily under the edge of the lily pad in pursuit of your plug.

*Lain in ambush.* How did he know that? How did he know it was four hundred yards? Because . . . Hell, he couldn't remember. But for the sake of argument, accept it as somehow given. A shot at four hundred yards would be taking a terrible chance. The shooter could miss, he could just cripple, the victim might even return his fire . . .

Unless . . .

Unless you were sighted in for four hundred yards. Unless you had a steady rest and a clear field of fire. Unless you were *certain* that your prey eventually would pass that way. Unless it was a *scoped* shot.

All of which was sheer nonsense.

Wasn't it?

# 6

Jarvis was still talking when David Ross covertly checked his watch and swallowed a yawn before it reached his face. Three hours going over and over the same core of material, like the machines that wound golf balls he had seen on a public-TV documentary. Almost none of it relevant, if he could believe Nicole's acerbic comments whenever he told her of these weekly strategy meetings that the governor seemed to rely on so heavily.

She had called earlier, no message, and he hadn't been able to reach her since. He looked back at Jarvis. He wished he knew what was bothering the man. It damned sure was going to affect Ross's future one way or another, and he'd like to know how.

"We're not talking about image, for Chrissake," raged Jarvis. During the working day he ran to three-piece suits with the coats off and vests unbuttoned, the inevitable dollar cigar in his fist. "We're talking about substance."

"Substance doesn't do you any good if nobody knows about it." It was Nicole's line, as most of Ross's best remarks were.

"Meaning what, for Chrissake?"

"Meaning it's mid-December, we've announced, we have to file for New Hampshire by Christmas and for Illinois three days later. Meaning we project the liberal good-guy image, but we don't have any *depth* to the projection."

Westergard again entered the fray on Jarvis' side.

"I think my record speaks to that. I overhauled this state's property- and income-tax schedules to benefit the working poor and the elderly. I rechanneled tax revenues to local gov-

51

ernments. Housing, family farms . . . In national terms, this adds up to one hell of a domestic record if I do say so myself."

"New Hampshire is the place where front-runners throw a shoe," said Ross, "and dark horses come from behind. We want to be that dark horse, so we have to—"

"We can show the Guv knows the problems of the cities, the economy, taxes, and the working poor," said Jarvis, warming to his own prose. "He's taken a public, open stand on AIDS and the need for supplying government-funded condoms to the queers and clean needles to the dopers to help stem the tide of the disease." Without a trace of irony, he threw his arms wide and exclaimed, "Jesus, what else do we need?"

Ross thought: Government-funded condoms—now, there's a sturdy plank to walk when we get to the old domestic platform.

"The man," young Hastings Crandall was intoning rather pompously, "who today has revitalized state government and who tomorrow will revitalize the federal bureaucracy."

"Reagan already pushed those buttons," snapped Ross, "and Carter before him. What if the red phone rings?"

"The governor served as a member of the Executive Committee of the Democratic National Committee. Firsthand knowledge of foreign affairs and national defense. He's been to China and Russia. During the hostage crisis in Lebanon he was a behind-the-scenes negotiator who—"

"How many people outside the Democratic National Committee know those things?" interrupted Ross.

"Dammit!" burst out Westergard. "My record speaks—"

"To *whom?* My whole point is that we have to spend a hell of a lot of money between now and New Hampshire to make sure everyone *knows* your record. *Then,* through your speeches, I can make it speak for itself. . . ."

It had been dark for three hours when Nicole pushed the electronic garage-door opener as she turned into their block. It would be so good to get home; she felt fatigued in her bones. How would David react to Dad being in the hospital? The few times the two men had gotten together, they'd not had too much to talk about. But who did have much to talk about with her father? That hour in his hospital room, she had felt closer to him than at any time since her college days.

As she heel-toed off her snow boots inside the back door, she called, "Hey! I'm home! Is anybody?" Where *was* David? It was nearly seven o'clock.

Then she remembered: Katie was having an overnight at a friend's house, Robbie would still be at basketball practice. She went through to the living room switching on lights, and was pouring herself out a can of pre-mixed margarita when lights swept across the front of the house. She heard the garage door open while she was in the kitchen getting ice.

David came into the living room shedding his overcoat.

"I could use one of those," he said. "A hell of a day."

She pecked him on the cheek as she opened another can of margaritas. "I called, but you were out to lunch."

"And I got nobody when I tried to get you back. Christmas shopping?"

She gave him his drink and sank down on the couch with a sigh and shut her eyes. She shook her head briefly. "I've driven over three hundred miles round trip on icy roads today, and I'm bushed."

"Over three hundred mi—"

"Cochrane."

Ross paused with his drink halfway to his lips. "I don't understand."

"That doctor friend of Dad's up in Cochrane called. Dad's in the hospital."

Ross almost dropped his drink. "You're father's—"

"In the hospital. Apparently some damn fool shot him a couple of weeks ago, thinking he was a deer."

"What? How? Who . . ."

Ross was spluttering. Seeing the stunned look on his face, she stood up and put her drink on top of the piano and went to him, touched by the depth of his reaction.

"He's okay, David, honest."

Ross nodded and sat down slowly on the arm of the couch. He began, "Yeah, but . . . *shot!* A hunting accident, or . . ."

She felt unexpected tears sting her eyes, remembering how wan and hollow-eyed her father had looked in the hospital bed. He had always been dark as an Indian. She resolutely picked up her drink and instead of answering David, said, "It was the doctor who called, not him. Never him. He almost died of pneumonia—exposure from crawling some incredible distance back to the cabin after he was shot. . . ."

Ross blew out a long breath; he still looked shaken. She went right on.

"I guess I never realized how much he loved Mom until today, when I saw him lying there, and understood that he'd buried himself up there in the north woods because he felt guilty about being out of the country when she died." She sighed. "Me acting like a shit at the time couldn't have helped much, either."

Seeing David was still shaken, she put her arm around his shoulders.

"C'mon out in the kitchen with me, I'll tell you all about it while I make spaghetti." She set down her drink on the piano again, told it, "I'll want more out of you later," and headed for the kitchen, saying over her shoulder, "I asked Dad down for Christmas."

Ross stopped to fire down his drink and grab another can. He followed her, saying, "The more the merrier."


Victor stopped the Chrysler and turned off the motor, thunk, thunk, kethunk. Without chains they wouldn't have made it this far in along the logging trace from the quarter-section road.

Fletcher reached for the door handle. "Your timing needs adjustment."

"Just so it runs," said Victor. "You know I think you're a damned fool to come back out here so soon."

"This is where I live. This is where I'm going to have to get used to it."

"Do I detect a note of self-pity?"

"Detect what you please."

Victor threw up his hands. "Fletch, you're impossible."

Fletcher grunted and stepped gingerly out into the cold morning sunshine. It was going to be a bitch in the snow with the cast on, but he wasn't going to admit that to Victor. He balanced awkwardly on his good leg and the walking stick Victor fortunately had insisted upon.

"I don't have to say thanks."

Victor chuckled. "Just pay your bill."

"A six-point buck every Christmas."

"*This* Christmas is at your daughter's house down in the Cities. I mean that, Fletch — as a doctor *and* as a friend."

Fletcher grunted again and closed the door firmly and plowed his uneven way through the calf-deep snow, unconsciously reading the sign that told him who had been by during his absence. Hundreds of birds, dozens of rabbits and squirrels, two . . . no, three whitetails, a *wolverine*, for God's sake, maybe just as lucky he wasn't trapping this season, they could strip a whole string of traps and never get touched . . .

Victor, who had his window rolled down, called out behind him, "You know our phone number."

Fletcher waved without turning, Victor already assigned to the past, and went around the corner to the unlocked door. Amazing how he had wanted to be here in his own cabin, alone, like a wounded animal lying up until it either knits or dies.

He leaned against the wall just inside the open door, his heart pounding wildly from even that negligible exertion. There was a catch in his side. His leg ached dully under the cast. His finger-stumps itched under the bandages.

The bastard should have killed him.

He hobbled over to the through-the-wall wood box, relying on the birch walking stick more than he liked to admit. Luckily, he'd filled the box shortly before he'd been shot, enough big oak splits to keep him going until he was better able to get around. He dragged one out with his good hand, carried it over to the fireplace and dropped it on the hearth he'd laid himself, stone upon stone.

He'd read somewhere that a man never totally recovered from a professional beating because his edge was gone. Was Fletcher's edge gone? Something essential he needed to be him? Not even the loss of Terry had done that; her death just had stolen his joy, his belief that there was something benevolent in the design of the universe.

He hobbled over to the door, opened it, stepped out, and overbalanced, so he kept himself from falling only by ramming the tip of his stick between the peeled logs of the cabin wall. His breath came in white puffs. Small white puffs. Splinting.

Bastard.

Would he ever be able to walk by that fire-blasted spruce down the burn without cringing inside?

Would he ever again walk at all with his former assurance?

*Do I detect a note of self-pity?*

*Detect what you please.*

He stepped back into the cabin, thoroughly chilled, and slammed the door. Got more wood from the box, log by painful log, lit a burner on the propane stove, and put on a kettle to boil for tea. Chilled a few minutes before, he was now sweating from moving around the cabin. Or from weakness. Still had to lay the fire, open some cans, drink some tea, and . . .

And what?

Other years, by this time he'd had his trap string laid out and had started the year's harvest of pelts: fox and the occasional mink or marten unwary enough to be taken. But not this year. This year . . .

His kettle started to shriek. He lurched to his feet, lost his balance, sprawled across the table. It tipped, dumped him on the floor with a crash. He lay there assessing; all that hurt was his elbow from hitting the floor. If he'd chipped that . . .

Do I detect a note of self-pity?

He levered himself to his feet through a complicated series of maneuvers with cane, chair, and table, then hobbled over to get the kettle off the burner and turn off the propane. He poured steaming water over the Red Rose bags in the ceramic teapot, which still held water despite the dark crack down one side. He'd also broken a triangular chip out of the lid and had epoxied it back in, because Terry had loved the pot and it was one of her few intimate possessions he still had left.

While the tea steeped he checked the larder. Store bread, still fresh—probably enough preservatives to make it last until spring. Eggs. Slab of bacon.

The kitchen of the West Newton shack was warm and heavy with frying bacon. The boy pumped icy water into the gray-and-white enamel hand basin in the sink and tried to work up a lather with the rock-hard water. He splashed soap-grayed water over his face and groped blindly for a towel.

"Here."

His father, standing by the kerosene stove with a spatula in one hand, flipped a towel around his shoulders.

"Whew, that's cold!" exclaimed the boy.

Early duck-hunting mornings his dad cooked in his long-john top with the sleeves pushed back so the boy could see the ridges of muscle work in his forearms as he broke eggs into the bacon fat and shook on salt. Each time the pan would spit hot grease onto his wrist he would jump and exclaim, "Ouch, son of a bitch, anyway," with no heat in his voice.

"Don't just stand there, boy. Eat your food."

They ate at the zinc-covered cupboard, bacon and eggs fried black and Post Toasties and steaming coffee in thick white mugs. Blackened toast made in the frying pan and flipped high in the air when the first side was done, with his dad never missing it, not ever.

By the time Fletcher had eaten, store bread and cold baked beans right out of the can, his awkwardly laid fire had caught and was drawing properly. He dragged up his big easy chair, the only article of furniture he'd brought away from Terry's death, and sat staring into the flames.

Well, he was back and settled in and able to care for himself. Maybe tomorrow he'd do something really tough, like walking partway down the burn and back.

Talk about your heroism.

# 7

Actually it was seventeen days, and Christmas had come and gone, before Fletcher took his first walk down the burn. In between, he had gone down to Nicole's for the holiday on the spur of the moment, after telling himself he wouldn't. What did one get? Neckties? Dresses? Toys? Books? A sweater? An air rifle? Terry had always done the present-buying.

He'd settled for gift certificates all around, purchased on Christmas Eve at a glittering Hennepin Avenue department store after the bus ride to Minneapolis. He had planned on spending the night in a hotel, but had made the mistake of calling Nicole to tell her he'd decided to come after all.

"You're in town." She made it a statement. "I'll be there in half an hour."

He'd limped into the front room for squeals and hugs from Katie—she loved it that he called her Katie the Kat—and a wave of the hand and half-turned head from Robbie, who at eleven had decided a man didn't get involved in undue displays of emotion. The full-size reproduction of a Vermeer cavalier over the fireplace gave him an unexpected wrench; it had been a wedding present from Terry's brother thirty-one years ago.

"We're hoping Santa will bring the tree tonight," said Nicole with a warning glance. Katie still clung stubbornly against all logic to the idea of Santa Claus.

Robbie took Fletcher up to his room; it had been the guest room when this had been his and Terry's house, and it was going to feel strange to be sleeping in it. The cast had come off the day before in preparation for the trip, but he did all the climbing with his right leg and still carried his walking stick.

"I think she's faking it," said Robbie in confidence.

"Faking it?"

"Katie. I think she knows there's no Santa Claus." Robbie's small serious freckled face was screwed up in concentration. "I knew for a couple years he wasn't real, but I had to pretend so Nicole wouldn't be disappointed."

Too late to duck out of it, Fletcher learned that Nicole was "having a few people in" for eggnog and munchies. David was late, so they ended up in the kitchen putting things on trays and getting out bottles and glasses and ice as the kids sat in the living room watching Christmas Eve specials on the box.

"I think the last time we really talked I was a freshman in college," Nicole said finally. She shook her head and laughed. "I remember I'd gotten sixty-seven out of a hundred on my humanities midterm and was in tears."

She was slicing Hickory Farms beef stick, very badly, giving him a momentary wrench; Terry had always sawed cold meats in that same slapdash manner which suggested fingers were expendable. Fletcher had learned just how *un*expendable fingers were, but already also had learned that since he wielded the knife with his right hand, his own missing fingers were more of a nuisance than anything else. He took the knife and began cutting thin even slices with the precision of a man who has skun and dressed out a great many animals in his lifetime.

Nicole went on, "You told me that grades were important *just then,* but that when I stopped being a student, they wouldn't mean anything anymore. You said I should remember the past and anticipate the future, but live in the present." She started opening bags of potato chips and cans of mixed nuts. "I never forgot that, even though in practice I keep getting locked into the present."

"You surprised me when you married a man with two kids."

"I've been really lucky with them. They think I'm okay.

Some of the horror stories you hear about people's relationships with their stepchildren . . ."

Fletcher, arranging crackers and cheese and beef stick on a platter, gave a grunt that could have been a chuckle.

"For a few years there I don't remember you and me getting on too red hot."

"I blamed you for Mom's death. Because you weren't here when it happened."

"I blamed me too. Still do. I know it was a drunk driver, but—"

"So you buried yourself up there in the woods."

He nodded. "A natural tendency toward misanthropy that finally surfaced."

Even as he said it, he knew it was flip. All his life he had guarded himself that way. Against what? Who gave a damn about his life anyway? In the weeks since he had been shot, he had felt a subtle shift inside him. Not a looking toward the future, but maybe an acknowledgment that for most people some sort of future was out there somewhere.

"How about you?" he asked. "Why did you just suddenly quit working for Gary?"

Nicole's resignation had surprised him, because she'd been interested in politics ever since high school and had volunteered for precinct work when she was seventeen. Two years later, during her sophomore year in college, she'd been a precinct captain in Westergard's reelection campaign, and had gone to work for him as a secretary directly after graduation. A year later she was his executive secretary.

Now she surprised Fletcher again; if she'd been an animal, it would have been an alarm sign.

"With the kids it got to be too much," she said shortly.

Lying, or at least deliberately trying to take him astray—a female catbird with nestlings feigning a broken wing to lead this predator away from her nest of secrets.

The doorbell rang; she made a quick relieved gesture.

"Our guests await."

Fletcher welcomed the interruption as much as she. God knew he had too many No Trespassing signs up in his own life

61

not to respect them in another's.

Against all odds, he was enjoying the party. Standing in front of the stately grandfather clock that had been another wedding gift, this from Terry's parents, he smiled down on Nicole's friend Iris, godmother to both of David's kids, a handsome blonde with wide frank blue eyes and a merry smile. Also, she could talk — God, could she talk!

"I knew David and his first wife, who as you know went off to England to find herself and found some Englishman instead, and was a terrible bore in the bargain and . . . Where was I?" Fletcher, who didn't have the foggiest idea, was saved when she exclaimed, "Oh, yes. When David married Nicole I told Norman: Thank God, someone interesting. You ever only discover a few — just a few — interesting people, and Nicole is a real find. Especially in Minneapolis."

"You're not from here?" Fletcher asked politely, although her accent already had told him that.

She gave her wide-open laugh. "I grew up on a ranch in Texas, and got my fill of the great outdoors." She put a confiding hand on his arm. "I got so the only wide-open space I liked was the main floor at Neiman-Marcus. Hiking is what you do between Saks Fifth Avenue and Lord & Taylor." She whirled, raised an arm, and yelled, "*Norman,* here's Nicole's dad!"

Fletcher lifted his head and saw Norman Bergman drifting toward them. He was a slight gentle man whose ambition had been to make a million dollars before he was thirty. He'd made it at twenty-nine, Nicole had told Fletcher, as a magazine and book distributor, and had gone shopping for a wife. He'd found Iris, at that time publicity director for the Minneapolis Dayton's: half a head taller than he, noisy, and unexpectedly shrewd. Her laughing spontaneity had flung wide the doors on his own dark quiet discretion.

Norman spotted the grandfather clock and sighed like a man coming home from a hard day at the office. His small delicate hands, as if of their own volition, opened the front panel of the clock. He pointed out the works to Fletcher in loving detail.

"A work of art. Pine-face grandfather, roller-pinion, eight-day wooden movement." His hands fluttered over the hardwood like fond butterflies. "See—American-made, not German. Early American clockworks were made of wood because they couldn't get iron, and the brass industry hadn't started yet. But these wonderful hardwoods were available, woods that had disappeared from European forests centuries earlier. My father could not get hardwoods like these in Germany."

" 'The Wonderful One-Hoss Shay,' " said Fletcher.

"Exactly!" said the delighted Norman. He declaimed, " 'The strongest oak, that couldn't be split nor bent nor broke . . .' "

" 'The crossbars were ash, the panels of whitewood . . .' "

" 'The hubs of logs from the 'Settler's ellum'!" He started to close the front panel again, chuckling with delight at the poem. "Clockmakers made the movements complete during the winter months, then in summer they sold them to cabinet-makers around the country. Each one unique. Like you. Like me. Like the women we love."

Fletcher was strangely moved at this small dark gentle man's benediction on his years with Terry.

Norman's eyes moved to Iris and suddenly twinkled. He shook Fletcher's hand and she embraced him warmly, leaving a red slash of affection on his cheek as she sailed full-bosomed after her husband through the crowd.

Nicole popped up at Fletcher's elbow with a wry smile on her face and an eggnog in her hand.

"The host has arrived, an hour late, if you can believe that. He's got Jarvis and Crandall and Quarles and Doyle with him, so I bet the work that kept him late at the office was a Christmas party."

"Only if you call sitting around with the Guv and those idiots a Christmas party," Jarvis was snorting a half-hour later.

Couples were leaving by then, calling "Merry Christmas"

before disappearing into the night. Quarles and Crandall had wandered off, and John Doyle, a heavy-faced fifty-year-old, was trying to recite *The Night of the Jabberwock* while slouched in his chair with an empty glass in his hand. He had leather patches on his elbows and smoked a pipe, and had gotten to the outgrabing mome raths before losing his way and lapsing into tipsy silence.

Nicole whispered to Fletcher that he was one of the best front men in the business—going around making sure all elements were in place before the candidate arrived in a given town for rallies or campaign speeches.

Jarvis, on his third eggnog, seemed loose and easy. He and Fletcher had met briefly the previous Easter when he had driven up with David to get the kids after their vacation at the cabin. Now his eyes studied Fletcher dispassionately.

"I heard you got shot or something."

"I love a tactful man," said Nicole. After a couple of drinks, she wasn't bothering to hide her hostility toward him.

"Whoever did it made a great shot," said Fletcher, smiling easily. "Just at the wrong animal."

"As to that . . ." Jarvis raised his eggnog in salute, then drank it down. "As to that."

Fletcher thought he understood the man's clumsy antagonism: the instinctual reaction of the healthy animal to the cripple. And Fletcher, with his red woolen Pendleton hanging to emphasize his lost weight and broad boniness of shoulder, knew he looked like a cripple.

"God, he's a creep!" Nicole exploded when Jarvis went to get his coat. "The others are kind of fun—Pete is a lovable bumbler, Hastings a marvelous mix of stuffiness and naked ambition, and Johnny Doyle tells the best awful dirty jokes in town. But if Kent had been with the governor for very long while I was there, I'd probably have quit a lot sooner than I did."

"What's his job?" Fletcher asked.

"Campaign manager, of course." Then she shook her head and chuckled. "I keep forgetting that not everyone lives and breathes this stuff the way we do. Hastings and Pete almost had me convinced to sign up again last month at Olaf Gavle's fund-raiser."

"Sign up for what?" demanded Ross, bringing outside cold back with him from noisily seeing off the last of the guests except Jarvis, who was in the john.

"The campaign. The excitement . . . the anticipation . . ." She gave a rueful little laugh. "Politics. A lot different from *hausfrau*. Speaking of which, guys, I hate to say it, but . . . we've got a tree to trim."

"I'll make some Tom and Jerries as soon as I send Jarvis out into the night," said Ross. Jarvis was a little the worse for strong drink, and needed a bit of handling.

Holy Jesus Christ, thought the killer. *How is that man still alive?* In his mind the scope showed him Fletcher's body roll facedown as the bullet entered his chest. Then he thought: Was Fletcher so stone cold that he could know, in that split second when the slugs were shattering his bones and ripping his flesh, that his only hope of staying alive was to play dead? Even though he might get a slug in the back of the head anyway?

No. No man could have that sort of iron control.

Still, Fletcher had escaped from the gooks during a winter storm or something, back in Korea in the fifties. The governor had told him about it. And here he was alive, when he should have been dead under the snow. The killer was sure he would never find the balls to try to put Fletcher there again.

The trimming went on until two in the morning. Fletcher strung the lights, Nicole and Robbie put on ornaments until Robbie, who had sneaked down again after his sister was in bed, was led off protesting and half-asleep in the middle of it. Fletcher and Nicole strung the tinsel, and they all tossed icicles — except Nicole, who hung hers strand by strand.

When it was finished, the two men sprawled in the living room with their final drinks of the evening, bathed in the warm reddish glow of the tree.

"I know what they're all going to say behind my back," muttered Ross. "They're going to say, 'Look at the way that damn fool trimmed that tree.'"

The remark called for no answer, and Fletcher offered none. Ross yawned and shook his head.

"God, I'm bushed. The way you got to hustle . . ."

"Why do you?"

"*Why?* Because we can't all go off and be hermits in the piney woods. . . ." He fell silent, as if dropping off to sleep—or passing out—but then suddenly roused himself again. "Politics, that's why. Politics and power."

Nicole appeared in the archway from the stairs. She was dressed in a pale violet negligee that brought out the color of her deep blue eyes and clung to her splendid thighs.

"The children will be up in about four hours wanting to open packages," she said. "So I suggest . . ."

"I'm telling Fletch here about politics. Politics and power and making it." Ross struggled to his feet, almost lost his balance, and looked challengingly at Fletcher. "*I'm* going to make it. Presidential speech writer, then segue into presidential press secretary." He swayed, owl-eyed. "You don't know what the hell I'm talking about, do you?"

"Of course he does," said Nicole. "Come to bed, Mr. Secretary."

"Merry Christmas," said Fletcher. "To both of you."

He sat up for half an hour longer, staring at the tree and remembering other Christmases when Terry had been alive. Then he went up to bed. And lay awake for another two hours, vainly and unconsciously listening for the Owl streetcars that had rattled by the house each hour of the night during the early years of their marriage, when he would return to Terry from each overseas contract telling himself that it had been the last one. Next to Terry's warm sleeping body spooned up against his in the bed, that familiar rattle-clank in the night had told him more than anything else that he was well and truly home again.

Nicole and David's home now.

"Presidential press secretary," he said aloud in the half-darkened room.

Ross was right. Fletcher *didn't* know what the hell he was talking about. Nicole had been married to the man for four years and Fletcher knew him hardly at all. Knew nothing of his hopes, dreams, ambitions.

Except that he wanted to be presidential press secretary.

Well, why not? Everybody had to be something.

# 8

On the day Westergard filed for the Illinois primary, Fletcher took his first real walk down the burn from the cabin. It was three days after Christmas and he was eager to get out into the woods. Until the cast had come off he had been unable to tramp through the snow.

He clumsily fastened up his overshoes one-handed, pulled on his heavy mackinaw, and went out, jerking the door shut behind him. Whoever had tried to kill him was long gone, of course, but he still felt his pulse rise slightly when he came out into the vulnerability of the relatively brushless burn in front of the cabin.

O the mind, mind has mountains. Or in his case, he thought abruptly, without knowing why he did, hills. The low hills off to the west, which, from here, couldn't even be seen because of the intervening growth. Hardly the cliffs of fall, frightful, sheer, that Hopkins had envisioned.

He walked down the burn, loving every breath cutting like a knife into his lungs. Every *shallow* breath. He was panting from even this small exertion, but already he was learning to avoid the pain in his side. It was like the first day of football training, running laps from goalpost to goalpost with a stitch in your side that, if you didn't throw up, you could get beyond. This one he could never get beyond.

All right, then, he'd learn to stay this side of it.

Some toppled finger-thick saplings caught his eye. The gnawed ends showed a cottontail's nipping, not the single clean hatchetlike bite of the larger snowshoe rabbit. He stopped, his half-smile fading. The tracks in the snow showed the cottontail suddenly had taken off from his meal, as the whitetail buck had done just before Fletcher had been . . .

He shot a quick look around, then returned to the tracks almost shamefacedly. They were this morning's, not over an hour old. But the rabbit had not been spooked by his approach; it merely would have hopped to the nearest evergreen and hidden under the sweeping lower branches until he was safely by.

Instead, it had fled in utter terror, jinking in zigzags so desperate they had sent miniature snowballs skittering out across the unbroken surface snow. What made the hairs rise on the backs of Fletcher's hands was that *nothing had been chasing it.* There were no other tracks, none at all.

Staying to one side so as not to disturb the sign, he followed. Twenty yards farther on he stopped and awkwardly crouched, leaning heavily on his walking stick.

The tracks ended in scuffed snow marked by a few bright red spatters and one quarter-size splotch. For the first time, other tracks appeared, three-toed devil tracks out of nowhere. Two yards farther on and almost a yard to either side, the snow had been brushed by a series of even strokes as if the attacker had tried to hide the evidence of his crime with a giant broom.

Fletcher grunted erect and used the stick to balance on his good leg while carefully extending and flexing the bad one a few times, working out the stiffness.

The story was complete. Each of the rabbit's zigzags had been a desperate attempt to evade the airborne attack. The scuffed area marked the final swoop, where curved talons had struck deeply into neck and body. Blood had flowed. Great beating wings had sent up clouds of powder as they strained to lift the burdened predator above the tops of the nearest trees.

A great horned owl, the only owl with that sort of wingspan that would attack in daylight. Snowy owls from up around the arctic circle also hunted in daylight, but they were much smaller and would seldom be found this far south. The great horned had gotten the rabbit out in the open, away from cover, had struck, and had carried it back to the deep pine woods, leaving only a few splotches of blood on the snow.

"Got him out in the open away from the trees," said his father. "There'll be blood on the snow tonight."
Fletcher coughed blood across the snow and fainted.

He felt tired, drained, abruptly chilled. He turned and started back up the burn toward the suddenly very distant cabin. God in heaven, how had he ever *crawled* this distance?

A week later Fletcher walked the distance with ease, stopping thirty feet from the fire-blasted spruce a split second before a flash of movement on the trunk caught his eye. He waited. After a few moments more, a big black bird burst from the far side and arrowed away with an angry ringing *cyk cuk-cyk*. It was the size of a crow but had a prominent red crest and white flashes on the wings and neck.

Fletcher was pleased. Pileated woodpeckers were not especially rare around the cabin, but they were very difficult to stalk and he had gotten to within twenty feet before he scared it out. Maybe he wasn't being as noisy moving through the woods as he had feared.

Then he thought: Why had he stopped here? His eye would have noted the movement of the woodpecker, cataloged it, ignored it. But he had stopped dead; stopped at the edge of the cleared space around the fire-blackened tree. Stopped when he was still in cover.

He cleared his mind as Old Charlie had taught him so many years before. See *through* the sign to the quarry. He saw. He had stopped here because of two facts.

Fact: he had been shot.

Fact: he had been shot three times.

He had stopped here automatically because the trees were shelter, shelter from

terrible sickening crunch against his leg, spinning with the force of it, going down. And . . . *crack*. The rifle shot, *a full second after he had gone down.* He had known it at the time, but shock had driven it from his mind until now. With the sound traveling at eleven hundred feet per second, and figure an average hunting load with the slug traveling at twenty-seven hundred feet per second . . .

Four hundred yards.

A third fact: four hundred yards. Not a fact of the certitude of the first two, but one he was sure of all the same, the way he was sure from the whistle of the wings what sort of duck had flown over his blind in the predawn darkness.

He limped up past the tree and then returned to it, his overshoes crunching through the crust as they had done that night. He paused with his gloved hand resting on the rough bark.

He had stopped right here to unstring his bow. Then he had moved forward, one, two, three paces. And *wham!*

He bent and felt just below the left knee, where the slug had carried away the head of the fibula and crippled him. He turned and looked west. Yes, everything was as he'd half-remembered. O the mind, mind has mountains. He was looking right at the unobstructed crown of one of the hills beyond the slough.

Four hundred yards away, and the buck had come trotting back toward Fletcher. Twelve hundred feet, a bit under a quarter of a mile. But the dull glint of light off the rifle bolt, just for an instant, would have been enough to alarm it. Nobody there now, of course, but would the shooter have left . . . *sign?*

Of course.

Why so sure? *Because the day of the shooting could not have been the first time he'd been up there.*

Unaccountably uneasy now, Fletcher used his glasses to scan the hilltop. Brushy, logged about twenty years ago at a guess. You'd need something to take a rest against, something to elevate you above the local brush for an unobstructed field of fire.

He had crawled from here. *Crawled.* For who? For goddamn who?

71

A hunter? No. A four-hundred-yard shot was a scoped shot, and the scope would have shown it was a man he was killing, and a hunter would have stopped firing. Unless he was hunting men.

But even a murderous hunter would have circled around to Fletcher's trail already broken through the snow crust so as not to be heard—and not to leave tracks in case someone *did* come looking before the next thaw or next snowfall wiped them out.

And a hunter, knowing that supposedly dead game, even after the eyes had begun glazing, could spring to its feet and dash off, would have checked the body to make sure its apparent death was real, not the bogus temporary death of shock.

Thrill-killer? No. A thrill-killer would never have come up here once before the killing day to . . .

*Before* the killing day? Let it flow, Old Charlie always said. Old Charlie, crazy dirty hermit who lived with his dog Spot in that one-room shack near the West Newton marsh. Fletcher's dad would leave him a sack of sugar and a box of salt and a two-pound can of coffee every couple of months. Old Charlie, best tracker, best hunter, best man in the woods Fletcher would ever know. Let it flow, he always said.

All right, why was he putting himself through this? Because he had crawled a thousand feet through the snow, leaking blood, to save himself? No. Because you played by the rules. The prey had to be at least as important as you. You killed, you didn't slaughter. You ate what you killed, or used what you couldn't eat. You went in after the wounded, because you didn't leave cripples.

And because, like any animal, a man had a life to joy in if joy was given, to endure if it wasn't—the broken wing, the shattered foreleg, the ruined paw, the parasite ants which burrowed up the nose until they reached the brain. The shortened leg, the splinting chest, the severed fingers.

Fletcher should have been dead. He wasn't. He had been left a cripple. The kill should have been clean.

Who killed so sloppily, with so little compassion?

Not a hunter. Not a thrill-killer. Not a professional killer. A professional man-hunter would have administered the same sort of *coup de grâce* an animal hunter would have.

An amateur. A murderous amateur out to kill Hollis Fletcher personally. How did he know? Because the shooter had to have planned it all ahead, coldly and with calculation. Had to have measured the distance from the place of ambush to the spruce tree, *and then had to have sighted in his rifle for that distance*. Only an amateur, after all that, could only maim; only an amateur could be too inept to hunt and kill cleanly.

An amateur would leave sign, as amateurs always must.

Fletcher didn't yet have the stamina to get up to the crown of the hill. But he could do the next best thing. He limped back to the spruce and took out the shiny red Swiss Army knife Terry had given him (along with a shiny new 1974 penny so the knife would never cut their love, which it never had). With it he began digging out the sighting-in slugs which had been fired into the fire-riven spruce by the man who had tried to kill him.

# 9

The man who had tried to kill Fletcher was drunk in the Algonquin Hotel bar on West Forty-fourth Street in New York City. He'd almost taken a bite of the Big Apple a few minutes before. He'd been lounging on a sofa at one of the small polished hardwood tables with the little silver bells for service on them, nibbling peanuts and getting smashed. And a girl with good legs wearing a short skirt, shorter than you'd see in Minneapolis, had sat down. Obviously the management hadn't spotted her as a hooker; they had got so far as to be talking price before he'd chickened out.

He'd told himself it was fear of getting herpes or AIDS, but he knew his unease really grew from Fletcher being on his mind. He looked around the tiny dark-paneled bar. The red-coated bartender was arguing about the Knicks with somebody two stools over.

"Another Jim Beam, please?"

What if Fletcher had been *watching* him as he approached? Had recognized him?

No, not possible. It had been dark, he'd have just been a shape behind a flashlight. But Fletcher was a hunter. What if he set out to hunt down the man who had tried to kill him?

He tossed back the shot of whiskey, sat blinking for a moment while he wondered if it was going to come back up again. It stayed down. The cold alcohol spread false warmth through his limbs. What the hell was he worried about? There was nothing tangible, nothing at all, for Fletcher to uncover if he did try to track down the killer.

Fletcher tossed the three bits of misshapen metal on the tabletop. So what did he really have? Three bits of lead. Since lead didn't rust, no real way to tell how long they'd been there. He'd never been a hand-loader, so he didn't have a delicate scale to weigh them.

Of course he could take them to Les Klumb in Cochrane, who had the requisite clamps and calipers and calibrators and micrometers to tell him the caliber — probably 30.06. Or he could take them down to a forensic lab in Minneapolis and probably learn they had all come from the same rifle, if they weren't too badly mushroomed from hitting the wood. If he ever brought in a rifle for test-comparison shots, they might be able to confirm it as the weapon that had fired them.

So what? It proved nothing. Knowledge without wisdom.

He'd gotten himself all worked up the other day, but it was a hunt he'd only waste his time in making. He had other things to do.

Fletcher dropped the slugs into his pocket, crossed to the gun cabinet, and got out his old 30-30 carbine and a handful of shells. He'd promised Victor a buck by Christmas, and it was January already. He'd have to use the rifle until he was better healed; he wouldn't be able to walk down any wounded animals. A clean kill or none at all. The bow just left too wide a margin for error.

It was a gray, raw day, spitting hard kernel snow. A mile from the cabin he cut sign that made him slip four 30-30 shells into the carbine and jack one up into the chamber with the harsh metallic *snick* which so often alerts animals to the presence of careless hunters. Only then did he crouch to study the tracks in detail.

A black bear, no doubt about it, a male by the size and depth impression of the tracks. Shambling along through the snow like a man with very wide feet wearing moccasins. Must have been fooled out of his den by the warm spell that today's raw weather had ended. Fletcher didn't want to tangle with a bull black bear grumpy from awaking, because in such a confrontation either man or animal had a good chance of dying.

The boy glanced behind him, away from the tall timber up through which Old Charlie would be coming, and there was a big whitetail buck a scant fifteen yards away, standing stock-still and staring at him. The trouble was, the boy was faced the wrong way and had his safety on.

He made his turn by infinitesimal degrees, very slowly bringing the old 30-30 carbine up and around to where he could fire it without shifting position. Any movement of his feet would rustle pine needles and the deer would be gone.

He eased back the hammer with the tiniest of metallic clicks and the buck gave a great whirling bound and came down angled away, was already into the air again in a twenty-foot leap, so the boy's shot merely scattered bark and cambium from a fir tree.

As he fired, there was a great crash behind him. He spun back; a huge black shape dodged aside and went straight up a lodgepole pine in long bounds of unbelievable strength and dexterity, digging into the tree with its acutely curved foreclaws as it shoved upward with its hind legs. In moments it was clinging to the tree thirty feet above the boy's head.

He had been so frightened he had dropped his rifle, a cardinal sin for a hunter; and, an even worse sin for a sixteen-year-old, he had wet his pants. Before he even let himself think, he snatched up his rifle, jacked another round up into the chamber, slammed the butt to his shoulder, and snapped off a shot.

Two things happened. The bear roared and fell straight down out of the tree like a shotgunned squirrel, landing hard enough to shake the ground; and Old Charlie broke out of the brush and yelled when he saw the fallen bear.

The bear was already on its feet, galloping for a dense thicket of hemlock and juniper and a deadfall tangle of pines blown down in some September storm years before. He went smashing and crashing in: then was only silence.

The boy turned for Charlie's expected praise. Charlie was so mad he knocked the rifle right out of the boy's hands again.

"Why you shoot that bear?" he yelled. "You got no call to shoot that bear!"

"But I . . . He came out and up the tree and—"

"We ain't hunting bear. We hunting deer."

"—and I'd just missed a big buck, and . . ."

From the thicket came a low moaning sound, so horribly human it raised the hairs on the back of the boy's neck. It rose in pitch and intensity to a near-wail, then dropped to low moans again.

"Is that . . . Why is he . . ."

"He's hurting," said Old Charlie. He sat down against the bole of the lodgepole from which the bear had fallen, his gun canted up between his cocked knees. He was looking straight ahead into the autumn woods. "You had no call to shoot 'im. Me, I'm from the Bear Clan." It was the first time he had ever openly acknowledged his Indian blood. "I'm Charlie Seven Bears."

The boy knew no answer was expected of him, nor would be tolerated. He sat down with his back against the same tree, at right angles to the Indian, unconsciously aping his position. They sat there for a long time, neither speaking. The bear kept moaning, then stopped. The boy had never heard such a total silence in his life. Not even the birds seemed to be calling.

"You think he's dead in there?" he asked at last, hopefully. He felt rather than saw Old Charlie's head-shake. He said plaintively, "What'll we do?"

"We wait for him to stiffen up. Then we go in after 'im."

The thicket was very dark and tangled and impenetrable. Somewhere inside it was a hurting, enraged four-hundred-pound black bear. He had difficulty swallowing. "Maybe if we just go away . . ."

"Sure. An' 'nother hunter come along, the bear go after him." Charlie was suddenly on his feet from his crouch, with no preliminary gathering of legs under him. He looked down at the boy from his beaky, hard-bitten face. "A *hunter* don't leave no cripples. Ever."

An hour later, Charlie went in after the bear. The boy found he was too terrified to go in with him. He was so ashamed his face flushed bright scarlet and tears came to his eyes, but he sat there in stubborn terror and let Charlie go.

Charlie made no sounds as he moved; the deadfall ate him alive. The cover was so thick and twisted he went on his belly, shoving his rifle ahead of him. A few branches shook slightly; the silky sack of a bagworm hanging from a juniper branch trembled slightly, that was all.

A lifetime, a dozen lifetimes went by. Suddenly Charlie's rifle exploded, shocking because it was so close. There was a roar, thrashing, the bagworm sack was ripped from its flailing branch. And silence, even as the boy sprang to his feet and, with a despairing cry, hurled himself against the thicket. It thrust him back. Crying and calling, he began worming and pushing and twisting in underneath it as the old Indian had done.

He found Old Charlie skinning out the dead bear; he had crawled so close his rifle muzzle had been touching the shaggy black fur when he had fired his single shot behind the foreleg and through the chest cavity into the heart. He had already made his initial cut from the chest to the corner of the mouth, proceeding as one would with a large deer; but he refused to let the boy help as he manipulated the heavy carcass in the skinning process, dumping the still-steaming intestines out on the red crystalline snow to get at the shattered heart.

Charlie didn't say a word, not one, during their whole drive back down to West Newton and his tarpaper shack. But he ate the heart and he kept the bearskin. It was the only possession he had left when he died.

Fletcher slowly raised his eyes from the bear tracks, stunned with memory, and was looking at an eight-point buck a dozen yards away. It was upwind and broadside to him, rooting with its nose like a pig for ground herbs still edible beneath the protective snow. He had been so immobile, and so far away in his mind, that he had been invisible to the deer.

He had one in the chamber with the hammer already cocked. It would be the easiest shot in his life that wasn't the result of a deliberate stalk. He very slowly raised the rifle and started to squeeze the trigger.

he was struck a terrific blow just beneath the left knee. it spun him partway around. he went down on his back. he started waving his hands desperately in the air above

He grunted and started to lower the rifle. The buck already was in flight like a released spring. Fletcher gave a great cry and hurled the carbine, spinning like a stick, after it. He stood stock-still, panting rapidly and shallowly, welcoming the sharp even stab of pain in his side.

A cripple. Crippled in his mind as well as in his body. He had *become* the prey, had *been* the buck. His own slug had ripped his own flesh before he could pull the trigger. He was maimed in body and mind, a hunter who could not hunt. A cripple.

The bastard should have killed him.

Hard kernel snow, falling more rapidly now, made tiny popping sounds against the blue fabric of his parka and a bristle of small scratchings as it bounced against the fallen needles and leaf-litter. Fletcher's breath smoked into the snowfall.

He had been shot, three times, from ambush, deliberately and personally, because he was Hollis Fletcher — and for no other reason. Shot and left for dead. Left a cripple by someone who had sighted in his rifle against the fire-riven tree Fletcher had to pass on his way to his cabin.

Fletcher started limping back toward the cabin without even retrieving the carbine from where he had flung it. Why bother? It was now as useless to him as a pair of running shoes. Until ten minutes before, he had been the best damned hunter, except for Charlie Seven Bears, he had ever known.

And since a careless speeding drunk had flung Terry, broken and bleeding, from the wheel of life to which he still clung, he had defined himself only as that. A hunter.

Now he could hunt no more. He had become prey. His edge was gone.

Someone had tried to kill him, and he didn't know who and he didn't know why. Something dark and bitter boiled up within him, so he swallowed repeatedly as if it were physical rather than spiritual.

He had to find out: Who? Why? What would the end of the hunt be? He didn't know. He didn't have to know. Right now, the hunt was its own purpose.

He realized without surprise, with almost a feeling of inevitability, that it was January. For Old Charlie, the Moon of the Wolf. The wolf, the greatest hunter the American continent had ever known, the hunter whose methods anthropologists now studied to learn how that other hunter, man, had done *his* work when hunting had been his business.

The Moon of the Wolf.
The month of the hunter.
And the hunt had begun.

# II

## Stalking

"To stalk" suggests the creeping of cats, stealthy and low profile. The use of the earth and the vegetation as cover, the mimicking of the prey and other animals, the speed and type of movement, the knowledge of when to rush, all are complex elements in the mosaic.

# 10

After he returned to Minneapolis to find his wife already in the ground, Fletcher went down to Hennepin Avenue that same night, at the time when the police report said the accident had happened, and spent two fruitless hours prowling the fatal intersection — hoping, perhaps, to find something of Terry. He had found nothing.

Only the dream, which had started that same night. Tonight it recurred for the first time in nearly five years.

As always, Terry emerged from a store on Hennepin Avenue dressed in the soft clingy powder-blue dress he had always loved so, wearing no coat, carrying a dress box under one arm. As she started across the street with the green light, he could see the Mercury Cougar come down Hennepin at sixty miles an hour and smash into her when she was four steps from the curb.

She was knocked catty-corner across the intersection and up into the air to strike the face of an office building just below a second-floor window, glance off, and float toward the sidewalk a dozen feet beyond. Fletcher ran as hard as he could across the intersection to the screech of brakes and bray of horns as cars slid and rocked to a stop, trying to catch her before she hit the sidewalk.

He was too late; she struck just as he reached her. But then she rose without effort and began to glide away, her head high and serene, her back straight and her body erect, moving very fast, away from him up the street. The movement was unhuman, but at least she was alive and whole again!

He ran after her, calling her name. She did not turn or slow down. They were suddenly in the country, him pursuing her along a blacktop road up a long gradual hill where he lost ground, his pounding boots now erratic on the blacktop, his shouts weaker and his breathing labored. She turned in at a gravel road and disappeared into leafless hardwoods and was gone.

He stopped, panting, a flicker of anger mixed with his tears. Why had she run away? Why had she ignored him?

Fletcher woke totally, as he always did at this point in the dream. The fire had fallen to red embers and it was cold enough so he could see the white streamers of his breath even in the cabin's dimness. Despite the cold, he was sheened with sweat. Tears were running down his face.

"Terry . . ." he said, then stopped. He was speaking only to a pocket of memory cells in his own mind.

The luminous hands of the bedside clock showed five A.M. In another hour it would start to get light. He threw back the beautifully cured bearskin that he slept under in winter, his only material legacy from Old Charlie, and sat up on the edge of the bed. He worked his bad leg a few times to limber it, then crossed to the fireplace and put two more oak splits onto the embers. Tongues of blue-tipped flame immediately began licking up around the dry seasoned wood.

He put water on the stove for tea and got back under the covers, shivering now, staring up at the tented ceiling logs by the moving firelight and waiting for the pot to boil. He had not bothered to pump up the pressure lamp. The light he needed was not external, but rather some inner illumination that could erase the shadows on his resolve.

Five years ago, he had dreamed the dream almost nightly until he realized that he actually had begun planning to shoot the drunken son of a bitch who had killed Terry. The man had killed someone else the year before with the same car, a judge had revoked his license and then turned him loose to kill again.

Fletcher had also finally realized that Terry was not running away from him so much as showing him the way. The

84

way out of the city, away from violence, away from vengeance.

When he had come to understand that, he had given the house to Nicole, had moved to Cochrane, bought the land, built his cabin.

The dream had stopped the day he had cut the first log for the cabin wall. Now, on the night of the day he had determined to find the man who had crippled him, it was back.

"I'm sorry, Terry," he whispered.

Sorry that the drunk driver had taken her life; sorry that his own amateur murderer had been too inept to take his. Sorry that he could not give her even this: he had not hunted down her killer but now was unable *not* to hunt down his own.


Unaware that the hunt for him had begun in earnest, the killer was with Westergard's fledgling campaign organization in Iowa, hunting for votes, one of the motley little crew in the unheated minibus from the airport to their hotel in downtown Des Moines.

Clustered in the back of the van were a couple of security people and four media types, none network—one reporter each from the Minneapolis *Trib* and the Des Moines *Register,* and two "television journalists" from KCCI and WHO; the third local channel hadn't bothered to be represented. Everyone assigned to the campaign knew that Fiksdahl was going to take the caucus anyway. Westergard sat up front with his usual aides: Jarvis, Ross, Crandall, and Quarles. Johnny Doyle, the front man, had met them at the airport and was riding into town with them.

"Fiksdahl's people got the best rooms at the best hotel, the best campaign offices, the prettiest volunteers, and enough booze to float the USS *Constitution,*" said Doyle. Then he added with the same seriousness, "But he lost the key to his mistress's apartment, so he ain't gonna get no noo-kie."

Doyle laughed uproariously at his own joke, then started coughing around the stem of the pipe clutched between his teeth.

As the bus took a curve and momentarily lost traction on

the icy highway, Jarvis raised his voice to be sure the newsmen heard. "You know what else Fiksdahl ain't gonna get? He ain't gonna get the votes. And you can make book on that."

Westergard's hunt for Iowa votes actually had begun nearly a year before the upcoming January 20 caucus. Late the previous February, Westergard and Jarvis had driven down to Des Moines for a reception at the leading hotel — the same one where Fiksdahl now was headquartering his campaign. They'd had food for about two hundred; besides themselves and the couple who had planned it, only three other people had shown up for the reception.

Westergard had waved a helpless hand at the mountains of useless calories. "Maybe you can give it to the poor. I'll go down and shake hands with the folks at the courthouse and try to salvage *something*."

Now, heaps of unused campaign leaflets and WESTERGARD buttons, result of an invoicing error by the printer and the novelty wholesaler rather than any failures in their campaign, littered the worn carpet around Ross's temporary desk. He was trying without much luck to insert last-minute changes into Westergard's television speech.

"The simple truth is, ladies and gentlemen, that *that* man in Washington is blaming depressed land values, low commodity prices, and high real interest rates on us — the American farmer! Do you believe that? I don't."

Last year's Des Moines fiasco had been before Ross had been hired as speech writer, but Jarvis had rehashed it *ad nauseam*, including the fact that it hadn't hurt them because no media people had shown up — Westergard's national recognition factor at that time had stood right around two percent. The national media reporters wanted meat and potatoes, not consommé.

"And now here we go all over again," Jarvis grunted as he stopped beside the desk. "Twenty-one fucking days of campaigning for fifty fucking delegates from Iowa — there'll be three thousand delegates at the convention in San Francisco.

So what's it all about, Alfie?"

"National recognition," said Ross dutifully. It was his invariable buzz-word answer to Jarvis' rhetorical complaints.

A hand-lettered sign on the door across the room read, DON'T LET THE CAT OUT. It was literal; the office mascot was a cat named Parity, after the return on their farm production that the farmers in Iowa wanted. That Westergard was from a neighboring farm state just to the north lent him credibility; among the Democratic candidates, he was coming closest to promising them what they wanted to hear. Not cynically, Ross knew: Westergard believed as they did.

"Whoever heard of a goddamned cat named Parity?" demanded Jarvis sulkily.

"*Full* parity," said Ross with a grin, watching the fat old tabby waddle across the room after another junk-food handout from one of the volunteers.

"You ain't shitting. Eight out of ten jobs in Iowa are farm-related."

Jarvis took out a cigar, ran it along under his nose, licked it, and returned it unlighted to his shirt pocket. Westergard was, temporarily at least, serving as his own media adviser, and a cigar-chomper image was not what he wanted for his campaign. Jarvis looked at Ross from the corner of his eye.

"You hear about the farmer over by Ames got charged with child abuse?"

"No, what did he—"

"Tried to will his farm to his kids." Without a break for the laugh, he added, "What time's the plane?"

Ross checked his watch. "Three hours."

They were scheduled to fly with Westergard to New York tonight because, as Jarvis had pointed out, what originated in Des Moines was *Midday* at 12:15, after their local news. The *Today* show, *Good Morning America*, and *CBS This Morning* all originated in New York. So Westergard had booked the New York flight. They would get the Iowa results there by phone.

Ross held the unstated belief that Jarvis had pushed for an early flight to New York not so much because of the media access if they did well, as because he wanted to get laid. Jarvis was always complaining there were too many church-sharpened eyes in Iowa for any overt sexual activity by members of the campaign staff. Westergard had even mentioned it as a factor in Iowa.

Ross returned to the speech.

"Is the American farmer being driven out of business because he's inept? Are his children being deprived of a college education because he's squandered his capital? No, *sir!* He's being driven out of business because he's been *too good* at what he does. And he's been left looking at gigantic surpluses of grain and butter and milk and honey, when on the other side of the world millions of people face famine and starvation . . ."

Ross crossed out the second "driven out of business" and substituted "mortgaged to the hilt," then did the same with "gigantic surpluses" by substituting "mountains of surplus."

He wondered if he should try to fit in Jarvis' joke about the Ames farmer, but decided against it. Westergard's audience probably all would have heard it already.

His mind crawled away to Nicole. Would he get a chance to call her, unheard, before they left? He was finding himself more and more dependent on her to hone his speeches before he presented the rough drafts to Westergard. When he didn't, the governor invariably felt they lacked the crispness he demanded.

He had to reach her. She was worried about her father, convinced there was more to the shooting than he was admitting to anyone, even his doctor buddy. It would be good for her to get her mind off her fantasies of deliberate violence about her old man's shooting accident, and onto the speeches where it would do some good.

Dammit, they *aren't* fantasies, Nicole told herself as she pushed the station wagon north along Minnesota 169. It was a clear day, the flat white landscape broken by growing congregations of evergreens that looked almost black against the snow. There *were* things about the shooting that Fletcher hadn't told her. When he had stayed with them over Christmas, she had been able to see in his eyes a shifting away, an inner calculation, whenever she mentioned it.

Like herself when he had asked her why she had quit working for Gary Westergard. She hadn't had any answer, not one she could give her father, as to why she and Gary had been sleeping together before she met and married David.

Wasn't it time she considered an answer, at least for herself? A pat psychological reason might be because Fletcher himself was no real force in her life, never had been, and Gary had provided a wonderful father figure. Or maybe it was heavier than that. He had been a close friend, a hero-worshiper almost, of her father nearly forty years before. In sleeping with Gary, was she *getting back at her father* for never being there when she was growing up?

Or maybe it *was* love, pure and simple. Or obsession, neither pure nor simple: obsession with the workings of political power, and those who possessed it.

Even tougher question: Why, three months after her marriage, had she started sleeping with Gary again? Could it just have been David's human limitations against Gary's magnetic attractions? David, with his surprisingly old-fashioned notions about marriage—legacy, perhaps, from the wife who had walked out on him—had quickly begun stifling her in the marriage. And there was Gary, dazzling in his physical presence and self-confident power, to restore her sense of self-worth.

While she was at it, why had Gary started it with her again?—because he *had* been the aggressor in the renewed affair.

The spectrum could run from the possibility that he had found her just too terrific a lay to give up, to the possibility that he had been in love with her, or had thought he was.

On the nasty side, maybe his pride had been hurt when she broke off the affair to marry David. His ego demanded that he reconquer her, make her sully her marriage vows as he had his, so when he broke it off they could share the guilt of betrayal.

But break it off he did. Every Thursday following the staff meeting, they had spent the hours until she had to go get the kids from school in that motel room out near the airport. A room with grotesque pink fake-flock wallpaper and a bed that brayed and banged the wall in its delight with their passion.

Every Thursday, until that day nearly ten months ago when Gary just wasn't there.

She looked off to her right across the vast flat white expanse of Lake Mille Lacs. Smoke came from the stovepipes of several scattered fishing shacks on runners; here and there patient men worked their lines through the holes chopped in the ice, or scooped skim-ice from them with kitchen strainers.

Gary hadn't been there, and had not mentioned it at the office the next day. He had been, instead, formal and precise, too busy for any personal discussion. He had left early that Friday afternoon "to spend a little extra time with my wife."

Through the leafless birch and aspen on the shore, she glimpsed an ice rink which had been made by shoveling back the snow. The movement of the car made it flicker between the tree trunks like an old-time silent movie. Goals had been set up at either end for impromptu after-school hockey games; the rink was deserted except for a tall graceful girl in a tall red knit cap, who was making loops and arabesques and figure eights. She spun up on one skate, going around in slowing circles like a top running out of spin, head thrown back as if in ecstasy, arms thrown wide to clutch at the inexpressible.

Nicole had left her resignation on his blotter after Gary had gone to join his wife that night, and had cleaned out her desk. She'd had just enough pride left for that. She didn't know if she would have hung up on him, but he never called. Jarvis had finally mailed her final check to her at home.

Only now, driving north alone through the frozen landscape, did she suddenly realize that Gary's renunciation had to do, not with her, but with his decision to try for the presidency. A cleansing of himself, a metaphoric vigil over his armor in the chapel of politics on the eve of knighthood.

Knighthood hell, she said to herself. A dalliance with his personal secretary as governor would be destructive if it came out after he was a serious contender for the presidency. His game was power, and in that game she'd been a pawn; but if he had told her that's what he was doing, she would have understood. She had always understood his motives better than he.

She thrust memory away and angrily jabbed the radio's On button, seeking mindless rock music. She got politics.

"Governor Gary Westergard has engineered a stunning upset in yesterday's Iowa Democratic Caucus, first test of political strength in this young election year. Westergard's twenty-seven percent of the vote to thirteen percent for his closest opponent, Fiksdahl of Mississippi, makes him front-runner in . . ."

*Front-runner*—and Gary would have been satisfied with second place. About fifty thousand voters turned out for the Iowa caucus, so some fourteen thousand Democrats had voted for him. Not even enough to get him elected to the town council in Oyster Bay, Long Island, but enough to make him presidential winner in Iowa.

Enough to give him the start of that national recognition for which he lusted. David, in New York with the governor, would be working on the ad-lib phrases Westergard would commit to memory for the media appearances that would follow the win.

# 11

Fletcher grasped another brittle winter-dead dogwood bush and pulled himself up the hillside. Along with ash and hickory saplings, this brush had replaced the hardwoods logged off a score of years before. It was a glorious winter day, cloudless, temperature in the twenties, the sky an aching blue, the air crisp as a bite of an October greening. Here under the brush, away from the sun's touch, the calf-deep snow was soft and without crust.

At the false crown of the hill, panting shallowly and quickly because of the damned splinting, he pivoted on his good right foot to look back the way he had come. His breath formed vapor clouds around his head. Once a few minutes' careless walk, now it had been a major project, planned in every detail. The frozen strip of marsh hadn't been too bad, despite the unavoidable tussocks hidden beneath the snow, but the climb up the hill had really taken it out of him. On this January 21 it was the farthest he had come from the cabin.

A chickadee sassed him from a bitter-cherry bush like a miniature berserker. A pair of pine siskins, yellow flashing in their sturdy little wings, flew out of the same leafless bush *tit-titting* disgustedly over the lack of edible seeds.

What did he know? What did he think he knew? And what did he think he could find out?

He knew: he had been shot from ambush.

He knew: he had been shot because he was Hollis Fletcher.

He thought he knew: he had been shot by an amateur lying in ambush on the crown of this hill — it gave the right angle of attack.

This inevitably implied that sometime previous to the attack, the amateur had sighted in his rifle on the fire-blackened dead spruce down in the burn past which Fletcher always went on his way home to the cabin.

He thought he could find out: what telltale sign the amateur might have left that could point Fletcher . . . *somewhere*. Perhaps at least suggest whether the assailant was from Cochrane or had come in from outside.

Which raised a nice point: if from outside, how had he known where to be, and when, to get in his shot?

It was late that afternoon, about a hundred yards from where he had turned to look down at the spruce, that he found the cut brush. His eye touched it, dismissed it as the work of rabbits, but then rested just long enough on the soft oblong under the snow behind it to understand what he was seeing.

A snow-covered log platform, six feet long and three feet wide, slightly below the crown of the hill. Man, not nature, creates obvious, not subtle, symmetry. This rectangular shape was obvious, therefore suspect.

Squatting laboriously, Fletcher brushed away the snow with a gloved hand. Half a dozen logs, each about six feet long and about six inches in diameter, had been laid side by side almost as if someone had been laying out a raft. These were not lashed together, but there was another similar log wedged at right angles across the downhill end of them, and lashed into place with thin nylon cord. Thus making an impromptu bench-rest for prone shooting, except for the thick undergrowth in front of it.

But there was that cut brush that had first caught Fletcher's eye.

He grunted down onto his belly on the makeshift platform, favoring his left side. When he raised his head above the cross-log to peer down and across the nearly quarter-mile of marsh and squaw grass between him and the burn, the cut brush formed a perfect keyhole. He was peering, as if through a rifle's sights, directly at the trunk of the burned-out spruce four hundred yards away.

He had found the point of ambush.

Fletcher rolled off the log raft into the snow, and got clumsily to his feet without putting any undue strain on the still-knitting wound in his chest. The lowered sun cast his shadow long and blue down the face of the hill. He panted smoke signals of emotion, not distress.

Amateur all the way. Three feet from where he was standing was a second-growth bur oak with a fork five feet from the ground. The killer need only have rested his rifle in that fork for as steady a shot as a sandbag at the rifle range could have given him. No raft of logs need have been laid, no brush cut, twig by twig, for an opening through which to fire. Just draw your bead and squeeze it off when the prey came up the burn.

Amateur, not from Cochrane — not after seeing this crude recreation of a bench-rest with a perfect oak crotch a yard away. Nobody in Cochrane was that unversed in firearms. Even a farmer who only shot deer to get them out of his cornfield would have taken his firing rest in that oak fork once he had chosen this as the site of ambush.

So the killer would have practiced, not up here in the woods, but at a rifle range, everything by the American Rifle Association rules, the sling wrapped around his left forearm and the breath drawn in and half-emitted. Prone is the way he would have learned, so prone is the way he would have gone about doing it for real when the time came.

It was like being at his own badly botched execution. Almost angrily, Fletcher dropped into his woodsman's crouch again to begin sifting through the snow for any further sign the executioner might have been so unwary as to leave.


Light shone through the window of his cabin in the gathering dusk, giving a golden tone to the snow it touched. Momentary fear rose like bile in Fletcher's throat, then was gone. He moved unevenly forward again. A bushwhacker would hardly have lighted the pressure lamp to advertise his presence. Probably Victor, come out to see how his patient was doing.

But when he pushed open the door, the smell of homemade venison stew came out at him like a blessing out of the past. From the back, just for an instant, Nicole looked like her mother despite the blonde hair. Then she picked up the kettle just starting to wail, and turned from the stove.

"I thought you'd be back about now."

She poured water over the Red Rose teabags in the pot as he knocked the snow from his overshoes against the edge of the doorframe, using one hand on the doorlatch to steady himself. The warmth of the cabin made him want to sneeze.

"To what do I owe the pleasure?"

"Dubious pleasure?" she amended. "David is in New York with the campaign, and—"

"I thought the caucus was in Iowa."

"Eight million stories in the naked city, but only a hundred ninety thousand of them in Des Moines. So the news media are in New York." She brought the pot over to the table, along with two mugs. "So you're stuck with me. I left the kids with Iris and gave myself an overnight pass from kids and cooking."

He pantomimed sniffing. "Smells like cooking to me."

"Some of the venison you sent home with the kids last Easter. I brought it up frozen, I'm just heating it up now."

"I don't have any extra blankets."

"Nice try. I brought a sleeping bag."

Defeated, Fletcher hung his coat on one of the hooks beside the door and crossed to the table to sit down rather heavily. He was suddenly tired. More tired than the day's physical exertion should have made him. He realized that his opposition to her staying had been more *pro forma* than real opposition.

"Tired?" she asked.

"That stew sure smells good."

"You have a hell of a time hearing a direct question, don't you?" She slammed down the sugar bowl and a can of evaporated milk for her tea.

He cupped a hand around his ear. "Eh?" As they both burst out laughing, he added perversely, "Just old and tired."

"You never used to talk that way."

"I never used to be old and tired."

"Did you find any clues?" she asked tartly.

"Clues to what?"

"Who shot you."

"A hunter—"

"Bullshit."

"What would your mother say to hear you talking that way?"

She cupped her hand around her ear. "Eh?"

He chuckled. He poured tea for them both, suddenly glad she was there. Perhaps for just this evening it would be as if the intervening years of disaffection and tension had never been, as if she were again the daughter he remembered from before her mother's death.

"My problem with someone shooting me deliberately is obvious," he said. "Who the devil would *want* to?"

"So you *did* go looking."

He stared at her for a long moment, then dug into the breast pocket of his red-and-black-plaid wool Pendleton. He tossed the cold metallic objects dramatically on the table, where they clinked and rolled and glinted in the hissing white light of the Coleman lantern.

Spent 30.06 brass shell casings. Eight of them.


"Why eight, if he only shot you three times?"

It was an hour later, they were at the sink, she washing their meager dishes in the scalding water in the washbasin, he drying them—which really meant just dipping the hot plates and flatware into the cold rinse water and setting them, still steaming, to drain on the sideboard.

"Five of them have to be from the first time he was up there, when he was sighting in the rifle. In the fall sometime, before the first snowfall but after the leaves had fallen. There was a perfect oak crotch to use as a firing rest, but he made a little bench-rest of logs and cut a keyhole in the brush for his field of fire. And didn't know enough to police up his spent brass either time."

"You only dug three slugs out of the spruce," she persisted.

96

"Add in the three times he actually shot you—"

"Probably missed the tree altogether with the other two when he was sighting in. I told you the man was an amateur."

He went to the fireplace to add more wood; she sat at the table to light a cigarette and watch him use the poker.

"I want in," she said abruptly.

"Nothing to get in on, Nicole. I'm doing this only to keep my mind occupied until my knee and chest—"

"Mom always said you were a lousy liar."

He gave a final poke, shifting one of the new logs, sending a red shower of sparks up the chimney, then went back to the table to sit down. Nicole squinted against the smoke of her cigarette. Watching her, he remembered that Terry, through their health-plan group, had quit the year before she had been killed. What good had that discipline done her?

"You're too . . . intense about it," said Nicole. "As if you lost something you have to find again."

He shrugged.

"Even if I wanted to go after him, Nicole, I'd have to face the fact that the chances of uncovering him are slight. He has no face, no name, no dimension, not even a motive."

"You've tracked down deer with no more to go on."

"Old Charlie's training isn't going to help me with this."

But even as he said it, he remembered his first solitary encounter with the old hermit his father had befriended—he hadn't known Charlie was an Indian then. He'd been out walking along the abrupt riverbank near the West Newton cabin, watching the cold brown autumn Mississippi rush past. The red-topped metal buoy marking the mid-river channel would disappear and reappear, dragged under by the current, then pop up again with the buoyancy of the air trapped inside it.

Something made him look back and there, three feet behind him, was Old Charlie, trudging along silent and unnoticed in his footprints. Charlie stopped to gesture back the way he had come.

"C'mon," he said. "I show you."

"Show me what?" The boy had stopped also, but now was edging away; the old man was funny in the head and smelled funny, acrid sweat and tallow and chewing tobacco and hound dog.

Not answering, Old Charlie turned and walked back the way they had come, along the path that edged the bank. It was one of those seminal moments that are important only in retrospect: a moment before, the boy had planned to back away and run. Now, perversely, he wanted to see whatever wonder was to be seen. He followed the old man back along the path.

Nicole's voice broke in on him. "You were gone a long time."

"Old Charlie," he said, coming back from the distant memory. "The first time I ever followed him into the woods."

"What did he show you?"

"A fox. A gray fox — they're the ones you'll find in the bottomland along the river. Reds like it more open."

Charlie squatted beside some tracks along the edge of the dirt tire ruts leading to the cabin. The boy squatted with him, not knowing what he was seeing. Earlier he had dismissed the tracks as those of a house cat from one of the other cabins.

"Fox," said Charlie. At that time he still had black thinning hair spiked with gray; his beaky nose and hard-lipped mouth were very Indian. Charlie's eyes were so dark brown as to look black, snapping like those of someone carrying a half-century less of time's weight. "Thick tail — see the drag mark? A gray. Smaller feet, bigger toes than the red."

His thick blunt finger turned over the fox's scat, a neat narrow cylinder sharply tapered at one end.

"Dark shit. Eatin' dried berries. Grays love berries." He stood. "C'mon," he repeated unnecessarily. The boy was hooked.

Charlie showed him one of the fox's dug-up meat

98

caches, then one of his temporary dens in the rotted base of a dying oak tree. A tuft of reddish-tinged gray fur was caught on a bit of protruding bark at the mouth of the hole. Old Charlie's finger pointed out scattered bits of bone, a patch of rabbit fur, three bright wood-duck feathers.

Finally he showed the boy the fox itself.

"How did he do that?" demanded Nicole. Her eyes shone; the fire gave her skin and hair a reddish cast akin to a fox's pelt. They had let the lantern go dim by common unspoken consent.

Fletcher put his lips to the back of his hand and sucked sharply. It made a thin squeaking sound.

"That's how a mouse sounds to a fox. They can hear it from several hundred feet away."

Charlie's bogus mouse had raised a sudden sharp nose against the leafless hardwood boles on a small rise at the far end of the clearing. The boy was seeing his first fox. It had been lying facing its own backtrail, full gray brush over nose and paws, all senses alert.

Five years later, under Charlie's tutelage, the boy had been able to make an upwind stalk on a sleeping whitetail doe and slap her on the rump to announce his presence. He sometimes thought the old Indian still lived in his mind just to lead him to game he would otherwise have missed. Maybe he was wrong in believing Old Charlie's tracking lore was useless for this sort of hunt.

"It might be that Old Charlie's going to help me after all," he told his daughter.

"I know I am," she said. "I'm not much use in the woods, but I'm very good at ferreting out information from bureaucrats and companies and corporations. And whether you like it or not, those are the thickets this hunt is going to take place in."

# 12

The next morning, before she returned to Minneapolis, Nicole extracted his promise to keep her current on what he was doing. Fletcher wasn't sure he accepted her easy reconstruction of the assault: so far, apart from the misshapen slugs and the spent rifle brass, all he had to go on was a filmsy edifice of conjecture.

Oh, sure, he agreed that the attack must have come from outside Cochrane, but . . . Something nipped at his memory. Something Nicole had said last night.

Yes. When he'd come home and found her in the cabin heating the venison stew, she'd said, "I thought you'd be back about now." She'd known his routine. Whoever had shot him had known his routine also. Locals would, outsiders wouldn't. But no local would be so inept with an ambush; and no local had any conceivable reason to want him dead.

Very logical. Yet the maddening anomaly was that only in Cochrane would he have any hope of finding the raw data he needed to help him look elsewhere. If it wasn't in Cochrane, it didn't exist. So, start looking in Cochrane.

But his search started with the easy rhythm of any real hunt. You can't begin with what you expect to find: you have to just make yourself open to whatever might be there. So it was only after a week of increasingly long rambles through the late-winter woods that he finally decided to walk into town with his limp and his eight empty cartridge cases.

The only person competent to read their sign was Les Klumb, Cochrane's resident gun nut. Klumb spent his spare time reloading new slugs and charges into used brass for half the county; there was at least a chance he could see something in the shell cases Fletcher himself couldn't see.

The spring-bell on the door tinkled his entrance into Klumb's Hardware Store. The hand-loader's pale-haired daughter, a high-school senior whose birth had raised an eyebrow or two because her parents had been in their forties at the time, was cutting a key for a farmer. The farmer was describing at length how he had locked himself out of his barn.

"Your dad around, Cindy?" Fletcher finally got in over the high-pitched whine of the finishing wheel. She looked up and grinned at him.

"Out in back, Mr. Fletcher."

He went down narrow, labryrinthine aisles past cast-iron spiders, roofer's nails, plumbing supplies — an unusually fine rack of hunting rifles — toward the back of the store. When locals needed something fixed or replaced, they usually had neither the time nor the means for a hundred-mile round trip to Grand Rapids.

Fletcher passed through a storeroom crowded with rolls of baled wire; a single corner was reserved for a battered roll-top desk bulging with messy paperwork and a sagging swivel chair innocent of occupant.

Klumb's shop was a dim, narrow, cluttered room that smelled of Hoppe's Number 9 and gunpowder. A bulb, directed by an old-fashioned green metal shade, puddled light down on the solid hardwood bench where Lester Klumb was locking a .577 Berdan primer into his vise.

He glanced over as Fletcher entered. "Be with you in a second, Fletch."

Fletcher nodded and stepped up to the bench, which was bolted into the concrete floor with cement screws for the total stability hand-loading demands. The tools of Klumb's avocation littered its hardwood top: a press, a powder scale, a measure with a trickler for absolute accuracy in meting out charges, a case trimmer, a loading block, and a resizing die to assure the uniformity of the cartridge cases being loaded.

Les Klumb was a grizzled sixty, with bushy eyebrows and a hawk nose and little lumps of muscle below the corners of his mouth which gave him a disgruntled bloodhound air only heightened by the drooping outer corners of his eyelids. The unlit spit-darkened stub of a cigar was clamped between his teeth.

Klumb's big calloused hands decapped the primer with a few delicate taps of his hammer on the punch. Fletcher spilled the brass cartridge cases rattling out across the wooden workbench. Klumb ignored them. His work was delicate; even factory-loaded cartridges will not always chamber in the rifle for which they were made, so hand-loaders had to strive for absolute uniformity in their bullets.

His task eventually finished, Klumb rumbled, "Finally decided to roll your own, eh?"

"Not exactly. I was wondering what you could tell me about this brass."

"Tell you?" Klumb leaned closer to squint at the cases. "Caliber thirty-aught-six, that's what I can tell you." He gave a booming laugh. "Heard you got shot by some damn fool greenhorn but I didn't know it was in the head, eh?"

"I know the caliber," said Fletcher patiently. "Is there anything else you can tell me?"

Klumb, still chuckling at his own wit, sent one of the casings spinning across the workbench with the snap of a finger.

"Not a hell of a lot. Standard factory cases, never been hand-loaded—"

"How do you know?"

"Eh?" Klumb looked surprised, as if his expertise had been challenged. He picked up the case he had snapped and pointed at the rim of the neck. "See here—never been trimmed back to length. You keep firing and reloading with one of these, pretty soon the brass starts to stretch. The neck can get so long that either it crimps into the lead or

102

hangs up on the rifling of the chamber. Either way, it can't expand to release the bullet just the way it should when you fire, so —"

"So," interrupted Fletcher quickly, "store-bought brass."

"Yep. Store-bought, but not in Cochrane."

"You know that just by looking at it?"

"I'm the only one sells guns and ammo here in Cochrane, eh?" A twitch of the jaw switched Klumb's maimed cigar stub across to the other corner of his mouth. "And I don't sell these. Only deal Remington, Winchester, and Western since these fellers stiffed me on an order and then tried to claim —"

"Any way to tell where they were sold?"

"Maybe send 'em to the factory, might be something on 'em to tell the manufacturer where he shipped 'em. But closest even he could tell you would prolly be the Twin Cities, eh?"

Fletcher nodded. He had gotten more than he expected: virtually certain confirmation of his belief that the killer was not from Cochrane. Of course the man could have bought his bullets elsewhere in hopes of leading pursuit astray should they ever be found; but if he'd been clever enough to think of that he'd have been clever enough to simply pick up the spent cartridge cases and put them in his pocket.

And he'd have been clever enough to make sure Fletcher was dead when he came down from the hilltop to check the body.

"Well, thanks, Les. I appreciate it."

Klumb nodded and struck an old-fashioned kitchen match on his trousered flank and hunched to relight his cigar. Acrid smoke filled the workshop with a blue-white haze. He spoke casually, without looking up.

"Must of found this brass out around your place, eh? Seeing as how you don't want it reloaded or anything."

"Must of," said Fletcher shortly.

"Must sort of wonder about whoever it was dumb enough to mistake you for a deer and take a shot at you."

"Sort of," said Fletcher. He felt a premonitory tingle in his

103

left knee, as if a tumbling bit of lead was about to smash into it. Hunting, hell. He was no longer a predator, but prey to some grotesque creature ambushed in his own mind.

Klumb added after a pause, "*Three* shots at you," and after a longer pause, "eh?"

Where now? Fletcher stood on the sidewalk in front of Klumb's and stared up and down snow-laden and almost deserted Main Street in the cold February light. He must be very obvious in his quest: first Nicole, and now Les Klumb, who wouldn't take any prizes for perception about human motivations, had understood that his search was not a casual one.

On the other hand, Klumb was a good hunter, and hunters noted seemingly unimportant sign. Probably everyone in Cochrane would realize he was looking for someone, without knowing exactly why; might even want to help. But that still didn't mean they could tell him anything useful.

During the next couple of days he canvassed the whole town, starting with the old white clapboard Cochrane Hotel where Main dead-ended, continuing to the rooming houses, then the hunters' bed-and-breakfast places, asking casual questions with impossible answers.

Do you remember back in November, just before Thanksgiving, someone dressed in hunting clothes . . . ?

Did a stranger with a gun come in to buy a license . . . ?

The trouble was, deer-hunting season. Scores of strangers around town with guns in their cars and pickups. They all had been dressed as hunters. They all *had* been hunters.

Especially one of them.

Each morning he walked the five miles to town, each evening the five miles back to his cabin, strengthening his knee and his resolve at the same time. Because he was coming to accept what Victor had told him: the knee was going to get only so much better. The limp was never going to disappear, nor the quickness return, because now the tendons were shorter than those in the other leg. No amount of exercise could alter that fact.

But that wasn't going to deter him from searching for the man who had done it to him. He told himself he didn't want revenge, because as long as he held nonviolence in his mind, the nightmare about Terry stayed at bay. He refused to think beyond the finding; whatever he did beyond that would not reverse the clock, would not turn him back into the man he had been before the shooting.

So he would seek. And if he found, he would know *who*; and then he could ask that *who* about the *why*.

"Why? Well, you know, Gene, I just thought you might have noticed someone gassing up his car that was acting, oh, I don't know, maybe a little spooked or something . . ."

"Well, you know, Sarah, maybe he asked you to fill him up a thermos of coffee 'cause he was going to be out in the woods all day. Or maybe he asked for some sandwiches or something . . ."

He felt, not impatience, but a kind of despair as he worked his way through town. This just wasn't his kind of hunting. But he stuck with it, asking his inept questions everywhere. At the restaurant and the two cafés, at Wilmot's General Store, the grocery stores — Yost's big old creaky one on Main Street, the new quick-stop by the highway between the town's two motels, then the motels themselves. Finally the bars.

Nobody remembered anything and everybody remembered everything. He had too *much* data, not too little, but none of it said: This man, on this day, did so-and-so and such-and-such that suggests he is the one you seek.

He collected scores of facts and duly noted them down by the light of his kerosene lamp each night, depressed by the knowledge that he might have crossed the killer's tracks a dozen times in his wanderings around town, and just wasn't versed enough in this sort of hunt to recognize what he had seen.

Bud of Dutch's Tavern remembered a nervous-acting hunter who downed two quick whiskeys and made two quick phone calls from his pay phone on some evening around the time that Fletcher had been shot. Lars Peterson at the John Deere place had rented a pickup to a man on the exact afternoon of the shooting, November 24, but he'd rented the same man the pickup on two previous afternoons. Neither of them gave him descriptions, but the facts went into the notebook anyway among the dozens of other such situations Fletcher had heard about.

It wasn't until two weeks after Nicole's overnight that he thought of the airfield a couple of miles on the other side of town from his cabin. Sixteen days, to be exact. February 25, the day after the first Democratic primary was held in the state of New Hampshire.

# 13

Gary Westergard was almost glad that his back ached and that his biceps felt cramped. Those physical twinges clamoring for attention, and his nonstop schedule, kept him from having to think about the fact he had been told casually two hours before.

A man in the crowd called out, "What happened to your boots, Governor?"

Westergard grinned. He was wearing a corduroy sport jacket, a sport shirt without a tie, and waterproof boots against the ankle-deep slush of the New Hampshire afternoon he had abandoned for Salem's town hall twenty minutes earlier. The boots were still covered with sawdust from his last whistle stop.

"I came here from a log-sawing contest, ladies and gentlemen, and I realized this is no state for old saws. So I'm not going to give you any."

The crowd laughed. Jarvis, at his side, murmured, "The car's here, Governor. We're running late." Westergard nodded, but then someone else yelled, "To hell with your boots, Governor. Do you think the man or the issue is more important?"

He called back, "Issues don't depend on personality. Whether a person is pleasant or not has no bearing on the truth of what he's saying." Then one of Ross's carefully memorized ad libs popped into his head. "But I think the old ideas, the old policies, the old agendas no longer work. Choose Senator Fiksdahl, you choose the past." He flashed that big honest Scandinavian grin again. "Choose me—you choose the future."

It was a good exit line. Never corner yourself with a straight answer to a simple question; those were the ones that came back to haunt you. He went down the steps with his legs wooden and his ankles thick from eight hours on his feet—and another six to go before he would be able to get off them. Working his way through the crowd behind Jarvis' broad back, grabbing any hand shoved his way, he headed for the door.

Tough campaigning but worth it. Most of the political pundits still were calling his Iowa win a fluke, but he was going to give them all a surprise. For over thirty years, nobody had won the presidency without first winning the New Hampshire primary, and by God he was going to win this one.

Icy outside air swept in at him. A major snowstorm was hitting the state, five inches of new snow expected before the polls opened in sixteen hours. He'd have to ask Jarvis whether the snow would help him or Fiksdahl, who despite Iowa was odds-on favorite in this first actual primary of the campaign.

Jarvis, bareheaded and barehanded, got the back door of the limo open, but Westergard spotted a woman with a baby carriage and also noted one of the television teams getting into its station wagon. Despite the predictions of a Fiksdahl win, hordes of newsmen now were following him around, thank God.

He needed all the publicity he could get, the six-P.M.-newscast kind of publicity that didn't cost anything; he'd been waiting for an opportunity like this. He went around the back of the limo and across the narrow street, Jarvis' surprised exclamation lost behind him, the network cameraman caught off-balance with one foot already inside his vehicle.

"Where the hell's he going?"

Nobody answered him. He got his foot back and, his

soundman dragging heavy cables and batteries behind, charged after the candidate.

Westergard was bent over the baby carriage and the rosy-cheeked face inside the little fur circle of parka. The mother was beaming as she waited for the candidate to kiss her child. Instead, Westergard found and solemnly shook one of the infant hands in a parody of what he had been doing all day. The crowd's roar of laughter was caught on video for the evening news.

Jarvis shepherded Westergard back across the street. The cameraman said as he passed, "Yeah, Kent, I been hearing you're the one having tough luck kissing the babes in this campaign."

Jarvis laughed, but his face was sour as he started into the limo after Westergard. To make it perfect, a slushy snowball hit him in the side of the head; wet snow splattered against the inside of the door. He slammed it, cursing the giggling boy who was running for his life with security people in hot pursuit. One of them landed on his butt in the snow as the limo pulled away, a sight which gave Jarvis a powerful perverse pleasure.

"Fucking brat!" he exclaimed. "I'd like to—"

"Shut up, Kent." The governor, smiling out through the closed window, handed him a handkerchief. "It was a vote-getter."

"He didn't hit you, I notice," snapped Jarvis. He wiped his face. "If this was what it took, we could all go home to Minneapolis and win the fucking primary long-distance."

Westergard said equably, "When I was a kid, they sometimes put rocks in the snowballs."

He was feeling confident: their pre-primary goal had been met, his campaign organization had contacted ninety-five percent of the Democratic voters in New Hampshire in person, by phone, or through the mails, and he felt that the crowds were with him.

Jarvis chuckled belatedly, his anger dissipated. "You mean I might have had rocks in my head?"

Westergard suddenly wondered if he had them in his own. The nagging worry he had been suppressing came back: Hollis Fletcher was still alive. That fact did not really bother him; but just why the devil had he been told the man was dead in the first place? What did it mean? He looked over at Jarvis' disgruntled face. Well, now was not the time to talk about it. Tomorrow was the primary.

"Minnesota Governor Gary Westergard, with forty percent of the vote, won a stunning upset victory over Senator Morris Fiksdahl of Mississippi in the New Hampshire Democratic primary yesterday," said the newscaster. He had a purple face.

"Hell," said Cap Bergstrom, fiddling with the color control inside the open panel.

He had flown a jet in Vietnam and wore an old-fashioned handlebar mustache and an ancient leather flier's jacket covered with sewn-on cloth badges that gave an unexpected touch of flair to his otherwise stolid appearance.

"Maybe that's his real color," suggested Fletcher.

"Yeah, sure, his mother was an eggplant."

They were inside Cap's tiny office at the Cochrane airfield. A kerosene heater glowed orange below an out-of-date girlie calendar. Snow swirled against the windowpane; three feet from the glass, Fletcher could feel the cold coming through.

"Fiksdahl, favored to win, got twenty-nine percent of the vote and, according to Westergard's campaign manager, Kent Jarvis, 'got sent to the showers by the New Hampshire voters, who value their Yankee independence of mind.' " The newsman's face was now bright gold. "Fiksdahl said in reply that—"

Bergstrom pushed the On-Off button and the gold face dwindled down to a white dot and was gone.

"Get out of *there*, you yellow bastard." He sat down behind the door laid flat across the tops of his two-drawer filing

110

cabinets to serve as a desk, and picked a fray-eared ledger book out of the rest of the litter. "November, you said, Fletch?"

"Yes. Just before Thanksgiving." He didn't want to suggest the exact date himself.

"Huh . . ." Cap's mustache quivered over the grease-darkened pages. "Here's one might fit . . ."

Fletcher felt a tightness in the chest: buck fever. He'd once seen a man in its grip empty his rifle into the ground a dozen feet in front of him, then swear he'd fired every round at the disappearing buck.

"What name?" He said it as casually as he could. He was starting to learn how to use his cover, blend in with the background, mask his movements in this new sort of hunting.

"November 24." Cap looked up, added, "Name? Doug Presnell."

Fletcher had never known a Presnell in his entire life.

"Doug Presnell." He made a show of thinking."What does he do for a living, you know?"

"Flies the plane, what the hell do you think?"

"Oh, I thought that was the . . . ah, the man who hired him."

"Oh, hell, I wouldn't know that." Cap swung the ledger around so Fletcher could see the pencil-scrawled entries. "All I do is log the planes in and out, but hell, I've known Doug for years. All-Weather Charter Tours, out of Robbinsdale."

"Do you remember anything about the man he brought up here?"

"He was on some sort of real-estate deal, I remember that. Flew up in the afternoon right after lunch, flew back down a couple hours after dark."

"Sure doesn't sound like the man I'm looking for. But maybe you'd better give me Presnell's address just in case."

Because it fit, it fit quite well. Fly up posing as someone on a land deal, go to the farm-equipment place and rent a

111

four-wheel pickup, drive out to the other side of town near Fletcher's cabin, drive into the brush where the truck couldn't be seen from the road, climb the hill, set up your ambush . . .

And afterward? That was easy. Come to town, excited and pumped up, find a bar and have a couple of drinks. . . .

Bud was behind the stick at Dutch's Tavern, setting up for the light Wednesday-evening trade, sprinkling salt in draft glasses, scrubbing them with a wet towel, sloshing them in soapy water, setting them upside down on the rubber mat to drain. He was a big man with thick hairy wrists, bright blue eyes, and a heavy jaw; his thinning blond hair, going gray, was parted almost down the center of his square Teutonic head. Chest hair darker than his head hair sprouted up from the open neck of his sport shirt.

He looked up when Fletcher walked in, automatically wiping his hands on his crisp white apron.

"Yo, Fletch. You're gettin' to be a regular. Twice in the same month."

Fletcher slid his bad leg across one of the red-topped bar stools, kept his other foot on the floor. The leg ached from the hike in from the airfield.

"It's that home brew of yours, Bud."

He picked one of the hard-boiled eggs out of the fishbowl, moved his hand enough to draw attention to it, then tapped it on the bar to crack the shell. Bud drew a draft beer, slushed some of the head away from it with a wooden tongue depressor.

"That's me, okay." He grinned. "Older Budweiser."

He topped it again from the spigot, and set the wet-beaded glass down in front of Fletcher.

Fletcher toasted him with it. "Skoal."

Whenever Fletcher had gone for a walk with his dad, the old boy would bring along a hard-boiled egg from the fridge

112

to crack against the point of his flexed elbow as he strode along. One day the boy had substituted a raw egg. His father had splattered it all over his coat sleeve, and had cursed so fervently that Fletcher had never told him it had been a joke.

"Still snowing out there?" asked Bud, nodding his head toward the front door.

"Yeah. I've been trying to walk into town and back every day, maybe strenghten the leg a little bit. All this snow sure makes it fun."

"Yo," assented Bud. He plunked salt and pepper shakers down next to the eggshells Fletcher was piling on an open napkin. "Ass-deep on a tall Swede by morning." He cocked one shoe on top of the beer cooler, put his forearm on it, and leaned toward Fletcher. "Listen, Fletch, how you making it, really? With the leg and all?"

Fletcher took a bite of egg and shrugged. "I can't work the trap line yet, not with this leg, but maybe next year . . ."

"Yo, she's a bitch, all right." Bud was silent for a long moment. "Anything I can do, anything at all . . ." He paused again, even longer, as if measuring his words so they wouldn't sound like prying. "I mean, you was asking me about some guy might of been around just before Thanksgiving . . ."

Fletcher wiped foam from his upper lip. His earlier surmise had been right: the whole town knew all about his quest, or guessed about it, and was silently trying to help him with it.

"Haven't found him yet, Bud. Listen, you said he was acting nervous. I was wondering, can you think of anything—anything at all—that might give me a line on him?"

Bud screwed up his face in concentration, finally shook his head. "Just what I told you before. Wore these yellow skiing glasses, that's why I remember him at all. Not much snow-glare that day, I remember thinking he was a phony, you know? Like somebody from TV nobody would recognize, acting like they would. And a little goatee and mustache like guys don't wear anymore. Not around here, anyway."

Fletcher nodded. "Could that have been the twenty-fourth he was in?"

"Just about then, yeah. I couldn't swear to it, but I remember I'd just got the Christmas decorations out of the storeroom before I opened up, and I always do that three, four days before Thanksgiving."

Fletcher grunted. "Seems like people in the Twin Cities start putting them up right after the Fourth of July. You remember anything more about those phone calls he made?"

"Just that there were two of 'em. He had a couple of shots, gunned 'em, went back and phoned somebody, came back, gunned another shot, phoned again . . ." His face suddenly lighted up. "Hey, he was nervous, y'know? Jumpy as hell—like a one-legged man in an ass-kicking contest."

Fletcher drank some more beer and finished his egg. Or jumpy as someone who'd just shot a man, he thought. He suddenly realized, those phone calls almost had to have been long-distance, and if he could get the numbers called . . .

"Listen, Bud, if those phone calls were long-distance, would they show up on your phone bill?"

Bud took his shoe off the cooler and spoke as he straightened up, disappointment in his face.

"Hell, Fletch, since it's a pay phone I don't get any bill or anything on it. I hadda even pay 'em to put it in. Hated to do it, but I went ahead last year after those Gunderson boys ran me up forty dollars here one night, calling some girl they knew out in Hawaii when they were in the service."

For a moment Fletcher considered opening the bag for him—somebody shot me, I want that son of a bitch—but that wasn't right either. The search was its own end. If by some miracle he ever found him, it would only be to ask *why*. Wouldn't it?

And just on an animal level it was hard for him to ask for help. He'd never been a herd animal, not even a pack animal. He liked to hunt alone—like the gaunt gray wolf he'd hallucinated crawling back to the cabin. If it had been a hallucination.

"Ax Gunderson still collecting the bounty on wolves?"

"Hell, Ax left, moved up around Bemidji way. Hasn't anyone seen a wolf around here in a sunth of Mondays." He laughed at his own witticism, added, "One for the road?"

Fletcher didn't really want one, but it was pleasant here in the warmth, pleasant to talk small talk, pleasant to nurse the momentary illusion that he had a community behind him in his search. He pushed his empty glass toward the back of the stick and laid a five-dollar bill out beside it.

"And one for yourself."

Bud grinned. "Yo," he said.

As Bud was drawing the beers, Fletcher realized that the trail seemed to have led him out of the woods into town, just as Nicole had expected it to. He didn't know where it would take him from here, but at least he had a place to start.

# 14

A cold wind blew straight down the river from the north, bringing with it the smell of snow. His father swung the boat off the slow brown reach of the Mississippi into one of the narrow channels leading toward the Weaver marsh. The boy sat on the front seat, twisted so he was facing forward. The eastern horizon was gray instead of black through the lacy silhouettes of leafless hardwoods rimming the slough, but when he heard the whistle of wings going over, it was still too dark to make out what kind of ducks they were.

The widening V of their wake splashed against the high mud banks on either side of the backwater, scaring up the carp lying in the shallows. The flat warning *splat!* of a beaver's tail over the staccato drum of their motor jerked his head around. He caught a glimpse of the big gray-brown pelted body slipping into the water and twisted back toward his dad, pointing.

His father nodded, then pointed himself, toward the northern sky. Long spears of faint white light pulsed perpendicular to the horizon, shifting and changing, shortening and lengthening, coruscating brighter and dimmer and brighter again as he watched. The Northern Lights.

A shiver of anticipation ran through him.

A shiver of anticipation ran through Fletcher as he approached the tied-down Beechcraft Bonanza, even though a wind-chill factor of right around thirty-five below made shivers from the cold more appropriate. The girl at the All-Weather Charter Tours office in Robbinsdale, a suburb a few miles north of downtown Minneapolis, had directed him out here.

"Here" was a snow-swept airfield tie-down and storage facility, with a double row of small corrugated iron hangars backed up against an ice-slicked but washboarded black gravel road half a mile west of Minnesota 169. Some two hundred yards away across bleak white fields was the single runway, the wind holding its weather sock straight out from the mast as if frozen there.

The struts of the tied-down planes vibrated as though the only thing keeping them from leaping up and riding the gusts were the tie-ropes lashing them down to heavy galvanized metal eyelets set into the blacktop. High-winged Citabrias with little sleeves over the wheels, a big Aztec twin-motor C, several Cessnas, even an old Cherokee Warrior.

A lanky redhead was working on the husky low-winged Beechcraft—big enough to be a charter plane, all right, with room for six counting the pilot. The man had his hands thrust deep into the engine cavity behind the three-bladed propeller as if seeking the plane's heart. He wore a fur hat with the earflaps down and a black leather jacket with several sweaters under it, and fit the description of Doug Presnell that Cap Bergstrom had given Fletcher. Cold had rimmed his mouth and eyes with blue-white flesh.

"Mr. Presnell?"

The redhead withdrew his head from inside the open engine cowling to look around from deep-set, faded blue eyes. Like Fletcher's, they seemed used to distant panoramas and picking out detail in vast landscapes. He held his hand up slightly, not quite far enough for Fletcher to shake but far enough to indicate he would shake if he didn't have oil on his gloves. They had fingers cut off at the first knuckle to give freedom and sensation to Presnell's fingertips.

"That's me. Doug Presnell. If you're looking to charter a plane, right now this one isn't it. Hundred-hour engine overhaul for the old Flying Rabbit here. Federal Flight Regulation ninety-one. It's too darned cold for a sane man to fly anyway."

"No charter." Fletcher, who liked the man on sight, returned the redhead's infectious grin. "Just trying to get some information for an insurance claim I might have against one of your charters last November—the twenty-fourth, I believe. . . ."

Presnell reverently laid his socket wrench on top of the engine cowling and climbed down off his stepladder to start away from the Beechcraft. "Now I've got an excuse to get out of this wind."

The wind took its cold hand from the boy's face as the roar of the motor dropped to a low drone and the boat lost speed; the keel cut into the coarse grass rimming the slough. He jumped out into black clinging mud up to his knees, the boat's chain painter in hand, then slogged ahead, pulling his feet out after each step with long slurging sounds. On slightly higher ground their flat-bottomed duck boat was chained to a willow sapling.

They transferred their gear into it, then his father rowed them into the marsh. Whenever the clinging black mud bottom rose to sheathe their keel, the boy would seize the pushpole and drive its triangular nose deep into the muck, holding the handle close to the water, then pushing it out, hand over hand, catching the pole at the very top with both hands, jerking it free, and repeating the process until they found deeper water again. Muck and vegetation often came with it, so he would shake the pole to get it free, leaving a muddy drifting trail behind them.

Ahead, through the half-dark of dawn, the number-one spot was visible: a little hump of swampy earth covered with trampled grass and surrounded by reeds and rushes interwoven with cut willows jammed down into the mud. It was the best hunting spot on the Weaver marsh because it was right at the edge of the reserve. The blind was empty.

"We beat them, Hal," said his father.

"To beat the other guy to that charter in Alaska, you gotta be willing to take your customers anywhere anytime," said Presnell. "It got so crazy I finally came back down here. But generally speaking there's not a whole lot of terrain scares me."

They were drinking coffee and eating yesterday's doughnuts at the counter of the Smuggler's Cup, a steamy-windowed flat-topped box appended to the wall of one of the hangars. A wide-hipped middle-aged waitress with impossible cinnamon hair took away their cups for refills.

Fletcher turned the conversation to the charter flight on November 24. Presnell remembered the man immediately.

"I flew him up there three times altogether: once in the early fall, September sometime—anyway, after the leaves had turned—and then two weeks in a row in November."

Fletcher was suddenly holding his breath. The September flight could have been for sighting in his rifle against the fire-blasted spruce; the first November flight a dry run because Fletcher hadn't happened to come up the burn past that particular tree. But if the second November flight had been *after* the twenty-fourth, he was ruled out.

119

"The last flight was the twenty-fourth?"

"That's it. We've already filed last year's records, but I can dig them out and mail you the exact data if it's important."

The broad-beamed waitress set their coffees down in front of them. "Here it is, boys—hot and sweet."

"Just like you, Emma?"

She gave a great whoop of laughter and slapped Presnell on the back so hard he slopped coffee into the saucer. He blew on his steaming cup from between chapped lips, then sipped at it gingerly.

"That Emma." He jerked his head at the window. "Out there, the wind sucks the juices right out of you, but I always feel I've got to check out the engine myself before I turn the Beech dealer loose on it. I don't like surprises that cost me money." He laughed. "You can always be sure that all airplane owners are cheap and always have a lot of credit."

Fletcher chuckled in sympathy, sipping his own coffee. "I understood from Cap Bergstrom that your charter was up there putting together some sort of land deal."

"That's what he said. A consortium of heavy money from the Twin Cities, looking to build a resort complex on the lake at Cochrane. Good walleye and sandy fishing, and it's right in the Mississippi flyway, so there's darned good duck-hunting. . . ."

Seven wigeon came out of the reserve in front of him, skimming the top of the blind as they never would after the shooting started, low enough so he could identify their dark fleeting shapes against the lightening sky. If the wind held from the north, keeping them nervous, they would fly all day.

The boy stood on the little postage-stamp of high ground inside the blind, his just-uncased shotgun under his arm, two boxes of shells at his feet, tasting the dawn with all senses.

His father was a black figure rowing away through the faint marsh mist, then a gray ghost, then nothing, not even the retreating creak of oarlocks. Then came the moist *plop!* of the decoys being dropped into the water one by one, fourteen in all.

As he drew his jacket closer around him and sat down on the empty wooden packing case which was the blind's only furniture, the splash of oars and the grate of oarlocks came from the other direction, west, where the highway was. These sounds, close to the water, carried distinctly through the mist.

Other hunters. Well, let 'em come, him and his dad were here first. The boy complacently opened his black metal lunch box and took out one of the doughnuts his mother had packed.

Fletcher shamelessly drowned the stale doughnut in his coffee. He wore a glove on his left hand, using as an excuse to himself the fact that the finger stumps were still too tender for the icy outside air.

"You don't remember what he looked like, do you?"

"Sure," said Presnell. "Dark hair and a dark goatee and mustache. Trimmed really careful-like — with those sunglasses it gave him a sort of actorish look."

"Sunglasses?"

"Well, yellow snow glasses actually. He wore 'em all the time, even flying back down here at night."

Fletcher finished the last soggy piece of doughnut and leaned back on his stool. The same description he'd gotten from Bud at Dutch's Tavern, right down to the mustache and goatee and the yellow snow-glare glasses. The important point was that any sort of tinted glasses both hid the eyes and disguised the shape of the face. Now, if he could get the jeep-rental dates from Lars Peterson at the farm-machinery company to correlate with the dates he was going to get from Presnell, and maybe jog Lars's memory on the description . . .

"And his name . . ."

"Hawkins, Hopkins, something like that." He suddenly snapped his fingers. "The flights were billed on some corporate credit card, shouldn't be much trouble to run him down once you have that." He laughed. "Closing in on him fast."

Through the haze, the boy would see the boats of the other hunters closing in on the number-one spot. He stood up so they could see the blind was occupied.

"Shit, somebody here already."

He felt his stomach muscles tighten when he heard the voice. Dieter Braun, the Rochester cop who was his father's only consistent rival for the number-one spot; a big-voiced, big-bellied bully who liked to shove the kids around when he was on patrol near the high school.

"It's the Fletcher pup," Braun said. Then, not realizing that water and fog were effective sounding boards for his words to the boy, raised his voice. "Your old man around, kid?"

"Over in number-two spot." He had trouble with his voice, a thickness in his throat.

"We got four men here, we're gonna have to take over that blind. You can get in the boat with your old man."

"I'm here, I'm staying."

The lead boat had reached the rushes; Braun jumped into the water and started to wade toward the blind. The boy's hands had started to shake, but he slipped three shells out of the pocket of his hunting coat and rammed one into the shotgun, pressing the release lever and pumping the gun to get it up into the chamber. Then he rammed the other two in; the gun, which normally held five, by

122

law had to be plugged for duck hunting.

Braun had stopped abruptly when he heard the first round go in. He stood still for a long time without moving, head up, looking almost quizzically at the boy like a Weimaraner testing the wind. Whatever he saw convinced him of something: he turned and slogged back to his boat.

It tipped when he got in, gear slid noisily, his knee hit the gunwale, and he cursed. Then the oars began to splash, rattle, and squeak and the boat retreated to the north, away from the reserve.

It was light now, light enough to shoot. The boy looked over at the number-two spot. The decoys were bobbing black specks on the icy water. Beyond them, over the top of the rushes which marked the blind, he could see his father's brown hunting cap. Even as he looked, it disappeared.

He already had dropped into a crouch himself, body bent low, head down, before he spotted the five teal rising off the reserve to fly up the channel against the wind. He clicked off the safety. They were on his side of the decoys.

The lead duck appeared over the top of the rushes; he came up, swung past it, pulled with the gun still moving. It dropped straight down, wings folded, stone dead. The others were rising almost straight up, beating frantically against the cold thin air. He fired again; a second duck went into a glide, one wing hanging, trying to reach the rushes instead of landing in the open channel.

The duck didn't make it. As it hit the water, the boy held high and toward the head, and pulled again. The gun bucked against his shoulder, the water around it was whipped with shot-pattern. Its head folded down and disappeared.

As his father poled out to pick them up, the boy reloaded. His hands had started shaking again, because he had realized that if Braun had kept coming at him, he would have shot the man as easily as he had shot the ducks.

mode the full contents turned Iretar a little from
where an instant later again saw for row, west
ay he had shot the dealer

# 15

The blonde leaving wet footprints across the hotel pool patio had the innocent face of a fourteen-year-old and the erotic movements of a porno queen. David Ross watched with carnal interest as her buttocks worked under the wisp of wet cloth, which emphasized more than covered, and tried with only modest success to consider the upcoming staff meeting.

Any hope of concentration went glimmering when the girl came back again, followed by Jarvis doing everything but lolling out his tongue at her busy backside. The man's blow-by-blow (often quite literally) descriptions of his endless seductions up and down the eastern seaboard were getting a little hard to take.

As if confirming the thought, Jarvis said as he came up, "Ah, that old callipygian cleft."

"That old what?" asked Ross in a pained voice.

"Callipygian cleft. The crack in a beautiful ass, sexiest part of a woman's anatomy." Looking down at Ross sprawled on his lounger taking rays, Jarvis slugged a long pale fruit-garnished drink and cackled loudly. "I thought you were supposed to be the big researcher-writer around here, you never heard of the callipygian cleft?"

"Nicole does most of the researching," admitted Ross, then, wishing he hadn't, quickly added, "I do *all* of the writing."

God knew when the admission about Nicole would come up in staff meeting, but he was sure it would; Jarvis always played hardball. The man seemed able to kill without compunction.

"Interesting. Good old Nicole. She and the Guv . . ."

He let it trail off. Ross, bothered, said sharply, "She and the Guv what?"

"Got a lot of work done," said Jarvis with a near-smirk. He turned his quick hairy body away. "C'mon, we've got a head-knocker with the Guv in twenty-five."

Ross picked his watch up out of his shoe and started to heave himself out of the lounger. "I called for this meeting, remember?" he asked dryly.

But as he went across the warm concrete toward the tall stacked structure of the hotel, what was in his mind was the two inches of cleft in the blonde girl's backside that had shown above her bikini bottom. Callipygian cleft. Damn.

He fought to get his mind back on track, but merely found himself desiring Nicole — brought on by the girl, no doubt, and by Jarvis' calculated hint that there might have been something between her and the governor before Ross had started courting her. He thrust both thoughts away.

Instead, he had better be reviewing the points she had made on the telephone two nights ago. Points which he was going to be making as his own in the meeting twenty minutes hence.

But up to his room, he still kept wondering about what Nicole might have been doing with Westergard in the past — and what she might be doing right then. And with whom?

Nicole tapped her notebook with the push-button end of her Bic Clic. She had listened to everything Fletcher had done, everyone he had talked to, and had made notes. Fletcher was sitting across the kitchen table from her, a tired look on his face and his hands wrapped around a mug of coffee with WORLD'S GREATEST MOM stenciled on it.

"What strikes you as the most significant point of these descriptions you got from Presnell and the bartender—Bud?"

"The fact that the descriptions match, I guess. They're obviously of the same man."

Nicole shook her head. She felt more alive than at any time since she had resigned as Westergard's secretary almost a year ago; it was as if in some part of her psyche she had been marking time. Now she wasn't.

"The significant thing is that both descriptions stress his *artificiality*. Actorish . . . like an unknown TV star trying to be recognized by acting as if he doesn't want to be."

Fletcher gave a little grunt. "I assumed he was wearing the glasses to hide his eyes and to deliberately disguise the shape of his face, but—"

"Taken with the obviously phony mustache and goatee, it suggests great lengths to not look like oneself. He wouldn't have done that just to keep from being described afterward."

"There wasn't going to be any afterward," objected Fletcher. "I wasn't supposed to turn up until the spring thaw."

She tapped the paper, frowning, then suddenly lightened. "Of course! He was afraid of being *recognized* if something went wrong—even if his name might not have been known."

"But no one in my past wants me dead, and if such a person did exist, when I moved to Cochrane my past stayed behind. There just isn't anyone, Nikki." Then he made an oops face and added, "Sorry, it slipped out."

Nicole grinned and stood up. "More coffee?"

When he nodded, she took his cup over to the stove with hers. Her nickname up through her teen years had been Nikki, and she had put up with it, saying nothing,

127

but the day she had departed for college she had served notice on one and all that she was Nicole from that day forward. And so she had remained—except to Gary during their motel trysts.

She brought back their cups, thrusting the thought of Westergard firmly away.

"Two other areas," she said thoughtfully. "The credit-card charge with the All-Weather Charter Tours people . . ."

Fletcher gave a deprecatory little cough. "I gave Presnell your address and phone number, because he said he would mail me copies of whatever he was able to dig out of last year's files. I hope that won't—"

"Don't apologize, for God sake!" she exclaimed. "I'm having more fun than I've had since . . ." She caught herself before "I got married" to finish lamely, "than I've had in a long time."

Fletcher nodded. He was seeing more and more of his own inner reticence in his daughter the more time he spent with her. Until their new association had started last Christmas, he had always thought of her as strictly her mother's child, an extension of Terry, and had been glad that any shadowy replica of his wife, no matter how attenuated, had been left upon this earth. Now he was coming to rejoice in Nicole's existence for its own sake.

"You said there was another area . . ."

"The phone calls the man in Dutch's Tavern was making."

"From a pay phone, and Bud doesn't get a bill there."

"But somewhere in the phone company there has to be a record of any long-distance numbers called even though it was a pay phone."

"But who would he be calling? You don't walk away from shooting someone and then call up a friend to tell him . . ." Fletcher paused, feeling a little silly and melodramatic. "You think he was *hired* to do this? And was

128

calling to say, 'Mission accomplished'?"

"What else? Granted he was a lousy killer, very few people would know how to find a *professional* killer. The man could be very professional in other ways. Maybe there's some sort of great hidden scandal in the payment for some road or bridge you built in a third-world country, and they don't want you around to attest to—"

"To what?" laughed Fletcher. "That sort of thing would be the concern of home offices and local politicians. The bridges and roads are there to attest to the fact that I built 'em. But you're right. If there's any way I can run down whatever number he called, I ought to try to do it. I'm going back to Cochrane tomorrow. I can—"

But Nicole had happened to see the kitchen clock, and had leapt to her feet. "Good Lord, I'm supposed to be picking up Katie from ballet class twenty minutes ago!" Pulling on her coat, she added almost sententiously, "Amateur or not, when we get that phone number we'll know who tried to kill you and who ordered him to do it. After that it's just mopping up."

"Before we can mop up the opposition," said Ross, "we have to win in Massachusetts the day after tomorrow. And I don't think we're going to do that."

They were in the Presidential Suite at the Sea Breeze Hotel—which wasn't, since Orlando was forty miles inland from the ocean beaches around Canaveral. The only way the local media could have loved it more was if it had been the Honeymoon.

The room was crowded with staffers there to pat one another on the back about how they were going to take three primaries in two weeks and glide into the nomination in July. Except now they were all sitting around with pained looks on their faces, especially Crandall and Quarles—David wasn't playing by the rules. He was bringing

129

up a subject the rest of them had stuck away in a corner and had pretended wasn't there.

Ross's point first had been made by the Massachusetts media and mentioned briefly in a memo by the absent Johnny Doyle as the Massachusetts Problem. Quarles and Crandall had jokingly referred to it as the Soft Support Syndrome; Kent Jarvis had taken it to his sort of logical conclusion by calling it the Limp Dick Constituency.

It all boiled down to the same thing. Media feeling in Massachusetts was that Westergard's supporters might not be firmly enough committed to the candidate to go to the polls, say, if the weather was rotten. Which meant that running hard in Massachusetts, where originally they'd had little hope for a win, and then losing anyway, could end up being worse than not running at all. This was the way Ross defined the problem. Jarvis disagreed.

"We called it a high-risk strategy when we decided on it last Tuesday night in New Hampshire," said Jarvis, "and that's what it is. But it's the *right* strategy for this campaign."

Clean-cut, ambitious Hastings Crandall, who subtly never let anyone forget that he hailed from an upstate New York political family himself, cut in, "Exactly. We will get a quick kill in Massachusetts, mop up—as Mr. Ross puts it so succinctly—here in Florida *next* week, and then face really very little between us and a nomination by acclamation on the first ballot in San Francisco in July."

"Sure," said Ross sarcastically, "we've got it made."

Westergard spoke for the first time in five minutes, a record of self-restraint for the candidate during one of these inner-circle debates.

"Kent and Hastings are right, and David is wrong." He marked off his points on his fingers. "This strategy will give us a farm-belt win—Iowa. A real Yankee win—New Hampshire. A northeastern industrial win—Massachusetts. And a southern-state blowout against Fiksdahl here in Florida. It's brilliant and it's gutsy and we have made a *major* commitment of resources—especially television money—to Massachusetts. Which you ought to know very damned well, David."

"He's been listening to his wife," said Jarvis with a snort of derision. "*She's* your speech writer."

Though Ross felt a flush rising, he kept control of himself. He was used to Jarvis' baiting, he just hadn't been prepared for his slip about Nicole's research to be used quite so quickly. How Jarvis would crow if he knew the ideas Ross was presenting in this meeting were also Nicole's!

"We haven't committed our *major* resource," he said evenly. "We haven't committed *you*, Governor. You haven't even *been* in Massachusetts for three days, and don't plan to go back before the primary on Tuesday. But the three-day forecast calls for snow. If the media boys should be right about soft support—"

"Massachusetts will take care of itself," said Westergard flatly. "Johnny Doyle says so, and he's up there on top of the situation. I feel it is much more necessary for me to maintain a high profile here in Florida. We have to show these voters that someone from a northern farm state can give the South a viable alternative to Fiksdahl."

"I'll be leaving for Boston in a few minutes," added Jarvis almost lazily. "If there's any fires up there, I'll put them out. We're not going to be embarrassed in Massachusetts."

"I know you don't want to lose up there, Governor," said Ross, "but—"

"That's right, I don't," said Westergard coldly.

"—but if the weather goes against us, I'm afraid that's what you're going to do."

"The voice of the prophet"—Crandall chuckled—"crying in the wilderness." He paused. "Crying wolf."

Crandall was taking his cues from Jarvis, and Ross didn't like it. "My point is that losing in Massachusetts might not necessarily be the worst thing that could happen to us."

"Losing is *always* the worst thing that could happen," said the governor, even more flatly than before.

"Unless by losing the battle you win the war. Winning *at the wrong time* can be disastrous. If you should decimate the opposition in this campaign too quickly, the congressmen who right now are ignoring you would panic. A Dump Westergard movement would start among the liberals from Washington that would be very hard to—"

"*I'm* considered the liberal candidate, remember?" demanded Westergard.

"Only in Florida," said Ross. He was ready to lighten up now; he'd gotten his points on record, which Nicole had felt was the important thing for him to do. "Up in Massachusetts the other candidates are trying to make out that the ayatollah sends you roses."

The remark brought laughter and a general release of tension in the room. Nothing had really been decided, the "high-risk" campaign strategy in Massachusetts would be pursued unchanged, but at least he had gone on record. The doubts had been aired and had been dismissed by the others as unnecessarily alarmist. But if events should prove him right, Westergard would remember who had been astute enough to foresee disaster.

Jarvis checked his watch and put on his jacket. "I've got a plane to catch," he said, causing a general shuffling toward exodus as the meeting began to break up. "I'll be back in two days with Massachusetts in my pocket."


Westergard put his hand on the killer's arm just as he started through the door, holding him back until the others had departed and they were quite alone.

"I know you're running late, but at Olaf Gavle's party back in November, you told me that Hal Fletcher had been killed in a hunting accident. Now I hear that isn't true."

"I was misinformed. Some hunter shot him, thinking he was a deer, but apparently he is recovering."

"I hope that you . . ." Westergard paused, picking his words. He was, after all, a politician. "I should be curious as to how anyone could hear about an accident up there in the woods so soon after it happened. Just an hour or two."

The killer said nothing for several moments. Finally he gave a slight shrug. "I should think that would be obvious."

Westergard nodded in apparent total understanding, even though the man had really said nothing at all.

"Of course. But I should also hope that what happened, or nearly happened, had nothing to do with what I said that day just about a year ago when . . ." He stopped just short again, with his usual superb sense of timing. "Anyway, I'd like a memo on the sequence of events which led to your knowledge of what you told me at Olaf's that night."

"A memo? In writing?" demanded the killer in astonishment.

"Just for the record," said Westergard softly, but with steel beneath his tone.


The killer pushed the Down elevator button, thinking for one dizzy moment that Fletcher had been in touch with the governor. But no. *It has come to my attention . .* He had learned it casually.

A *written memo?* Making sure the gubernatorial backside was covered, just in case . . .

The elevator door slid open, he entered. Punched the

133

button for his floor. Empty, thank God: he didn't want to talk to anyone just then. Because, oddly enough, he felt his gut strangely twisted by something like guilt at what the governor had said—right along with his fear of Fletcher.

Well, dammit, he'd done it. Couldn't undo it. Couldn't ever do it again, either. He would not be going back to try to finish the job. He'd hurt enough people already. And Fletcher probably wasn't after him anyway.

But then his old highly developed instinct for self-preservation bubbled up again. He couldn't undo what he'd done, but he couldn't be sure Fletcher was going to leave him alone, either. Fletcher was a hunter—now a maimed hunter. Maybe buy himself a handgun? Self-defense if Fletcher came looking?

Maybe buy it here in Florida—but no, too scary trying to get it on and off planes in his luggage. When they went back to Minneapolis before the Illinois primary would be soon enough. Right now they had Massachusetts on their hands.

# 16

Kent Jarvis stood in the disastrous still-falling snow and watched the foot traffic move along Boston's lower Washington Street. The storm had stopped most of the auto traffic, although the big lazy flakes now were deceptively soft, deceptively pretty as they sifted through the pale haloed streetlights.

Fucking snow.

He strode along through the infamous Combat Zone's moving stream of street life and lowlife, eyes busy, unfocused anger constricting his chest. It was after midnight, but despite the weather, people were still on the move: hookers who hadn't scored yet; a few college kids wearing letter sweaters meant to impress; diehard out-of-town johns determined to taste some big-city sin before returning home.

The porno houses were closed due to the storm; only wedges of oddly old-fashioned yellow light from a few peep shows and dirty-book stores shone out across the falling snow to suggest shelter from the cold. He didn't know what he wanted but he knew he didn't want to go back to an empty hotel room.

A black whore in spike heels that made her a good two inches taller than he stepped out of a doorway to hook her arm through his. Despite the icy weather, she wore no hat over her stacked blond wig, no coat over the summery frock which showed her bra-compressed cleavage to full advantage. Shivering with the cold, she managed to find a seductive smile.

"You look lost, sugar."

"A long way from home," he agreed, suddenly short of breath.

"I'm *real* reasonable tonight, sugar."

He had never paid before, but now he knew why he had come here. Though she was barely out of her teens, her eyes, older than stone, said she knew too. She gave a little giggle.

"Anything you need—like maybe a little head . . ."

He had to dominate the situation here; he wasn't going to have some fucking whore laughing at him.

"Yeah, if it'll fit into your mouth."

"Ohhh!" she exclaimed, and giggled again. "I get through with you, sugar, you gonna need salt tablets for dehydration."

Jarvis got back to his hotel an hour later, undehydrated; despite her skillful ministrations, he hadn't even gotten a full erection. The trouble had come from the fact that he'd been sure there was laughter lurking somewhere in her head even as she crooned and exclaimed over it.

And violence obviously hadn't been anything new to her: on her left breast had been a black-and-blue mark old enough to be turning yellow around the edges. So in his frustration and disappointment he'd doubled up his fist and struck her in the face with all his might, breaking her nose and knocking out one of her teeth and mashing those suddenly hateful red lips flat and bloody. Panicked, he'd run, chased down the hall and out into the snowy street by her mushy shrieks and curses.

When he walked into his own hotel room, bone tired and self-appalled, the phone was ringing. He ignored it to go into the bathroom and wash himself off.

The water stung his skinned knuckles. He was *glad* he'd hit the bitch, it had felt good. Everything had started with

136

that blonde cow after Olaf Gavle's party back in November; he'd failed then and he hadn't been able to get it up, really get it up, since. That's why he'd gone looking for a whore tonight: his failures with staff volunteers were starting to get around. Even that goddamned newsman up in New Hampshire had heard some rumor about them.

It wasn't that he'd become impotent, hell no. And it wasn't anything he'd done in the past catching up with him, either. Too much career pressure now during the primaries, that was all. At least he'd learned something valuable: not even the goddamn pros knew what they were doing, so you had to hurt them to keep them interesting.

He came out of the bathroom into the plush suite he'd taken for celebrating their Massachusetts win—none of that now—and the phone started to ring again as if on cue. He sighed and picked up. As expected, it was Westergard, voice icy with rage.

"What the hell happened up there, Kent?"

Jarvis said tiredly, "A fucking blizzard. Only fifty-five percent of the Democrats bothered to get out and vote, and they weren't *our* fifty-five percent."

"How bad is it?"

"If this was a horse race, you'd have finished out of the money."

There was a long silence. "You mean that I'm coming in fourth out of four?" Jarvis said nothing. There really was nothing to say. Westergard asked, "What's our percentage?"

"If we break fourteen we'll be lucky."

Another long silence. His voice finally under control, the governor said, "Get down here on the first available plane, Kent. We've got a lot of work to do."

Jarvis rang Johnny Doyle's room. The Irishman answered on the first ring, as if he had just been sitting there waiting for disaster to strike again.

"Get packed," said Jarvis. "First available plane south."

Doyle said, almost as if he were programmed by a computer, "Confucius say, 'Girl who fly upside down—'"

137

"Fuck you," snarled Jarvis.

" '—end with crack up.' " Doyle laughed and hung up.

Packing his suitcase and phoning for a bellhop, Jarvis was glad to be on his way to Florida, even with Doyle's awful jokes for company. And if there should be no planes moving, that was all right too; he'd rather wait at the airport than at the hotel. Boston now had for him a feeling of impending doom, as if something unknown and unexpected was gaining on him.

"September 23, dot was de first time he needed a vehicle, *ja.*"

Lars Peterson was a ponderous bovine man who reminded Fletcher of the late movie actor Leif Erickson, with those same heavy brows and chiseled face. He was a gentle soul without spark until he'd downed three or four Christmas shots of aquavit. Then he became the wit of any social gathering, telling one and all his only joke, a dumbest-Swede story that ended with the punch line, "Yesus Christ, yingle! yingle!" His wife always left the room when he started telling it.

Fletcher said, "And he rented the pickup so he could go out and look at the land they were thinking of getting an option on, is that right, Lars?"

"*Ja,* dot's it."

"You didn't keep the mileage, did you?"

Lars shook his head. "*Nej.*"

Fletcher took that to be no. It would have been nice if there was just about enough mileage showing to go out to his cabin and back, but the three dates were really enough: September 23, November 15, November 24. He was sure they would match up with those of Presnell's charters.

But he still was unable to confirm the description. Lars just didn't remember what the man had looked like.

\* \* \*

Fletcher did no better with trying to get the numbers called from Bud's pay phone on the night of November 24. He hooked a ride up to Grand Rapids with red-faced wheezy Gus Gustavsson, who over the years had graduated from lineman to phone-company rep; Gus had arranged for him to talk with Thelma Edwards, one of the public-communications operators in the Grand Rapids phone center.

Thelma was plump, solid, and frankly middle-aged, but she wore glasses amazingly chic to Fletcher's unaccustomed eyes, with the earpieces coming from the bottom of the ornate scored plastic rims rather than the top. When Fletcher insisted on buying her lunch she became more than willing to help; this was an Adventure, a rendezvous with a man other than her husband. The trouble was there was very little she could tell him.

"Bud Bauer there at Dutch's Tavern pays a monthly fee for the pay phone because the revenue doesn't justify our keeping one in there ourselves. So he doesn't get an itemized bill."

"But you have a listing of the long-distance calls, don't you?" asked Fletcher. "The phone company, I mean."

"On credit-card or collect, yes. But . . ."

"But there's no way I could see them?"

Her eyes, slightly magnified behind those glasses, looked distressed as she salted her cream-of-tomato soup and stirred two pats of butter into it. "A court can subpoena them, I guess. Oh, dear, I'm not helping you much, am I?" She gave a surprisingly girlish giggle. "Of course, if you could figure out some utterly nefarious way to get a look at our records . . ."

Unfortunately, Fletcher realized, she wasn't the person who would be willing to help him with that; and certainly no court would give him a subpoena for the records. He said, "I leave all the nefarious stuff to my daughter."


Leaving herself plenty of time to get back and pick up

Katie after school, Nicole drove north and west to Robbinsdale. She was disconcerted at the avidity with which she had taken up her father's search. Was she really so bored in the roles of wife and mother that she would grab at anything that gave her the illusion of involvement with the larger world out there? Or was it simple outrage because someone had tried to kill Fletcher?

What would her dad do—as opposed to what he *thought* he would do—in the unlikely event they got lucky? Did his compulsive search represent something deeper at work in him than he acknowledged even to himself? The dark side, as the psychiatrists loved to say? Or was he hiding his real intentions from her?

Whatever her father was doing, a week had passed and Presnell hadn't sent anything yet; day after tomorrow was the all-important Florida primary. Stuck at a red light, she drummed the steering wheel impatiently; ahead was a station wagon the twin of hers, same color as her own, the back end a restless tumble of black Labs.

Thank God David had taken her advice and made his pitch about the possibility of losing in Massachusetts before it actually happened; on the phone last night she had urged him to prepare a new memo to Gary and the campaign staff about substance in future speeches.

A spiteful serves-you-right thought about Gary surprised her, but then it was instantly replaced by a deep wave of feeling for him: he would be needing her tonight, to turn his angry disappointment wry and gentle. She could do that for him, no one else could. Certainly not Edith, the plump-breasted chickadee.

She thrust the fruitless thoughts aside. Ross was her husband, and his career was hers also. If he appeared to base his thinking on different reasons for different outcomes, this one memo would work whether they won or lost in Florida. He hadn't agreed to it, but she knew he would. Original thinking was not his forte.

She realized cars were honking angrily behind her. The

light had long since changed, and she started forward with a jerk. Lord, she was a mess! David would be home for a day or two before they started to prep for Illinois on the seventeenth, and here she was playing detective while feeling real twinges of resentment over her husband's current success. She didn't know what she wanted; she wanted to help his career, but resented the fact that he was where she had always wanted to be—indeed, deserved to be.

Hurry home, David, she thought suddenly. I need some loving. I need to be held. I need you to keep Gary's presence at bay.


All-Weather Charter Tours stood high-shouldered in a narrow storefront on west Broadway, Robbinsdale's main street. The sweet-faced brunette behind the desk wore heavy eye shadow and a nylon aloha shirt, as if suggesting charters to balmy Hawaii, but Nicole saw thermal underwear peeking out from beneath a flowered cuff. The girl caught the direction of her gaze and started to giggle.

"Doug says I have to dress like far places to make people think positive, but they don't keep the heat high enough for that."

"Why not raise it?"

"Dad . . . um, Doug," she grinned, "he's real economy-minded."

Nicole nodded and smiled, and sat down in the chrome-and-plastic chair across from the girl. She was there for a reason and she hoped the tone of her voice made that clear.

"Your father was to have sent me some material relative to one of his charter clients last November. If there's some—"

"Oh!" The girl's face was stricken. "You must be Mrs. Ross! Wow, I'm really sorry, I . . ." She pawed wildly through an overflowing Out basket, came up triumphantly with a six-by-nine manila envelope, already addressed, sealed and stamped. "I forgot to mail it. When he finds out, my dad's going to freak . . ."

Nicole took the envelope from her hand, unable to keep from grinning; a bubbly nature that made even embarrassment a kind of joy was infectious.

"I won't tell if you don't," she said.

Back in the car with the defroster clearing the windows, she tore open the envelope and checked the contents. She ended up staring at the photocopied charge-card receipt for the plane leasing on all three dates.

Gerard Hopkins, employee of Primary Power, Inc.

She drew a deep breath, but still had a feeling of oxygen starvation. Not a public-utilities corporation, as the name might suggest: she knew this company well, because she had carried on stacks of correspondence with it during her last year with Gary.

It was a fund-raising entity that had been set up to get Westergard elected President of the United States. Someone in her former lover's organization had tried to kill her father.

Someone named Gerard Hopkins, which she didn't believe for a second. Gerard Manley Hopkins was a poet she had introduced her father to, who had become one of Fletcher's favorites.

For God's sake, who was this man they were looking for *really?* And why had he done it?

# 17

Westergard, shirtless, took off his shoes and sat down on the foot of the bed. The eleven P.M. news was giving him a rare glimpse of Edith at work. On the tube, the stage of the high-school gym in Vero Beach, Florida, was bedecked with red-white-and-blue bunting. Edith was wearing her white linen suit with the blue blouse and a red-and-white hat of the kind that gets votes from middle-aged women to whom value is at least as important as fashion.

"Yes, my husband has always been considered a liberal, and so have I. But not anymore, not on the really important questions that demand practical, across-the-board answers."

"Isn't he trying to outconservative Fiksdahl here in the South just to get votes?" demanded a strident female voice.

The camera panned around to find the woman, rail thin, her print dress and dowdy hat right out of *Tobacco Road*—but with a too-expensive handbag that gave her away. They shouldn't have tried it, he thought; Edith's forte was turning loaded questions back on the asker. The camera had returned to the dais for Edith's response; Ross was leaning down to whisper into her ear. Westergard grinned. He had heard about this exchange.

"Didn't I see you wiping the sweat of politics from Mr. Fiksdahl's fevered brow out at the marina yesterday afternoon?" Edith asked. The crowd roared. She went on, "But the fact that you're in the employ of my husband's opponent makes me eager to answer your question. My Gary's people have always been farmers—and farmers are conservatives by nature. Yes, Gary left the farm, but there are still two brothers at home tilling the land." She paused. "He's the underdog here in the South, just like you all, and we wouldn't have it any other way . . ."

Edith's voice said, "Yourself as others see you." She hit the Off button and the set went silent. She was wearing a terry cloth robe and her hair was wrapped in a towel; the mingled scents of shampoo and steam and powdered flesh had come from the shower with her.

Westergard stood; even in his stocking feet he was nearly a foot taller than she. The unbidden wish flashed through his mind that it should be Nicole instead of her inside the robe, and he felt unexpected desire mixed with guilt: Nikki was his only affair as a married man and, as the only model he had, always represented sexual abandon to him. He slid his arms under the terry cloth and around his wife's damp plump body, but she pushed him away, laughing and blushing at the same time.

"Are you forgetting, Mr. Candidate, those people from the Florida UAW who asked to drop by just for a minute?"

"Damn!" he exclaimed.

The campaign came rushing back. He was going to try to get them to go against the National's Fiksdahl endorsement, and he wasn't sure how much he was going to have to promise them in exchange. They weren't that important, here in Florida—but auto workers were damned important in Illinois. Getting the backing of these locals might give him a chance to take a bite out of Fiksdahl's union domination in Illinois.

He started to pull on his shirt again, impatience escalating to annoyance. For a flashing instant he wished again she was Nicole. Nikki had given him more than loving: she'd given him a keen political mind to bounce problems off.

"Damn that loss in Massachusetts! I had it all planned—ride the bandwagon from Iowa to New Hampshire to here. But I let that fool Jarvis sidetrack me into his campaigning-by-the-numbers road plan right into the Massachusetts massacre, and now . . ."

But Edith had gone into the bathroom to get dressed again; there was a slight chance she might have to shake hands with the union men, and that couldn't properly be done in nightgown and curlers. She knew he hated talking with her when he couldn't see her face, but she kept up the conversation from beyond the half-open door.

"I agree with David—it's not going to be as bad as it seems. A blizzard in Massachusetts can't hide the fact that you're drawing support . . ." She emerged from the bathroom still talking. ". . . right across the board here in Florida—rednecks and blacks, liberals and hawks, corporation executives and, . . ." she paused at a discreet knock at the door, ". . . labor leaders. We all were getting pretty cocky anyway, so . . ."

The door opened enough for Ross to stick his head in. "The union people are here."

"Tell them to come around to the corridor door."

The head nodded and withdrew.

"Thank you, dear," said Edith in a suddenly tired voice. "I've had enough politicking for one day."

"So have I," said Westergard. "But . . ."

He gave her a grumpy grin and went to the corridor door and opened it enough to slip out into the hall. Thoughts of Nicole made him mildly guilty, so he was almost glad to get away from Edith for a while.

Ross had just settled down in front of the TV, but he stood up and hit the remote's Off when Edith came out of

145

the bedroom. He kept his expression interested and alert, even though all he really wanted was a little time alone to consider the position paper his wife was urging him to write. Now that Jarvis had stubbed his toe in Massachusetts, it was just a matter of time before Hastings Crandall made his move to break out of the bunch for the rail position. Nicole felt it essential for Ross to make his move first for the inside track with Westergard.

Edith was dressed as if for the street, but wore no makeup and had her hair in curlers covered by a terrycloth turban. He hoped all she wanted was something to drink from the kitchen unit's little refrigerator.

But she said quickly, "Don't mind me. I just get restless when Gary has one of these little 'off-the-record' meetings."

Which meant she wanted to talk. Cursing inwardly, he gave her the wide meaningless smile he had developed for what he called "campaign situations."

"The dread cabin fever," he said. "It strikes at the most unexpected moments."

She nodded and sat down in one of the chairs facing the couch. "You ought to feel pretty good, David. You were right about Massachusetts after all."

"I wish I hadn't been."

"Maybe you'll also be right that in the long run it will be a blessing in disguise. Jarvis is always so cocky, it'll do him good to eat a little humble pie." She sighed. "I guess he only knows one way to go . . ."

"For the jugular."

"Has he been giving you a bad time again?"

"About Nicole researching my speeches," Ross admitted, grabbing the opportunity she had offered. Edith had a lot of influence—many staffers felt too much—with the governor. "He would like to make out that she writes 'em too."

"She probably could," said Edith with an almost ruminative expression on her face. "She and the governor . . ."

146

She had stopped on the same phrase Jarvis had paused on. Ross felt a slight flush mount his cheeks. "She and the governor what?"

Edith gave a soft chuckle. "She and the governor worked very well together, David. Jarvis might have been jealous of that." She was silent for a moment, then stood up with a sigh. "Good night, David."

"Good night, Mrs. Westergard."

He watched her go back into the bedroom and shut the door. He felt suddenly tired and sullen. What had she been saying to him? Or not saying? That Nicole probably had slept with the governor before Ross had been in the picture, but that she, Edith, didn't mind? And that Ross shouldn't mind either?

*Did* he mind? He'd done plenty of playing around after his first marriage had dissolved. Hadn't Nicole had the same right?

Maybe it was just because the governor was supposed to be above lust, above subterfuge and lying. Ross stood up. Who was he kidding? Westergard was out rambling the corridors in his stocking feet right this moment, making some sort of unspecified deal with the half-dozen United Auto Workers officials thinking of secretly throwing their Florida locals behind him despite the National's backing of Fiksdahl.

Rambling down the half-bare burn with Nicole, Fletcher paused where the low hills beyond the bog became visible through the leafless undergrowth. He pointed at the lacework of brown starting to creep up the white slopes from the valleys.

"In another month the snow'll all be gone."

Nicole was furious with him; he hadn't yet reacted to her news about Primary Power, Inc. She said tartly, "They're talking about storm warnings for tomorrow afternoon."

"Doesn't matter," he said. "Mid-April it'll be gone."

A mixed flock of grackles and redwing blackbirds passed over them, driven north by their migratory instincts. Their raucous voices faded and the woods were still again except for the incessant tinkle of melting snow.

"Damn you," she exclaimed, "let me hear something that does matter. Like what you thought of my news."

"I'm still trying to get my mind around it," he said. "There just isn't any—"

"I'm not wrong," she said in an almost threatening voice.

"Then I am, in my reconstruction of the guy who chartered a plane to come up here three times last fall as the guy who shot me. If it involves Gary's campaign staff, then whoever used that credit card really did come up here to look at real estate, and didn't have anything to do with my getting shot."

"Do you really believe that?" she demanded scornfully.

"I can't believe anything else. Nobody on his campaign staff would shoot me on his own, for God's sake—but there's no way on God's earth that Gary would *tell* someone to do it."

"It's *Kent Jarvis!* It *shouts* at you, for God's sake!"

"It wasn't his name on the card."

She gestured impatiently. "I told you I checked that out. No such person as Gerard Hopkins works for them or *ever* worked for them. Since that's the name of the poet—"

"I know it's the name of the poet," he said rather tartly. "That still doesn't mean it's Kent Jarvis. I only met the man twice. Once at Christmas, and once here at . . ."

His voice trailed off. She nodded vigorously; dapples of sunlight through the trees spun gold into her hair.

"Yes. Last Easter—when he came up with David to collect the kids after the school vacation. So he would know about the layout here. Of course, *why* is another matter,

148

but . . ."

Fletcher had squatted beside a set of staggered tracks in the snow, about an inch and a half in diameter and nine inches apart. Nicole, realizing she had lost him, turned back.

"What the *hell* are you doing?"

"I think these are marten tracks," he said. "In soft snow they're hard to tell from a mink's, but—"

"For God's sake, I've just told you who shot you, and—"

"You get sore, I study animal tracks," said Fletcher.

"Pop psychol . . ." She stopped. She suddenly laughed. "You think you know me so well, don't you?"

Fletcher chuckled in turn. "Well enough. At least the half of you that's me."

She came back and squatted beside him. "All right, Dr. Jung, tell me about marten."

"Bigger than mink, smaller than fisher, but all of them—as well as the weasel—have similar track patterns you could easily confuse in loose snow."

"And all of them together," said Nicole at her most pedantic, "along with ferret and wolverine and otter and skunk, make up one family. Mustelidae."

Fletcher applauded softly. He pointed at the tracks again.

"Anyway, whatever he is, the little devil, in winter the marten gets the bottom of his foot covered with hair. The toe pads don't make any impressions in the snow. But just to confuse things, in late winter, like now, the toes become visible in their tracks again as the hair wears off."

"No toe tracks on these," said Nicole triumphantly.

He led her a dozen feet beyond, where the sun had reduced the snow to a midday-softened film on the trail. On this perfect tracking surface, three of the tracks were clearly visible—with toe impressions.

"You cheat! You knew these would be here!"

"Guessed," said Fletcher.

149

"But why can't it be a mink or a fisher?"

"Size. Stride. And because mink like to be around water, while marten like dry woods like these. And fisher have become very scarce—in five years here, I haven't seen even one of them."

They started back up the burn toward the cabin. Nicole was thoughtful. "You've been trying to tell me something with these tracks, haven't you?"

"When you start trying to decipher tracks and sign, you quickly learn—"

"Patience."

"The very word," said Fletcher. "But there's more to it than that. What we think is a marten track might be a mink—or a weasel or a fisher. So we have to get our tracks on something that takes good prints before we can be sure of what we have."

"We *are* sure," she said. "That plane was chartered with a Primary Power, Inc. charge card. There's no doubt—"

"I agree," said Fletcher. "But is the Hopkins who charters a plane three times, flies up here, and rents a jeep pickup three times, the same man who shoots me and tries to kill me *once?*"

"You're saying we can't *make* them be the same person?"

Fletcher nodded. "Either they are or they aren't. Common sense says they aren't. Our desire to end the hunt says they are. Because *if* they aren't, we're back at trailhead again—"

She interrupted with total conviction, in contradiction of everything they had just been agreeing on, "It's Jarvis."

They both burst out laughing. Fletcher put an arm around her shoulders to hug her close. He realized that he loved his daughter very much, whether she agreed with his hunter's logic or not. And if she was right about Jarvis, then they had their man but no *proof* of anything. Without proof they had nothing to push him with for the who and why behind him.

150

* * *

Ross watched Westergard shaking hands under the orange trees. He hadn't slept very well the night before. Why was Nicole pushing so hard? Her and her damned new campaign memo, and then not able to stop thinking about her and Westergard. The final straw, out of left field asking him to check up on Jarvis' whereabouts the night her father was shot.

He had a moment of empathy with her about her father. But empathy or not, asking questions about Jarvis' movements that night was one thing he wasn't going to do for her. Any campaign organization was a hotbed of gossip. Start asking questions like that, and you started rumors flying.

Besides, he was doing enough for her by struggling, against his better judgment, to write the damned memo she wanted. Was she pushing for it because she and the governor . . . ?

Oh, hell, she was pushing because she was bugged by the fact that she wanted to be where he was, not because of anything sexual that might once have gone on between her and Westergard. She was jealous, plain and simple.

For this she was jealous? Sweating his brains out here in the middle of five thousand acres of oranges outside Orlando, Florida? The area had been hard hit by the unusually severe winter, with a lot of crop damage, and of course the local growers wanted to know what Westergard intended to do about it if he became president, and the governor was giving them one of Ross's predigested ad libs-for-every-occasion.

"It was a southerner, Mark Twain, who said that everybody talks about the weather but nobody does anything about it. I can't do a whole lot about the weather either, but I *can* do something about the climate — in Washington. I'm a people's Democrat. Put me in office and I'll stand

151

up for the people."

Nicole had been right, as usual: Westergard hadn't said anything of substance at all—which was fine out here on the stump, but pretty soon the press was going to be demanding more liquor in their drinks. He'd finish the memo tonight.

Half an hour later they stopped at a marina on Lake Monroe, off Highway 4, where a lot of retirees spent their time fishing. Ross and the now-constant gaggle of newsmen and an unusually subdued Jarvis—he'd been that way ever since his return from Boston—followed the candidate out to the end of the pier. None of them wore hats in the blazing Florida sun, so Ross sweat as he pondered the "revelations" Nicole had hinted about on the phone last night; she had "something to tell him" about someone connected with the campaign.

A returning fisherman cut his outboard and glided his aluminum boat up to the dock, the V-shaped wake catching up and passing him to slosh gently against the sandy shore. The waiting Westergard caught his thrown rope and expertly snubbed it around one of the pilings. The newsmen loved it.

"How are they biting?"

The fisherman, a chunky, deeply tanned man in his sixties, wearing a billed cap of blue nylon mesh, said, "They aren't."

The newsmen loved that too.

"I guess that's what makes fishing interesting," mused Westergard. "Just when you think you have it all figured out, it changes and they quit biting."

"Or voting," said the fisherman. "I've always voted Republican, so why should I vote for you? When are you going to engineer some breaks for retired folks that make sense?"

"Soon as you cross party lines and get me elected."

"Maybe I will at that."

They shook hands as the cameras whirred. The exchange made the national news on two networks, and all of the Florida stations. It was months before anyone, including Westergard, learned that Johnny Doyle had paid the crusty oldster a hundred dollars to arrive when he did, and had carefully coached him in his lines ahead of time.


Ross had filched a portable word processor from the press room for the night, so he was up until three in the morning working on his memo. He printed it out two different ways: one for a loss in tomorrow's primary, the other for a win. Westergard took 34.3 percent of the Florida Democratic vote. Fiksdahl took 30.6. The win made Westergard a truly national candidate; as such, he now needed a national press strategy. Ross was just the boy to give him one.

# 18

MEMORANDUM
To: Governor Westergard, Kent, Hastings, Peter, John
From: David Ross
Date: 11 March
Subject: Control of Media Coverage

Now that we have won in Florida, we must avoid the greatest danger of a national presidential campaign, the arrogance of early and startling success. We have taken three out of the four target primaries, and must now control and dominate media coverage. Success in utilizing the press to send our signals and messages to the electorate is vital. Without it, we will lose this campaign.

I propose a series of speeches be developed on "Issue Themes." These will not replace the governor's off-the-cuff remarks. Rather, these addresses, national in character, will supplement the more parochial speeches of the state primaries and will give the semblance of real substance.

We know that exact detail always has a potential for disaster, but broad specifics in support of substantial points do not. These speeches will articulate thematic approaches and priorities which will satisfy the press that we are being "presidential" and which will send "signals" to elites, special-interest groups, and eventually to the public. At the same time, these points will not be so specific that they lose flexibility or box us in. They must be easily adaptable to the constituency being addressed.

Despite the governor's aversion to them, I believe that set, formal addresses, keyed to ongoing events so as to ensure maximum national attention, should be made every ten days. Thus we can shift positions without seeming to, and can make the press work for us, not against us, as it sometimes has done in the past.

(Sample speeches appended.)

Gary Westergard had planned on sleeping during the flight to Chicago, but forty-five minutes with a *Rolling Stone* reporter had left him keyed up, so he read Ross's memo first. He thought it was brilliant but handed it to Edith without comment. Since Johnny Doyle had arranged a rally at O'Hare Field, Edith was no longer in a simple suit with a sensible hat. She was dressed for the big time, the Windy City, which included a fur coat stowed in the overhead rack.

When she finally looked up from the memo, she said, "Well, I haven't read the sample speeches, of course, but—"

"I did. They're just as good as this is."

Across the aisle and two rows up was Kent Jarvis, in vest and shirt sleeves and a pall of cigar smoke, his nose buried in a sheaf of papers.

Westergard added, in a not particularly guarded voice, "*He* didn't see it coming in Massachusetts."

"And David did. Maybe you ought to tell him how much you admire . . ." When her husband visibly hesitated, Edith said immediately, "You get some sleep, honey. I'll do it. Coming from me, it won't commit you to anything."

155

Westergard nodded gratefully. "I am tired," he said.

But after she had slid out of the big first-class seat and had gone back through the partition to cut Ross out of the press contingent in the back of the plane, Westergard dug out the would-be killer's memo, handed to him without comment two days before. Not Edith, not anyone had seen it. Nor would they.

He reread it, not believing much of it, struck by its vast difference from Ross's brilliant Media Control Memo he had just finished reading. It profoundly disturbed him because he didn't know how to react to it, much less what to do about it.

After a time, he slept.

Fletcher slept badly, his rest ruptured by the endlessly unrolling dream: Terry's body flying through the air, gliding effortlessly away from him, her disappearance into the leafless hardwoods . . . He kept trying to convince his subconscious that his hunt was not for vengeance but for understanding, but his subconscious wasn't having any.

*Was* he planning vengeance? Against whom? Jarvis? He doubted very strongly that Jarvis was their man; but even if he was, then he had attacked on behalf of someone else, whom he had twice phoned from Dutch's Tavern. Except that Hopkins, for lack of a better name, the Dutch's Tavern/Presnell's Beechcraft man, could not have been the attacker: the very fact that he was attached to Westergard's organization would have to mean that Gary had commissioned the attack. Which was utter tripe.

Nicole was convinced, however, against all logic, that Jarvis was their man. And even if Hopkins was not Jarvis, he was *someone*. That someone, Nicole insisted, was the attacker. He could have stolen the card just for this purpose, she said, knowing it could never be traced back to him.

Having abandoned all pretense of sleep, Fletcher realized that Nicole was up when a match flared; one of the burners on the stove popped into soft blue-flamed light, which lit her face and made her twelve years old.

"I've been awake for an hour," she said, "listening to you being awake."

She put the kettle on, then started pumping up the Coleman lantern. Fletcher shoved down the covers—with the approach of spring the bearskin was too heavy to sleep under—and sat on the edge of the bed massaging his knee. As always, he bubbled with the temporary anger his wounds gave him upon waking.

Nicole was boring in again as the water heated. "The night you were shot, Jarvis had David working in the office late on a list of names—but wasn't in the office himself. In fact, David told me that Jarvis hadn't been around all afternoon."

"Was he at the fund-raiser later?"

"Yes, but he got there just a little before David. It isn't much of a drive from that airfield at Robbinsdale to Olaf Gavle's house. He could have flown in, gone straight there . . ."

"If I really believed that Jarvis was the one, our smartest move would be to go ask Gary about it."

"No!" she exclaimed with startling vehemence. There it was again, that sensitivity when the subject of Gary came up. As if realizing her reaction had been too strong, she added quickly, "Don't you mean *tell* Gary about it?"

Fletcher shrugged. "Ask, tell . . . what's the difference?"

With the lamp lit and tea steeping, the fire stirred up and another log blazing, he explained why he believed that an attack from Westergard's campaign corporation necessarily would have to come from Westergard himself. Nicole grilled bread for toast over the burner, more relaxed now that Fletcher was making no further suggestions that they talk with Gary directly about it.

"I don't believe Jarvis's it, but I would like to know whether he was ever in the service," said Fletcher. "The shooter was an amateur but he *did* hit me—three times at four hundred yards. He used a good rifle and the right ammo for a scoped shot through brush at that range. If he didn't learn that in the service, where did he learn it? Somebody had to teach him, probably somebody down in Minneapolis. How did he know what sort of ammo to use? Where did he get it? Where did he get the rifle? What did he do with it afterward?"

Nicole brought over the toast and some marmalade from the cupboard and sat down, then didn't eat. She lit a cigarette instead. The lamp hissed steadily. Her face was moody.

"David can find out about the army and whether Jarvis's familiar with firearms or not—"

"Can he dig into why that credit card was used and who really used it? It just makes so much more sense that it wasn't Jarvis in the first place, just some harmless somebody actually named Hopkins, so low on the campaign totem pole that just about nobody knows who he is."


Fletcher walked Nicole out to her car in the icy pre-dawn blackness, then, because he knew he wouldn't sleep any more anyway, followed the car out to the blacktop, his boots squeaking unevenly on the hard-packed snow.

Uneven steps. Splinting if he should try to speed up his pace. A cripple.

*Gary?*

No, he couldn't credit that. Somehow they hadn't even seen each other in almost forty years, but during four of their teenage summers they had worked together as yardmen at Crowley's Lumberyard, getting into shape for football and hockey. Gary had looked up to him, almost

158

worshiped him, and their long years of noncommunication owed more to Fletcher's own elusiveness than to any real estrangement between them.

A startled whitetail crashed away through the brush. It was still too dark to see him, but Fletcher's ears could follow his flight as it dwindled away to predawn silence.

Stunned silence.

"You want us to do *what?*" demanded Fletch. He, Gary, and Mr. Babs, the yard boss, were in the half-basement under the lumberyard office. It was the summer he was eighteen; Gary was sixteen.

"Dig a tunnel back the length of the building so we can put heat and air-conditioning ducts in it," said the red-faced man.

"That must be a hundred and fifty feet. How are we supposed to do it?"

Mr. Babs smirked. "Why don't you blast?"

When he had gone back upstairs, Fletch grinned. "All right, we'll blast."

He came back from lunch with a sackful of cherry bombs. They laid out a dozen each for easy throwing.

"On three," said Fletch, "one, two . . ."

These were the kind of fireworks that exploded by impact instead of by a fuse, going off with a great bang and a puff of smoke when thrown against any hard surface. They hurled them as fast as they could against the wall, so it sounded like one huge explosion rocking the office. Smoke rolled, a gunpowder stink filled the air, their ears rang from the roar.

From upstairs came a totally satisfying chorus of shouts and shrieks, the thunder of running feet, the slamming of doors. That at the head of the stairs flew open; through the smoke they could see the choking, backlit silhouette of Mr. Babs.

"What the hell happened?" he roared.

"We blasted," said Fletch.

His breath smoking around him like the detonated cherry bombs, Fletcher laughed aloud in the first hint of false dawn. Remembering that, he knew that Gary could never have done anything to make him dead. They hadn't seen each other in almost forty years, not since that drunken night with Old Charlie, but friendship doesn't die as easily as accident victims. And Nicole had been Gary's trusted associate . . .

Why, he wondered, her panic reaction when her resignation came up, or any suggestion was made that they contact Gary? Something personal between them?

Driven deep into his wife's body, Ross came so hard and long that ecstasy was almost pain. Nicole was with him every moment, heels digging into the backs of his thighs, fingers raking his back in frenzy. She had done that only twice before in their lovemaking. Finally he rolled off and lay beside her, chest still heaving.

Nicole remained supine, legs wide, belly and thighs glistening with sweat, totally vulnerable, totally spent. She reached over and found her glass of champagne. It tipped, spilling to trickle down between her breasts, cool and sticky.

"Hand me some Kleenex, will you, honey?" she said in a soft slurred voice.

But Ross was staring at the ceiling, his hands clasped behind his head. "Jesus, baby," he said, "everything's coming up roses. The campaign . . . my memos to the guv . . ." He shook his head. "After the first one, the guv was ice. Just ice. Jarvis was the fair-haired boy, and the rest of them were ringing around me like hyenas, especially Crandall. But then—"

160

"Honey, I'm sorry, but the Kleenex . . ."

She felt her loving mood evaporate when he casually tossed the box of tissues over without even glancing her way, barely aware of her in his self-absorption.

*His* memos? she thought almost angrily. Who had thought them up, pushed him into writing them? He wouldn't have done it on his own. *Couldn't* have done it on his own.

". . . when Jarvis came back from Boston really subdued, I knew I'd made the smart move. But it was when the guv read my second memo on the plane yesterday that I—"

Still trying to hang on to her postcoital euphoria, she broke in, "Jarvis is acting strange?"

"Ever since Boston, yeah." He turned his head to give her a lascivious grin. "I know you've been dying to tell me something about the campaign, but getting my ashes hauled seemed more important."

"You sound more like Jarvis every time you come home."

His eyes had sought the ceiling again. He said musingly, "I hope what you have to tell me is about Jarvis. He's such an ambitious bastard, I need anything you've got I can use against him."

Nicole had already abandoned all hope of maintaining a loving mood. Now she exchanged it for one of almost naughty delight.

"Oh, it's about Jarvis, all right."

She started right at the beginning, with Fletcher dumping the used cartridge cases out on the table at his cabin, ending with the Primary Power, Inc. credit card being used to rent the airplane *three times*.

She was aware of her husband getting more and more still beside her, and felt a surge of triumph. Unlike the memos, David couldn't take this away from her.

"It was after I got the material from All-Weather Charter Tours that I really started to zero in on Jarvis as the attacker."

"The attacker," said David in a flat strained voice.

"He was up to Dad's cabin with you to pick up the kids last spring, so he'd know the ground. I imagine you told him just casually, in conversation, that Dad always walks up that burn in front of the cabin when he's coming back from the woods . . . and stops to unstring his bow by that big burned-out tree. He has access to that charge account, he could dummy up a card under a phony name. Dad's still trying to find out who he called from that pay phone in Dutch's Tavern, because that will probably tell us who hired him to do the shooting. If you can find out if he ever served in the military—"

*"Stop!"*

The near-hysteria in that single word made Nicole spill the last of her champagne in astonishment.

"What's the mat—"

"Holy shit, are you *crazy?* Are you and your fucking old man *nuts?*" He literally leapt out of bed as if impelled by the disbelief bubbling up inside him. "Are you trying to destroy this campaign? The governor? Me?"

She was getting angry in turn. She sat up in bed facing him, hugging her knees as if cold, her anger suddenly and inexplicably mixed with something that was almost fear.

"Nobody's implying that Gary had anything to do with this. Of course Jarvis was acting on behalf of somebody else. But—"

"Just fucking *give it up!*" Ross shrieked. He lunged forward to jab a forefinger at her face. "I know why you're doing this! Because you're jealous of me! You're trying to ruin me with the governor—"

"Don't talk like an asshole!" she yelled. She slapped his hand away, anger at the half-truth of his accusation overriding her uneasiness. "It doesn't have anything to do with

162

you. If you won't help us—"

Her head was over to one side, her ear ringing, before she realized that he had slapped her very hard across the face. He seized her bare shoulders and started to shake her with a power she hadn't known he possessed.

"God damn you," he panted, "I said *stop*. I mean it. I . . ." His fingers unclenched from her shoulders. He stepped back from the bed once more. He said lamely, "I . . . I won't have my . . . my chance at Washington ruined because you and your sick fucking old man . . ." He grabbed up his pants, started hopping on one foot as he pulled them up. "Just . . . just *fuck you!*"

He grabbed the rest of his clothes and almost ran out. Nicole stared at the empty doorway, numbed, barely aware of the stinging heat where he had struck her.

"Oh my God!" she half-whispered. "Oh God in heaven."

She knew, beyond any shadow of doubt, beyond proof, beyond reason, who had tried to murder her father. Vomit welled into her throat as it had into her husband's after he had shot Fletcher in the woods up by Cochrane. The onslaught of nausea was so sudden that she barely made it to the bathroom in time.

# III

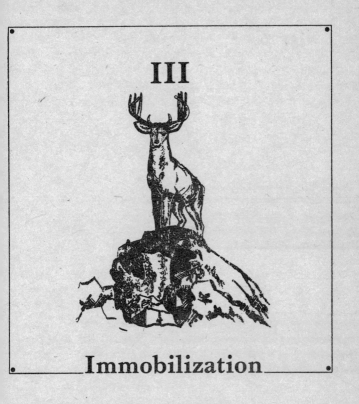

# Immobilization

The animal may be driven or captured first to avoid transporting the dead carcass or to put the hunter in more favorable terrain. Animals are also stampeded into pits, over cliffs, into swamps, into a cul-de-sac, or taken by snares.

# 19

Ross sent the car shooting backward down the driveway into the nighttime-deserted suburban street, then slammed it into drive. The rear wheels spun on the ice and caught a patch of clear pavement; the car fishtailed away, tires smoking as his breath smoked in its still-cold interior.

She knew. Instead of his pathetic outburst, why hadn't he just written her a notarized deposition that he'd tried to murder her old man?

The trouble was he'd been waiting for something he could use against Jarvis, and all of a sudden she was unraveling his whole goddamn life right in front of his eyes. Maybe if he'd kept his mouth shut he might somehow have sidetracked her, pointed the loaded gun that was her old man in someone else's direction.

*Anyone* else's direction.

No. Not Fletcher. Shot three times, lying there in the snow holding his breath and not moving. Listening to his killer approach and knowing that any second a slug might crash into his brain. Then, when it didn't, crawling a thousand fucking feet . . .

Ross's hands convulsed around the steering wheel. This madman might be coming along his back trail. Not pursuing a faceless somebody with some vague connection to a Westergard campaign-funding agency. No. Coming after David Ross himself. By name. By face.

He needed a drink.

They had always liked Vasili's because it was a totally conventional Midwest steakhouse—with touches. The owners were 1930's Greek immigrants, so there were bowls of bitter salt-cured olives on the tables, ouzo and Greek salads on the traditional steakhouse menus.

The walls, also, were Greek. There were bearded Orthodox priests and stern-faced Greek women. There were crossed scimitars with curved shiny blades, long-barreled rifles probably used during whatever Greco-Turkish war Byron had fought in, battered metal cook pots, bright peasant skirts tacked up to display the full flare of material, soft caps with red tassels, old cracked leather shoes with pointed, turned-up toes and tassels on the tops of the insteps.

Tradition. Family. Honoring the old folks through the generations. But nobody smashed any saucers on the floor in Vasili's. Here was none of the hustle and joie de vivre of a taverna on Rhodes.

Sitting on a leather-topped bar stool, Ross thought that it had all seemed so clear. Carry out the governor's unspoken wish, ride to the top with him. The act itself had seemed unthinkable, yet somehow he'd just . . . edged into it.

The bartender, his short white jacket straining under the arms with twenty extra pounds of good Greek cooking, set down a napkin and bowl of pretzels. From the tables came the low hum of conversation and occasional bursts of alcohol-loosened laughter.

"Hey, Davy, what'll it be?"

"Oh, uh, hi, Fred. A, uh, Jim Beam, water back, no ice."

Fred poured the two-ounce shot glass brimming, carefully set it down on the little paper napkin with its drawing of a vinegar-faced woman and the caption, "If you can't say anything nice about someone, come here and sit by me."

Ross drained it in a single gulp. "Hit me again."

"You got it, babe."

Fred had pale protuberant eyes and a beefy, clean-shaven face smelling of freshly applied English Leather. He poured, Ross fired it down as quickly. God, how he'd needed that! Then he realized he had muttered that exact thing to himself in that crummy little bar in Cochrane after shooting Fletcher. Fucking Fletcher. He had to deal with his fear rationally, instead of emotionally as he had with Nicole.

Okay, treat it like some unfortunate publicity story about the governor's campaign that was in danger of being leaked to the press. He gestured for one more drink.

Assess the seriousness of the security breach; identify the most dangerous potential adversaries; work out the steps to limit the damage.

First, degree of danger. By his blowup, he had virtually told Nicole that it was he, not Jarvis, who had tried to kill Fletcher. Take it as a given that she now believed, or at least feared, that he was the shooter.

Second, potential adversaries. Fletcher, of course; but Nicole was trickier. He sipped at his third shot. Would her main loyalties lie with her father? Or with her husband? A strong bonding with the kids had occurred; this would work in Ross's favor. If only he'd somehow been a better husband to Nicole when it would have counted. Kept lines of communication open, talked things through with her.

If he'd been doing that all along, he never would have done it in the first place. Or if he'd done it, he wouldn't have stormed out of the house a half-hour ago. But he'd had no other option. His guts had been churning and tension had gripped his temples with iron tongs.

169

Be cool. If Nicole hadn't already phoned Fletcher, she would have realized by now that Ross hadn't outright *said* he'd shot her old man. She was a strong-minded woman, a rational woman, a *fair* woman—she'd *have* to be worrying about the mathematical chance she was wronging Ross in her assumption of his guilt.

Theoretically, then, Fletcher didn't yet know who the would-be assassin had been. There was still time to do something about containing the situation—limiting the damage, as they said in the campaign.

Two options now. Go home and admit it. Or go home and deny everything, flat across the board. He had once read that if your wife discovered you were having an affair, no matter what she knew, or thought she knew, deny it.

Deny it, assess her reaction, then take the offensive.

He put his head down for a moment, rubbed his eyes with the heels of his hands. So tired. If he could just go *talk* to her, tell her how scared he was, how badly he'd fucked up.

He couldn't do that. Sharing had never been his way. Guts it through. Attack her about her jealousy—her obvious wish to be where he was, be doing what he was doing. Then . . .

Then, claim to believe that she'd been sleeping with the Guv before he'd started courting her. That could have been what Jarvis and Edith Westergard had been hinting at in Florida. Claim Nicole had quit the governor's office because she was still attracted to the man. It wasn't so, of course, but it would make powerful ammunition for their pitched battle when he got home.

At the very least, it would buy him some time.

But as he slid off the stool, he knew he needed insurance against that cold-minded son of a bitch who could lie bleeding in the snow while the man who had shot him came to check his kill. The sporting-goods shop a few blocks down the street would still be open. Now was his time to buy the handgun that he had thought about buying down in Florida.

Wrapped in her winter robe, Nicole strode up and down the living room, hugging herself as if cold, taking mechanical drags on her cigarette. Her eyes were a mess from crying, her cheek hot and red where David had slapped her.

Why hadn't she been able to see it before? Because it was so monstrous? Because he might as well have tried to kill his own children as her father?

Twice she picked up the phone to call Fletcher, twice put it down again. Despite all of Fletcher's rationalizations about the hunt being an abstract exercise in logic, she knew how he would react if she called and told him that David was the one who had shot him. He would come storming down here from his great north woods like a hungry wolf.

When she'd been really little, in her dreams Fletcher had seemed the hugest man in the world. Indestructible. Filling her horizons. Then he'd kept going away, and his strength had faded.

Now . . .

Now, the trauma to the kids if he came down from the north after David . . .

Shouldn't David have thought of that himself? They were *his* kids; she was only their stepmother.

Resolutely she tried again, but then on the first ring slammed down the receiver.

What if David's burst of rage, his striking her, were because he thought she was jealous and feared her jealousy would destroy his desperately sought chance at Washington?

No, he had struck out of fear, not in rage.

171

As she ground out her cigarette in the ashtray on top of the piano, the garage door, activated by David's car remote, rumbled open beneath her feet. She lit another, stood rigid in the middle of the room, arms crossed, face set, eyes flinty, tension building as she listened to him come up the cellar stairs, pause on the landing, then come up into the hall to shed his coat and gloves before finally entering through the wide arched doorway.

"You fucking bastard!" she burst out.

"Honey, I'm really sorry I slapped you." His smile was like that of a hyena finding an absent predator's kill. "I was overwrought, and then you—"

"Then I overreacted because you tried to murder my father?"

"You can't really think . . ."

She shook off his hand furiously.

"How could it take me so long to see? Everything I thought about Jarvis fits you so much better. You're a petty mean little man with a mean crabbed little soul. You could have done all the things I thought Jarvis had done, only easier. You were late to the party that night—"

"I phoned you from the office!"

"You phoned me from Dutch's Tavern in Cochrane. That's who got those two phone calls Daddy's been trying to trace—Nicole, the damned fool! Jarvis was at the office, you were up there shoo . . ." Her voice broke. "Shooting my father. But *why?*"

He shook his fisted hands in apparent frustration. "But I didn't *do* anything! That's what I'm trying to tell you. I was there at the office and—"

"Let's ask Jarvis, shall we?"

"He'd just lie anyway, just to fuck me over."

"And you wouldn't? You, you filthy . . . You're the one, I know that. I'm calling my father right now to tell him."

172

Ross gave an uneasy chuckle. "Honey, if you do that . . ."

"You're afraid of him, aren't you?" She was growing ever more furious. "You'll hide in the woods and shoot him from ambush, but the thought of facing him—"

"He . . . he's a crazy man, that's all," said Ross lamely. "He was the big survivor in Korea, everything's by instinct with him. He wouldn't wait to hear the truth, he'd just—"

"Why won't you tell *me* the truth, murderer?"

"Nobody's dead, Nicole. Now if you'd just—"

"He might as well be dead, crippled inside and out. All you've left him with is hate."

Ross yelled, *"Goddammit, Nicole, I didn't shoot anyone!"*

"Let's ask Jarvis, shall we?"

"You've already used that line." He sneered. "Maybe we ought to ask him about your affair with the governor instead."

"What?" she demanded. "What did you say?"

"Do you think I'm stupid? Do you think Jarvis and Edith Westergard and the governor's staff are blind? They all knew you were sleeping with him before you started going out with me—maybe even after we started dating. Here's a man old enough to be your father— hell, your father's best friend. But you're a power-fucker, so you got him into bed and—"

"Maybe after you I just needed a good piece of ass for a change."

Ross was shocked. "You're saying you *did* sleep with him?"

"Of course I did—*and* picked up the affair again three months after you and I were married."

"What? You . . . I don't believe . . ."

She laughed into his stricken face. "That really gets to you, doesn't it?" She was advancing now, smiling scornfully, her eyes furious. "You want me to tell you about

173

it the way that Jarvis would? With the name of the motel and how many times who did what to whom?"

"You *wouldn't* sleep with him after we were mar—"

"I would and I did. Do you expect me to apologize? I'm only sorry that I broke it off to be wife for something as low as . . . Oh, God *damn* you! You're nothing without me to tell you what to do! You're a coward and a murderer and . . . and get out of this house! Right now! Tonight! I'm sick of looking at your lying face!"

"Honey, if you'd just listen—"

"To what? You haven't given me anything except lies. Until I have the truth . . ." She demanded suddenly, "Did you shoot my father?"

"Nicole, if you'd just—"

"Did you shoot my father?"

"Can't you understand, it isn't just a simple—"

"Did you shoot him?"

He spread his hands. "You can't just . . ."

"Did you?"

He covered his face with his hands. So tired. So scared. He had to let it go. Had to let it out. There were tears in his voice. "Well . . . yes, but . . ."

"And you admit it to me!" she cried in illogical despair. "You sorry excuse for a . . . *Why?*"

He raised his head again. "Can't you see that it isn't just black or white, it—"

*"Why?"*

"Are you going to tell him it was me?"

"Unless you tell me why you did it!"

"He'll kill me like swatting a fly."

"Do you really think I'd care?"

"Nicole . . ."

He sank down into the chair beside the fireplace where he usually read the evening paper, and suddenly, like a dam bursting, it all poured out of him. The governor, foot up on his desk on that rainy afternoon eleven months before. Reacting to the poll showing him with a distant dark-horse shot at the presidency, his big right hand fisted in frustration.

*"The presidency of the United States. Right here. And out there a man who could, if he wanted to . . ."* The fist opening, the presidency escaping forever. *"Like that."*

"My father? He meant my father?" she exclaimed in a rising, amazed voice. "What could my father . . . ?"

Ross didn't know, but he made her see it all, everything that had happened, as it had happened, even made her understand what had been going through his own mind as the idea of killing Fletcher somehow had gradually formed. It was the greatest public-relations job of his career, because he *had* to tell someone, and he had shared his life with her for the past four years. And because without her silence he feared he wasn't going to stay alive.

Even though he knew he was no good at this, he was never going to try to kill anyone again, the one thing he didn't tell her about was the handgun that he had put in the drawer of the file cabinet on the cellar stairs landing.

That handgun might just conceivably have even more to do with his staying alive than Nicole's silence.

# 20

As Ross choked out his justifications for murder, Fletcher was crunching his way back to the cabin through the midnight woods. It was clear and cold; the full moon cast lacy patterns of naked hardwood branches and bearded silhouettes of lance-topped pines onto the snow. But spring was not far away. During the daylight hours it was getting slushy in the open glades, and, surest sign of the changing seasons, hoarse arrows of ducks and geese were honking their way north.

Fletcher stopped as a pregnant doe, followed by her previous spring's fawn, picked her way across the trail a dozen yards ahead. They moved carelessly, cracking twigs as they went, pausing for a mouthful of sere grass or a nibble of secretly budding ash, more appealing forage than the bitter willow twigs of the deeryard. The doe's flag was down, the fawn's up, the underside of his tail a creamy gray in the moonlight.

A dozen yards closer and Fletcher could have run an undetected hand along their sides as they passed. He'd done it many times under Old Charlie's tutelage, dreaming of one day doing the same thing to a timber wolf. But predators are often more wary than their prey; as a boy he'd never seen one.

A brace of cottontails hopped gingerly out of a tangle

of brush into which his arrival had sent them. They started gnawing on nascent gooseberry buds at the edge of the burn.

When—if—David dug up anything on Jarvis would be soon enough to leave the fifty square miles of forest, woodland, marsh, and hillside he had come to think of as *his* woods.

So enjoy the night.

Enjoy the night, the boy thought. He brushed snow off a fallen log to sit down. The sky was brilliant, its stars blinded by the overriding radiance of the January moon. February's would not fall on a weekend, so, with Christmas vacation over tomorrow, this would be his last full-moon night of the winter snows.

The rest of the forest was not even grazed, but this open parklike corner edging the plowed fields had been logged a dozen years before. Imagination could make death's heads of raspberry bushes, hide demons in brush piles, see corpses in rotting logs.

Of course Old Charlie said you never had to be afraid of anything in the woods. Just get so good you never surprised anything and were never surprised *by* anything.

He slid off the log into the snow, after a few moments lay down on his back, parallel to it, staring up into the winter sky, protected by his layers of warm clothing and letting his thoughts drift like the wisps of cloud periodically obscuring the moon.

Maybe he could get his Dad to drive down to the river next Saturday so they could hike in and check the fords across the West Newtons sloughs. Once there, what more natural than to drop off some supplies for Charlie and the current Spot?

All of Charlie's dogs were called Spot. None of them seemed to last very long—one had been killed by a bobcat, a second had been drowned in a slough by a big old coon it had been dumb enough to chase into the water, a third had died in its sleep. Somehow, a month or so later, there was another one.

What dog *wouldn't* want to live in a tarpaper shack down in the river bottoms? On a night like this, with school starting the next day, the boy sure wished that he could.

The veinlike markings on the full moon's plump, creamy surface were like the veins on the half-glimpsed breast of a nursing woman he'd seen in the Town Talk Café last year. It had given him the same hot and heavy feeling in his groin as the bouncing of the bus after school. At his stop he'd hold his books in front of him, knowing he'd die if any of the girls saw the front of his pants sticking out that way.

Dying. Lying all warm and toasty in the snow, he remembered the Jack London story where the guy froze to death. Just sort of went to sleep and never woke up. . . .

The boy woke up. The moon was much lower in the sky; it had to be after midnight. In his sleep he had turned on his side and had picked up, even through his earflaps, sound waves being transmitted through the frozen earth.

Thump, thump-thump, thumpity-thumpity-thump . . .

Excitement and fear shortened his breath and made his heart pound. The only potentially dangerous animal he'd ever met had been that black bear, three months ago; he could still barely think

178

about it running, even shot, into that deadfall to hide rather than charge him.

But there weren't just animals in the woods — often there were people. Old Charlie's never-acknowledged ancestors entered his mind: Chippewa or Winnebago or Sioux braves ghosting through these forests on silent moccasined feet. Crazy, of course, but what about *real* people?

Well, what about them? Old Charlie had taught him that in the darkness you need be wary of no man. Outside the circle of light other people felt they had to surround themselves with, you were a piece of the night, unseen, unseeable.

The thumping had continued. No longer scared, the boy pulled himself up to stick a cautious eye above the log.

Cottontails! This meadowlike land was dotted with their burrows — beneath brush piles, between the roots of stumps, under logs. Here were dozens of them at this meeting of three trails, more arriving even as he stared, more rabbits than he had ever seen in one place before. They cavorted and hopped in the pale blue light, their twirling moonsoft shadows blurry beneath their feet, forming a rough circle with all of them facing inward. Up on their back legs, bouncing like the square dancers at the American Legion Hall on the Fourth of July.

In the center of the circle were half a dozen bucks, alive with passion, erect, capering, leaping, their long springy hind legs making moonlit blurs of the feet they pounded with an almost sexual fervor on the hard-packed snow.

*Thumpity-thump, thumpity-thump, thumpity-thump thump thump!*

He hiked himself up for a better look, but in-

179

stantly furry moon-grayed bodies went flying in every direction. Warned by their sentries, they tumbled over one another in panicked flight; within seconds the little patch of beaten snow was deserted.

The chagrined boy remained totally motionless for half an hour, but not a single rabbit returned. Before trudging back home, he paused to feel the tamped-down snow with a bare hand. As hard-packed as if men, not rabbits, had been cavorting there.

To heck with school, tomorrow night he'd—

The sound of busy teeth cutting through slender branches on the still night air made Fletcher once more aware of the brace of cottontails grazing a dozen feet away. When he'd gotten home that night long ago, bursting with excitement, he'd told his folks all about the rabbit dance. He doubted they'd believed him. Rabbits didn't dance—never had, never would.

He'd gone back for several nights thereafter, but he'd never seen the rabbits dance again. He came to believe he'd just dreamed it; but years later he ran across a book of reminiscences by the naturalist Charles Livingston Bull. Bull, during a midnight winter ramble through the Maine woods, had seen the same ritual.

Sudden anger suffused him. Why was he wasting his time trying to find the man who had shot him? Here in his wilderness was where he belonged. If he was without inner peace, at least he was not at war with himself. Here he had worked out his truce; here he could live by it.

Fletcher rose, stiff from his hour of total immobility. The rabbits fled back into their deadfall. Phone Nicole, tell her he was giving up the hunt. Predators couldn't be

Hamlets, agonizing over their actions. If he found his man and a killing moment was called for, it had to be unthought, as natural as breathing. His would not be so. His inability to shoot the deer had shown him what he was: a crippled predator that had become only prey.

# 21

Chicago was having a heat wave in the middle of March. Temperatures just were not expected to soar into the high seventies while exhaust-blackened snow banked the side streets and ice rimed the rivers. Especially not when frigid Canadian winds would soon be booming back down across Lake Michigan again.

Warm afternoon sunlight slanting through the tinted double-paned window of his Carl Sandburg suite cast attractive crags and highlights across Gary Westergard's rugged features. In a television campaign, rugged features meant votes. He blessed the warm weather. The primary was in just two days, on the seventeenth, and he was tired, bone tired. He wished this false hint of summer would melt some ice at his weekly staff meeting.

"Jackie Jefferson is a local boy who made good in the big bad world of national politics." Jarvis raised his voice to be heard over the rush-hour Loop traffic, audible even up here thirty floors above the street. "He hasn't got a chance in hell at the nomination, but he's a spoiler—he's gonna scoff up seventy, eighty percent of Chicago's black vote. That means—"

"Exactly squat."

"Your wife tell you to lay a couple of nifties on me?" he snapped at Ross around his sodden cigar butt. After the rude shock of the Massachusetts loss, Jarvis had developed a belated sense of caution about the campaign. "Jefferson's clowning around means we've got only eighty percent of the Illinois popular vote left to play with. And the polls are giving Fiksdahl over half of that—forty-five percent overall."

"The polls are wrong. The governor has fielded full slates of candidates for all one hundred sixteen slots on the Chicago ballot." Ross turned to Hastings Crandall. "How many potential delegates has Fiksdahl qualified?"

"At last count, forty-two." Even at this informal meeting, Crandall was dressed with an Ivy League perfection which only emphasized Jarvis' rumpled-politician exterior. "And with the election only two days away, he's not going to qualify any more."

"He doesn't have to," snapped Jarvis. "When Austin and Reubin and Liebert dropped out, he picked up the thirty-four officially uncommitted delegates to appear under his name."

Crandall said, "Making seventy-six total if all of them should get elected. Since they won't appear on the ballot as pledged to Fiksdahl—"

"Who gives a damn about the popular vote anyway?" demanded Ross. "The governor's just won ninety-nine delegates in Michigan and Arkansas combined, and I think we're going to win over half the hundred eighty-one delegate votes here in Illinois no matter which way the popular vote goes."

"You're dreaming!" said Jarvis. "Jefferson's getting the blacks, Fiksdahl's getting the union vote—"

"Like he did in Florida?"

Westergard, thanks to his secret hotel-corridor meeting with the UAW local honchos, had carried the Florida union vote by a paper-thin margin.

"Christ, Ross, the guv was able to cut a deal with organized labor in Florida. Here—"

"He can cut a deal here too."

"Not so goddamn likely," muttered Jarvis. But it had little force: they all knew Westergard had been meeting privately with the leaders of the various Chicago locals.

"Except for Chicago, Illinois is a Republican state," said Ross. "Republicans and independents like to cross over here, and the Republican yuppies out in the suburbs are going to vote for the governor just to screw the Cook County Democratic machine."

Westergard watched them almost dispassionately, weighing, judging. Way back in November, at the fund-raising party, Ross had told him that Fletcher had been shot dead in a hunting accident. Only in New Hampshire, Jarvis had casually mentioned seeing Fletcher alive and well at Ross's place on Christmas Eve.

The discrepancy could be a political land mine, and he had planned to get the truth about the whole damned incident out of Ross after tonight's meeting broke up. Now he wasn't so sure. The man had become the sharpest current political voice on the campaign staff. It didn't matter whether his ideas were his, or, as Jarvis claimed, Nicole's: they were the *right* ideas.

Maybe, right now, he needed Ross.


Ross's hands tremored visibly as he poured himself a second shot from his suitcase bottle and added water from the bathroom tap. He stood at the window to sip his drink and look up South Federal toward the Board of Exchange, guiltily aware of the telephone on the bedside table. The phone's winking red eye announced a message waiting. He'd just left the other staff members a few minutes before, so it could only be from Nicole up in Minneapolis.

He needed to know her state of mind but equally dreaded learning what it was. What if she were calling to say she had decided to tell Fletcher after all? Or, worse yet, that she already had? The Minnesota primary was just two days after this one, but he couldn't ask for Secret Service men to tag him around Minneapolis. And he couldn't tell the governor the truth.

If Fletcher had indeed been dead, he could have let Westergard understand, obliquely, that he had been the one who had lifted that particular burden from the gubernatorial shoulders, and could have looked forward to an appropriate reward once the candidate made it to the White House. But he had failed.

The telephone started to ring. Ross drained his glass and walked past it out the door.

# 22

Nicole paced the kitchen, glad that the children were in the living room involved in the TV. She had to think. Why was David avoiding her? She *had* promised to do nothing while he was gone, but that had been two days ago. Two agonizing days. And now he was ducking her calls. As a result, all she could think of was the fact that *he had shot her father!* Tried to kill him. *Wanted* to kill him. Had crippled him instead.

*Crippled* him. *Forever.*

She poured herself a seltzer from the fridge, then rolled the cold glass back and forth across her forehead. She had a splitting headache.

Her father was an honorable man, her husband what they had called in the Old West a bushwhacker. So why the agonizing? Why the hesitation? Honor, truth, honesty all demanded that she get hold of David and tell him she was going to . . .

Not that easy. There was another side.

The children.

Gary's campaign.

The scandal.

Even David, sitting in the big easy chair, confessing his sins, moving her to compassion as he was somehow always able to do no matter how mad she was at him. More than compassion: in his moments of weakness and confession, almost to a rekindled love.

But what about her father? Didn't he deserve her compassion more than David did, no matter what she had promised?

The phone rang.

It was the unlisted line so she was across the room in two strides, to pick it up before a second ring would bring one of the kids to the living-room extension.

"David," she said into the phone, "I've decided to—"

"From your tone of voice, I'm glad I'm not David."

"Oh. Dad." She couldn't breathe. She wasn't ready for this. "I was going to call you—"

As Fletcher said, "I decided to call you—"

They both stopped, with only the sound of the miles between them. Literal and figurative miles, she thought. She took a deep sighing breath. Almost painful—like splinting. The inability, ever, to take a really deep breath again.

"Dad . . ."

She had only to say: *Dad, it was David who shot you. He thought he was doing a favor for Gary.* Just say it, and let . . . well, let her father and David work it out. And Gary.

But then the father of her childhood swirled up before her eyes again. The man who filled her world from horizon to horizon. Who could handle anything, take anything. When he was angry, do anything he wanted to do.

And David . . . hunched crying in the easy chair . . .

*Do you, Nicole, take this man to*

In a rush of words, she said, "Dad, David found out it . . . wasn't Kent." There was no response from Fletcher. She went on blindly, panicked by his silence. "He was in the office that night, and the credit card was a stolen one. So I was wrong . . ."

She heard herself ending almost on a rising, almost a pleading note, and thought: Oh, God, what am I doing? I'd made up my mind to tell him, hadn't I?

Fletcher said, "It doesn't really matter, honey."

187

But his long pause had so unnerved her that she was just tumbling out words in a high strained voice, any words to fill the accusing void of his silence. "Yes, and I guess it's just as well he wasn't able to find out anything . . ." The gaunt gray wolf would come loping down from the north, and David would die. ". . . Because I won't be able to help you look for . . . look. For a while. I . . . I might have to . . ."

"Nicole. Honey. I said it didn't—"

"I . . . David has asked me to . . . accompany him on . . . on the campaign trail." Her tinny laugh was mere sounding brass. "You know how I am about politics."

"What about Robbie and Kate if you go off down to Chicago?"

"Oh, ah, David suggested that maybe his mother could come and stay with the kids for a week or two."

"A week or two? Isn't Illinois in two days?"

For the first time she realized he wasn't enjoying the silences any more than she. "Yes, but, ah, I might even go with him for the rest of the campaign, at least off and on, right up until the convention in San Francisco in July. I've never been to San Francisco and—"

"Reason I asked, I could stay with the kids if you couldn't get anybody else."

"Oh, no," she exclaimed instantly with her forced gaiety, "David's mom would *love* to." She was babbling faster and faster, like Iris Bergman during one of her periodic reversions to Southern belle. "Or if she wouldn't, there's Iris and Norman, you met them at the party, and I couldn't ask you to do that now that I'm defecting from the ranks, so to speak." Bleak despair lurched through her, a clumsy monster. "I guess you'll just have to . . . go on all by your lonely, just . . . keep on looking . . ."

Him, anguished, looking for his murderer, while she, with a word, able to give him what he wanted. *Needed.*

"It doesn't matter, sweetheart," he said again, "I'm giving it up."

That brought her up short. "Giving . . . I don't understand."

"I'm going to quit looking for him. Even if I did ever find him, what then?"

"Then you . . . you'd question him, find out who and why . . ."

She stopped, appalled. He was giving her the solution to all of her problems, and here she was urging him to go on with the hunt. Needlessly go on, because with a single word she could give him his prey; but she was incapable of it.

"I've thought about this a lot," said Fletcher. "What if I found him and . . ." Sudden rage and anguish entered his voice. "Nicole, I can't even kill a goddamn deer anymore. I'm not a hunter, I'm not anything." His voice began rising. "I can't hunt, I can't trap, I can't . . ."

He stopped himself. She said in a small voice, formal as a party dress, "I . . . I'm sorry, Daddy."

"Yeah, so am I." He tried for a chuckle, almost made it. "But I'll sure be free to baby-sit the kids if you need me."

"I . . . thanks, Daddy, but maybe I won't . . . maybe the trip won't . . ."

They hung up by mutual accord. Nicole waited for a flood of relief. *He was giving up the hunt!* David was out from under, she was out from under . . .

No rush of reprieve. Because now she had to live with a moral issue merely removed, not faced. She burst into tears, great wailing gawps of sound that brought in the children, wide-eyed, from their television. She could not tell them what was wrong, could only cling to the puppy comforts of their love.


Ross had been right.

Westergard took forty-one percent of the popular vote in the Illinois Democratic primary, Fiksdahl thirty-seven percent. Jefferson, who took eighteen percent—virtually all in Chicago—claimed it was now "a three-man race" for the Democratic nomination in July. Nobody but his most avid supporters paid any attention to him.

Thirty-nine percent of the union vote for Westergard, to Fiksdahl's twenty-eight and Jefferson's twenty-six.

Ross had also been right in assessing the delegate count. Westergard eighty-nine, Fiksdahl thirty-six. The other fifty-six were officially uncommitted until after the first ballot on the convention floor.

Nationwide, with a total of 1,967 needed to nominate, Westergard now had 629 delegates selected or allocated, Fiksdahl had 357. Jefferson was a distant third with sixty-one.

Westergard, 1,338 delegates yet to go.


Jarvis wasn't needed for the Minnesota shoo-in, so he fabricated a campaign-connected excuse to stay behind in Chicago for an extra day. And night.

First of all, he needed time to think.

He had lost a lot of ground since Massachusetts; and worse than that, he seemed to have lost his balls as well. Chickening out in front of the Guv by predicting a loss in what he now saw had been somewhat of a sure thing.

He had no center to his political reasoning, no core. He had to reorient himself. Had to figure out what he could do for the Guv that nobody else on the staff could do. And then he had to do it, thus making himself indispensable once again.

After New York and Pennsylvania, they'd be halfway to the Democratic convention in July, the guv was in the lead, and the Republicans didn't have a Ronnie-babe this time around. If Westergard went all the way, by God,

Jarvis was going all the way with him. There was no reason an indispensable man couldn't segue from campaign manager to cabinet member.

So he was going to find whatever it was that would make him indispensable. Maybe not today, maybe not tomorrow, but before the campaign was over. He would find it. And exploit it.

Meanwhile, there was a second reason he had wanted to stay behind in Chicago. In the course of wangling the guv's fifteen percent of the black vote—three percent better than Fiksdahl's—he had made a connection with a black pimp called Sharkey who ran a string of street whores on South Drexel Boulevard in the Kenwood area. Sharkey would do almost anything if the price was right, and certain of his girls would do even more—things too dangerous to look for in Minneapolis.

The fiasco with the black whore in Boston had taught Ross that professionals couldn't blow the whistle if things got a little rough; that dark-skinned whores excited him; and that there was something else that excited him even more.

He talked to Sharkey about it, man to man, and Sharkey, far from being shocked, had just the right girl for the job. For a price, of course; people with special needs had to expect to pay for them.

Or maybe it was the girl who paid. She was very good, but as he had expected, even her skillful ministrations couldn't get him stiff enough to get where he was going. He felt his now-familiar rage, just as he had in Boston, and, just as in Boston, he doubled up his fist and knocked her right off the bed.

But this time he was ready. He was on her in a frenzy of excitement, beating and kicking and breaking her arm and cracking two of her ribs and, as she started to scream with pain and fear, messing up her face rather badly.

Also, as he'd half-anticipated, half-feared, getting where he was going.

He left her lying in a welter of blood and semen beside the bed, confident she'd find her own way to the hospital. After all, that was what she'd gotten paid for, and Sharkey had assured him there would be no repercussions. Hell, she probably got off sexually herself on the rough stuff.

Sharkey went home counting a lot of hundreds, and Jarvis went back to Minneapolis feeling like a million.

# 23

Fletcher sat on the foot of the examining table, the vinyl cold against the backs of his thighs through the paper sheet, and wondered why Nicole had been lying to him on the phone.

"What?"

"Your hand looks absolutely splendid." Victor Kroonquist, M.D., stuck a blue Scandinavian eye close to Fletcher's brown one. He looked very much like a heron hunched in the shallows with its eye bent downward for an unwary minnow. "You aren't hearing a damned thing I'm saying, are you?"

"Should I be?"

Victor grunted, tall and stooped and rawboned. He jerked the blood-pressure cuff tight around Fletcher's arm, pressed the stethoscope to the inside of the elbow, and inflated the cuff.

"Before I waste the time and effort of a physical exam, I may as well find out if you're still alive."

"Affirmative — unfortunately."

Victor flung his arms wide to declaim:

> *If you can force your heart and nerve and sinew*
> *To serve your turn long after they are gone . . .*
> *Yours is the Earth and everything that's in it,*
> *And — which is more — you'll be a Man, my son!"*

Fletcher barely heard him. He'd noted all the hesitations, the changes in the timbre of Nicole's voice, the slight shortness of breath as she had poured out her reasons for withdrawing from the hunt. Children had been lying to their parents since Adam and Eve invented Cain and Abel, but still . . .

"One-twelve over sixty-four. High blood pressure doesn't seem to be a problem with you—and you aren't listening again."

"I tuned you out when you set the dial on *If.*"

"I admit Kipling's a bit hard to take in his inspirational mood. But there are worse poets—"

It was Fletcher's turn to emote. " 'I'd rather flunk my Wassermann Test, than read a poem by Edgar A. Guest.' "

"Exactly."

She probably had feared him taking the law into his own hands, and so had just quit helping him. It didn't make any difference anyway. His scarred left knee was tapped with a little rubber hammer; the leg jumped obligingly.

"Splendid! A galvanized frog could do no better!" exulted Victor. "Kroonquist, you're a hell of a surgeon!"

Just as well he was giving up the hunt. It wouldn't be much fun alone. He had come to depend on Nicole for her enthusiasm and identification with his outrage.

The stethoscope was cold against his bare chest. "Breathe normally. You aren't running a race."

"Not many of those in my future."

"Do I detect a note of self-pi—"

"Oh, ashcan it! You're like a preprogrammed computer."

Victor put the stethoscope on Fletcher's back. Told him to breathe deeply. Kept moving it from spot to spot. He finally folded it up and stuck it in the breast pocket of his white smock and put his butt against the edge of the file-littered desk.

"Healthy as a horse and sour as a lemon. And *that,* my friend, is something no computer can do. Make similes. To a computer, 'sour as a horse' and 'healthy as a lemon' would be equally valid."

Fletcher reached for his pants. "Are we in the middle of a conversation I don't know about?"

"It can't arrive at an understanding of the unfamiliar by relating it with the familiar, and without the ability to evoke images and emotions—"

"Words would be meaningless?"

"Very good! You're wasting yourself up here in the great north woods, Fletch."

"What about you?" He gestured at the framed degrees and certificates on the walls. "How many years of med school and internship and residency to be sitting up here in the piney woods yourself, playing word games at a two-bit private clinic?"

"Hardly two-bit." He chuckled dryly, as much at his own sharp tone as at Fletcher's comment. "Don't try to make me sore, and don't try to change the subject, pal."

"What is the subject?"

"You and the fact that you're not a computer."

In his own way, Victor was as much of a hunter as Fletcher was. Had been.

"When you finish looking for whoever shot you, why don't you come over to the house for a good dinner and some good talk? Ingrid has some pheasants that—"

"Who says I've been looking for—"

Victor flopped the local phone directory open on the desk.

"Just about anyone in here except for the sheriff—and not him only because you never bothered to officially report the shooting. But . . ."

Fletcher angrily shoved an arm into an appropriate shirt sleeve. "But you put it all together?"

"At least enough to know that a hunter putting three

shots into you because he thought you were a deer was about as probable as you winning the hundred-meter dash at the next Olympics."

Fletcher pulled on his boots and stood up. "Well, it doesn't matter now."

"You're giving up."

"I didn't say—"

"You don't have to. It's obvious. You're feeling sorry for yourself. You've had all this input—getting shot by someone you can't imagine who, for some reason you can't imagine why—without anything to compare it to. A computer would say 'INPUT ERROR' and do nothing. But you *acted*. In human terms you did the right thing— even the heroic thing. You survived. Survived suffering God knows what damage to your psyche right along with the physical damage. Then you . . ."

He paused. Fletcher was looking around at the walls.

"What are you doing?"

"Looking for your diploma in psychiatry."

"How do you make 'psychiatry' sound like 'witchcraft'?"

"I got shot because secretly, deep down inside, I *wanted* to get shot? No thanks."

"Well, you sure as hell ought to thank whoever did it— he broke you out of a five-year groove of self-pity."

Fletcher jerked open the door. "Thanks a lot for the exam, Doc. Send me a bill."

Victor detained him. "Goddammit, Fletch, I'm just saying that you can get over psychic trauma the same way you can get over physical trauma."

"The fact that I can't shoot a deer right now doesn't mean I'll never be able to shoot a deer?"

Victor did not notice that the excitement in Fletcher's voice was bogus. "Exactly! You can—"

"But didn't you say I'll never be able to walk without a limp? Never be able to breathe deeply without—"

"As I said, it's a sour bastard." Victor chuckled. "Okay.

196

Just tell me all about why you can't shoot a deer any-more."

"Some other time."

"Today. Wednesday is my golf day so I've got—"

"There's still snow on the ground and there's no golf course in Cochrane and you don't play golf anyway."

"See? My afternoon is free." He put an affectionate arm around Fletcher's shoulders, starting him out past the admissions desk. "Come on, I'll drive you out to the cabin."


Fletcher opened the bag for him: the dreams of Terry fleeing him into the hardwoods continuing even though he had determined to give up the search; and feeling again, with the defection of Nicole, the disgusting burden of self-pity.

"Seems to me that Nicole quit 'cause she got scared of what you'd do if you found the guy."

"I'm glad she did," Fletcher said, not sure he really meant it. Enough snow had melted so that Victor was able to pull the old Chrysler right up beside the cabin. The engine ka-thunked to a stop. "It still needs a timing job."

"And will until the day it dies."

Fletcher had his hand on the door handle. The engine creaked in the icy air. "Nicole didn't know that even if I had him in my sights I wouldn't be able to pull the trig-ger. So—"

"Do *you* know that?"

"I just told you. When I tried to shoot that deer—"

"The deer hadn't shot you first." He made an exagger-ated shrug. "But it's all academic anyway, isn't it? You've declared closed season on ambushers."

Fletcher grinned. "I thought you were a healer, not some bloodthirsty murderous bastard who incites his

197

friends to—"

"I *am* a healer. What the hell do you think I'm trying to do right now?"

"Get sued by the Minnesota State Psychological Association for practicing psychiatry without a license. Hell, even if I had scars all over my psyche, Victor, finding the man who shot me wouldn't heal them." The car-door hinge squealed; it needed oiling, just like his knee. Him and the tin woodsman. "Or anything else."

Victor ignored him. "The phone calls from the Dutch's Tavern pay phone are crucial to identifying him."

"But there's no way to find out who made them, and even if there were, I'm out of it for good. That's final."

A vocal cloud of startled grackles flowed up from the open space in front of the cabin, voices raucous, feathers a purple oil-slick sheen in the sunlight. Victor gave a single bark of laughter at Fletcher's back, then began coaxing the Chrysler back out toward the quarter-section road.

His face wore a speculative, chess-move expression, as if he were thinking about Dutch's Tavern and phone calls.

# 24

Westergard waited alone in a La Guardia VIP lounge for the one-on-one he planned with David Ross. He would hate to lose David, but he had to know the truth. At this point in the campaign, ignorance was just too dangerous. If Fletcher spoke . . .

He made a disgruntled face at his newspaper. The election news was creating a proper mood for his upcoming confrontation.

### DEMO PRIMARY RATED A TOSS-UP

At the beginning of last week, Minnesota Governor Garrett Westergard appeared to enjoy a healthy thirteen-point lead in the ABC-Washington *Post* Poll. Last night, the same poll found that Morris Fiksdahl has surged to a virtual tie with Westergard in the significant New York Democratic presidential primary.

Political punsters are offering a variety of explanations for the apparent shift in voter preference, but most feel that Fiksdahl's media blitz is beginning to make itself felt.

The door *shushed* shut behind Ross before he reacted to the fact that Westergard was alone in the otherwise deserted lounge. "You shouldn't be here alone without any—"

199

"The Secret Service people are outside. I sent the rest f the staff on ahead to the hotel and the midtown head-uarters to draw off the press." Was that a spark of wari-ess in Ross's dark eyes? "I want to talk about your letcher memo, David."

Ross sighed. He sat down facing his employer.

"All right, Governor, what do you want to know?"

"On the night of the fund-raiser at Olaf's house, you old me Hal Fletcher had been shot and killed in a hunt-1g accident."

"That's what I thought at the time."

"Where did you learn that?"

No hesitation at all. "From Nicole."

"I spoke with her a few minutes before you told me bout Fletcher and I'd swear she didn't know anything bout it then."

Ross was meeting his eyes directly, but Westergard was oo old a political hand to believe a steady gaze necessar-ly meant the truth was being spoken. "Why don't you sk her yourself?"

"She's in Minneapolis, you're here. I'm asking you."

Ross shrugged. "All I know is that she asked me to tell ou, and then just left the party."

"David, she knew her father and I were great good riends. If she thought he was dead . . ."

"She couldn't handle telling you about it just then."

"And since? She couldn't handle telling me he was 1live?"

Ross stood up to make two tight, oddly aimless circles. "Can we be frank here, Governor?"

"It might just save your job."

Ross made a dismissive gesture. "That's just a fucking :heap shot, Guv. You see, I know about you and Nicole."

Westergard was on his feet, the back of his neck scar-let. He had not briefed himself for this sort of confronta-tion.

200

"David, that, er, that was before you and she—"

"And after."

Westergard sat down again. "I . . . I see."

"I know it's finished now," said Ross quickly, "but . . ."

"Yes," said Westergard dryly, "but." After a long pause he put his hands on his knees as if to stand up. "Well . . ."

Ross blurted, "You said yourself that Fletcher could stop you from being president. If he *had* been dead . . ?"

"I exaggerated," said Westergard. "Hyperbole. Too many drinks. Casting about for reasons why I couldn't become president. Unable to face the enormity of it all, I suppose."

Ross met his eyes for a moment, then just nodded and turned away. Westergard watched the door *shush* shut behind him.

Well, Ross was the key right now. Ross, the injured party who all but apologized to the man who had seduced his wife. That was understandable—Ross wanted power, position; Westergard might be able to offer them. But he had also said about his wife's father: *If he had been dead*—with the inevitable implication of *then everything would have been all right and we wouldn't be here having this discussion.*

As if he had been involved in trying to *make* Fletch dead.

Yet Westergard had never *said* he wanted anything done to Fletcher, just wished aloud. *His* hands were clean. But Ross . . .

He sighed. Nicole he would believe; but there was nothing he could do until he could ask her about it face-to-face.


Ross splashed his face with cold water, sloshed out his mouth, wiped his face dry with a fistful of harsh paper towels from the dispenser. He should have felt on top of the world. He'd just faced Westergard down! Matched him tone for tone, icy look for icy look, all because Nicole had told him on the phone last night that Fletcher was giving up the search.

So why was he here shaking and close to tears and almost throwing up into the toilet in an airport men's room?

Because he had pulled the trigger. In Westergard's office that April afternoon it hadn't been just booze talking, or any crap about the guv's inability to carry off a presidential campaign. No, Westergard had believed that Fletcher could knock him out of the race.

But it was David Ross who had pulled the trigger, so it was David Ross between Westergard and Fletcher now. Westergard with his power for life; Fletcher with his power for death.

Ross took a deep breath. Fuck 'em both. Hadn't he found the courage to shoot Hal Fletcher? Hadn't that taken a man of strength and daring, a man of guts, a man of *seeds?* In the woods by Cochrane, and again here in the airport lounge, that inner man had been in control. That inner man could be president himself, could handle the red telephone, could even push the doomsday button if he had to.

Except that David Ross, apart from those isolated explosive moments, wasn't that cool, ruthless, totally competent man. David Ross was a man in terror of being gunned down by one whom he had dreadfully wronged — one who *was* all of those things. And there was the *real* reason why he was dry-heaving in men's rooms.

He was never going to grab the brass ring. Not unless he could satisfy Westergard's self-serving fears once and for all, not unless Nicole would confirm his version of events to the guv. And Nicole wasn't going to do that.

Or was she?

He stared at himself in the mirror. He wet his pocket comb and began running it nervously through his tight black curls.

This David Ross might not be brave, but he had broken through to Nicole once before, when he had admitted shooting her father. He had cried, she had held him in her arms.

Maybe . . . just maybe . . . Maybe he could do it again.

# 25

Garrett Westergard bit into his pickle — kosher dill, of course. Here even the smells were Jewish, controlled, rational, or at least civilized: fresh-baked bread, onion bagels, pickles, gefiltefish, kosher meats. Zuckerman's Deli had been at this same address just off Broadway on New York's recently trendy Upper West Side for well over half a century. If he'd been trying to woo neighborhood voters in the twenties, he would have been wooing bearded *hassidim* in forelocks; but the local yuppie vote he was after now was still just as Jewish.

He wiped his chin with a paper napkin. Campaigning eighteen hours a day for three solid days, with no relief in sight. After the primary tomorrow, right on to Pennsylvania for the following Tuesday. No time right now to worry about Ross.

He waved his maimed pastrami on kosher rye around at the media people and the shoppers who had assembled for a firsthand look at the candidate.

"Any questions — about me or the sandwich?"

"Since New York is considered a media state second only to California, what impact do you feel Fiksdahl's outspending you two-to-one for television ads will have on the primary?"

"His ads speak for themselves."

"You want me to quote that? He's standing on his record?" The reporter had a strident voice and big round mauve-tinted glasses that made her look remarkably like a bug.

"That isn't what he said, lady," snapped Jarvis. His tone suggested he'd like to step on her. Westergard shushed him.

"Perhaps instead of standing on his record, you should say: standing still. I'm moving forward."

"He says the past is prologue."

"I say the past is passé."

A field reporter from one of the New York television stations popped out, flanked by his cameraman with a shoulder pack. He wore his hair in a single ponytail down his back, with a U-2 concert T-shirt under a trendy Italian linen jacket with the sleeves folded back the obligatory single turn. Shoes, no socks. He never appeared on screen anyway—his questions were looped by the on-air personality before airtime. He started laughing and snapping his fingers.

"Hey, Guv, I think the story"—snap, snap, snap—"is gus-ta-tory. But what the public wants is elim-i-na-tory." He gestured to his cameraman to roll tape and deepened his voice in conscious parody of the on-air personality who would replace him in the newscasts. "So tell me, Governor—word is that the New York primary's a toss-up, with the tide running strongly toward your opponent. Would you care to comment on that?"

"What's the catch phrase? 'It ain't over till it's over'?"

"You're still claiming that you'll win?"

"I just want the New York voter to ask himself this: What does Morris Fiksdahl stand for? There's no question of where I stand—on every issue. But there's no answer to where *he* stands—on *any* issue!"

A patriarchal-looking Jew with well-tended gray hair and a bushy gray-flecked beard rapped his cane on the edge of Westergard's table. The already-moving Secret Service agent stopped; the cane-taps were more symbol than substance. The crook of the cane was darkened and smooth from many years of use and the old man's suit had the soft creases of drawer-folding. He smelled faintly of mothballs.

"With all due respect, sir, do you think you can represent this neighborhood honestly in dealing with the Middle East situation?" Despite his courtesy, his voice had unexpected ringing tones. "Could any man who did not come out of a ghetto in Eastern Europe, who never fought the sand storms of the Sinai or the Palestinian terrorists of an East Bank *kibbutz* be such a Solomon as we need?"

Westergard knew better than to try clever retorts to a mind trained from birth in analytic thinking. Instead, with a warm smile he turned away to an overweight, strong-featured, black-haired young matron who was buying deluxe meatloaf at $5.99 a pound. In the crook of her arm she cradled a tiny boy wearing a white skullcap.

"Madam, do you find me a false pretender in your midst?"

"By me, you're okay."

A newsman had his mike in her face. "Does that mean you're going to vote for the governor?"

"Hey, I'm sorry, I can't. I'm so kinky I'm a Jewish West Side *Republican!*"

The crowd burst into delighted laughter. Westergard turned back to pat her son on his white-capped head.

"Madam," he said, "don't you realize that the time has finally come when a man is not barred from the White House because he is wearing a prayer shawl and a skullcap—except if he's Jewish, of course."

He made the six-o'clock news surrounded by laughing Jews in a Jewish deli; Fiksdahl was seen pumping blue-collar hands in a singularly unphotogenic South Bronx garment factory.

* * *

206

Standing at the kitchen counter, Nicole read the scare headlines of the New York *Daily News* she had bought at an out-of-state newsstand in downtown Minneapolis:

WESTERGARD WIPE-OUT IN N.Y.!
45% of the Popular Vote!
133 Delegates!
FIKSDAHL'S MEDIA BLITZ FAILS TO IGNITE VOTERS

She read on while waiting for the microwave to heat her cup of coffee. Instead of the usual podium victory-speech photo, Westergard was in some fancy Upper West Side deli in front of a crowd of laughing customers, all of whom looked Jewish.

Yesterday, Garrett Westergard won a smashing victory in New York's Democratic presidential primary. Morris Fiksdahl only narrowly edged out Jackie Jefferson for a distant second place. The Minnesota governor, unlike Senator Fiksdahl, seems to have mastered the art of winning the big industrial states.

The phone rang. It was David. He demanded, his voice full of enthusiasm, "Did you hear?"

"I'm just reading about it in one of the New York papers." Then she added in a totally neutral voice, without animosity and without excitement, "Congratulations."

"A great win. The governor—"

"Where are you? Still in New York?"

"Philadelphia—in the guv's suite at the Bellevue-Stratford."

She said with her careful neutrality, "How jolly for you."

"I wish you were here to share it with us."

My God, how she would love to be with the campaign

207

right now! Her voice took on the slightly accusing tone she hated but couldn't help using with him.

"You know why I can't be."

"Even the governor wishes you were here."

Now he was starting his phone call; the rest had been prologue. "You've been discussing your wife with your boss, who just happens to be her former lover? Wonderful. That's the sort of throbbing sensitivity I've come to expect from you, David."

"It wasn't that way at all."

She pinched the phone between jaw and shoulder as she got her steaming cup of coffee out of the microwave and added a flat spoon of sugar.

"What way was it?"

From the fridge she got the two-percent milk she had trained herself to use.

"Actually, Nicole . . . honey . . . he trapped me in the VIP lounge at the airport the day we got to New York." She could hear the strain in his voice. She took her first flat slurp of coffee and thought dispassionately: Here it comes. "He wanted to know who at Gavle's fund-raiser had told me that your father had been shot."

"And you told him what?"

"You."

"*Me?* For God's sake, David, he'd know that wasn't . . ."

She caught herself, sat down, shook a cigarette out of the pack on the kitchen table. She still hadn't been able to quit again. She wasn't going to get emotional, and she wasn't going to get involved. This was David's problem. He'd created it, let him deal with it. Through the sulfur tang of the match she drew the first delicious drag deep into her lungs.

"You may as well tell me about it from hello-hello."

David did, ending with him almost getting sick afterward in an airport men's room. "We haven't spoken of it again, but I know damned well he's going to want to talk

208

to you about it."

"If he asks, I'm going to tell him the truth."

"You can't. I looked him right in the eye and said you'd learned of it after you spoke with him at the party, and asked me to tell him while you went home."

"Even if he *would* believe that, why didn't I call to tell him that Dad hadn't been killed after all?"

David hesitated. There was a what-the-hell shrug in his voice when he said, "I said I knew about your affair with him."

"You utter *bastard!*"

"It was the only thing that would convince him." Asperity entered his voice. "After all, you did it. *After* we were together. I told him that too."

Her affair with Gary had actually hurt him! But nothing she could ever do would compare with what he had done to her and hers. And even though he was playing hurt right here, he was still finding it very handy to use against her in a tight situation. She ground out her cigarette viciously in the ashtray until it was just shredded fiber lisping smoke.

To her silence, Ross exclaimed defensively, "Dammit, I just didn't have any other options. That was the only thing he'd believe. You *can* get my mother to stay with the kids while—"

"No, David," she said very deliberately, "I won't do it."

"You lied to your father for me."

Lied to save your life, she thought. Because there's no way you could stand up to him. Then she had another, more uncomfortable thought: maybe lied to get a little of her own back for all those years of neglect when . . .

She said hurriedly, not wanting to look too closely at the web of motive which seemed to keep her tied to this man, "I've already started to regret that."

Ross was wheedling. "Honey, if you won't square me with Westergard, I'm going to get dumped from the campaign."

"*I* got dumped from the campaign a long time ago," she burst out. "Hasn't it ever occurred to you that there's a moral issue here more important than your damned campaign? You tried to *murder* my father! You've gotten me to go along with that for the moment, for Christ knows what obscure reason inside me, but—"

"If you don't back me in this we *both* lose our chance at Washington."

"I saved your life—you'll have to save your own job."

"Nicole—"

"I have to go pick up the kids. Good-bye."

"Nicole . . ."

But she already had hung up the phone.

# 26

*The night of the Pennsylvania primary, Fletcher dreamed. Not of politics. Not even of Terry fleeing him down the labyrinthine ways. He dreamed memories.*

The truck slithered down the road almost sideways. Ahead the way was unmarked except by animal tracks; behind the churning tires of the new '49 Willys Jeep was just a slurry of April mud. Young Fletch reached down and pulled the stubby four-wheel gearshift lever back to engage it as he jerked the wheel over.

The still-unfamiliar truck jumped out of the ruts and shot forward across the beaten-down saw grass. He pumped the wet brakes, slithered to a stop nose-up against a leafless willow. Discarded cans and bottles were scattered around in obvious signs of habitation, but winter-dormant vines covered Charlie's tarpaper shack so completely it seemed only a thicket, not a man's home.

He got out and slammed the door loudly, sure signal for the current Spot to burst joyously forth, leaping and barking his delight. The air was cold after the heater-warmed interior. No Spot appeared. No Charlie either. Fletch set down his gunnysack on the square-topped front fender to thrust an arm through the sleeve of his hunting jacket, picked up his sack of goodies, and trudged back, pulling on the jacket awkwardly as he went.

The door was shut, no smoke leaked into the gray

afternoon from the stovepipe poking up precariously through the shed-style slanted roof. Three years earlier, Fletch had helped Charlie put up new support wires for the rusty, soot-blackened relic.

*"Charlie!"*

No response.

"Hey, you! Charlie! It's me. Fletch."

No response.

He went around the broken-down rocking chair mired in front of the shack to pound on the door with a bare fist. Nothing. Always unlocked; but Charlie's code demanded that visitors be invited inside before they entered.

Out in the woods with Spot?

Not too likely, this early in the spring with patch-snow still on the ground and rim-ice still on the river. Worried now, Fletch went around to the back. Anything could have happened to Charlie since he had been here during Christmas vacation.

Cupping his hands against the dirt-grimed little window, he belatedly sensed someone behind him. He leapt and whirled, coming down facing the way he'd come, heart pounding. Charlie was a foot away, his beak of a nose almost touching Fletch's chest, his seamed, lined face an explosion of wrinkles.

"College no damn good for you! Old Charlie walk right up and pinch your ass if he want, you no hear 'im!"

Fletch wanted to hug the old devil, but settled for shaking hands. "What the hell were you doing? Hiding?"

"Yeah," agreed Charlie unexpectedly. "Me'n Spot."

Given permission by Charlie's silent arrival, Spot had appeared to bark and whine simultaneously. He was a golden Lab and Irish-setter mix; Fletch crouched to hug the big red-gold head and get his face licked. Spot looked gaunt. Fletch straightened to hoist the sack of goodies to his shoulder.

He began, "We had this stuff left over at home," in his father's dignity-sparing formula, but Charlie cut him off.

"Any snoose in that sack?"

He held up a couple of flat round tins of Old Copenhagen. Charlie grabbed one and began twisting off the top.

"Hiding from who?"

He was talking to Charlie's back. He followed, Spot leaping and barking for a handout. Old Charlie's hair had gone white from the remembered salt-and-pepper, was twisted into the beginnings of a single heavy braid down the nape of the wrinkled neck. Beside the mired rocking chair, Charlie paused to stare at his shack as if seeing it for the first time.

"Me, I was born in a Winnebago tepee . . ." His hands sketched a half-sphere in the air. "Shape like beehive, mebbe."

Fletch was astounded. Only once before, when mad at him for shooting the bear, had Old Charlie admitted his heritage.

"Not pointed like the Sioux tepees." The hands tensed to bend something into a half-circle. "Made of bent willow poles. Covered with grass and hides. Hole in the middle for the smoke to get out. When I was little an' the packets was runnin' on the river, sometimes used canvas 'stead of hides. Pretty good houses." The door of the shack made a harsh grating sound as he pushed it open. "Better'n this," he added disdainfully.

The room, not over ten feet square, was murky except for the light coming in past them through the open door. Tarpaper walls lent the pungency of pitch to the sweetish smell of age, the half-wild marsh smell of wet dog, the memories of rancid bacon and hobo coffee and fried fish and onions.

Dominating the left wall was the ancient potbellied

213

woodstove Fletch's dad had donated, its crazily canted stovepipe going out through a hole in the wall stuffed tight with rags. Beside it a stack of *True Detectives*, tinder for the stove and toilet paper for the lean-to out back. No pictures, no books, no photographs, no mementos of wife or family. Nothing personal except the ancient army cot covered with the bearskin from the autumn before last—and Spot and Charlie, two live animals sleeping together for warmth under the pelt of the dead one.

Fletch thudded the gunnysack of supplies down on the table in the center of the room. Charlie sat down on the cot in the corner by the stove, where it would get enough warmth to put him to sleep during the early hours of the evening.

"Hiding out from who?" Fletch repeated.

"Those guys from the county, wanna put me in a home'r somethin'," Charlie muttered darkly.

"Home?" Fletch didn't understand. "You got a home."

The old Indian lifted a shoulder in an irritated manner. His jaws moved rhythmically as he chawed his snoose. His skin lay closer to the skull than last December.

He said with shame, "Poor farm."

Fletch felt as if he'd been kicked in his lean belly. The poor farm was for people at the end of their lives, people without any friends or resources.

Charlie had a lot of friends. The fishermen and hunters who frequented this portion of the Mississippi wetlands could always get from him where the walleyes or sunnies or crappies were hitting, could always learn which way the ducks were coming off the reserve. He didn't really need what old-timers like Fletch's dad always brought him—he could trap and shoot and catch whatever he needed, better than any man in the bottoms.

"Wait until my dad hears about this!" Fletch burst out.

"He knows."

Another kick in the gut. Fletch stood beside the table, disoriented by feelings he couldn't even identify, let alone understand.

"He can't know! He hasn't been down here for . . ."

"They come, took me in January. Durin' the thaw." Old Charlie's black gaze left Fletch's face for the first time, wandered away to the slapped-together wooden cabinet that served as a food chest. It was as empty as Charlie's eyes. "Your dad hear about it, come to see me at that place. Said there wasn't nuthin' he could do. So I left. Come back here. Then the cold come back . . ."

And nobody had been down since. Fletch realized he was panting like a dog, with that unexpected and unfamiliar emotion belatedly recognized as fear.

"They're gonna come back after you again now that the weather's breaking."

"Won't find me." Charlie chortled again. "Why you think I wait until I see who's comin' in fancy new truck? They come, I'm gone. Don't gotta live here." He jabbed a finger in one direction. "Live there." Then in another. "Live there." He stood up to make an unexpectedly graceful sweep with his right hand. "Live anywhere. Live everywhere. It don't matter."

"But *this* is your home."

Charlie said, "Wanna go for a ride in that Jeep."

Before they left, Fletch unpacked the supplies. Canned beans filched from the basement fruit cellar, a mason jar of his mom's pickled watermelon rind that Charlie loved, a slab of bacon out of the freezer, the already-opened three-pound can of J&B coffee from the shelf over the sink, a ten-pound sack of flour and another of sugar, some dry dog kibble . . .

And an unopened fifth of Seagram's Seven.

Fletch got the Jeep back into the ruts to drive on toward West Newton. Charlie was wearing the heavy red mackinaw Fletch had outgrown a couple of winters back, his dark eyes glowing as he watched everything the youth did in driving the vehicle.

They parked behind the cabin and got out. The sun had melted the thin skim of ice on a pothole in the road and Charlie crouched, elbows on thighs and hands hanging laxly between his knees, to study the muddy water.

"Frog in there," he announced as Fletch joined him.

At the same moment, a green mottled snout appeared above the surface and beady eyes looked at them unwinking.

Fletch stood up and walked away, around the cabin to the river. When he'd been eight or nine, he'd seen a frog in that same pothole and had pumped his BB gun and had shot at it to scare it. He'd shot its left eye out. The frog hadn't moved; had just sat there staring at him with unwinking wisdom from the remaining eye, with unwinking evil from the bloody socket.

He walked out to the end of the dock, the rough-sawn two-bys bouncing under his boots. The cold air carried the woken tang of thawing marshland, brown water swirled great chunks of ice down toward the Gulf of Mexico. Soon stern-wheelers would be shoving their tows of barges up the river for another season.

He'd never told anyone about the frog, but he'd never frivolously shot even a BB gun at any living thing again. From then on when he had pulled a trigger, it had been to kill.

Old Charlie was standing beside him on the rough, warped finger of dock thrust into the current, holding out the now-open bottle of Seagram's Seven. The old devil must have brought it unseen in the pocket of his mackinaw.

"*Patchanina.*" He had to almost yell over the incessant roar of the river. To Fletch's blank look, he chortled,

216

"Firewater!" and took a grand slug from the bottle.

He held it out again, unmoving and patient, because he understood what Fletch was feeling. The youth had long since accepted that the old Indian could track an emotion through his thoughts as easily as he could a fox through hardwoods. He took the bottle and drank. It was the first time he'd ever tasted anything stronger than beer. The alcohol burned on its way down his throat.

"Whew!"

Charlie took it back and lowered the level another inch. The whiskey was starting to warm now in Fletch's gut. Charlie turned back to the river.

"When I was born back in sixty-eight, weren't no cabins here. Tepees. A riverboat went ashore up on the point 'fore they had them channel markers in . . ." He pointed upriver toward the spot where he had followed the boy to show him the gray fox's den. "Broke up. The wheelhouse set here for a long time, when they come to build the cabin they used it as a bedroom."

No wonder he knew these bottomlands so well! He'd lived here eighty-two years—and still chopped his own firewood! Minnesota had been a state for only ten years when he had been born. The Civil War had been over for only three years.

". . . 'member them river packets from way back then." Old Charlie nodded—and sipped. It seemed just right to share another nip from the bottle. His eyes, looking into the past, were as empty of emotion as standing water. "Used to dive for coins they threw off them boats. Nickels an' dimes an' quarters. Used to shoot for 'em too."

The old Indian's face was beaky and passionless against the rushing muddy water. Fletch took the bottle.

"With a twenty-two?"

"Injuns couldn't have no guns. Bow and arrow. Whites from them packets stuck the coins in split sticks, walked off fifty feet, you shot 'em there. Anything you hit, you

217

got to keep."

Fletch gave Charlie back the bottle. He'd lost track of its journeys back and forth. He was feeling really great.

"You hit much?"

Charlie's beaky face split into a huge grin. "Got rich."

They went back to the Jeep. Charlie insisted on driving. Fletch knew he could; when he'd been a kid, there'd been an ancient Model-T parked off to the side of Charlie's shack.

"You got any money?" Charlie demanded.

# 27

*When his father came home, young Fletch was cleaning the crusted mess off the dashboard of the Jeep. His dad was sore.*

*"Where the devil were you last night? Your mother was worried sick when you didn't come home."*

*"You knew I went to see Old Charlie," he said defensively. "I took him down some supplies . . ."*

*His father's face changed. He had a round stubborn chin and a big nose and was totally bald except for a salt-and-pepper fringe over his ears and around the back. In lighter moments Fletch called him Curly. This was not a lighter moment.*

*"You took him down a bottle."*

*"You used to, sometimes."*

*"Not for years." He paused. "And shared it with him?"*

*Fletch told it. All of it.*

*"Do you realize what you've done? You've given the people who want to put him in the poor farm their chance."*

They started off with a jerk and a roar. Charlie pulled a U-turn through the wet matted brown grass, then sent them lurching back down the track toward his shack. Fletch almost gave a wolf howl, just to see whether he could do it. The half-empty bottle was upright between his thighs.

"You ever scalp anybody?"

"Naw." Charlie chuckled. "Early spring, late fall, Injuns used to bring in ducks, mushrat, beaver to the store in Fountain City. Twelve cents apiece for a big mushrat. Didn't get nuthin' for the little ones. Storekeeper'd say which ones was big enough to pay for. Mallard ducks, they'd bring a dime."

Fountain City, five miles south on the Wisconsin side, had some really good spring smallmouth fishing in the sloughs north of town; they'd hit anything that wasn't bigger than they were.

"Canoes was ash or cottonwood logs hollowed out. Squaws did the paddling." He chuckled again. "Used to give war whoops when they see them white kids at town. Scare hell out of 'em."

"Do one."

Charlie put back his head and whooped, high and piercing and ululating. It would have raised Fletch's hackles if evolution had left him with any. He did his wolf howl. They'd come up parallel to Charlie's shack; the old Indian slammed on the brakes and opened his door as the pickup squealed to a stop.

"Spot wanna go to town too."

The big rangy red dog tried to drive, thrusting his heavy blunt head under Charlie's arm and putting a paw on the steering wheel. Charlie batted him on the nose. He settled down between them with a contented sigh as Charlie drove on into town.

*"But why?" Fletch had finished the dashboard and had swept out the muddy cab and hosed down the outside of the Jeep. The water numbed his hands. "Why can't they leave him alone?"*

*"Because they're well-meaning people doing good by their own lights," said his father. "Christian people. Practicing the cardinal works of mercy."*

*"Would you want to live in the poor farm?"*

220

*"It's better than dying in a tarpaper shack."*

*Fletch didn't answer, but he thought: No, dammit, it isn't.*

Kellogg was separated from the wetlands by Highway 63 meandering its way north along the Mississippi through Wabasha and Lake City and Redwing to the Twin Cities of St. Paul and Minneapolis. Its single paved main street—dusty in the summer like the towns in the western movies, now filmed with mud—had a general store, a gas station, a grocery store, a bar where his dad bought their fishing and hunting licenses each year, a feed store, and a farm-equipment place.

The false fronts of many of the buildings bore the faded dates of their turn-of-the-century construction. The church had a wooden steeple and the houses were white frame.

Pedestrians scurried. A shiny Olds 88 bounced up across the sidewalk, horn bawling like a bogged calf. Faces mouthed silent imprecations at Fletch's closed window.

Charlie jerked the wheel over and hit the brakes. The front bumper crunched into a phone pole. They got out. Charlie gave his war whoop. Fletch, not to be outdone, joined in with his wolf howl. Spot peed on the pole. A matron wearing a black cloth coat and a kerchief over her head, knotted under farm-country jowls, stopped to glare.

"Well, I never—"

"An' I always," chortled Charlie triumphantly.

They paraded across the sidewalk into Ole's Bar. It was a barn of a place, with faded linoleum turning up at the corners, dark wood walls, smoke-clouded front windows. The back bar featured signs from the beer distributors: Miller, Pabst, Busch, Hamms, Heilman's Old-Style Lager. It was midweek-deserted, only a pair of passing salesmen to prop up the bar. The smell of stale beer lingered like the memory of old hangovers.

Ole himself had pale blue go-to-hell eyes and a shock of brown uncombed hair and the tattoo of a half-clothed woman on the back of the right hand he thrust out to shake with Charlie.

"Hey, Injun, ain't seen you in here in a sunth of Mondays. What'll it be?"

"Boilermakers. For me'n"—he jerked his head—"him."

Ole looked hard at Fletch.

"You old enough?"

"The dog," said Charlie.

"*He* old enough?"

"Old enough to bite your ass you don't give us them drinks."

Ole set two shot glasses on the bar beside the gaudy punchboard. He got two Leinenkugels out of the cooler. Spot stood between their stools, wagging his whole hindquarters with his excitement.

"Okay—for the dog, then."

He poured their shots, flipped the tops off the beers with an opener affixed to the underside of the bar by a gilt-colored chain. He picked up his own glass.

"Mud in your eye."

Watching Charlie from the corner of his eye, doing what he did, Fletch gunned his shot, followed it with a gulp of beer. He wiped tears from the corners of his eyes.

"That'll sit on its chest and hold it down." For some reason Ole was laughing. He leaned across the stick. "Saw you trading a word with Old Lady Sorenson outside."

"She don't like Spot," said Charlie with great dignity.

"She don't like *you*. Leastwise not running around loose." He leaned closer yet. "She's one of them wanna put you in the poor farm."

222

Charlie tossed off his second shot, following it with a big sudsy gulp of Leinenkugel's. Fletch sprinkled salt on his own beer to make the head come up again. Charlie chortled.

"Old Injun like the wind. Don't catch 'im."

He poured some of Fletch's beer into an empty pretzel bowl off the bar, set it on the floor by the brass footrail. Spot slurped loudly, delighting the salesmen. Fletch tried to focus on the framed picture behind the bar from one of the beer companies; it depicted Custer's defeat at Little Big Horn in lurid detail.

The picture began to swirl and dissolve. Fletch shut one eye and held on to the bar with both hands and squinted. Better. It was alive with cavalry and Indians, shooting, stabbing, tomahawking one another. In the middle was Custer in his fine buckskins and golden hair, shooting a charging brave. Fletch remembered the Errol Flynn movie where Sitting Bull said that Custer was like the last stalk of corn standing in the field.

Ole leaned across the stick and laid his tattooed hand back-up on the elbow-polished wood.

"Lookit this, soldier."

He clenched and unclenched his fist. Before Fletch's popping eyes the half-naked woman gyrated and pumped her hips.

Old Charlie said, "One for the road."

Fletch didn't want one anything for the road. Sweat was falling in a circle on the bar below his face. The room was going around in circles. He put his cheek down on his forearm and, head to one side, shut one eye again to give Custer's Last Stand one last squint. A warrior was scalping a still-yelling soldier, with the hair half-pulled off to show the gory skull beneath. That spot of lurid red stood out just like the frog's red eye socket in the puddle half his lifetime ago.

"Mebbe time we go now," said Old Charlie judiciously.

223

"Money all gone."

Fletch threw up into the gutter, glad Old Lady Sorenson wasn't there to see him do it. The night air was frigid, he literally reeled under its assault. Why was it dark out? Maybe he was going blind. His head was pounding in a terrible way. He was reduced to dry heaves.

He rode with his head lolling on his chest, hugging himself against the icy night wind coming in the open window. Spot was moaning. Charlie was sobbing softly.

"Poor ol' Injun, all alone." He cast a lugubrious sideways glance to see how Fletch was taking it. "When Ol' Charlie was mebbe twelve, sojers come an' rounded up all the Injuns like a lotta cattle an' took 'em to Nebraska."

Fletch was panting, quick even breaths through his mouth that helped keep him from feeling even sicker.

"Said they was gonna have to be farmers. Was gonna give 'em cattle an' horses an' seed wheat an' houses. Took ever'body but me. I hid." He gestured out at the hardwoods cast into stark patterns by the truck's headlights. "Lived hard mebbe three, four years, then everybody come back, one, two at a time."

Fletch aroused enough to ask, "Your mom and dad too?"

"Ha! Them Injuns was dead in Nebraska!"

That was when Spot threw up against the dashboard.


Fletch woke up lying in front of the long-dead stove, Spot curled inside the curve of his body for warmth. They were covered with Old Charlie's bearskin. He had never been so cold. The memory of last night's whiskey made him want to start throwing up all over again. The cot was empty.

It was mid-morning before the old Indian showed up. By that time Fletch had brought a pail of water from the

224

piped well in the willows behind the shack, had washed his face and scrubbed off his teeth with salt and the tail of his T-shirt. He had started the fire and made coffee the way that Charlie had shown him, with an eggshell in it, and had given Spot some dog kibble.

Charlie arrived with a brace of red squirrels in one hand and in the other a couple of homemade arrows and a short thick stubby Indian bow Fletch had never seen before. His face was drawn and gray and one knee of his pants was ripped, but his eyes glowed triumphant. He took the big gleaming hunting knife off his hip and started to skin out the squirrels, making the back incisions and putting one muddy boot on the tails to hold them down while he pulled the skins off inside-out.

"One of 'em wouldn't fall, hadda climb up an' get him."

Fletch remembered a year and a half ago, the disastrous deer-hunting trip when he'd shot the bear. Each evening hard-bitten bulky-clad men had shown up at their hunting camp with already-skinned and dressed squirrels in their pockets to assure themselves a share of Charlie's stew — cut-up squirrel simmered with potatoes and carrots and onions and red wine and little cubes of crisp-fried salt pork. And a few herbs he picked in the woods.

Fletch poured water from the pail into the cooking pot and set it on top of the stove.

"You coulda left it, one would be enough for—"

Old Charlie grabbed his arm, glared fiercely at him.

"You don't leave no cripples! Never!"


Fletcher came up out of sleep in the cold cabin, speaking aloud those same words from almost forty years ago. He threw back the bearskin blanket brought down through the years with him, then sat on the edge of the bed massaging his knee and cursing the man who had shot him.

He'd sure dreamed about Old Charlie last night, he thought. And about his dad.

He sighed. He knew with an almost sad finality what he was going to have to do.

*You don't leave no cripples. Never.*

Not even when that cripple is yourself.

Maybe *especially* not when that cripple is yourself.

# 28

Pennsylvania was history.

Five days before, it had looked like a disaster, with new polls showing Fiksdahl leading by two percent. And the Guv still sticking pigheadedly to his lunch-bucket issues from New York and Illinois. Then Fiksdahl had used the Pittsburgh League of Women Voters debate, seen throughout the state in prime time, to contrast their experience in national politics.

"I know what I'm doing, I've been in Washington doing it for years, while Mr. Westergard has been hiding out in his farm state pretending to solve his constituents' problems."

Westergard started jumping up and down on Ross's spine as soon as they got into the limo, with Hastings Crandall and Pete Quarles listening white-faced on the jump seats facing them.

"Why in hell didn't you give me some useful briefings?"

With Nicole refusing to back up his lies about Fletcher, Ross knew his job already was at risk; so he said to hell with it. When all else failed, try the truth.

"I briefed you fine, dammit. You just weren't listening."

Both Crandall and Quarles visibly winced. Westergard, with the ominous restraint that usually presaged one of his blowups, said, "I'm listening now."

"In thirty years, this state has lost a hundred thousand

227

manufacturing jobs in steel and heavy industry. But—"

"Exactly what I said on the podium—and got clobbered!"

"Let me finish, dammit!" yelled Ross. "During that same time the state gained *two* hundred thousand jobs in service industries. You were talking to half the populace tonight—and half the populace ain't gonna cut it for the nomination."

"*All right!*" roared the Guv. To their surprise, he modified his tone as he went on. "All right, we blew it. *I* blew it. Now, what do we do about it?"

"Now we blitz 'em," said Ross.

"Fiksdahl did that in New York, he fell flat on his face."

"You won't." Ross brought out Nicole's points as his own. "The traditional Pennsylvania young urban professional is from a blue-collar family. He watches the Steelers on Sunday with his high-school buddies—who are driving trucks or working steel or not working at all. He's already in your pocket, so to hell with him for the moment. Go after the one who isn't."

"And who might that be?" asked Westergard with a certain note of sarcasm.

Ross ignored the sarcasm. "The new high-tech boy. He isn't from Pennsylvania—hell, he isn't from anywhere except maybe Harvard Business School. He's into money, he's into defense, his wife's into world peace. He doesn't give a damn about Fiksdahl's entrenched power structure—or about you. You're just another hayseed out of the boonies."

Crandall tacitly agreed by asking, "How do we change his perception of the chief?"

"We spend three, four hundred thousand dollars on a series of new thirty-second TV spots that concentrate on the issues."

Westergard was silent for a full city block, staring out

228

his smoked window at the mostly deserted streets. Finally he turned back to the two men facing them from the jump seats.

"Hastings? Pete?"

Crandall said, "I like it, Chief," and Quarles, who knew a bandwagon when he saw one, added, "Check."

Westergard nodded. "Then let's do it."

From then until the primary, you couldn't turn on a TV set in Pennsylvania without seeing Westergard talking about the state's problems against some appropriate state scene.

Gary Westergard on the issue of the laboring poor:

"For eight long years the Republicans have been throwing money at the working poor of this state, hoping you'll go away. But you want a hand *up*, not a hand *out!* We can affect the balance of payments by revitalizing America's international trade so that Pennsylvania's heavy-industry manufacturing products will be competitive in the world marketplace again. That's the best welfare program there is, and it's going to take smarts and guts to carry it out. I've got plenty of both."

Gary Westergard on the issue of smokestack industries:

"I wish my worthy opponent would get off his pork barrel and onto the issues. Sure, I'd like to see the battered old smokestack industries rebuilt too — but that's yesterday's news. What about the *other* Pennsylvania constituencies? I'm talking insurance. Real estate. Computer software. High-tech robotics. Corporate management. Research. Universities. Government. Where's *their* representation in Washington?"

Gary Westergard on the issue of special interests:

"When you're a Washington power broker you find yourself so beholden to those other power brokers, the lobbyists, that you forget *the people* — the ones who put you in Washington in the first place. If you want a president who is nobody's puppet, who *owes* no special interests and

229

is *owned* by no special interests, I'm your man. If you want just another backroom boy in the White House, vote for my opponent. Are you listening, Senator?"

Someone was. Westergard took forty-six percent of the popular vote, Fiksdahl limped in with thirty-four, Jefferson was just a memory at eighteen—true, an impressive three-quarters of the black vote, but who cared? That vote would not win an election.

Ross's media blitz had paid off. At four A.M. after the polls closed, Ross was using ideas suggested by Nicole on the phone to finish Westergard's victory statement. Jarvis, meanwhile, was already on his way to New York to get whatever network goodies he could pick up.

Because now Westergard had a chance to take it all at the nominating convention in July. The Pennsy victory had upped his first-ballot electoral vote total to 1,069 of the 1,967 needed to win by acclamation in San Francisco. Only 898 delegates to go, with half the state primaries still to be run—mostly west of Chicago, where Westergard figured much of his strength lay.

Nicole called from Minnesota to congratulate Ross, adding in almost loving tones that the children missed him—thus opening the door a crack. He went through it, saying he'd be home for the two weeks before the next big one, Texas.


While Ross was getting his personal shit together, Jarvis wasn't *just* arranging network coverage for the Guv (*Today* on Thursday, *Face the Nation* on Sunday); he was also arranging a little personal reward for himself. The girl Sharkey's local contact found was Puerto Rican, not black, and more expensive than Sharkey's; but she screamed just as loud and bled just as red, and Jarvis, standing over her, made himself come just as hard. And later, through her broken teeth, she told the admitting nurse on the emergency ward at Bellevue only that she had been "beat on by some bastard john."

Even as she spoke, Jarvis, in a luxury suite at the Essex House overlooking Central Park, was sleeping like a baby.

Nicole awoke to the faint aromas of frying bacon and brewing coffee. She had a moment of utter peace—all was well in her world. David was home, had gotten up early to surprise the family with breakfast, and they would . . .

Then she remembered, and her heart turned to stone.

Stopping off on her way downstairs, she found Katie sitting on her already-made poster bed under its frilly French canopy, reading aloud from her book on rabbit care to the black-and-white miniature Belgian hare in her lap. Her tone was tart, even minatory. The rabbit was wriggling his nose and looking dull-witted. Nicole found that a normal state for rabbits.

She sat down beside the girl on the bed. "Katie, do you think maybe Thumper already knows how bunnies behave?"

Katie shook her head, ringlets flying around a thin, serious face lent extra beauty by the soft light of the ceramic-doll lamp Nicole had given her for Christmas.

"No. He chews my bedspread and tries to eat the cord on my lamp whenever I let him out. And his cage is always full of droppings. He has a real attitude problem."

"Maybe all rabbits do."

"Not in the book," she said darkly. She brightened. "He only makes droppings when he eats. If I quit feeding him . . ."

"I don't think that'd be such a good idea."

Katie sighed and nodded. "I guess it's pretty hard to be best friends with someone who keeps biting you on

231

the neck."

Nicole's bark of laughter came from deep in her chest. "There are them what would say you're wrong." The laughter choked unexpectedly toward tears; she grabbed the little girl and hugged her. Katie remained solemn through both manifestations.

"Nicole, are you glad Daddy's home?"

"Of course, sweetie. Don't I seem to be?"

"You always look mad when he comes into the room."

"Sometimes your daddy has an attitude problem—not unlike Thumper's, as a matter of fact."

At Robbie's room she knocked softly, waited, when there was no response opened the door and went in. What a different scene from Katie's orderly burrow! A wild animal's lair, rank as the tiger cage at Como Park Zoo. Unwashed clothes littered the floor like the aftermath of a terrorist attack. An eight-foot Styrofoam dinosaur skeleton dangled from the ceiling. Whitesnake and Motley Crue and Aerosmith lit the walls in four colors.

Robbie was still asleep, face angelic except for an inflamed pimple at the base of his nose.

"Hey, Tiger. Time to get up."

No response. Nicole gently shook the thin naked shoulder, feeling a wrench of almost unbearable emotion as she did.

"Your dad has breakfast ready."

One brown eye opened with distaste directed not at her, but at a world in which one had to face a cold dawn. " 'Naminnit."

"Now, Tiger. School day."

Robbie got up on one elbow, drawing the covers higher so no trace of bare flesh showed; he was at the age when boys are more secretive about their bodies than nuns in habit. He looked at her covertly, measuring her mood.

"Is it okay if I miss supper tonight, Nicole? I just gotta be down at Wally's—it's the most important night of my

232

life."

"In that case, Tiger, sure. What'll you be doing?"

"Hanging out."

She smothered a laugh and went downstairs to find Ross hanging out by the stove, flipping pancakes. He'd always made breakfast during their courting weekends at her bachelor pad near the U—with the memories of her mother still sharp in her mind, she'd been renting out this house her father had given her. She and David would eat together in bed, the Sunday *Trib* scattered across the covers, then would make love with *Washington Week in Review* or *Firing Line* unnoted on the TV across the room.

As if remembering those days himself, Ross put his arms around her. She stiffened. He stepped back, not pushing it. She poured coffee, sat down, told him Katie was giving her rabbit tips on proper behavior and Robbie was still in bed.

"But they'll be down in a minute, we can all eat together."

Ross looked dubious. "If Robbie wasn't up yet . . ."

"Okay, two minutes."

As she drank her coffee, the unexpected tears started again; she wiped them hastily away with her napkin just before the kids burst in. She knew she was being more sentimental than realistic in her memories of the good, early days with David; but she also knew that when she had covered up for him with her father, she had made a decision of sorts. David was trying now, he really was trying; maybe the next move in trying to repair their life together might be up to her.

Evenings, Ross found himself giving Nicole his ideas on the remaining primary races—Texas on Saturday, May 2, the intervening ones of little relevance, then

Tuesday, June 9 — California, Ohio, New Jersey, South Dakota, West Virginia. And he found that she was willing to listen. Usually she generated the ideas and he listened.

They went up to bed together in a civil, almost a warm mood; Nicole seemed to fall asleep right away, so he spooned his body up behind hers and tried to keep from thinking too much about his resultant hard-on twitching uselessly against the backs of her thighs.

He dreamed he was in a vast dim cavern with dark pools of standing water and stalagmites reaching up from the floor like calcified demons. Nicole appeared, terrified, threatened, battered. He had great wings like an angel's, so he enfolded her in them. They crouched together within their shelter, he protecting her from harm — but at the same time trying to slide himself into her from behind.

He awoke with his hand over her hip, pulling her back against his erection. Though Nicole still seemed asleep, her negligee was rucked up around her waist. He whispered in sudden desperate need, "Darling, please . . ."

She slumbered on. He pushed himself fractionally forward; to his astonishment, he slid into her as if her body had been only waiting to accept him. Gently, then stronger, then stronger yet, she clenched rhythmically around him. It was a wordless ecstasy so intense it was almost agonizing. He finally came at the same moment that Nicole stiffened and gave her own low, nearly inaudible moan.

Then she breathed on evenly, continuing to feign sleep. The shared, unspoken duplicity gave Ross an extraordinary sense of peace — strangely compounded with guilt. By shooting her father he felt he had somehow jeopardized her as well as himself, but at the same time knew Fletcher would never be a threat to his own daughter.

Until this moment he had never really loved her. He

234

had never really loved anyone. He craned forward to drowsily kiss her shoulder blade. Now, he loved. In that moment, he felt that if destruction came upon them, he wanted it to strike him, not her. It was an extraordinary thought of a kind he'd never had before.

He whispered, "I love you, my darling."

They lay together in the numb safety of sleep's counterfeit death, like unwary children at the start of one of those archetypal fairy tales that always turn out badly in the end.

# 29

On the bus to Minneapolis, Fletcher's eye was caught by the woman across the aisle, and he realized with a wrench that since Terry's death, no woman had stirred him sexually or emotionally. He couldn't love, he couldn't hunt—he couldn't even kill. He could only look for his attacker in the probably vain hope that the search might bring him alive again emotionally.

So review your hunt's possible assets.

The chartered airplane had come from Minneapolis with the attacker, had returned there with him. Then the credit-card charges. Nicole said the card was stolen; Jarvis and others associated with Westergard's campaign were thus eliminated. Another dead end.

The telephone calls the attacker had made from Dutch's Tavern in Cochrane. Since he was unable to get from the phone company whom they had been placed to, also a dead end.

The rifle used in the attack. A 30.06, certainly scoped. The most common big-game caliber in America. No way on God's green earth to find it. A dead end.

The slugs dug out of the tree. Of use only in identifying the rifle. Without the rifle, dead end.

The shell casings. Even with Les Klumb's analysis, they could not take him beyond the fact that the attacker had come from outside Cochrane. Dead end.

Cochrane itself. Already checked out. Dead end.

What *wasn't* a dead end?

Minneapolis. And the man.

But the man was only a shadow who shot from ambush. What did Fletcher know that might bring that shadow image up like a developing Polaroid print, until it became sharp and focused?

—He had been wearing tinted glasses on a day that didn't call for them. A disguise of sorts? Suggesting that his mustache and goatee might have been the same?

—He had built a bench-rest to shoot from despite a forked sapling three feet away. Had not policed up his spent brass after firing, yet had known enough to sight in his rifle and hit Fletcher with all three shots. So, no military training.

—Though not trained in firearm use, using them well. So he had to have asked someone questions—questions for which, despite their being distinctly odd, he had gotten answers.

An amateur at killing. A goddamned amateur who . . .

Do I detect a note of self-pity?

At the bus station, for Fletcher, now sunk in thought, the woman had become invisible. Like the man he sought.

How to make him visible?

If his mustache and goatee hadn't been real, maybe he'd recently bought them here in Minneapolis.

If he hadn't learned to shoot in the service, maybe he had asked his questions about shooting here in Minneapolis.

Slight sign, to be sure, to follow in thick cover on a cold trail. But Old Charlie had taught him well; and if he *did* ever find the attacker . . .

Worry about that in the event.

From a cheap hotel close to the bus station, he started to call Nicole's house but hung up with the number half-dialed; he had left a message on Victor's machine about coming down here; and besides, Nicole was on the cam-

Nicole wasn't, but she might as well have been. Each day she became a more willing conspirator in her own involvement; and each night, they made love. It was no longer unacknowledged: face-to-face now, sometimes she on top, sometimes he.

But never, there in the dark, did a soft word pass between them. Never a moment of tenderness, never a caress, never a whisper of love, never a giggle at the gracelessness of the two-backed beast. Only in the light of day did they talk, and then only of politics. The same competition, the same ferocity went into their dialectic as into their sex.

"For God's sake, David, you people can't ignore the District of Columbia just because you're getting ready for Texas! Gary has to be a strong second in D.C."

"Why? Jefferson will win there, and—"

"Why? Because *they* will be watching who comes in second. A strong showing will make a lot of congressmen jump to Gary's side of the fence."

"The Guv doesn't see it that way."

"Dammit, *make* him see it that way."

"Why don't you?"

That was the core of their wrangling, also unspoken: he needed to present her ideas as his own, but also needed her to confirm his lies to Westergard—or be dumped from staff. Because it was a choice she strenuously avoided being forced to make, they fought verbally—rapier thrust and parry, not saber slashes, until finally, *touché,* straight to the heart.

"Goddammit, Nicole, Texas is *next week!* We have to concentrate on that. The rest of these piss-ant states—"

She made a dismissive gesture. "Your Texas issues are laid out for you like a pike on a plate." They were on their way up to bed for their nightly rutting; she stopped on the landing to smile almost coldly back down at him. "I know how to give him a win there. The Latinos. Insist he brush up his infinitive Spanish—I'll give you the most likely phrases. . . ."

Thus Nicole lived politics and frustration between the rhythms of her life as mother, homemaker, and bawd. She wanted to be on staff, or even, occasionally, the candidate herself; but all she could do was try to manipulate from afar.

Until the day she opened the door and Fletcher was standing on the threshold.

But that was later.

First, Texas and California had to happen.


Texas was anticlimactic. Westergard crisscrossed the state armed with set speeches and answers for probable questions furnished by Nicole through Ross. Jarvis, only half-joking, suggested a novel approach to the hurting rich of Houston and Dallas, newly (and only relatively) pauperized by oil prices, tax changes, low beef prices, the chronic stock-market instability. Westergard rejected it almost huffily.

There were the urban cowboys who wore ten-gallon hats and high-heel boots and Texas silver belt buckles— and rode a desk five days a week. For them, Westergard went hootin' and hollerin' and sippin' Lone Star at Gilly's on a Saturday night. Rode the mechanical bull, got up on the bandstand to smoke out a not-half-bad down-home fiddle to "Your Cheatin' Heart," then told them what they wanted to hear:

"I don't believe anyone can be elected president of these United States without carrying Texas. You are the mainstream of America, you are at the core of the traditional American political process. When the time comes around for me to pick a running mate, there are going to be Texans on that short list."

Then there were the *real* cowboys and roughnecks: rifles racked in their pickup cabs and the backs of their necks burned red by the Texas sun. They had been getting screwed since cattle still wore long horns and oil rigs still were made of wood, and they expected to be screwed again. Westergard gave them Andy Jackson, because Andy Jackson had been for the little feller:

" 'The rich and proud too often bend the acts of government to their own purposes, but the farmers, mechanics, and laborers have a right to complain of the injustice of their government'!" When the inevitable rebel yells died down, he added, "Those words were true almost a hundred and sixty years ago when President Andy Jackson vetoed the Bank Bill—and they're still true today!" Then he tipped them a wink. "Wish I could have a JB and ditch over here with you-all, but the little woman don't like me drinkin' while I'm campaignin'."

Finally there were the Texas blacks, the only constituency Westergard would admit was out of his reach because Jackie Jefferson had it sewn up. But Jefferson also was trying to sew up the Texas Latinos, and Nicole had made the Guv aware that that couldn't happen.

The Latinos, with twenty percent of the Texas population and counting, had gotten themselves some mayors and judges and state officials, and wanted some cabinet posts, maybe a vice-president. They had political muscle to flex, so he went right after them down among the Gulf Coast sand flies outside Brownsville.

"I hear you Latinos are the most civic-minded constituency in this great state of Texas. I hear you Latinos are finally getting the vote out in percentages that match your share of eligible voters. I hear you Latinos—"

"Hell, you don't hear 'em at all, Westergard!" The heckler, an obvious Fiksdahl plant, wore a white shirt and a tie and his suit jacket even though it was a broiling hundred degrees in the shade. "Why *should* they vote for you? Hell, you don't see but about two Latinos a year up there in Minnesota—and you got them mowin' your lawn! I bet you don't even have *one* Spanish-speaker on your staff."

"*No ganas, mi amigo,*" Westergard shot back in an amalgam of the phrases Nicole had insisted he take coaching on. "*Hablo español también. Y mis empleos serán feliz para darles una posición, por cualquier cosa crean es importante . . .*" He tried to finish him off by adding, in English, "In Spanish, of course."

"*Putana mierda chinga, no puedes hablar español!*"

Westergard didn't know what he had said, but it didn't matter: the exchange had brought down the house. In the limo back to their hotel, he asked their Texas coordinator what had been yelled there at the end.

The Texan laughed. "Let's just say it involved the fact that you don't really speak Spanish. You broke that pinto back there, Governor—now all you gotta do is ride it."

"Any suggestions as to how?"

"Just hang on and wave your hat." He chuckled. "As we say down here, looks like Fiksdahl is *all* hat—and no cattle."

The political analysis in a Fort Worth Sunday newspaper the day after the primary put it in a slightly different way under a headline reading, EMPTY SADDLES IN THE OLD CORRAL.

"Governor Garrett Westergard," he wrote, "rode into Texas on a big white horse, six-guns blazing, and left the campaign of Senator Morris Fiksdahl dead or dying in the dust.

"With Westergard's overwhelming Texas win, he needs only 733 more delegates to take the Democratic nomination by acclamation on the first ballot in San Francisco. It might be time for both Senator Fiksdahl and Jackie

Jefferson, who lost the shoot-out for the crucial Latino vote forty-two percent to seventeen, to hang up their spurs."

# 30

On Fletcher's infrequent spells at home during Nicole's high-school years, they had always bought her the latest workout tights or leg warmers or leotards at this Danskin shop. Be they French-cut, bias-cut, or candystripe, by the next month they would be of as much interest as last year's lecture notes.

"May I help you, sir?"

The woman was well into her forties, lean and slight, with a face almost too young for the gray-streaked hair down her back nearly to the waist and the dancer's body which had aged without sag or weight. Her eyes were merry and direct, heavily shadowed and accented in a blue to match her clinging wool dress.

Even overwhelmed with nostalgia for the shop, Fletcher found her striking; he felt again that twinge of regret at the loss from his life of sexual interest.

"I hope so, though I'm not really here to buy anything."

Through days of trial and error at theatrical supply houses and costume shops, he had perfected his approach, dissembling with the ease of an Indian brave wearing a coyote hide in the old days to stalk a buffalo herd. He was, he explained, with Primary Power, Inc., whose fiscal year ended on June 30. A whole drawerful of their charge receipts had been water-damaged during a fire . . .

"So you see, I'm just looking for a charge-card transaction with a man named Gerard M. Hopkins."

"Say no more." She was smiling with her voice as well as her disconcertingly direct eyes. "Bookkeeping is the bane of my life too, and we *do* keep copies of charge-card receipts, Mr. . . ."

"Oh. Fletcher. Hollis Fletcher."

"Hi. I'm Alison."

They shook hands almost formally.

"It'd be September, October, November of last year, something like that. Hopkins probably would have been interested in theatrical beards and goatees."

She disappeared into the tiny littered office partially visible through a half-open door past shelved boxes of dancing shoes and ballet slippers.

Fletcher thumbed through some dance magazines full of impossibly flexible women and improbably wispy men. Since this was the nineteenth or the twentieth place he had been to during his week in Minneapolis, the search had become rote, with no real expectation of possible success.

Even if he did get a lead, he was running out of money to pursue the hunt. Go to Nicole? No way. She had her own life to lead, her own expenses to meet. He was glad he hadn't tried to call her since his arrival. Just too much to explain.

"Are you a devotée of the dance yourself, Mr. Fletcher?"

He limped back to the counter. A devotée of the dance? A cripple.

"I'm not up to a lot of dancing lately."

*Do I detect a*

"I didn't mean your leg. It's those men in the magazines—no matter how beautiful they are, they're usually not much interested in women." Then, with an air of triumph she held up an untidy sheaf of papers for him to

244

see. "September."

His heart was pounding. Buck fever. At the same time, he felt ashamed of his lies to her. They leaned over the receipts from their opposite sides of the counter, heads almost touching. He could smell shampoo, a trace of freshly applied perfume.

There it was: a flimsy receipt duplicate for one mustache-and-goatee set. Black. With the scrawled signature at the bottom of the card, "Gerard M. Hopkins." Beside it, on a hand-drawn line with *ph #* in front of it, was indeed a phone number.

*Hopkins' phone number!* He must have reacted strongly; she drew back slightly, a startled look in her eyes. It barely registered.

"I know it's been months, but is there any chance—"

"That I remember him?" She shook her head. "See the initial in the upper-left-hand corner?" She bent closer, so their heads actually were touching; again her perfume disturbed him. Her hand brushed his. "J.L.—Judy Leffert. She handled this transaction but she doesn't work here anymore."

"It doesn't matter," he assured her. "This is so . . ."

"If it helps as much as you say . . ." She paused, suddenly self-conscious; a flush rose up her neck. She checked her watch. "It's nearly lunchtime . . ."

"Hey, I'm really sorry I kept you past . . ."

"You didn't. Really." She smiled, waited, when he said nothing more, gave a rueful little sigh. "Well, then, I'm glad I could help you out."

"You have. Very much. Thank you."

He shook her hand again and left, mildly puzzled by the disappointed look on her face. At a pay phone, he got out a quarter with his maimed hand, realized that until this moment something in him hadn't really believed it. It had all been conjecture. Sure, logical. But just a constructed edifice of guess and circumstance. He could have been wrong.

But not now. *This* Gerard M. Hopkins had purchased one mustache-and-goatee set. Black. And had left a phone number. He slid his coin into the slot and began tapping it out.

Of course the number had been a phony; but as he sprawled on the bed in his motel room that night, eating a Whopper and listening to the noises coming from the TV his eyes weren't seeing, Fletcher didn't care that much. If the number had been genuine, there would have been a blade-thin chance that Gerard M. Hopkins also was genuine. The poet didn't own the name. But the three-digit prefix not only didn't exist in Minneapolis or St. Paul, it didn't exist in any Minnesota area code.

Alison had given him more than a bit of information: she had renewed his enthusiasm for what he was doing. Funny how disappointed she had looked when . . .

Fletcher grunted and sat up straight on the bed. The perfume, the heads touching, her hand sliding across the back of his unmaimed one as he wrote . . . She had been expecting him to take her to lunch! A little repayment for her effort in going through all the old receipts.

Suddenly, vividly, he remembered Bette Anderson. A student at the Kahler School of Nursing he'd met the night after he'd got drunk for the first time with Old Charlie. Because of Bette, he hadn't gotten back down to West Newton again that vacation. Each night they'd go to the movies; on the last night before he had to go back to school, they'd parked in the driveway of a darkened farmhouse outside town.

As the radio played *"The Gypsy,"* Bette's mouth

opened wide to receive Fletch's questing tongue. His left hand slid under her skirt to the feverish heat of her soft inner thigh; his right, awkwardly under her sweater, could just cup one breast through her brassiere.

Her sweater was pushed up. Her head was back against the window, she was breathing hard, beyond stopping him. He was so hard it actually hurt. His thumbs under the elasticized bottom of the bra pushed upward to pop her breasts free, heart-stopping resilient cones by the dashboard radio's dim light.

His mouth tried to engulf her. Her nipple was in his mouth! Stiffening. He could taste her perfume. He twirled his tongue around the nipple.

"Fletch! Fletch! *stop* . . ."

Bette was pounding on his shoulders with both fists, panicked. She was bathed in light. He twisted awkwardly on the seat to be struck in the eyes by a flashlight beam.

"Godless heathens!"

The light quickly jerked from his face to Bette's naked breasts, as quickly slid down to shine between her parted thighs. Despite the steamy car windows, Fletch could dimly see the farmer's enraged yet avid face on the other side of the glass behind the light. Bette was struggling with her bra.

"Get outta our driveway or I'll call the police!"

Her knees were together, she was jerking her sweater down. Fletch was fumbling at the car keys. *"Linda"* was on the radio.

"We're Christian people, my wife's in the car!"

He got his dad's car started, let off the hand brake, started backing out past the farmer's sedan.

"Slut!" yelled the farmer. "Whore of Babylon . . ."

Bette was crying beside him on the seat.

Even now he remembered the farmer's shouted curses as his popping eyes had feasted on her bared breasts and opened legs. Even now, Fletcher's face burned with shame at his then inadequacy: he had been unequipped to protect her from that symbolic rape.

Impotent then, psychologically. Impotent now, physically.

Nothing he could offer a woman now. No longer an emotional being, no longer a sexual male, no longer a *man*.

Prey then. Prey now.

But now, right now, after getting confirmation that he actually was on the trail of a real attacker, maybe also just a little bit predator. Maybe a shrew-size predator.

Build on it. Tomorrow, take this newfound confidence to look for firing ranges. The man who called himself Hopkins had to have learned about man-shooting from *someone*. Someone who surely would remember such very strange questions and the man who had asked them.


Ross was slurping coffee at the kitchen counter, already late for the Guv's early-morning strategy meeting. When the phone rang, he answered; Nicole was in the shower and it might be Hastings or Pete with a modified day's agenda. The situation was fluid, changing by the minute, the Guv would be leaving for the coast this afternoon.

"Ross residence."

An unknown voice asked for Hal Fletcher. Ross hadn't thought about Fletcher much lately, not since he and Nicole had made their strange truce. Fletcher had quit looking, the incident was closed — if shooting someone could be called an incident.

"Mr. Fletcher is not in Minneapolis. He's up—"

"Oh, he's in Minneapolis, all right. I'm sure he's down there looking for . . ." The voice paused abruptly. "Could you have Nicole call me when she gets the chance? This is Dr. Victor Kroonquist in Cochrane. She knows the number."

Ross hung up sweating. His hands were clammy.

*Oh, he's in Minneapolis, all right. I'm sure he's down there looking for . . .*

Looking for whoever the fuck had shot him. Looking for, unwittingly, David Ross. Or was it unwittingly? Ross looked involuntarily out the kitchen window at the backyard, half-expecting to see Fletcher charging the house in camouflage fatigues and boots, bow and arrow in hand like fucking Rambo.

He shook his head in self-chagrin.

Get real, for Chrissake. Looking and finding were two different things. There just was no way, from the meager collection of facts Fletcher had recited to Nicole, that he could ever identify his assailant. Hell, Ross had been very careful with that drunken ex-assassin who ran the firing range, always wearing the mustache and goatee to change the shape of his face, the tinted glasses to hide the color of his eyes, the hunting cap to cover his curly black hair. And he'd used the poet's name.

His fear was subsiding. He was more sure of himself, more in control now than he had been when he'd hatched that half-baked scheme to kill Fletcher.

Tell Nicole? No. If she knew her father was in town, she might start having attacks of conscience again, which *could* be dangerous. This way, Fletcher would poke around, find nothing, and go back to Cochrane. End of story.

But on his way down to the garage, he stopped at the filing cabinet on the landing to get out the boxed automatic from the back of the bottom drawer. Under the car seat was a handier place for it than the filing cabinet, even if he did know there was no way that Fletcher's kind of hunter could successfully operate in a city like Minneapolis.

# 31

This was the next-to-last target range on his list. Just going through the motions now, Fletcher ducked under the striped barrier arm for autos and walked in beneath a signboard reading:

TWIN CITIES RIFLE RANGE
Target — Skeet — Self-Defense
Members Only — No Trespassing

The Greyhound from downtown Minneapolis had dropped him a dozen blocks away; though nearly twenty miles from the city, it was not far from Robbinsdale, where All-Weather Charter Tours was located.

May sun was drying the puddles alongside the road; puffs of spring cloud drifted overhead as if fired from cannon below the horizon. His shoes crunched gravel. Cordite from the flat pop of firearms drifted through the dark smell of evergreens, taking him back to the rifle range at camp during his ninth and tenth summers.

The trees ended in a gravel parking lot with a Saturday dozen cars and pickups. A bullhorned voice thundered, *"Cease firing!"* The office was pale yellow frame-and-clapboard, about the size and shape of a railroad boxcar. Its peaked roof, brown-shingled, sagged slightly in the middle. Despite white-painted window frames and ends of roof studs, it still somehow harked back to the old mustard-yellow army barracks of his service days.

Beyond the office a two-story observation tower, rough wood also pale yellow, overlooked the firing line. Targets were being pulled against the earth banks at the far end of the range. Fragrant lilacs flanked the whitewashed gravel walk, but even so its stripped-down look was more military than civilian.

To complete the illusion, a towheaded youth with body-builder biceps put down a *Guns Magazine* and stood at attention behind the desk when Fletcher entered. Even his name tag was sewn on his shirt pocket in the military manner.

"Yes, sir, can I help you, sir?"

"I'm trying to locate a man named Gerard Hopkins who might have been a member of your gun club last year."

"Sorry, sir, our membership lists are confidential."

"This man would no longer be a member, he—"

"Sorry, *sir*."

The "sir" was hit hard in the military manner: impeccably correct but derisive at the same time. Fletcher ambled around the room looking at trophies in glass-fronted cases. No guns; they would be racked under lock and key elsewhere. A group photo of the Fifth RCT . . . Regimental Combat Team—of Korea's old Twenty-fourth Battalion brought memories flooding back: he recognized not only faces but the picture itself. He'd had its duplicate for years.

Outside, the loudspeaker blared from the observation tower: "READY ON THE RIGHT." A pause. "READY ON THE LEFT." Another pause. "READY ON THE FIRING LINE."

Fletcher tapped a remembered face in the photo. "Sergeant Jerzy Hrock. Thirty-five years ago."

"Do you know Sergeant Rock?" Awed surprise momentarily stripped the ironic "sir" from his reply.

"Just for drill," said Fletcher in conscious mimicry of

the Rock's growl. "Is he up in the tower? I have to talk to him."

"THE FLAG IS UP. THE FLAG IS WAVING. THE FLAG IS DOWN."

The starch was back. "No civilians are authorized to—"

"Civilians?"

"Non-employees."

"COMMENCE FIRING."

These guns with their measured cadence so unlike combat's confusion reminded him of his second eight at Fort Leonard Wood, Missouri. Little Korea, they had called it. With three days' leave en route (he and his father had spent it hunting mulies in Wyoming), he had been shipped directly from there to Seoul.

His finger tapped another remembered face in the photo. "*Me* thirty-five years ago."

He went past the gaping youth to the range. The shooters were firing from the prone position on sandbag rests, legs splayed, slings wound around their left arms. Sandbags with the same function as the framework of logs on the hilltop overlooking his cabin. It was enough; even thirty-five years later he knew the Rock had instructed Hopkins in his killing ways. *Almost* killing ways.

But Fletcher waited with both elation and resignation. He had found the place, but the attacker would have been just as wily here as elsewhere; wily as a feral old tomcat.

It was a day of killing.

Four A.M., first day home, summer vacation stretching away for three months before the start of his sophomore year. Next week, back to work at the lumberyard; but this week was his.

The predawn air was cool and delicious; wet grass soaked his pant legs as he went down through the hardwoods and out across the open field of young corn. After loading his rifle with .22 hollow-point long-rifles for extra shocking power, he took his stand in a clump of chokecherry and juniper that commanded the long-since-abandoned wood-chuck burrow.

Feral cats killed more birds and small game than all the wild predators combined, and here, the sign told him, the battle-scarred old tomcat slept between his nightly forays. Last winter he had cleaned the rabbits out of the hedgerow; now he would be starting on the pheasant chicks. His time had come.

Twenty motionless minutes later the blackbirds started making alarm calls in the developing dawn. The old predator's scarred, whiskered visage parted dew-wet grass to glare at Fletch from a dozen yards away. The bead of the front sight, already nestled in the slot of the rear, covered the tiger stripe between the tomcat's eyes. Fletch squeezed.

*Crack!*

The shrieking brain-dead animal leapt and spun and turned cartwheels. Blood splattered leaves and grass and brush stems. Fletch snapped off three more shots as fast as he could, all body shots; nothing died as hard as a cat.

"CEASE FIRING!"

The dead tom thudded to earth twenty feet from where Fletch's first shot had sheared off the top of its head and smeared brain matter down its spine like scrambled eggs.

The shooters were sitting up, unslinging their arms, bolts open to show no rounds were still accidentally chambered.

Instead of carrying it back to razz his dad with, as

he had planned, Fletch laid the dead cat in its lair and used the butt of his rifle to knock the bank down over the burrow for a shallow warrior's grave. He used a handful of new leaves to wipe a smear of brains from his sleeve.

At the far end of the range, targets were being pulled so firing scores could be checked.

Boots grated on two-by-four rungs. Jerzy Hrock's bulk, larger than life, blocked out the sky above him. Fletcher could hear him panting. He had become immense: too much weight, too many cigarettes, a sea of booze. A killer with no killing to do.

"Sergeant Rock," said Fletcher.

Hrock stepped off the last rung before turning to look at him. Recognition dawned in the mean little pig eyes.

"I'll be fucked! Fletch! This calls for a fuckin drink— just for drill!"

Pitiless noonday sun through unwashed windows exposed the dust-filled corners, slashed vinyl, garish pretentions of the country-western bar. Crude sexual intentions had been hacked into the top of their table. The Rock's massive paw engulfed his shot glass; he was on his seventh, Fletcher on his second. The half-empty bottle stood on the stick between them. The Rock's ashtray overflowed with stubs.

"Fuck, Fletch, the fucker said he was a fuckin newsman."

Fletcher already had checked the Rock's ill-kept records at the rifle range; nothing there except the Hopkins name and the same stolen charge-card usage already established at All-Weather Charter Tours and the Danskin shop.

"Working on a story?" he prompted.

"Fuckin-a! Said he wanted to write about how I'd do those fuckin assholes in Central America."

"So you thought you'd *show* him how you'd do them instead."

"Shit, Fletch, you know me. I could teach a fucking monkey to fuck a football — *an'* teach the football to like it!"

"Describe him," Fletcher said dryly.

The Rock's growl of uneasy laughter turned into a rasping cigarette cough. "Who the fuck remembers?" He rapped his shot glass on the bar. "Lotta this piss down the fuckin' gullet since then."

The Rock, who'd had a good war against the Nazis, in Korea had been assigned as a sniper shooting enemy officers behind the lines. After some kimono-and-sake R&R in Japan when he'd started waking up screaming in the middle of the night, he'd somehow got himself reassigned to a line company for normal battlefield duty. There Fletcher had met him.

"You remember," said Fletcher pitilessly. "Picture him in your scope, then describe him as you'd see him going down."

After an almost pleading look that Fletcher stared down, the Rock shut his eyes. His fingers whitened around his glass. Sweat popped out on his porcine face. But he spoke in a flat recitative voice, as if he were seeing Hopkins, not against his eyelids, but through his sniperscope.

"Five-ten, five-eleven, medium build, pretty good shape — push-ups in the morning maybe. Mid-thirties."

"Describe his face."

"Couldn't see much of it. Black goatee, mustache . . ."

"Eyes."

"He always wore tinted glasses."

"Hair. Dark? Light? Curly? What?"

"He wore a hunting cap all the time too."

"Could the mustache and goatee have been phony?"

But the Rock opened his eyes and drew a deep shuddering breath. He downed his shot. The panic was gone from his eyes.

"Who the fuck knows?" He grunted his way to his feet, a fat and ugly killing machine rusting out from lack of use. "Gotta go tap a fuckin' kidney—just for drill."

It continued to be a day of killing.

Noontime found Fletch five miles from the dead tomcat's hedgerow grave, sitting on a sun-bathed sidehill close-cropped by the farmer's Jerseys and Guernseys. Gopher holes dotted the hillside with little mounds of brown earth. Because he didn't want, somehow, to remember the tomcat's exploded head, he was deliberately remembering Bette in the car with her sweater and bra pushed up. Would she ever go out with him again after that fiasco in the farmer's driveway at Easter?

Far down the slope a stripy gopher came out to stand up straight beside its burrow—really the thirteen-lined ground squirrel, also called the federation squirrel because its patterns resembled stars and stripes; but everyone just called them stripy gophers.

Hundred yards? Hundred and fifty? A hell of a shot, downhill with an unscoped rifle. He rested his elbows on his knees, estimated elevation, angle, the negligible windage. At this range the gopher looked like a stick upright in the ground.

He released his pent half-breath, squeezed off the round. The flat *snap* of the .22 was like a breaking twig. The upright stick fell over.

Fletch whooped and leapt to his feet and skidded and slid down the slope, trying to count paces as he did. He made it 113 yards to the gopher from where he had been sitting. There was a little dot of blood between the yellowed buck teeth, one eye was half-popped out of its socket.

"Hell of a fuckin' shot!' grunted the Rock.

Fletcher looked up at him, blinking. "What?"

"That guy Hopkins. Worst fuckin' shot I ever saw." He slid back into his chair, fired up another Lucky, coughed, picked a fleck of tobacco from between his teeth. His sparse hair, chopped short in the World War II cut known as a heinie, stood up off his head exactly like hog bristles. "But the fucker kept tryin', he got better."

"Good enough," agreed Fletcher.

"Better'n good enough!" He guffawed. "I can't fuckin' believe it, Fletch! Christ, on patrol you was the best fuckin' point man in the whole fuckin' outfit!"

"All these years I've been thinking the war was over."

The Rock shook his head. "No war ain't ever fuckin' over. Just shut your eyes an' there it is again." He grabbed the bottle by the neck, drained it, heaved himself ponderously to his feet. "Gotta go teach fuckheads how to defend their homes 'gainst the fuckin' crazies." He chuckled. "Just for drill, find the fucker, Fletch. Find him an' kill him."

*What is the spirit of the bayonet? To kill.*

It was a day of too much killing.

When he got home, Fletch took the rifle out on the front lawn to clean it. Despite the shimmering dusk where things lost definition, movement caught his eye. A chipmunk, compact little striped body hunched, was eating birdseed at the base of the oak tree a scant ten feet away.

Fletch slowly put down the cleaning rod and just as slowly picked up the rifle, easing off the safety without a click. The chipmunk, used to human comings and goings, ignored him.

The rifle popped, the little animal fell dead on its back in a comic sprawl, legs and arms flopped wide in a parody of sexual abandon, white underbelly gray in the failing light. The body was warm and soft and flexible in Fletch's hand. He slid down the oak tree with his back against the rough bark, sat there holding it. Why wasn't it still alive?"

He stayed there unmoving until darkness had fallen and the body had gotten cold and stiff and

the bus had pulled into the Minneapolis Greyhound station. Only then did Fletcher get stiffly to his feet and follow the others off, somehow surprised there was no dead chipmunk in his fist and no smear of cat brains down his sleeve.

After that day, except for Korea, he had never again killed anything he couldn't eat or sell for money.

# 32

Gary Westergard rubbed tired eyes as he waited to take part in the three-way Democratic national television debate. During the past twenty-four hours he had logged 6,200 miles by plane, limo, and bus: Newark, Charleston, Dayton, Pierre, Albuquerque, San Francisco. Since leaving L.A. last night, his only sleep had been catnaps on the plane and two hours in a Newark motel room early this morning. Tomorrow, the round-robin of primary states those cities had represented: New Jersey, West Virginia, Ohio, South Dakota, New Mexico, California.

But tonight, in the green room of the Burbank TV studio where Johnny Carson also taped, his tired brain could reconstruct the last frantic hours only as shards of disconnected memory.


The Cleveland TV host hoping to goad him into indiscretion said, "In this final week of a bone-crushing and mean-spirited campaign for the Democratic nomination, what is your final impression of Ohio, Governor?"

"It's got everything except an ocean and a mountain range."


The managing editor of the Sante Fe *Herald:*

We're comparing Garrett Westergard with Franklin D. Roosevelt because he's a man of ideals at a time when our country's ideals need clarifying.

The editorial in the East Rutherford, New Jersey, *Standard:*

Gary Westergard and Morris Fiksdahl are a pair of punch-drunk pugs answering the bell for the final round, tired, battered, and near bankruptcy. But Westergard hits below the belt in his campaign, a nasty habit that will kayo him with the American people.

"Governor, California is known as the ultimate media state. We expected slick commercials from you instead of old-style door-to-door campaigning. What happened?"
Westergard, cornered by a reporter from local KCRA-TV in the Sacramento airport lounge, found himself being candid.
"I ran out of money."

Pete Quarles amplified on the theme to a reporter from Rapid City, South Dakota, on *Air Westy,* the guv's campaign jet.
"Money problems? Hell, no. We've come to think of our expense checks as a good California burgundy — they have to be properly aged before we can cash them."

Kent Jarvis showed his usual inimitable style in San Jose, California, before a rally with local Chicano field hands.
"Christ, Guv, did you see the statistics? One registered Democrat in six is a spic in this state."

261

In the back of the limo in Charleston, West Virginia, there was a sudden flare-up with David Ross.

"Governor, put your bucks in the East and your butt in the West. Press the flesh out there. You'll have a blow-out in New Jersey and Ohio anyway, but the new polls show Fiksdahl leading you forty-one percent to thirty-nine in California."

"Two percent? That's paper-thin."

"Paper cuts can be painful."


Handing out I SURVIVED AIR WESTY T-shirts to the staff on the plane ride back to L.A. . . .

Pete and Hastings and Johnny Doyle making up quasi-obscene Fiksdahl songs in the back of the plane. . . .

A reading of the "wimp list" in the jet's press section—the names of newsmen assigned to his campaign who had chickened out of making this final relentless campaign swing. . . .


Of the regular staff, only Ross had elected to stay in Minnesota—working, he said, on a series of statements for Wednesday morning to cover any permutation of possible wins and losses. Real anger spurted through Westergard. Had he gone through all of this pain and effort, nearly bankrupting himself in the process, just so that the presidency might be snatched from him at the last minute? Ross hadn't done one damned thing to get him the truth about whatever really had happened up there in the pine woods last November.

*Had* somebody shot Fletcher deliberately? Unthinkable as it might seem, could that somebody have been Ross? God knew he couldn't ask Fletch—or anyone else save

Ross—about it. He could never appear to have known that the incident had occurred—just in case the unthinkable was real. Whatever the outcome tomorrow, or the day after tomorrow, or the day after that, he would have to act.

Meanwhile, tonight . . .

Tonight he faced Jackie Jefferson (mahogany skin and smooth good looks and bandido mustache) and Morris Fiksdahl (rumpled three-piece ward-heeler suits and party-hack cigar breath) under the TV lights. Well, he had been elected to the Minnesota state legislature while still a student at William Mitchell College of Law; if he couldn't dismantle those two clowns in a head-on political debate, he didn't deserve to win the nomination. Especially since Ross (Nicole?) had clued him in on how to do it.

### WESTY AND THE BACK-ROOM BOYS
### by Lester Warga
Los Angeles *Times* Political Correspondent

The three Democratic presidential hopefuls brought three different agendas to the nationally televised debate which last night officially closed the long, grueling political-primary season.

As he has from the beginning, Jackie Jefferson sought legitimacy; he needs to be taken seriously as a contender.

As he has since the beginning, Morris Fiksdahl sought to shed the back-room dealmaker image rightly or wrongly thrust upon him by Gary Westergard.

As front-runner, Westergard—Westy, his supporters have taken to calling him—had only to hold his own in the debate.

Westy did much more than that.

After stressing there was nothing illegal about such an arrangement, Westergard claimed that over the weekend, Jackson and Fiksdahl had pooled their resources to try to control the West Virginia delegation to the convention.

When the other two candidates tried to deny the allegation, Westy further charged they had done the same thing in Iowa, Missouri, Wisconsin, Indiana, Mississippi, Virginia, Kansas, Tennessee, Oklahoma, Alaska, and even in Westy's home state of Minnesota.

They finally admitted there had been some "cooperation" but tried to minimize it, claiming it was "just at the state level, not a national strategy."

The damage was done. Westy turned to the cameras and said, "Ladies and gentlemen, I give you . . . *The Back-Room Boys!*"

With a single brushstroke, he had painted them into a corner: Fiksdahl, the Washington power-broker of more pragmatism than integrity; and Jefferson, the candidate who feared he could not make it on his own merits. In the process, Westergard won not only last night's debate but also the Democratic nomination for President of these United States.

New Jersey and Ohio landslides, narrow wins elsewhere—except for the eleven-delegate loss in California foretold by Ross. Fiksdahl ended up with 1,212, Jefferson became only a moral force with 367, Westergard emerged with two delegates over the 1,967 he had needed to win the nomination.

He would be the Democratic presidential candidate in November. As such, he would no longer need Ross and his acumen—Nicole's acumen, if he could believe Kent Jarvis. In the heat of the campaign, that sort of expertise could seem irreplaceable, worth any danger; but what good the expertise if, through a scandal involving a putative attempt on the life of his oldest friend, it cost him the presidency?

He had kept putting it off. Now it was time to do it.


Ross was on top of the world. He and Nicole had spent the previous evening working out statements for Westergard to give the press before the weekend, then had spent another of those sinuous quasi-hostile hours of sex that were becoming more exciting to him than conventional loving.

He went through the massive hardwood doors of the governor's office, past Maggie, the middle-aged and married (Edith's work?) secretary who had replaced Nicole. Westergard was behind the ten-foot antique desk he hoped to take with him to Washington, every inch presidential material in his midnight-blue suit and conservative tie. He looked up from his papers when Ross put down a new sheaf on top of them.

"Governor, before the convention next month you're going to have to pay off your eight-hundred-thousand primaries debt, zero in on foreign issues over domestic, and make peace with the other candidates—including those who dropped out of the race early. I have a breakdown for you of the figures on—"

"On Hollis Fletcher?"

Ross was floundering. "Why, I . . . we . . . I thought . . ."

"Thought I had forgotten about it?"

He swiveled away from the desk, elbows on the padded arms of the executive chair, fingers tented in front of him. Outside, statehouse secretaries in their summer dresses were taking coffee breaks under the shady elm trees.

"Do you realize how dangerous this whole situation has

become for me?"

"Governor, I assure you that Nicole can confirm—"

"Can but hasn't."

"Well, it's very embarrassing for her—"

"As embarrassing as losing the presidency would be for me?" He spun his chair back to face the room again, swept a hand over the papers Ross had put down on the desk. "Thank you for these analyses. I'm sure they will be, as always, brilliant." Then he added pleasantly, "But the truth is, David, that you've become an unacceptable liability for this campaign."

Ross's face was ashen. "What . . . do you mean?"

"David, you're fired."

# IV

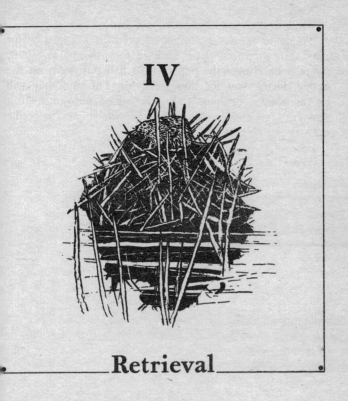

## Retrieval

By its own self-imposed limitations the ritual hunt
keeps before the hunter the immanence and mystery of a world not created for him alone and
over which he has only partial control.

# 33

David Ross said, "Everyone has to believe in something, Fred. I believe I'll have another drink."

He should already have been drunk as a skunk. Drunker, in fact. His first time had been in college, swigging from a bottle of cheap sauterne while walking back to the campus with two other guys—and then throwing up for the rest of the night. This drunk, deliberate and cold-blooded, wasn't as much fun as even that; and despite numerous Jim Beams at Vasili's, not nearly so effective either.

"Be cool, Davy," said Fred in a slightly worried voice.

Ross winked at him and said, "Total control, my man."

Waiting for the drink, he stared vaguely at the Greek artifacts on the walls, meaningless to him now as men's-room graffiti. He'd tried with Nicole, he'd really tried. And what had happened? He'd lost his job. Because she wouldn't go *all the way* for him. So far, and then: Fuck him.

Yeah, he'd shot her old man. But at least the guy was still alive. David's career was *dead*. Westergard was the one going all the way, all the way to the White House, he really was—and David Ross wasn't going with him.

He fired down the bourbon, heaved himself off the stool, almost lost his balance, winked again at Fred, and scattered paper money across the bar. Hey, maybe better not be so free with the old green. Out of a job. Off the campaign.

He went out the door squinting against the summer sunshine. He'd realized he really wanted to go home and tell Nicole off. All her fault he'd lost his job with the campaign.


Nicole was feeling invincible. Their work-ups for Gary last night had been damned good; it was as if she were running his campaign from afar, putting him in the White House single-handedly. *I give you . . . The Back-Room Boys!* Inspired. And *hers.*

Of course, to be honest, David was starting to come up with some excellent ideas of his own too. And somehow all of this trouble seemed to have brought them closer together, more like it had been at the start of their marriage. They were becoming husband and wife again instead of just two sex machines pumping blindly away at one another.

Then she found it.

David had taken her station wagon to work that morning because it had been parked behind his car in the driveway, so she had used his to take the kids over to Iris'. On the way back she'd had to brake for a dog, and a box the size of a shoe box, not so deep but very heavy, had slid out from under the seat.

Back home she opened it, then stood in the driveway beside his car, staring down blindly at a brand-new Python .357 Magnum with a three-inch barrel. She didn't know that it could shoot through the engine block of a Chevrolet. She only knew it could shoot through her father—*and* through her life. Already had.


David drove up as she started into the house with the boxed gun under her arm. All of the tenderness she'd been feeling about him was gone. Surprised, still stunned, unprepared to deal with him, she demanded, "What are you doing home already?" Then, smelling his breath, she added accusingly, "And drunk besides."

"Don't you fucking start on me, Nicole."

"You must have seen that in a movie, lover."

He grabbed her arm. He was almost crying. "I just got fired because of you."

She dropped the gun to push him away with both hands. It hit the porch between them with a loud thud.

"No, you got fired because of *you*."

But he was staring at the box at their feet. All the color had drained from his face.

"What are you doing with that?"

She stalked into the house without answering. He grabbed up the box and followed, slamming the door behind him. She turned to face him.

"Why do you have a *gun* hidden under the seat of your car?"

"*Not* hidden! *Left* in the car. *My* car! You wouldn't have found it if you hadn't been snooping around." He waved an arm and almost lost his balance, making her realize just how drunk he was. "Jesus, all you had to do was tell the Guv—"

"*Lie* to the Guv."

"Better a lie than my whole goddamn life down the drain."

"I'm *glad* it's down the drain." The past weeks came rushing in upon her again. "Shooting my father and now planning to do it again!"

"The gun wasn't for that, it was just—"

"For burglars? You hear someone in the house, so you jump out of bed and run down to get it out from under the car seat?"

"All right. Your fucking father's in Minneapolis. That doctor from Cochrane called, asking to talk with him."

She stared at him, rancor momentarily forgotten. "If Dad was in town, he surely would have called me . . ."

"Unless he was planning to murder your husband."

"He doesn't know that you're the one. I lied to cover up for you so he *couldn't*. . ." She suddenly, literally, began wringing her hands. "I did that to him! For you! *You!* You . . . you . . . and then lying about why you got the gun . . ."

The doorbell rang.

They looked at one another, frozen in that moment of time when both parties suddenly realize an argument is out of hand and that someone—in this case, Iris Bergman bringing the kids home from the municipal pool—is about to catch them at it.

"I'll never forgive you," said Nicole, getting in the last word as, hand on the knob, she turned to look back at him with real loathing. "The lies . . . the self-justification . . ."

She opened the door.

It was Fletcher.


"Oh! Dad!" She put a hand over her mouth like a stricken soap-opera heroine. "I didn't . . ."

". . . sorry I didn't call, honey. But I knew you'd

been out of town with the campaign, and . . ."

He stopped there. Waiting to be invited in. She was trying to listen over her shoulder without looking away from him. Where was David? Where was the gun? Then she saw him outside, beyond Fletcher, running bent-over from the garage past his own car to her station wagon, the still-boxed gun in his hand.

She drew her father quickly inside, embracing him with a strange ambivalence. She felt stricken with guilt at hiding from him that David was the man he sought, yet at the same time felt almost angry with him for being so much in her life *now,* when she had so much else to cope with. Where had he been when she had been little, when she had needed him so desperately?

"Dad, you should have told me you were here in town . . ."

"I was ashamed to admit I'd taken up the hunt again."

She led him back to the kitchen and the coffee on the stove, dreading David's possible return, or, almost as bad, the kids'. They would inevitably blab that she hadn't been away at all. Despite her fears, she made herself listen with a semblance of interest to Fletcher's oddly disconnected update of the hunt, from Old Charlie's stern admonition, *You don't leave no cripples—never!* to the Rock, the man from Fletcher's past who, ironically, had taught the man calling himself Hopkins how to almost kill him.

Her ambivalent guilt jolted her again like a shock from a faulty appliance: the man calling himself Hopkins was really the man calling himself David whom she had married and who at this moment was driving around Hennepin County in a drunken frenzy with a .357 Magnum under his car seat.

Fletcher was saying, ". . . but the Rock was a dead

end too, so — finished." He chuckled without mirth. "Anyway, Victor thinks getting shot was the best event of my life for the past five years. Said I was in a groove of self-pity."

*"Dad . . ."*

He patted her hand almost impersonally, as if gentling an uneasy horse. "I'll just go back to being whoever I was before all this happened, honey."

She said in a small voice, "Victor called. He wants to talk with you."

He nodded as if it didn't matter very much.

After he had gone she sat at the kitchen table and cried. Then she splashed cold water on her face so the kids wouldn't see she was upset when they got home. She knew she would never tell Fletcher now. Couldn't. She had let it go on too long. To tell him now would destroy them all — him, her, David, their marriage. Everything. Maybe even end up getting someone killed.

Better go on from here, with the imperfect man she had married. Fletcher had chosen his life, to live almost like the animals he hunted. For five years he had lived like that. She told herself that he would get over his hurt as an animal does, he had said it himself: *I'll just go back to being whoever I was before all this happened.*

Which was at least partway a wild man. Not like David. He had committed an inexplicable act, but at least him she could control. In his very weakness was civilization. Civilization she could handle.

As she started making sandwiches for the kids' lunch, she wondered if she should get David his job back with the campaign. Not *tell* him she would, but . . . Maybe do it. Maybe even work herself into the campaign officially at the same time.

274

Suddenly she felt a great deal better.

Smelling mesquite smoke and roasting meat, Fletcher went past the house to the partially enclosed patio area. Victor and Ingrid had the old Doc Sigurson place south of town, two-story white frame with green shutters and a narrow winding drive up through the oaks. The drive had to be plowed out after each winter storm.

Victor was a lanky scarecrow in at-home chinos and a black short-sleeved sport shirt covered with huge yellow tropical flowers. He had a long-tined barbecue meat fork in one hand.

"Fletch! Just in time for dinner under the stars."

Ingrid came from the house with a can of beer in each hand.

"Hal! How nice!"

She put them down to embrace Fletcher with enthusiasm. She was a strapping Scandinavian woman as attractive as Victor was ugly. They made a striking couple.

"You're staying for supper. Let me get another beer." She handed them the two she had brought. "If Victor insists on these high-cholesterol cook-outs, the least you can do is sin with us."

Fletcher slapped at a mosquito zizzing around his head as Ingrid returned to the house. Victor was slicing into one of the steaks to get a peek inside.

"I remember you now," he said without looking up. "The man who was going to shoot me a buck by Christmas." He gave Fletcher his sly and ugly grin. "*Last* Christmas." He gestured at the grill. "Since you didn't come through, I'm reduced to this."

"Prime Four-H beef," said Fletcher. "You poor devil."

He moved closer so the smoke would keep off the mosquitoes.

"Now, why don't you show me how clever you've been about the phone calls made from Dutch's Tavern? I'm sure that's why you called me at Nicole's."

Victor nodded. "Well, I kept thinking about how to trace those calls, until I suddenly realized that old-timey country docs like me, who still make house calls, always have people in their debt. We get babies named after us, sometimes even colts if we happen to be around when the vet isn't. Then . . ."

Fletcher took a swig from his beer. It was icy and good.

"Let's take it as a given that you're a prince."

"Let's." Victor was enjoying himself also. "Y'see, last summer the manager of the phone company from Grand Rapids was fishing for walleyes on Lake Cochrane and got hit with a backcast—both sets of triple hooks right in the face." Victor made horrible grimaces and exaggerated gestures. "Well, sir, if I hadn't been available he might have been running around with his right eye hanging down to—"

"We get the picture," interrupted Ingrid loudly, arriving with another beer and place-setting for the screened-in-patio table. She set them down and disappeared back inside for vegetables and rolls and scalloped potatoes.

"You just called him up and asked him," said Fletcher in admiration.

"*Told* him. Said I needed the information for the treatment of another patient. Strictly speaking, true of course. Bring over those plates."

Fletcher did. Victor put about a pound of steak on each.

"And?"

276

"The calls were made on a credit card issued to a Gerard M. Hopkins by an outfit called Primary Power, Inc."

"Calls to whom?"

"Ah-ha, quick tension in the voice! Calls to an unlisted number in Minneapolis."

"Couldn't your man at the phone company—"

"Wouldn't. In-house he was willing, but the Twin Cities have a different carrier. I almost called the number myself just to see who would answer, but then I thought—"

"Just tell me the damned number!" burst out Fletcher.

But Victor still wasn't through. He squinted in phony concentration. "The number . . . Hmm, I should have written it down, shouldn't I?"

"Victor, I swear—"

"All right. Two-eight-nine, three-seven-six-six."

Fletcher felt as if he couldn't breathe, felt as if he were going to fall down. It was like being shot all over again.

"That can't be right," he said in a hollow voice.

Victor was staring curiously at him. "I saw the printout myself. Fletch, what . . ."

But Fletcher had turned away, only vaguely aware of the voice raised behind him. He was trotting, almost running. Then he *was* running—or at least moving with the odd quick skipping gait a crippled predator might think of as running. Running down the long gravel driveway through the cool woods, away from the place where the blow had been struck. Already the pain was stabbing at his side, but he welcomed it.

The would-be killer had made two calls to the private, unlisted phone number of Fletcher's daughter, Nicole, less than an hour after leaving Fletcher for dead in the snow.

What besides pain did he have left that hadn't just been taken from him?

# 34

Nicole's first impression of San Francisco from the air was of fog-washed crispness, of a clarity she had not seen elsewhere except the Greek isles. There was a red and smiling Golden Gate Bridge, a surprisingly small financial district of glittering high-rises, finally a tumble of homes like stunning-white children's blocks strewn haphazardly over the hills.

But David was there to spoil it for her.

"Honey, what are you going to say to Gary?"

She didn't answer. When she had opened the door to her father, she had made a snap decision she was going to have to live with—but she wasn't up to explaining it yet. Or perhaps, she thought as they waited in the baggage area beneath the Northwest (Domestic) Terminal, she didn't have any explanation—beyond keeping her husband alive and protecting her father from his own rage. Or did she have other, less-obvious motives that would, as Hamlet was fond of remarking, be scann'd?

"We're going to have to talk about it sooner or later," he persisted. But she merely pointed at the carousel.

"There's my overnight case, David."

Outside it was bright and windy, less muggy than the Midwest. An energetic gull was pumping its way over the wind-chopped water, trying to keep up with their cab speeding north along the causeway past Candlestick Park.

David tried again, this time using his wry and deprecating grin.

"Honey, you've got every right to be angry, but—"

"Angry?" She turned to look him directly in the face for almost the first time since he had staggered home drunk and sick and fearful after her father had left. "'Angry' is such a wimp word for what I feel toward you, David."

An hour later she was angrily trying to run Westergard to earth at the Fairmont Hotel.

"All right, then, please get me Hastings Crandall. He's with the campaign." She looked up from the phone to meet David's sappy look—which meant he was going to tell her something she didn't want to hear. That he loved her, probably. "What?" she demanded in irritation.

"I . . ." He made a vaguely conciliatory gesture. "Why—"

"'Virtue debases itself in justifying itself.' Meaning, don't look a gift horse in the mouth, buster." Into the phone she said, "Crandall with two L's. He'll be registered here at the hotel." She put her hand back over the receiver. "I'm going to have to work very hard on Gary to make him change his mind on this. So if he does then I'm in all the way, understand?"

Mr. Nice Guy slipped for a moment. "Yeah, I understand. You want everyone to see that you know how to run a campaign."

"Just be glad I do. Gary will protect you with his campaign security only as long as he doesn't know he's doing it."

David was silent. He had no retort. She was glad, because she was preparing herself to cold-bloodedly and with calculation lie to Gary to get David back in.

And herself.

Fletcher had hiked the three miles to the river bottom because he couldn't stand being cooped up with his bitter thoughts any longer. While the ground was bare of undergrowth, the receding floodwaters had left a springy bed of driftwood that crackled underfoot. To be totally silent in moving through the hardwoods he could advance only about three feet a minute. His concentration was bogus, of course; he sought nothing, hunted nothing except relief from the fruitless round of thought.

Who had known the terrain around the cabin reasonably well for an outsider? Had known Fletcher's routine when coming back to the cabin from a hunt? Had, discounting mustache and goatee and tinted glasses, fit the attacker's description perfectly? Had been in an ideal position to steal and use a Primary Power, Inc. credit card? Was the only person who might call Nicole after his bloody work was done? Was, finally, the only person Nicole would try to protect from him?

So, all questions answered. His hunt was over. All he had left to do was go to his daughter's husband and politely ask why the son of a bitch had tried to kill him. Right?

Wrong. Because he already knew the answer. Such a strong wind of hate blew through Fletcher that he bent into it as into a blizzard. Over Christmas Eve drinks, David had offered a rationale for his existence: *politics and power and making it.*

Only Gary Westergard could offer David these things after which he so openly lusted.

Again that icy inner wind whipped through his guts and balls and brain. And through his injuries, so that they stabbed with pain so intense he almost cried out.

Why, for God's sake, Gary, *why?*

He hadn't seen the man in almost forty years, so it had to be from the four years of distant summers they had worked the boxcars together at Crowley's Lumberyard. Getting in shape for football and hockey, earning money for college.

He found himself standing with one foot raised, a scant two yards from the head-high stump of a lightning-blasted hardwood which the years had hollowed out. He'd disappeared so thoroughly in himself that a big brown blunt-nosed woodchuck came thrusting up out of the opening at the top of the stump unaware of any human presence.

Nicole had worked for Gary for years; ask *her* why the man would want him dead. Ask Nicole. Ask his daughter.

A wind of emotion even stronger than hatred raked him. His silent howl of anguish finally made him visible, blew the groundhog back down its hollow tree like a shotgun blast.

Nicole. Flesh of his flesh. Blood of his blood. So *why* had she done it? For what had Nicole betrayed him?

A dozen people crowded the sitting room of the suite; Nicole automatically worked the room, embracing here, shaking hands there, feeling wholly, truly alive for the first time in months. Most were unknown to her—well-heeled local volunteers, Westergard's San Francisco campaign coordinator, reporters from the *Chronicle* and *Examiner,* a high-profile network reporter she had known slightly at WCCO-TV, Minneapolis, who had gone national. The woman now sought an exclusive interview with Westergard.

At last Hastings got Nicole to the campaign-staff regulars, which also meant Kent Jarvis, even more objectionable than she had remembered. As if the man knew something about himself—about her too?—that he hadn't known six months earlier.

An ease with political power? Or something darker? The one thing she knew for sure was that here was the foe. Despite her perception of lurking danger, perhaps because of it, she submitted briefly to his stale-cigar embrace.

"I know, baby, you just couldn't stay away from me."

"Not really. I wanted to confirm earlier impressions."

"What the hell does that mean? I gotta lie awake nights trying to figure out whether I've been insulted or not?" He took her arm to steer her through the crowd. "Came to hustle the Guv to get your hubby's job back for him?"

Instead of answering, she said, "Where's Edith?"

He shot her a shrewd sideways look. "Like that, huh?"

"I just want to say hello to her."

"Sure." He gave his meaty chuckle. "Madame Defarge is out shopping." He opened the door to the bedroom, stood aside. "So for the moment it's safe for you to try to get the Guv back into the sack for old times' sa—"

"Has anyone ever told you what you really are, Kent?"

"Nobody knows what I really am, baby."

"I think I could come close in five words or less."

Gary Westergard, in jeans and stocking feet, was alone on the balcony in the sunshine with a stack of paperwork in his lap. Behind him, bracketing his head, were those two very different symbols of San Francisco's economic might, the glum dark marble shaft of the Bank of America monolith and the airy white marble spire of the Transamerica Pyramid. Nicole's voice brought his head up with a jerk.

" 'My name is Ozymandias, king of kings:/Look on my works, ye Mighty, and despair!' "

She was framed in the bedroom doorway against the dim interior. He sprang up to embrace her, dropped his papers on the floor, in retrieving them noticed the symbols of commercial power which had bracketed his head. Understanding, he answered: " 'Nothing beside remains. Round the decay/ Of that colossal wreck, boundless and bare,/ The lone and level sands stretch far away.' "

She was in his arms. She was trembling—or was it he? He quickly dropped his arms and stepped back.

"Is that how you see me? A colossal wreck?"

She shook her head fondly. "I see a man on the way to his dreams—a man at the height of his powers, unstoppable."

He walked over to the little round two-tier decorative fountain gurgling softly in the warm air. He had to be very careful here, no matter what his personal emotional responses. She was here to sue for her husband's job back, and he didn't know how much she knew, didn't know how much—if anything—there was *to* know. Maybe she could tell him.

"Except your husband?" he asked belatedly.

She had come up beside him to stare down into the sparkling water. "There should be birds splashing around in it."

"I'll order up an exaltation of larks right away."

She took a deep breath and turned to look up at his face. "I know you've got some crazy notion that David might have had something to do with shooting my dad, but—"

There it was immediately, right out in the open. "Crazy?"

"Utterly. He didn't even know about Dad being shot

284

until I told him at Olaf's house that night."

"How did you learn about it?"

She met his eyes easily, with none of the false challenge of concealed falsehood. "My friend Iris called—you remember her . . ." He nodded. "She was baby-sitting the kids, the doctor in Cochrane called the house as soon as he got Dad to the hospital."

Westergard realized that for weeks there had been a lump of lead growing in his belly like an unacknowledged tumor; now, as if from a miracle at Lourdes, it had gone into remission.

"So it was . . . just an accident."

"According to Dad."

He was silent for so long that she walked past the fountain to rest her forearms on the railing, staring down over the city laid out below Nob Hill like an ad for The Golden State.

He came up beside her, saying "Nikki" softly, as if tasting the name. But she said without looking at him, "Anything else left unsaid to come back and haunt us?"

"You keep showing me how to be a candidate," he said wryly. "All right. I can understand why you didn't tell me Fletch had been shot before you left the party that night. But why didn't you call and tell me once you knew he was all right?"

Only now did she turn to look at him.

"I just assumed David would have told you. Meanwhile, he had . . . found out about us, so it was difficult for me to . . ."

He nodded. "Edith knew too. Guessed, anyway." He took her arms in his big clever hands and turned her toward him. "You know why I . . . broke it off between us, don't you? I finally found the guts to do what we had so often talked about, run for president. When I did, I felt it wasn't right to be—"

"I know," she said softly. "The knight's vigil in the chapel over his armor. I should have figured it out sooner." She stepped back from his hands. "Gary, I want David's job back for him, and I want back in myself."

"Nikki, I . . . The campaign . . . That is, Edith and I . . ."

She said quickly, "Not that way. Not . . . us. I just miss it all so damned much . . ."

"Done," said Westergard over the butterflies in his stomach. For a vivid moment he wanted her in bed, under him, but . . . Too risky for a would-be president.

In synch with his thoughts, she said, "Edith isn't going to be too happy when I come sashaying back into your life—"

"Edith wants to be first lady," he said bluntly, "almost as much as I want to be president."

Nicole gave a glad little laugh, spun from the railing.

"That investigative reporter who used to be with WCCO-TV is waiting in there for an exclusive interview. I think you should talk about choosing a running mate— you can use a very public search to our political advantage."

"Shouldn't I win the nomination first?" he asked lightly.

"Too late then." She was pacing, thinking. "By considering them now, you honor all the groups who might be passed over when you actually make a choice. You're looking for . . ." She kept tapping the air with her forefinger as she walked and talked. "For someone you're personally compatible with, that's it. Someone who can . . . conduct foreign negotiations at the highest level. Can cut through the federal bureaucracy, advance your programs on Capitol Hill, be in charge of long-range planning for the nation . . ."

She stopped and whirled and pointed at him.

"Go change your clothes and . . . No, don't. In fact,

leave your shoes off and put your feet up again. Let her talk to you out here where you'll be the Viking conqueror of the city."

He blew out a delighted and relieved breath. In that moment it seemed as if the final necessary element for a successful run at the presidency had fallen into place.

"My God, Nikki," he exlaimed, "it's great to have you back!"

# 35

"We've missed you," said Victor. "Since the night you came back from Minneapolis we've seen you zero times."

Fletcher had found him in his office writing up notes on a just-completed physical exam. He said nothing, so Victor sighed and swept a hand across the open medical history on his desk.

"Emphysema. She says she never smoked a day in her life. Her X rays say she smoked a pack a day for twenty years. Whom should I believe?"

Fletcher said, "I want you to sell my cabin for me."

"Gee, I'm swell, Fletch. Nice of you to ask."

He made an impatient gesture. "Victor, you said it yourself—five years of self-pity is enough for any man." He put down on the desk the heavy accordion file he'd been holding. "Here's the title to the property and a power of attorney to handle the sale. I hate to stick you with this, but—"

"—but a man's gotta do what a man's gotta do," finished Victor in ringing ironic tones. He leaned his butt against the edge of the desk, his arms folded on his chest. "I'm not so sure I did you a favor tracing those phone calls from Dutch's Tavern."

Again Fletcher ignored his remark to say roughly, "One other thing. I'll need some of the money right away."

An hour later, Victor stood on the sidewalk in front of the First National Bank of Cochrane, watching Fletcher go unevenly down the street toward Lars Peterson's used-car lot to buy a pickup. A man under tremendous pressure, a man full of sadness.

"Fletch, why?" he had asked in the bank.

"Victor, why not?" Fletcher had said.

"Why not indeed?" said Victor aloud in the empty street.

He guessed that coming to him to sell the cabin and get some money was probably the hardest thing Fletcher had ever done. Well, maybe the second hardest. Crawling a thousand feet through the snow, shot three times, that probably had been harder.

Or, he thought, turning away back toward his clinic, maybe escaping from the North Koreans and working his way to American lines through the ice and snow and subzero winter temperatures north of the forty-second parallel. Korea had been Victor's war too; he remembered those winters. Even in Minnesota he remembered those winters.

"Damn her," he said to himself, again aloud.

He had no doubts at all about whom the unlisted phone number belonged to: there was only one person still living who could anguish Fletcher in this way.

*Damn* her!

He decided he wouldn't sell Fletcher's cabin right away, just in case. No telling when the man might need a place to come back to, a place where he could lie up and lick his wounds and hopefully heal himself yet again.

*Damn her!*

Kent Jarvis dropped off the rattling cable car a block short of the turnaround at the foot of Powell. This wasn't too smart just before the convention, but he was dangerously near the edge of his control. And it somehow didn't seem like all that big a deal in San Francisco—hell, here in Sin City S&M probably was a way of life.

The fog was in; he pulled his inadequate topcoat more tightly across his chest as he went out Ellis toward Taylor and the heart of the Tenderloin District. What was that saying? *I spent the coldest winter of my life one summer in San Francisco.*

He turned in at the porn shop to which he'd been directed by a bellhop at the Fairmont for twenty bucks. To the left was a short-order counter half-full of street types with quick, on-the-hustle eyes; to the right, racks of magazines and paperbacks organized by fetish, preference, or perversion. The "marital aids" were beyond a waist-high counter in the back. On the counter was a cash register and a sign, "B 21 or B Gone," behind it a toad in a three-piece suit.

Jarvis spent a few minutes among the dildos, merkins, dancing eggs, inflatable dolls, vibrators, and self-help items that plugged into auto lighter sockets, checking whether anyone had entered the place after him. He could just see some enterprising reporter's feature in the Sunday paper's "Life Styles" about what Westergard's campaign manager did in his spare time.

Hell, who was he kidding? Since Nicole's return two weeks ago, the focus was all on her. She was taking over everything. Too late he had realized that she, not Ross, was the one with the smarts and the drive and the determination. Poor old ineffectual fucking Ross had never been anything but a hand-job until she could get back in tight with the Guv again.

Soon she'd be dicking him, no matter how watchful Madame Defarge might be. How the hell could he compete with that? Damn her! He imagined her nude, in a porn-magazine pose, and suddenly, vividly, could *feel* his fists thud against her naked flesh. Made resolute by the stirring in his groin, he strode across the room to the toad.

"I'm looking for Jimmy," he snapped.

"Never heard of him."

"Carl at the Fairmont said—"

"Never heard of him either."

But the toad's hand happened to have fallen, palm up, on the counter. Jarvis belatedly understood and put the card Carl at the Fairmont had given him into the palm. The toad nodded.

"How remarkable. You found Jimmy after all."

"Good. Now what can Jimmy find me?"

"Fuckin' near anything you want."

Jarvis found himself taking out a head shot of Nicole he had snipped from one of the guv's old state campaign brochures.

"How about a woman doesn't mind getting roughed up a bit, looks something like this?"

The toad squinted judiciously, said, "Sure," then warned, "But you gotta understand, this gal I got in mind won't be any Doublemint twin."

Jarvis automatically checked his watch and flexed hands that would soon be fists. He didn't worry about AIDS anymore. Now, when he'd finished punishing a girl, he would do himself by hand onto her as she lay there moaning.

"Close is good enough," he said.

Over three hours before he had to be back to the Fairmont. Whoever the toad found for him tonight, whatever she looked like, he had time to make her pay

291

for Nicole's return. Pay plenty.

Hell, *somebody* had to.


Fletcher never needed a watch in the woods; his innate sense of sun-time even on cloudy days was nearly perfect. Four-thirty — and, as if on a timer, the woodchuck popped up out of its hole in the hollow stump like an overweight furry jack-in-the-box. Fletcher, no longer battling the tortured progress of his thoughts by concentrating on silent movement through the woods — his thoughts had won — swiped an ineffectual hand at the swarms of mosquitoes massing about his head. The quick movement dropped the panicked animal back into its hollow stump like a stone.

Fletcher barely noticed. This was his good-bye to these woods. He had come over the low hills from which Ross had ambushed him; his meandering return would take him one last time up the burn past the fire-blasted spruce; tonight he would sleep in the cabin for the last time.

Redwings chirped and rode the wind-danced cattails in the brackish water at the edge of the slough. A brace of raucous crows flapped up off a bloated carp filling the air with its sweetish stink of death. An eight-point whitetail buck still in velvet crashed away through the brush.

An eight-point whitetail buck with its gleaming antlers fresh out of velvet was swimming the river fifty feet away. Old Charlie leaned forward to grab Fletch's arm and point through the deepening dusk. He was getting progressively more Indian; his long white hair was braided in brave fashion; he wore beaded doehide moccasins in the old style.

292

Over the summer, since finding a stand of paper birch, they had been making this birchbark canoe together on weekends, when Fletch could get down to West Newton.

The buck was angling upstream against the current, its shoulders working to drive its chest up out of the churning water with each stroke. Excitement constricted Fletch's chest. Ever since the old Indian had told him of doing this as a boy, he had rehearsed the moves in his mind.

"We gotta try it, Charlie!" he yelled.

Charlie dug in his paddle, the fragile craft shot forward like an arrow from the bow. This was the first time they'd taken the canoe out; tomorrow evening Fletch would catch the *Burlington Zephyr* back to college for his sophomore year. They'd wanted to test whether the resined joints between the overlapped sheets of bark would leak. Birchbarks made the lightest and best of all canoes, Charlie said, but if pierced or leaking, quickly became waterlogged and lost their buoyancy. This one was holding fine.

The buck was casting wild looks over his shoulder, panicked at the canoe's approach.

Fletch said aloud, "We aren't going to hurt you, old boy."

It was just dusk; against the chinook-salmon sky an arrow of resident mallards careened down-channel at sixty miles an hour on their way to the reserve for the night. Charlie brought the canoe up alongside and downstream from the quarry; Fletch laid his paddle in the bottom, crouched with his hands on the gunwales to keep the craft from tipping when he shifted his weight.

"Now!" yelled Charlie.

The boy reached out across the deer and grabbed the far antler with his left hand, hesitated, grabbed the near antler with his right hand, then shoved down hard for the leverage to flip himself out of the canoe and onto the buck's back.

His weight drove the animal right under the water, but it came up instantly, blowing, pumping hard, twisting its powerful neck, trying to throw off the unexpected weight. Fletch hung on for dear life with knees and hands, the working shoulders alive between his gripping knees, the antlers hard and knobby and unforgiving under his fists.

The old Indian had dropped the canoe back to keep the deer from hooking it in his frenzy. Over the animal's snorting Fletch could hear Charlie's yell, "Yahoo! Ride 'im, cowboy!"

They were coming up fast on the Wisconsin side, where a pale strip of sandbar had been left by last summer's channel-dredging. Fletch wondered for the first time how he was going to get off without being gored. Charlie hadn't covered that. He tried to *feel* the quality of each movement by the animal under him. *There!* One shoulder had lurched with the unexpected solidity of bottom under its hoof.

Fletch had already let go of the antlers to hurl himself sideways into the water with great splashings even as the deer thrust himself up from it with even greater splashings. Without looking back, the boy dived as deep as he could, swam hard underwater straight out into the current.

When his lungs felt like they would burst, he surfaced to look back at the sandbank past which the current was quickly sweeping him. The buck, far from turning to attack, was fleeing up into the undergrowth without a backward glance, shaking itself like a wet dog as it went.

The next time he saw the birchbark canoe, its bottom had been smashed out by the people from the poor farm so the old Indian couldn't use it for yet another escape attempt.

In the slanting dawn light Fletcher locked his cabin for the last time. He left the key under the usual stone for Victor, drove away in the old Toyota 4x4 without a backward glance.

Apart from clothes and toiletries and camping gear, he had brought only Charlie's beautifully cured old bearskin. Old Charlie, always somehow present in the soft, tanned hide, might sometimes be a comfort on his travels.

With his three rifle blasts, Ross had stolen it all from him. He was thunderingly angry, but he didn't know what to do about it. To go after Ross, he would have to go through Nicole; she had obviously made her choice. Just like when Terry had died: she had dismissed him then, she was dismissing him now.

He wished he could do the same, dismiss her completely from his feelings and emotions. But he couldn't, even though he had come to suspect that treachery was part of her nature; maybe because she was the last bit of Terry on earth.

For the moment, anyway, like Charlie at the end of *his* life, Fletcher was no longer a hunter, not of men nor of animals nor of anything else that lived upon this earth.

David Ross had seen to that, on behalf of Gary Westergard.

Perhaps some adventure on the road would change all of that. Perhaps that was why he was going on the road.

# 36

At 10:03 P.M. on July 14, PDT, when New Jersey's 115 votes gave Westergard eleven more than the 1,967 delegates needed for the first-ballot nomination, Gary and Edith were holding hands on the couch in front of the suite's big-screen color TV. He kissed his wife and held her, emotions pouring through him: pride, unease, triumph, dread, a profound excitement.

Finally he stood. "Come on, darling." Unconsciously he echoed Nicole from earlier: "They want their Viking conqueror."

His day of Viking conquest had begun prosaically with a six forty-five A.M. working breakfast in the Fairmont's posh Brasserie.

"It needs final blue-penciling, but I think we've got the important points covered," said David Ross about the twentieth draft of the acceptance speech. "Economic growth, prosperity, jobs, justice, human dignity, opportunity, peace, security, freedom."

Underground in the cavernous Moscone Convention Center, Kent Jarvis was explaining their first-ballot-nomination tactics to a batch of reporters.

"Since eighty-five percent of floor management is rumor control, half our convention budget goes on communications so we can reach any of our people anywhere in Moscone Center anytime."

"Reach how?" asked a newspaper reporter with an old-fashioned notebook in hand just as a younger, hipper one with micro-mini-cassette recorder demanded "What sort of rumors?"

"Oh, Mondale's coming back from the dead, for instance, to have his name put in nomination." For the older reporter, he added, "You can't get anything done out on the floor, so we oversee the fourteen key delegate trackers from trailers backstage. They talk with pairs of cluster leaders, who each watch three hundred delegate whips on the convention floor."

"Sounds like a lot of chiefs for not a hell of a lot of Indians," commented the young reporter.

"Stencil titles on their chests to hang on to your delegates," returned Jarvis with a cynical grin.

Nicole had another batch of early-rising media people, mostly TV and radio, at the hotel's convention press center.

"We want the convention to be the starting blocks for the general election rather than the finish line for the primaries."

"Are you saying Westy can pick up all the marbles *tonight?*"

"Tune in after the first ballot," Nicole said with a grin.


Twenty minutes after his first-ballot nomination, Westergard was on the convention floor. Moscone Center was a sea of WESTY posters and tricolored bunting, the roar of the crowd echoing off the high ceiling like surf battering a seawall. The feeling it gave him was worth anything on earth. Anything at all.

"Tomorrow I will accept your nomination," he told them from the podium after ten minutes of pandemonium. "Tonight . . . well, tonight I just want to tell you that my heart is . . . full. Of joy. Of gratitude. Of kinship with all of you who worked so hard to put me here. Thank you."

The crowd thundered. He was in. He was The Chosen.


Who was he? wondered Fletcher, standing barefoot and bare-legged in the dark on the short gray-green buffalo grass that early settlers had used for their sod houses. He had put out his groundsheet and sleeping bag, had taken off his pants and wrapped his shoes in them for a pillow—and had been hit with another bout of fruitless soul-searching. He shook his head.

"To hell with it," he said aloud.

He slipped into his bag beside the 4x4 and lay staring up into the night. The truck was parked under a solitary cottonwood well away from the highway's barreling long-haul rigs and flat-eyed intrusive highway patrolmen. Under the new moon it was very dark; a warm breeze sighed across the Wyoming grasslands.

A band of coyotes began an abrupt serenade of barks, howls, and whistles. Fletcher dozed off as the mice and gophers began their rustlings and squeakings again.


The mule deer was surprised when Fletch's first shot broke its left front leg. It ran three-legged for a few steps, then stopped, puzzled by its sudden infirmity. The untested rifle fired low, so the second round hit it in the left hip and knocked it down. As it struggled up again, Fletch's overcompensated third shot went into the neck too high to

299

touch the spine.

"For Chrissake," said the guide in disgust, "that's Jesus Christ enough."

He was in his mid-thirties, lean and whipcord but with his face already eroded by summer sun and winter wind. As he raised his own rifle, Fletch charged the deer, tears of humiliation in his eyes. Sixteen weeks of training as an army rifleman seemed to have made him good only for the gross firepower of the M-1.

The buck was standing splay-footed and patient-eyed under the enormous weight of imminent death. Fletch slashed its jugular with a quick jerk of his knife. It dropped to its front knees, then fell on its side, arterial blood staining the crushed al-kali grass almost black. Fletch, still shamed by the grossness of the kill, rolled the dead deer onto its back to gut it.

The guide panted up, followed more slowly by Fletch's father, still recovering from his previous year's heart attack.

"Hey," said the half-angry guide, "that's my job."

But Fletch, having already severed the root of the dead buck's genitals between the rump bulges, was unzipping the deer from groin to rib cage as easily as slitting an envelope. His forefinger along the back of the edge-up blade kept it from prick-ing the innards.

"And mine's shooting—I know," he said tightly, face dark with self-disgust. "But it looks like that's more than I can handle, so I may as well do this."

They finished field-dressing it out together in hostile silence. An hour later, after Fletch had be-latedly fired a few sighting rounds through the borrowed rifle, they were hunting again. Skirting a tumbled area of scree, he grabbed the guide's arm and pointed, but was shaken off. The guide too had spotted the big mulie buck up on the ridgeline three hundred yards away.

"Too far without a scope. Hell, even *I* couldn't hit it from here. We'll drive around, come up behind it—"

"Just stop the jeep," said Fletch's dad.

After a tense moment the guide made a long-suffering face and stopped. Fletch got out. It felt right; this time he knew his gun. He fired one round, a chest shot, rock-steady without support. Easier than a hundred-yard unscoped downhill .22 shot at a stripy gopher, wasn't it?

The buck pitched forward off the ridge, came rolling and flopping down the scree to land at their feet in a clattering shower of dislodged rocks. Fletch actually had to step aside to keep from getting knocked over.

"You're getting sloppy," said his dad happily. "Usually you drop 'em right into the back of the jeep."

"For Chrissake!" exclaimed the guide. "Three hundred yards uphill without a scope? This one *I* skin out."

The three of them got half-drunk around their campfire. In the morning his dad drove back to Minnesota while the guide drove Fletch down to Cheyenne to catch a bus to San Francisco—and, a week later, Korea.

He sat up covered with sweat. The breeze had fallen, the night was still and close. He threw open the sleeping bag; dream had turned to nightmare. Until Terry's death had driven him back into the woods thirty years

301

later, his killing had been of men in Korea—and he'd been damn good at that.

Korea. For the first time since Inchon he wished he had a bottle to get drunk with, because now he couldn't even hunt men.

Not even one man.

David and Nicole climaxed together for the first time since leaving Minnesota. As their hearts slowed, she realized that, incredibly, yet another healing had begun. Perhaps it was inevitable. Since she had chosen to protect David from her father—at least in part because her father would never need protection from anyone or anything—perhaps such a healing was inevitable.

Who knew how she might have acted in David's place? She knew that hunger for success, that fear of failure. And she had chosen him, hadn't she? Didn't that imply an acceptance of what he was? Of what he had done?

She looked over at him, sleeping. Had he shared her warmth or feeling, or had it still been basically sex for him? She finally drifted back into sleep thinking that actually what she felt now, what David felt, even whatever her father might feel, were no longer important. In sixteen hours all of their lives would be changed forever by Gary's acceptance speech.

"My fellow Americans. With humble heart I accept your nomination to lead the fight that now surely follows."

He felt the first wave of sound washing over him in his guts, his groin. This was what sex was supposed to be but never was; this was flashpoint of nuclear explosion.

"Since this has been the most wide-open race in the history of American politics, usually this would be a time of healing. Of reconciliation within our party."

Another thunder of sound to interrupt his words. He did not mind. All time was his.

"But tonight, my friends, the primaries are history and out there the Republican party, grown fat from years of public power, is strapping on its armor and sharpening its sword like some corrupt medieval nobleman seeking easy spoils."

Again the deafening roar. No faces, only mouths; no voices, only sound. Multiple orgasms of sound for him alone.

"Instead, in November the Republicans will find disaster. Why? Because the very life of our great nation is at stake, so we must not fail. We *will* not fail."

The roar of sound, *the roar!* He *was* the sound. He *was* the faces. He was the party. He was Power.

"Because we Democrats are just that—*democrats!* Look at us assembled here, from every state of the union, from every race on earth. This is our shield against the elitism of the enemy."

WESTY! Roar of a thousand throats acknowledged his vision, acknowledged *him!* WESTY! He was their be-all, their end-all, their chosen. WESTY! He would lead them out of the twilight of nuclear terror into the sunshine of destiny. WESTY!

"Here we are foregathered. Black and white and brown and red, young and old, native-born and first-generation, urban and rural, male and female. From Porsche to plow, from hot tub to swimming hole, from high-rise to hovel, from sea to shining sea."

The rolling thunder filled him: he was a drum, resonating their needs. They had given him their power, no one would stop him. No one *could* stop him. No one had the right. In his two hands was mankind, only he could save them.

"Tonight we bring you the new political realism. The realism which says we Americans can recapture our future without losing our past. Let the Republicans fight for what is already gone—they belong to it. We will fight for what yet can be—because *it* belongs to *us!*"

They were interrupting him now with applause and roars of agreement at almost every sentence. His ears were deafened with his own praises.

"We are wiser than they are, stronger than they are. They focus on past payoffs to the rich of the earth—we focus on *saving* of the Riches of the Earth for future generations."

WESTY! And again, WESTY! His own sweet name, chanted by them like medieval warriors chanted their liege lord's name during that age's bloody hand-to-hand battles. Thunder of acceptance, thunder of human need.

Yes, God, the thunder! Oh, God, the power!


"It was honest, plain-speaking old Harry Truman who said a president has to be able to say 'yes' and 'no'—but most often 'no.' 'No' was all right for Mr. Truman's day. But for today's president, the words must be, 'No more.' "

Even through the static of the pickup's indifferent radio, Fletcher could hear the rich stew of non sequiturs and the roar of approbation they evoked.

"*No more* is what I say to the military's bloated defense spending. *No more* is what I say to fat cats' tax breaks. *No more* is what I say to pork-barrel congressmen raiding our nation's treasury."

That mindless roar of approbation, *that* was why

304

Fletcher had never been comfortable in groups. Groups so easily became crowds, which could even easier become mobs. Tonight's adoring WESTY could become tomorrow's hate-filled NIGGER or KIKE or WOP.

"Our great President Lincoln once called for government of the people, by the people, and for the people. What the Republicans have given us is government of the powerful, by the influential, for the wealthy. Well, my fellow Americans, we aren't going to put up with it anymore! We, the people . . ."

The platitudes rolled forth from a man he had worked with, drunk with, picked up girls with, a man he would have backed, voted for. A man who had hero-worshiped him but now had . . .

"As president, I intend to reassert the true American values. Strength at home, strength abroad. At home, cut the deficit, reduce interest rates, make our exports affordable."

This very son of a bitch spouting these platitudes about the noble things he would do as president had seduced Fletcher's son-in-law into trying to kill him! *Why?*

"Abroad, I will press the Soviets for more nuclear accords, because our two nations can destroy this planet, wipe all life from the face of the earth. It was our party's own great President John F. Kennedy who said we must never negotiate out of fear, but must never fear to negotiate. . . ."

Or was it only jealousy on Fletcher's part? Once hero-worshiped, now a cripple and a failure. A man who let his wife die unavenged, a man who could not defend himself against attack, could not even avenge *himself.*

No. It all boiled up within him. Fletcher suddenly knew that he was angry, not apologetic. Blindingly angry.

He wanted a drink. *Needed* a drink.
Maybe a lot of drinks.
Maybe it was going to be a crazy night.

# 37

It was a crazy night.

Cottonwood was an east-west, north-south grid, flat as
a pancake, with a diagonal slash of highway through it
like someone winning at ticktacktoe. There were a church
and a gas station and motels and stores and houses, one
of them an old gingerbready two-story that perhaps had
once stood lonely and proud with the prairie winds rustling the cottonwood trees around it.

Only now there wasn't a cottonwood in town.

But there was a bar, Carrothers Big Game Bar;
Fletcher parked in front beside a new Caddy with
smoked windows. Inside, three people were watching the
color TV: cheers and tears by women dancing in the
aisles at the Moscone Center because one of their own,
Della Weinberg, ex-mayor of San Francisco, had been
unanimously nominated as Gary Westergard's chosen
running mate.

"Mayor of the Year," said the early-thirties man on
Fletcher's side of the bar. "She'll be a good veep."

He was smooth-bodied and handsome, with an athlete's
trained physique and ruthless competitor's eyes. His tight
slacks and striped short-sleeved Italian sport shirt made
him look like a pimp.

"She's a creep," said the tawny young woman beside
him.

"Shut up, Maria," he said.

The walls of Carrothers Big Game Bar were covered

with hunting trophies. Elk and moose and mulies and pronghorn, a woolly-polled bison, coyotes and badgers, a cougar and a bobcat and a snarling timber wolf, two black bears and a grizzly mounted upright, mouth gaping and great clawed arms outstretched.

The new vice-presidential nominee was trying vainly to make herself heard. "My fellow Americans . . . My fellow Americans . . ."

"The needle's stuck," said the tawny woman as Fletcher limped by. "Change the record."

She was not far into her twenties, probably full-blooded Indian — tawny skin and strong nose and high cheekbones, utterly straight black glossy hair, deep-set black liquid eyes with a predator's fierce gaze. More handsome than beautiful, yet feminine in a lithe, full-bosomed, border-town way. She also looked very drunk.

"Shut up. I want to listen to her."

"I wanna listen to her," she mocked. "What for, Arnie? You know they're all just playing the power game."

He turned on her with half-raised hand. "I said shut up."

She put her hand over her mouth in an exaggerated gesture. Fletcher took a stool three down from them. She didn't dress Indian, more casino-girl-trashy: tight sateen blouse to show unbrassiered nipples, glittery miniskirt hiked up to show thigh all the way to the curve of her buttocks. The TV finally spoke.

"My fellow Americans, welcome to the future. I am Della Weinberg. Tonight my heart is full of the American dream —"

"And your mouth is full of American moose shit," said Maria. She was slurring her words slightly. Fletcher laughed.

Arnie shot him a hostile, appraising look. "Who were Pocahontas' parents?" he asked, then answered himself. "A couple of fucking Indians." He turned away and leaned closer to Maria and sneered. "Squaw lady no can hold her firewater."

An angry look flitted across Maria's features. Della Weinberg said on the TV, "That great American Martin Luther King once told us, 'There are moments which cannot be expressed by words, only by the inaudible language of the heart.' Here upon this stage I want to tell you that—"

"The name's Buck."

Fletcher shook the bartender's proffered knotty hand. Buck was a grizzled mountain-man type with scraggly beard and gray hair to his shoulders. His twinkly blue eyes looked as if they could take a man in with one casual glance and have him forever.

"Ain't them trophies the damnedest thing you've ever seen?"

Big game had not been the sportman's only killing urge. There were curlew and killdeer and sharp-tailed grouse, marsh hawks and prairie falcons and kestrels, short-eared owls and burrowing owls and horned larks and meadowlarks and crows and magpies and rattlesnakes and jackrabbits and foxes and prairie dogs and mice and even voles and a tiny shrew.

"Who was Carrothers? A taxidermist?"

Buck grinned. "The Carrotherses was first settlers and made this town. Made a lot of money too. What'll it be?"

"Give him a tequila," said Maria in her slurred reckless voice. She gestured at Arnie. "On the Big Spender here."

Buck got out a bottle of Cuervo Gold, set out in front of Fletcher a two-ounce shot with salt and a wedge of lime.

"Just passin' through?"

"Just passing through," said Fletcher.

"Not fast enough," said Arnie in a challenging voice. Fletcher turned to look at him, more in curiosity than

309

in reaction. Arnie was twenty years younger, with a mean mouth and hair that could only have been styled by an expert because it looked so perfectly unstyled. The sneer was back on his face.

"Don't be scared, old man. I don't pick on cripples."

"Sonny," said Fletcher, feeling high and reckless even before he'd had a drink, "don't let my grey hair and bad leg make a coward out of you."

The Indian girl gave a smothered laugh. She signaled for another tequila. Arnie curled one hand around the shapely inner curve of her thigh and squeezed. Pain entered her face.

But not her voice. "Autoeroticism, that's Arnie."

"Railroad," said Buck quickly to break the tension. "Grandpa Carrothers was here first, sold 'em the land for the right-of-way, built the station, later on built the school and the church. Made a lot of money. The son, he made more. The grandson, he hunted."

Fletcher licked the salt from his knuckle, toasted the girl silently with the tequila, downed it, sucked the lime. The shot burned like that first one with Old Charlie so many years ago.

"Hunted just about everything, looks like," he said.

"Yep. Women, too, down in Denver. Wife found out, took him for a bundle, he sold me this place in May, nineteen hundred and fifty-two. I never regretted buying it. The American way."

"The American way," agreed Della Weinberg on the TV. "Play by the rules and work hard, and expect to be rewarded with your share of this great nation's blessings. But the Republicans . . ."

". . . shot things that ain't found anywhere else except right around here." Buck shut an eye in a calculating manner and gave a vigorous nod of agreement with himself. "Take that varmint up above the Coors sign, now. Whadda ya see?"

310

"The American dream," said Della Weinberg.

"The damnedest-looking jackrabbit of all time."

"And what does he have on his head?" demanded Buck.

"The earth as we found it, green and fecund and unpolluted by the spoilers," said Della Weinberg.

A pair of pronghorn spikes had been glued to the top of its head just forward of the ears to look as if they had grown there.

"Horns," said Fletcher in his best I'll-be-damned voice.

"Yep. Horns. That there's a jackalope. Cross between a jackrabbit an' a pronghorn antelope. You'll never see another, once you leave these parts."

"And so I'll leave you with my love," said Della Weinberg.

"I'll drink to that," said Fletcher.

Buck poured him another tequila and hit the remote to kill the TV. Fletch downed his shot. It didn't burn as much as the first. It tasted fine.

"Turn it back on," ordered Arnie from down the bar.

"Turn it back on," mimicked Maria.

Fletcher shrugged. Buck turned the TV back on. A famous black gospel singer was starting "The Battle Hymn of the Republic." Everyone was singing. The camera came in on Westergard. There were tears in his eyes. Fletcher looked away.

"Autoeroticism," said Maria drunkenly in his ear.

"Get fucking back here," said Arnie from down the bar.

Maria was on the stool next to Fletcher, looking at him from solemn black eyes. He'd eaten little that day and could feel the tequila in him speaking to the pain in those eyes.

"Arnie's taking me to Chicago. From Vegas. In his Caddy with the smoked windows. Autoeroticism is what he's into."

"I'm warning you, bitch."

311

Maria was pressing the firm round side of her breast up against Fletcher's arm. He could feel body heat like a stoked furnace through her thin blouse.

"He's always wanting me to go down on him while he's driving through the desert. Autoeroticism. That's his price for getting me out of Vegas. He says it makes him feel—"

The back of Arnie's hand made a sound like a gun going off against the side of her face.

"I warned you, bitch," he said.

Maria was standing straight and defiant in front of him, a thin trickle of blood coming out of one nostril.

"Do it again," she said thickly. "I didn't feel that one."

Fletcher thrust past her to block the next blow with his forearm; the third was a hard left jab under his heart. His stool skittered away to dump him against the bar. A vicious kick missed his head only because Maria jumped on Arnie's back, yelling. He drove the heel of a hand up under Arnie's nose, snapping the head back; his palm came away smeary with blood.

Arnie grabbed for a stool as Fletcher staggered to his feet, splayed fingers groping the bar for support. Buck seemed to be taking no sides in the dispute, but the hand found a still-capped bottle of beer that hadn't been there a moment before.

The bottle exploded against Arnie's good looks just as the stool exploded against Fletcher's head. Blood obscured his vision. He didn't feel himself sliding down the front of the bar, but he heard Maria's voice as he faded out.

"We've got to get him out of here right away . . ."

"Damn, right!" exclaimed Old Charlie.

He looked almost guiltily around the deserted porch in the June twilight, then reached out a clawlike blue-veined hand to snatch the half-pint that Fletcher was offering. He was dressed in cast-off clothes, with his hair chopped short. The poor farm was a flaking white frame house a mile from Kellogg, set under a clump of bur oaks half a mile of sand road from Minnesota 63.

Charlie tipped up the bottle and it said glug-glug-glug. Fletch got a hollow place in the middle of his gut at the fear in Charlie's eyes and the speed with which the bottle disappeared between his legs when the screen door creaked open.

Outside it was clear and dark, the stars looking close enough to reach up and grab a handful. Some Indian girl was dragging him backward across the sidewalk with surprising strength, her hands hooked under his arms from behind. Charlie's daughter, maybe? No. Charlie didn't have a daughter.

A matron in white with a shadow of hormonal hair on her upper lip was looking at them from suspicious eyes through the intervening screen of the door she was holding open. But she spoke to Charlie in the saccharine voice fools use with oldsters.

"Are we having a nice *visit*, Mr. Smith?"

"Just great," said Fletch hurriedly. He felt tears behind his eyelids but blinked them quickly back.

Quick strong hands were going through his pants pocket. He heard the keys to the truck jingle.

He managed, "Wha . . .?"

"Mr. Smith will have to come in now. No residents are allowed outside after dark."

When the screen door creaked shut after a suspicious pause, he said, "Jesus, Charlie, why don't you just run away again?"

"Keep runnin', they keep findin' me. They're wearin' this ol' Injun down."

The door slammed. He was slumped halfway across the cool vinyl seat of the 4x4. His head hurt. His hand came away wet with something that looked black in the streetlight.

Charlie said querulously, "Tomorrow you're goin' up to Alaska, Spot run off, they busted our canoe." Again his turtle head craned, then tipped back, for the bottle's quick furtive glugging. He grabbed Fletch's arm. "I wanna go home."

The truck engine started, it jerked forward. A warm strong hand on his back was gentling him. "Steady, old-timer. I'll find us a place to hole up in a few minutes. You can do it—"

"Can't nobody do nothing," said Charlie, then repeated fretfully, "Canoe busted up an' the dog, what's his name, he's run off, an' now you're runnin' off to Alaska . . ."

The tequila, far from making him high, was making him feel depressed. Or something was. He said aloud, guiltily, "I'll be back in three months, Charlie."

"To hell with Charlie," said the girl. "I just hope you've got a first-aid kit in this duffel bag of yours."

The room was very hot and the light of the bedside lamp hurt his eyes, so he closed them to shut it out. Which was his pattern all right: when things got tough, shut them out. Get drunk for the first time in twenty years because you can't stand Gary's triumph in this world where you are a failure.

He and Gary had gotten drunk the night that old

314

Charlie . . .

By the time Terry died, he didn't get drunk anymore. When he'd come home to find her in the ground, he'd mourned and fumed and hated—and then had given away the house to go live in the woods, shut it all out. Or in. Now, five years later, he'd run away again. Run away from what he couldn't stand. Or crawl away. Crawl a thousand feet through the forest when he was shot three times. He'd been pretty good in there a time or two.

What the hell was he thinking about? High-sticking Canuck bastard giving him a concussion? It sure made his head ache.

"My head aches," he said thickly.

"Hush," said a girl's soft voice.

Surprisingly deft fingers were doing something to the side of his head, where the ache was centered.

His knee ached. His missing fingers ached. Excuses. How did he really even know that Gary had put David Ross up to the attack? He wouldn't track an animal this way, would he? Why not just let the sign tell him whatever had really happened?

A fight had happened. He was starting to remember. A fight in a crazy bar full of dead animals. Fight. Anger. Rage. And a breast pressed against his arm. A breast now four inches from his nose, bare, sweat-stippled, the nipple slightly erect.

"Maria?"

"Be quiet. You sure bleed a lot." He could feel a scissors going snip-snip. "You're going to look pretty silly for a while. You ought to get stiches but I'm going to try to butterfly the sides together with Band-Aids and hope it holds."

"Where are we?"

"Motel. I hope you have twelve bucks for the room."

"You do a lot of hoping. Why are you here?"

"Arnie sure as hell isn't going to take me to Chicago now."

Arnie. Fight. The rage he was feeling at Westergard and Ross and Nicole had gone into his fight with the smooth man in the bar. As usual, rage won against lesser emotions. There was a savage pleasure in hitting and being hit. For the brief duration of the fight, he had been *alive* again. Without hesitations, without regrets, without remorse, without guilt.

"He would have if you hadn't jumped on his back."

"Hold still." A bloody towel fell to the floor. Snip, snip. Salt-and-pepper hair fell to the pillow beside Fletcher's head. "I hope you don't have a concussion. There's no way to bandage a concussion. How do you feel?"

"Like I've been in a fight."

"Don't you remember? You *were* in a fight."

"Of course I remember. The more I remember, the more I feel like I was in the fight."

"Good. Here, try this."

She leaned forward, a simple movement, and her dark-areolaed nipple was in his mouth, already starting to stiffen. *Bette's nipple was in his mouth! Stiffening.*

Fletcher turned his head quickly away like a baby refusing a bottle. There was an offended look on his face.

"I lost my wife," he said flatly. "Since then . . ."

Maria drew back quickly. "I'm sorry, man." Her voice was small. She worked awhile longer. "When did you . . . did she . . . ?"

"Five years ago."

She unexpectedly burst out laughing. "You're telling me that for five years you haven't once wanted to—"

"Can't." He made an unconsciously graphic gesture at his crotch, winced. Moving hurt. "Nothing . . . there."

316

She nodded. "Just as well you can't. Or won't. The fight made me horny." She shrugged. "That's what always gets me into trouble." She paused. "I don't know what they call you."

"Hollis Fletcher. Hal."

"I'll call you Fletch." She held out a hand. "Maria Amore." She giggled like a teenager. "I thought maybe you and this Charlie you kept talking about—"

"Charlie was an old Indian," said Fletcher. "A friend. My best friend." The tequilas were dying in him, his bumps and scrapes and the gash in the side of his head were starting to sting and ache. "He's been dead going on forty years."

"Charlie what?"

"Seven Bears."

"Yeah," she said, suddenly bitter, "I used to be into that 'Bull Bison Farts in the Thicket' crap. It's all bull-shit."

"Not to Charlie," he said. "What's your Indian name?"

"I don't have one."

"What was it when you did?" he persisted.

"Navajos don't ever tell anyone their secret names." After a long pause, almost inaudibly, she said, "To the *dinah*—the people—I was Daughter-of-Horseman. Horseman was my daddy's name." Her eyes sought distance. "Horseman." She threw another bloody bath towel on the floor beside the bed. "All finished."

She slid down, leaving sweat smears against the headboard. Fletcher's head on the pillow was even with her hips. She wore only a pair of sheer panty hose with a high-cut French-lace panty built into them, and he could smell the warm animal scent of her sex a few inches from his nose. It left him unmoved. He felt like crying because it did.

She had found a half-pint of whiskey in her handbag. She broke the seal on it. "Since all we're going to do is 'talk, tell me about Old Charlie."

They passed the bottle as he and old Charlie used to do, and he talked to her the way Old Charlie used to talk to him there on the poor-farm porch in the twilight with his voice grown reedy and with long pauses between sentences.

Maria was the first person he had been able to talk to about the old Indian without feeling somehow a betrayer. But not even to her could he tell how it finally ended. Not yet, anyway.

# 38

No way to finish the document so that she and David could go over it and get it just right, not before the Republican convention in Miami next month. Until then, they wouldn't know if Gary's opponent would be the vice-president or the senator.

Meanwhile, there were speeches to block out while Gary was up at Gunflint Lodge on the Canadian border for six days of walleye fishing. He and Della Weinberg would then be appearing together at a labor convention in New York, an Urban League meeting in Cincinnati, and a Mark Twain festival in Hannibal, Mo. It was important that the voters see them as a team; their speeches had to be hard-hitting and direct against an enemy not yet known.

Distracted, she dropped the pages she was holding onto her bare belly. She hadn't been able to get her dad on the phone. She grimaced and lit a cigarette. Maybe a quick drive up to Cochrane? Just up and right back, ease her still-present feelings of guilt at having chosen David over him?

In the house, the phone started to ring. She had a moment of panic: it was bad news about her father. Or was it fear that he somehow had found out . . . Oh, stop it. Just guilt speaking. It would be one of the kids, or something about the campaign.

She set aside the papers, stubbed out her cigarette, got out of the rustic redwood chaise longue, went inside. The kitchen linoleum was cool to her bare feet. She lifted the wall phone off its cradle on the fourth ring.

"Mommy?"

Oddly, now that Nicole had rejoined the campaign, she had become "Mommy" instead of Nicole. But Kathie's phone style hadn't changed: a breathless rush of excited run-on words.

"I-just-called-to-ask-if-I-could-eat-over-at-Michelle's-but-I-already-did-so-it's-a-little-late-to-ask-isn't-it?"

"We'll pretend I said yes, hon. Is Iris there and available?"

She was.

"Nicole? Good news! Norman has informed me that we'd be officially delighted to take both kids whenever you have to be away. Now go out there and win one for the Westy!"

"Bless you both, Iris." She lit another cigarette. " 'Win one for the Westy.' Not bad. Maybe you should come aboard as a slogan writer."

Iris gave a low throaty laugh. "You know me, honey." The remnants of her Texas drawl became obvious and intentional. "Between politics and pimples, I'll take pimples. At least you can pop 'em and make 'em go away."


Her father had gone away; the forest already had started taking back the cabin. The first grass was showing in the path around to the front of the cabin; a squirrel was insolently slow to hop off the front stoop. The shutters were closed over the windows, the door was locked. She got the key from under its rock and prowled the cabin, jolted viscerally when she saw the bearskin missing from the bed. If it was gone, he was too.

The knowledge put a little knot of fear in her gut. She carefully relocked the place and put the key back under its stone. Why would he just leave like that without talking to her?

"Maybe he was afraid of what he'd say to you if he did."

Nicole had gone directly to Victor's clinic from the cabin; they walked side by side in the enclosed yard that gave patients something pleasant to look at while waiting for doctor.

"What's that supposed to mean?" she said coldly.

"You can think of no possible scenario?"

Victor was being formal to the point of rudeness. The knot of fear got tighter in her stomach; she *could* think of such a scenario. Only one.

"No, of course not," she said.

Victor walked in silence for a few moments, hands clasped behind his back, lowered head and gangly gait giving him a remarkably storklike appearance. She realized that in his own way he was a strong, perhaps even a hard man. Anachronistic general practitioners in backwoods areas, coping with emergencies in primitive conditions, probably had to be strong and hard.

"I learned that an hour after your father was shot, the man who shot him telephoned two-eight nine-three-seven-six-six in Minneapolis."

A ruby-breasted hummingbird darted and swooped above their heads like a bit of colorful windblown chaff. Nicole suddenly felt her whole body trembling. She had never needed a cigarette so badly in her life.

"I don't know whose number it is," said Victor with that almost hostile precision. "When I called your house looking for your father, I called a different number. But your father obviously recognized it."

"Is that number why you tried to reach him at my home?"

"Yes. Of course, it had no significance to me at the

time."

"And now?"

"Now? You're here, aren't you?"

"God damn you!" she burst out, surprising them both but herself more. He stopped to face her directly. No gun muzzle was ever colder than his eyes. He surprised her even more.

"And God damn your soul to hell, lady, for what you've let that poor man go through."

He left her standing there on the brink of the abyss trying to blink back the tears. Oh God. Oh God. What had she done? What had David done?

And what was Fletcher doing? Where had he gone? Was he out there somewhere in despair at the depths of her betrayal? Or was he even now, in a frenzy of revenge, drawing a bead on David's unsuspecting head through the living-room window?

As she looked around wildly, instinctively, for a phone to call her husband and warn him, another part of her mind was thinking: Oh God, where is my poor father?


Fletcher and Maria spent four days in the motel at Cottonwood before moving on. For the first thirty hours neither of them had left the room, not even for meals; Maria had paid Jimmy, the proprietor's teenage son, to go down to the McDonald's for junk food. She explained to Fletcher that Arnie would be looking for them and that he was a dangerous man.

"Looking why?"

She shrugged, emotion easily read on her face. Under the crude Vegas veneer was a rather wide-eyed girl of twenty-three.

"To hurt us. Hurt us bad. You really messed up his face with that beer bottle, and he loooves his face like all the pimps do. So he'll be really mad. But I don't think

322

he'll find us. Jimmy's in love with me, he'll say we aren't staying here."

"How do women know things like that? About Jimmy?"

"How do you know what animal you're tracking?" She made Fletcher laugh by adding, "That's the way we predators are, man."

He said, "If I messed up Arnie's face bad enough, he'll be on his way to Cheyenne or Denver or wherever he can find a good plastic surgeon."

"You really flattened his nose." She giggled, suddenly the little girl flattening her own stern Indian nose with a finger. "Flatter than mine. And the glass cut his cheeks pretty good."

"*Mensur* scars," said Fletcher, then to her blank look added, "dueling scars. Initiation cicatrices."

"That too," she said, making him laugh again. "When you first saw me, Fletch, did you think I was a whore?"

"Didn't and don't."

She got abruptly off the bed and went into the bathroom. When she came out, her eyes were red. She stopped in front of him.

"I have been, kind of. That's why I was using Arnie to get away from Vegas. I was going to ditch him in Chicago."

"Why Chicago?"

"It wasn't Vegas. Anyway, thanks for what you didn't think. Even if you were wrong."

"I wasn't wrong," said Fletcher.

Which sent her back into the bathroom for more Kleenex.


Once on the road, they drifted. Sometimes they got motel rooms, sharing a bed but not their bodies—after that first night, Maria was chaste as a nun—sometimes

323

just pulling off the highway and tossing out their sleeping bags.

For Fletcher it was a return to early days. After Korea and going back to college for an engineering degree — suddenly he wanted to build things instead of blowing them up — he'd ranged across the West from one construction job to the next. First alone, then with Terry until she was big with Nicole. Those had been their best days, their closest days. But with Nicole had come a heightened sense of responsibility; he had started taking long-term overseas jobs because the money was so good, and pretty soon they had become a way of life.

"But she never complained," he said aloud.

"Terry?"

It surprised neither of them that two people of silences, of solitudes, shocked by circumstance into talk of anything and everything, could anticipate each other's thoughts.

"She was just always there for me when I got back." Ahead, a scudding rain squall's incredible rainbow arched the prairie from horizon to horizon. "Then all of a sudden she wasn't."

"It would have happened if you'd been there," Maria said.

"But I wasn't."

He had told her about getting shot and who had done it and who he thought had asked for it to be done, but wasn't sure. He had even told her about what he considered Nicole's betrayal.

"Not because she stuck with David instead of me. Even the Bible tells a woman to do that when she marries. But she should have told me . . . *something.* Instead of letting me keep on looking when she knew who had done it."

She said abruptly, "I would have told *my* daddy. He was a sheepherder, had grazing rights out around Chaco Canyon way. We had a round stone hogan with an old cast-iron stove and a stovepipe up through the smoke-hole. I remember once . . ."

She fell silent, overwhelmed by memory. Fletcher said, "I thought there wasn't any individual ownership of land among the Navajos."

"There isn't really, but if you got grazing rights and mark the corners with little piles of stones, everyone respects it."

They had driven into the rain squall; water flew from the wipers. Translucent water-prismed light patterns played across her face. Her eyes were shiny with memory.

"I loved it there. It was all open space. You lived by the sun and in the winter the sheep would sleep in the hogan with you to keep you warm . . ."

The squall had passed; blazing sun beat down on the truck, the tires sang against the steaming blacktop.

"Daddy died when I was eleven. Ma moved my sister May and me to the HUD housing in Window Rock." She blew out a long breath. "I tried—high school, even a year of community college at Flagstaff. If we'd stayed in the hogan, maybe . . ." She shrugged. "We didn't. May went to L.A., I went bad."

"You aren't bad now," said Fletcher, really meaning it. The sun behind one of the drifting thunderheads haloed its dark soul with silver. She sighed.

"May married a Mexican named Martínez, he does the Anglos' lawns in Beverly Hills and . . ." She giggled. "May. May wanted babies—lots of babies. Me, I wanted bright lights. When you think of bright lights on the reservation, you think of Vegas."

Fletcher nodded, remembering his early days. "It's close, it's gaudy, but it's still sort of western."

"I couldn't sing, I couldn't dance, I was too lazy to wait tables, but I had something I was good at and sort of liked doing, so . . . here I am." She made one of her clown faces. "But sometimes I wish . . ."

"Not too late to go back," said Fletcher carefully.

"It is for me."

"After Terry died, I went back."

"And Nicole's husband shot you." She added abruptly, "I'd of killed *him* when he did that, if I'd of been your daughter."

# 39

David had worked like a dog on the document, but it was her triumph, hers alone. *Her* ideas, *her* perceptions, *her* beliefs—*her* document, down to her name first as author. If Gary did what she outlined, she would be kingmaker: he would be president. She knew this with an unshakable certainty. The high was better than religion, better than love, better than sex, better than anything. Anything at all.

PERSONAL AND CONFIDENTIAL

To:   Garrett Westergard
       Della Weinberg
From: Nicole Ross
       David Ross

The following is an analysis of your present political posture and what we see as the strategic premises for the upcoming general-election campaign. With Vice-President Arbor confirmed as your opponent, we must begin to make commitments in terms of scheduling, media relations, and organization.

Political campaigns are traditionally *dis*organized and chaotic, yet they needn't be. The points of this memo may seem simple and self-evident, but so is chess strategy: protect your own, attack your opponent's. In both cases, a simple basic strategy requires very complex tactics for successful execution.

*Introduction*

How do we allocate our finite and limited resources for the general election? The facts we have to work with:

1) Between Labor Day and Election Day we will have at best forty-five active campaign days.

2) We will have no more than $29.4 million to spend.

To meet our political goals, we must establish a realistic and precise framework and mechanism to allocate these finite resources most effectively with maximum flexibility.

*Image*

Your rise has been so dramatic, so unexpected, that your political image is not yet fully developed nor of much depth. "New face" and "outsider" still best describe you. To an American electorate chronically alienated from their government and its leaders, these are not pejorative terms. They suggest a new dedicated leadership unpolluted by merely political considerations. With time between now and Labor Day, we should be able to mold an image which will correct wrong impressions and magnify your very real strengths.

*Strategic Premises for the General Election*

Five premises are the building blocks of our strategy:

1) *We must win 270 electoral votes.*

We must not be seduced by polls or surveys into losing sight of the 270 while scrambling madly for 400 and a landslide. 270 electoral votes will make you president. To be president is why you are here.

  2) *Early in the campaign we must challenge Arbor in those states traditionally considered Republican.*

If we deny Arbor a region or political grouping of states that he can count on, we deny him a mathematical base for a majority of electoral votes. Without such a base, he lacks a clear strategy for winning. By attacking early in the twenty states he considers his heartland, we can make Arbor spend time and money in states he should carry while ignoring those he must carry.

  3) *The midwestern and western states which are our base of support must not be fragmented or jeopardized.*

We cannot let Arbor do to us what we plan to do to him. If we spend early campaign time in such key states as Minnesota, Wisconsin, and Michigan to create a solid lead, we can later reduce our campaigning there to periodically "showing the flag" while pushing hard in contested states such as Texas, Illinois, New York, Pennsylvania, and Iowa.

  4) *Garrett Westergard and Della Weinberg must play their separate strengths.*

Westergard, as head of the ticket, must campaign everywhere while playing the leading role in protecting our base. Weinberg must work the areas of the country and units of the electorate where her unique qualifications make her strongest. This would include big cities (Governor of the Year), liberals, minorities (women, gays, Latinos, Orientals, blacks), government workers and welfare recipients, and (since the primary exposed our weakness there) her vital home state of California.

5) *If we have a commanding lead by mid-October, and have retained our flexibility in allocating our resources toward the objectives of our strategy, then we can broaden the goals and objectives of our campaign.*

Our basic strategy is to get 270 Electoral College votes. If our surveys show this is probable by mid-October, then we can expend our remaining time and resources seeking a massive voter mandate rather than a mere win. A landslide victory would make it easier for us to bring real and effective change to government once we are in the White House.

Kent Jarvis finished reading his copy of the "Personal and Confidential" memo a little before midnight and was so enraged that he stormed down to the wedge of light spilling out across the dim statehouse corridor. Maggie Fenton looked up from her computer, her astonishment showing two rodential front teeth beneath her wriggling rabbit nose.

"Why Mr. Jarvis, what's wr—"

He was already yanking open the door of the private office.

"Well?" snapped Westergard, looking up from his work.

The months of campaigning had stripped away extra flesh lent by the years; with the almost fanatic depths of his ice-blue eyes, his rugged Scandinavian features, and his hockey-player shoulders, Westergard could as well have been a fundamentalist preacher as a candidate for president. His first-ballot convention win had given him more than confidence: it had given him righteousness. Jarvis' rage broke the spell.

"Who the *fuck* does she think she is?" he yelled. He threw the memo down on Westergard's desk like the pelt of a vanquished foe, scattering papers in every direction. 'Miyamoto Musashi writing *A Book of Five Rings?*"

"A rather apt comparison, actually," said Westergard with surprising mildness. "I was expecting you, Kent. You're my campaign manager, and Nicole's—"

"Yeah, goddammit! She's trying to take over my—"

"Is her analysis right?"

"What the fuck difference—"

"Is this brilliant?"

"I don't care what—"

Westergard suddenly roared, "Goddammit, man, is this an election-winning analysis or isn't it?"

Jarvis' agile brain belatedly had begun working again, seeking ways to turn near-disaster to his own advantage.

"It is," he admitted finally.

"Good. Then, as campaign manager, implement it."

"But I'm the one who's supposed to—"

"But you didn't." Those icy blue eyes chilled him from across the desk. "You couldn't. I couldn't. Nobody could except her. She has a totally political mind. Are you saying that we should discard it? That staff power games should keep us from utilizing that mind?"

"Well, no, but . . ."

"The presidency, Kent!"

Westergard came around the desk. He exuded power and concern; for one shining moment Jarvis almost imagined him as a knight in armor, was dazzled by the certainty that this man *had* to win at any cost.

"No one's been more important to this campaign than you, Kent. I know my trust in you is not misplaced."

"I won't let you down, Governor." But the purity of the moment had already been adulterated, sieved through the filter of self-interest. "It was just seeing her name on it after the rest of us have been busting our balls on this campaign for a year. But I've got a lot of ideas for implementing it in the two weeks until Labor Day. Tomorrow

I'll run down to Chicago . . ."

Tomorrow Sharkey would find him a woman who looked like Nicole. But right now, Westergard was right, she was doing a brilliant job. The unique service that was going to make him indispensable to the governor — could it have something to do with her, her husband, her father? There was a mystery there he would somehow have to pierce. Knowledge was power.

Meanwhile, two of the Guv's words had come together in his mind. *Utilize. Discard.*

Nicole's work was open against her drawn-up knees, her forehead was wrinkled with concentration, a cigarette smoldered forgotten in her bedside ashtray. David looked at her with pride; it had been he who had insisted her name be first on the document. But now he realized with a shock that he had fallen in love with his wife.

She was sitting up under the covers in her frilly blue nightgown, totally immersed in creating a complicated state-by-state formula based on three key factors — size, potential, need — that would let the governor allocate campaign time and money in the optimum way. Of course he had believed he loved her when he married her. He had been crazy with possessing her and thought it was love.

After the terrible time of discovery, when they had come together again, there had been a flash of *something.* Something fleeting, more a momentary dream of love than love itself.

But now he was in love. Smitten. Proud of her, yes, grateful and amazed at her forgivingness, yes. And beneath all the reasons, something abiding that he had never known before.

She looked up and caught his look and smiled at him.

"What's so fascinating?"

"You," he said.

She gave an ironic chuckle. "Ain't it the truth?"

She returned to her work. He went to the window, parted the curtains enough to look down into the backyard. Light filtering through from the street fell on their seldom-used redwood lounges side by side on the patio. The symbolic closeness of the inanimate furniture pleased him.

She *was* fascinating, unexpected. Like calling him from Cochrane to warn him that her father knew his identity as the attacker and had disappeared.

"I've realized it isn't in him to kill someone from ambush," she said from behind him.

He jumped. "Who?"

"My dad. He *stalks* his prey. He doesn't just slaughter."

He felt a flush rise on his cheeks. He would have settled for slaughter. But she wasn't making comparisons, just analyzing.

"So what keeps him from stalking me?"

"Pride. He'd have to warn you before he came after you. Also he'd have to be satisfied in his own mind why you did it."

"To please the governor."

"Not enough—why would *Gary* want him dead? He and I talked about this a bit—the idea that he could be a threat to the campaign is just a joke to him."

"Not to the Guv." Ross let the curtains fall shut and started to take off his robe. Nicole was regarding him with a strange expression.

"You aren't afraid of being attacked anymore, are you?"

"No. You told me I didn't have to be."

In a wondering voice she said, "You love me, don't you?"

"Yes," he said, "I love you." And knew he meant it.

"Too bad you aren't wearing your pajamas with the little red hearts on them."

He hadn't worn them since . . . since the night of the shooting, when his need for her had been only lust, a need to affirm his own existence by his wild thrusts into her body.

He was naked under his robe; he looked down at his bare chest and made an exaggerated face of surprise.

"Well, whadda ya know!" he cried. "I'm breaking out in little red hearts!"

She was smiling at him as she untied the bow that held her negligee closed.

# 40

Dawn, September 5. Labor Day. Traditionally, the day candidates started their final sprints for the presidency.

Gary Westergard, following Nicole's advice, was defending the home turf against the Republican philistines; Della was doing the same out in San Francisco. He checked his appearance again in the bedroom mirror, then went downstairs to wait for the car. No limo today. No suit and tie either; just another horny-handed son of toil bound for the Farmer-Labor party picnic.

Edith was waiting by the front door, her hair expensive but her dress a print and her coat against the morning chill a plain cloth. She took Westergard's big hand in her two small ones.

"Well, darling, the beginning of . . ."

"Of the beginning," he said. "I want you to know . . ."

But the motorcade had arrived; a Secret Service agent wished them good morning and led them down to the cars in the cool deserted dawn. Jarvis got out of the second one; the first was Secret Service, the two behind press-pool. In his casual clothes, Jarvis looked like an ill-tempered bear.

"Off we go to honor all the blue-collar workers and white-collar workers," he said sourly. "If somebody came up with a way to call rednecks red-collar workers, this could be the *truly* All-American Holiday."

He must have had a rough night; the knuckles of both hands were skinned. Westergard, who didn't like his people drinking, made a mental note to ask Johnny Doyle about it: they'd been in Chicago together setting up tomorrow morning's El-station handshaking and carefully rehearsed impromptu speech.

"We leave the picnic after the sack races but before the softball game," Jarvis said. "At the AFL/CIO stock-car race in St. Paul, you'll do two laps around the course in the lead car, then try to find some good ordinary everyday American folks who aren't shitface to watch the first race with. From there, you go to Fort Snelling for the working-Vietnam-vets presentation . . ."

The search for the Grail.

Nicole woke with a start and the guilty feeling, left over from guilty dreams about her father, that she had overslept. She shrugged them off. He hadn't exactly made a happy affair of his life even before she had contributed her measure of woe, had he?

David was singing in the shower. There had been a time when she would not have believed either of them would ever feel like singing again. The staff had gone crazy over her twenty-two-page numerical state-by-state formula for optimum use of campaign time and money. She had a husband who loved her. She had a leader to believe in — Gary as lover no longer occupied her mind — and a campaign in which she had a critical, perhaps even vital role. Even Jarvis seemed to have accepted that she was good at her job.

She reached for the day's first cigarette, but instead disciplined herself to roll out and make up the bed with fresh sheets. They were a must, in case David's mother came up from Sioux Falls to spell Iris with the kids.

She hadn't heard the shower stop; but as she stooped to pull up the bedspread, David, dressed only in a towel, wrapped his arms around her and pressed up against her backside.

"No you don't!" she exclaimed, stepping away quickly. "I've got a million things to get done before four-thirty, so there's no time for a dirty old man to—"

"You have to admit, honey . . ." Ross dropped his towel. He struck a pose. "A *great* dirty old man!"


A time zone west, Fletcher swung his legs out of bed and massaged his mangled knee. He could smell perking coffee and frying bacon. West Newton. Duck-hunting mornings. But instead of the wild marsh smell of Minnesota wetlands, through the open window came the fresh Rocky Mountain scent of pines.

For the next month, this was home. The motel owners, who took their vacation each year after the tourists but before the hunters, had asked them to fill in for a while. "You folks have honest faces"—just like that.

Maria appeared with a cup of coffee. She sat down beside him on his bed. "What time'd you get to sleep last night?"

"After two." They'd been told to hold "hot-sheet" rooms, weekends, for the local bar pickup trade. "A couple of cowboys got lucky with tourist ladies down at the Wild West Saloon."

Don't think. Don't remember. He slurped carefully at the hot black brew. Just live, day by day. Equilibrium. Eventually what he should do with himself would come to him and he would give Maria half of whatever money he had; she was more of a daughter than Nicole had ever been.

"And you?" he asked in that odd telepathy between them.

"Back to Vegas? Eventually?" A question, not a statement.

"Maybe anywhere else," he said.

"Maybe," she agreed.

The office bell tinkled with someone wanting to check out, cutting off further conversation. That was okay. Equilibrium.


September 6: The Chicago El handshaking turned out to be a nightmare. Lousy advance work by Doyle and Jarvis had put them at a station where there was more press than people, so Westergard ended up chasing constituents around the platform as if they were wealthy intestate relatives in ill health.

September 7: Brooklyn College. Westergard was forced to abandon the prepared text because there was no lectern and the P.A. system wasn't working. Grabbed a bullhorn—it wasn't working either. Narrowly avoided falling off the auditorium stage, good for a lot of laughs but not many votes.

September 9: Another near-disaster: abortion on the agenda for a rally at Our Lady of Sorrows Church in Philadelphia, but instead of an abortion briefing, some idiot handed him an ACLU text calling for reduced church-property tax exemptions. Nicole saved the day with a page of hasty *ex-tempore* notes on the ecumenism

338

of Pope John Paul II, first Polish pope in history.

September 12: Pittsburgh's Polish Hill, a major ethnic triumph for Westergard as a result of Nicole's notes of the ninth. He made the six-o'clock news wearing a red-and-white Polish Power sweatshirt while being kissed on both cheeks by the Right Reverend Ryszard Orzeszkowa, Archbishop of Pittsburgh.

September 19: The last straw. In Green Bay, Wisconsin, he stood outside a factory gate for nearly an hour waiting for a shift change. There was none: no workers, pro or con, showed up. Later the same day he got conked on the head by a misdirected pass at a Dubuque, Iowa, high-school football practice.


The meeting in Westergard's Ramada Inn motel suite in Tupelo, Mississippi, started at ten P.M. and didn't break up until well after midnight. He was steaming.

"I want to know what the hell is going on with my front men. Every time I show up somewhere, there's nobody there to talk to. And I *do* mean you, Kent, and you, Johnny."

"We gotta please the locals, then they don't deliver—"

"We just aren't thinking far enough ahead," interrupted Nicole. She looked smashing in charcoal mantailored slacks and matching narrow-lapel suit jacket. "What we need is more rallies. More speeches. Not so many visual events like shaking hands outside pickle factories."

Westergard nodded. "A forum for remarks of substance that will appeal to the voters in the most compelling way possible."

"We *do* have to give the electorate the candidate close up," said Nicole, on her feet. "But in a communications age, that means the tube. Precinct politics are dead."

"No they aren't, dammit." Jarvis was bristling. "The Guv has to be out there *in the flesh —* "

"In the media is better," said Ross dryly.

Nicole backed him. "We need a media consultant whose full-time job it is to design and produce *all* of the governor's print, radio, and television advertising. Still hold your traditional campaign events — the school auditoriums, the factory gates, the local town-hall meeting — but not to win votes. Just to furnish background for the media coverage."

"Coverage of *what*, goddammit?" demanded Jarvis. He was getting red in the face again. "Handshaking? Dicky-jerking?"

"Of the remarks of substance the governor was just talking about. We tailor his words and ideas to the needs of — "

"Tailor how?" demanded Westergard. His voice had that ominous containment that signaled a major blowup.

"The *themes* will always be yours," amended Nicole quickly. "But the *words* — and *when* you say them — will be tailored by the media consultant."

"Nobody's going to package me into something I'm not."

"Nobody's trying to." Her voice was soothing. "But can't someone pinpoint the issues and candidate qualities the voters care about most — and then direct you to them?"

"Hell, we're paying sophisticated poll-takers a hell of a lot of money for data," said Ross. "Let's use it."

Nicole again. "I admit what I'm proposing is pretty damned radical, but I feel that something radical has to be done."

The next day Westergard announced that Ross would be in charge of "scheduling and preparation of events," and that Nicole would be the campaign's media consultant. Face it, what it took to attain the goal was what he had to be willing to do.

# 41

Fletch was just back from Alaska and drunk; he'd gone down to West Newton to see Old Charlie that afternoon, but Charlie had been back in the poor farm again. What would he do? What could he do? In two days he went back to college for his junior year.

Up on the Hollywood's stage four black men were belting out as dirty a ditty as Rochester would stand for. Gleaming sweat rolled down the dark faces behind their sunglasses

> *M is for the many times you made me,*
> *O is for the others that you tried . . .*

"Hey, Gary, you ol' bassard you!" Across the smoky jammed lounge he had glimpsed Gary Westergard's familiar face.

"Fletch!" Gary's eyes shone at his hero from four summers of work together at the lumberyard.

Fletch was still dressed as for Alaska, black Frisko jeans and a black T-shirt and hack boots and a mustache and goatee that he thought made him look tough and mean. Tough and mean had done all right for him in the Yukon. So had getting drunk.

*T is for the trips to tourist cabins,*
*H is for the hell that's in your eyes . . .*

"Shit, I heard you were in Alaska!" yelled Gary above the music, tough of language and mien himself in Fletch's presence.

"Jus' got back. Goin' back t'college in a couple days."

*E is for the ease with which you laid me,*
*R is for the "reck" you made of me . . .*

"How was it up there?"

"Wild an' woolly."

*Put them all together they spell Mother—*
*And brother that's what I'm about to be.*

Up the Alcan in his old '41 Ford. Thought it was two thousand miles to Fairbanks, drove two thousand miles and was still in Idaho. In Fairbanks, two weeks in the union-hall shape-up, no job, no food for three days, sleeping in a gravel pit. Finally got a job, but lived in the gravel pit the whole summer. Eight flat tires in two days on the way back—with no spare and no jack. Got home last night and, shit, today found out Old Charlie was back in the poor farm.

"God, what a bitch!" exclaimed Gary in his newly minted tough-guy voice. "But I guess there isn't anything you can do."

"I can break him out."

Saying it, Fletch realized that now he'd have to do it. As for Gary, this was his big chance. Extend the moment, make himself a peer of the role model in emulation of whom he already had taken up hockey and football.

"*We* can break him out," he said.

"He got better at both of them than I ever was," mused Fletcher to Maria. They had been watching TV while waiting for customers, but election news had set him off on his story.

"Both what?"

"Hockey and football. Especially hockey. Gary was with the Olympic team that beat the Russkies in fifty-six."

And with Fletch to bust Old Charlie out of the poor farm.

They crouched in the bushes beside the sand road. A half-moon gave pale light for action.

"Two things we gotta do," Fletch whispered solemnly.

Gary was giggling. "Whazzat?" He was no more used to hard liquor now than Fletch had been a year earlier.

"Be *quiet*. An' leave a drink for Ol' fuckin' Charlie."

Charlie's room was on the second floor, but there was an oak tree and his window was open a crack. With scraping of boots on bark, muttered curses, skinned knuckles, Fletch shinnied up the tree while Gary kept watch below in the half-dark. Fletch edged out along the thickest branch. He could just, by hanging under it with one hand, his feet locked around it, get the other hand under the window and push upward. It squawked but moved.

Old Charlie appeared to shush them, panic in his eyes.

"They hear you, won't let me sit on the porch no more!"

"Be sittin' on your own porch in an hour, Charlie!"

That's when his feet unlocked. He was suddenly swinging below the branch by one hand.

"Fletch!" Gary, on the ground below.

"Fuckit!" exclaimed Fletch, "frontal assault," and let go.

He landed in a heap twenty feet below, staggered to stinging feet with Gary trying to help him, stomped around in circles. Charlie was desperately waving for him to go away. He lit out for the front of the building at a dead run.

He was pretty drunk.

Toughened by a summer of tossing fifty-five-gallon drums around at the Standard Oil Bulk Plant in Fairbanks, he went right through the door in a rush, smashed it off its hinges, slid across the entryway on its remains, scrambled to his feet, and charged up the stairs like Teddy Roosevelt at San Juan Hill.

"Yeaaahooo!"

By now Charlie, barefoot under the shapeless nightgown they made him sleep in, had caught the spirit of it: he came charging down the stairs as Fletch charged up. They collided in mid-flight, went tumbling down to cut Gary's legs out from under him just as he burst through the front door. Lights were going on. With the fragile old Indian between them, they hustled out as a voice started yelling loudly behind them.

*"What are you doing? You can't . . ."*

"Charlie out, ain't goin' back," boasted the old Indian.

On the way to West Newton, Fletch went in the ditch twice; the four-wheel drive got them out. The door of the shack, lit by their headlights, gaped on darkness and the smell of mildew. No Spot. An owl hooted above them; they could see their breath.

"You gonna be all right here?" asked Gary worriedly.

"Charlie's all right wherever he is!" Fletch had an arm around the old Indian's shoulders. "He's wily. Right, Charlie?"

"That's me," said Charlie sagely. "Wily. You got any more booze in that bottle?"

"You see those people from the home around here again—"

"They won't see me," bragged Charlie.

Forgetting he was leaving for college, Fletch promised to come back down in a day or two. They left Charlie there alone with the last of the booze, half-drunk under the cold half-moon.

The ten-o'clock news started. "I don't remember a whole lot about the rest of the night," Fletcher told Maria. "Gary wasn't as drunk as I was, so he drove back to Rochester . . ."

Fletch remembered another bottle, both of them drunk and getting tossed out of the Rainbow Dance Hall and two girls in the Jeep with them and later being in a motel-room bed, naked, with one of the girls. Was she naked too? Or was there an argument?

Just fragments. Somebody saying something about love, and then . . . Then what? They were gone?

"Then what?" asked Maria with a giggle in her voice. She loved Fletch to tell stories of his youth.

"Then nothing. I don't remember."

Not quite true — he almost did, right then, but then it was gone again. Something happened, all right, something . . . momentous? Couldn't remember. Woke in the morning on the floor between the bed and the wall, all alone and still buck naked. Girls gone, Gary gone, booze gone, just an empty bottle on the floor. Somebody had been sick in the toilet and hadn't flushed.

"Terrible headache," he chuckled to Maria. "I *do* remember that. Started to drive home with the sun already up, and went right into a cornfield. Missed the road. Still drunk." On the ten-o'clock news a talking head was explaining the rules of the upcoming presidential debate. Fletcher nodded at it. "Haven't seen Westergard again since that night."

"What about Old Charlie?"

"I didn't see him again ever." She had been laughing, but his flat voice tone made her eyes somber. "When duck hunting started in October, they found him in his shack wrapped up in his bearskin. Dead from exposure — he'd been too weak to get in wood for the fire."

Remembering, he felt like crying. Maria put her arms around him. She quirked an eyebrow at his

347

bed. "That bearskin?"

"Yeah. My dad got it for me. They didn't tell me about Charlie until I came home for Christmas. I quit college after that semester—joined the Army and ended up in Korea."

She still held him. "You know, Old Charlie . . . hell, Fletch, I'd wanta go that way too."

"But you see, he really *didn't*. He wanted to stay in the old folks' home but he didn't want to look bad in my eyes."

On the TV, Gary Westergard was talking about jobs and the homeless in front of a group of Latino migrant workers waiting for a farm truck on an L.A. corner. Maria jerked her head at the set.

"It isn't fair," she said.

"I can live with it."

"Not him. What your daughter did to you."

He almost said: You're my daughter. But the anchorman was saying that after the debate, the governor would be taking a two-day rest at El Tovar Hotel on the South Rim of the Grand Canyon.

"El Tovar?" said Maria. "I worked there one summer as a maid. I know all about . . ." She stopped talking abruptly.

Their eyes met and held in speculation.

Rehearsing The Candidate for the debate was like a hockey team practicing slap shots at the goalie: rapid-fire impersonal exchanges. Nicole no longer found it odd that she thought of him only as The Candidate; he had become objectified, depersonalized, almost deified for all of them—even, probably, for himself.

Jarvis: "Ninth-most-important issue. Arbor says

348

the Republicans inherited a legacy of forty-two un-balanced budgets in the last fifty years. You say . . ."

"Stop wrapping yourself in the American flag. It worked for Reagan but we won't stand for it here tonight. We—"

Nicole: "Verbose."

"Who's been in the White House for the past four years?"

"Better."

Crandall: "Second-most-important issue. Arbor says the Republicans have launched the greatest crusade against illegal drugs this country has ever seen. You say . . ."

"A Band-Aid for a hemorrhage. During their great crusade, crack and coke have reached epidemic proportions. I propose—"

Ross: "Save that, we don't have the proposals worked out yet. Seventh-most-important issue: Arbor says that for the first time in history we have a treaty for reduction in strategic nuclear weapons on both sides of the curtain. You say . . ."

"A treaty unratified by this country thanks to knee-jerk congressional opposition by Mr. Arbor's conservative cronies."

Quarles: "A newsman brings up the Iran-Contra affair and Arbor's still-undefined role in it. You say . . ."

"I want a cheeseburger."

"Great. That gives us the Ronald McDonald vote—except it's twelve-year-olds. You say . . ."

"I say it's the thirteenth issue of the campaign, dead last. The polls show only twenty-nine percent of the electorate want to hear more about it. Sixty-four percent are sick of it."

"It's two in the afternoon and this man is a contender—a *hungry* contender," said Nicole. "Let's *all* have a cheeseburger."

"Let 'em eat cake," snarled Jarvis.

Everyone laughed. Military observers listening to their banter about the debate would have said: Confidence is high.

# 42

Nicole was on the mezzanine overlooking the lobby of El Tovar Hotel, eating a muffin and drinking coffee and reading the *Atlanta Herald* on that city's first presidential debate. The governor had taken an early-morning donkey ride down from the South Rim of the Grand Canyon, leaving her unexpected free time.

### ONE PUNCH DEBATE KNOCKOUT?

"Chesty Westy" leapt into the ring against "Gentleman George" last night and gave him a bloody nose. It was a bare-knuckle brawl from the opening bell.

The sprawling hundred-room hotel, built of native boulders and Oregon pine in 1905 when the Santa Fe Railroad extended service to the canyon's South Rim, was rustic yet luxurious, remote yet hospitable, historic yet modern, with spacious rooms beautifully appointed. The coffee steamed in a heavy pewter pot. There was real cream. She spread one of the best strawberry jams she had ever tasted on a muffin and continued to read.

The hotel had been built at right angles to the canyon rim instead of facing, as would be done today; Westergard's party had taken over one whole wing and sealed it off. David, still in pajamas, was at the window when she came in. Their room looked at the adobe Hopi House where native artifacts were sold.

She set down the tray of coffee and muffins on the unmade bed and said, "I'm going to spend money at the gift shop."

Ross was tucking into the muffins. He waved a coffee cup at her.

"I'll grab a shower and see you down there."


Jarvis, frustrated, was stewing about Nicole as he started down the broad stone steps from the wide veranda, then paused for a crippled janitor, in hotel workclothes and a Harvey Hotels workcap jammed down hard over his eyes, to limp up past him with bucket and mop. Jarvis just couldn't get fucking Nicole out of his mind. Media consultant. If the Guv made it, who would end up with a cabinet post? Madam Secretary, sure as hell.

He ended up sitting on the stone guardrail of the Crater Rim Trail, staring out at the view. It had taken rain, snow, heat, frost, wind, and the Colorado River six million years to carve out the peaks and spires, the buttes and bluffs. Red and green and pink and blue, shale and limestone and sandstone, eroded by the elements to lay bare a large hunk of the earth's two billion years of fossilized history.

But the eerie beauty of the 4,500-foot precipice

was lost on Jarvis. His eyes saw only the flyspeck dots on the canyon floor with their tail of dust: the governor's mule train going out along Bright Angel Trail. Would fucking Nicole be with him, sucking up as usual?

He needed one of Sharkey's women under his hand, that was it. As if in response to his frustration, he felt a soft touch on his little finger. He looked down and jerked his hand away with a grunt of alarm. A gopher or squirrel kind of animal was sitting up a few inches from his hand and going *chit-chit-chit* at him. Its feet and belly were washed with yellow. When Jarvis didn't react, it began to beat the rock with a tiny angry paw.

Was the damn thing rabid, for Chrissake, coming right up to him like that? A woman's laughter jerked his head around.

"Don't be scared. He's just mad at you because you didn't give him a peanut or a piece of chocolate."

"Scared?" He was immediately bellicose; he didn't like broads laughing at him. That jig whore laughed in Boston, see what she got. "I oughtta knock the little bastard off the wall."

The woman sat down beside him. She looked Indian or something, long shiny black hair twisted into a single heavy braid down her back. Even had a blanket tossed over one shoulder like a squaw in the old western movies. Good body, what he could see of it, lots of chest.

But it was the face that caught him. A real Indian face, hawk nose, dark eyes both challenging and bold. Proud, proud as a bastard. He felt it in his groin; he wanted to humble that face, put fear and pain into those eyes.

353

"He's a cliff chipmunk," she said.

They're tame because the tourists from the hotel feed them all the time."

"You a tour guide, Pocahontas, or part of tonight's entertainment?" She lifted an eyebrow quizzically, so he continued, "You know, the big Indian dance they got laid on for the governor tonight." She still looked puzzled. You know—Gary Westergard? Running for president?"

She shrugged. Jesus, not even interested! Maybe he could . . . No. Cool it. Try something out here in the boonies with an Indian broad, the whole damned tribe might show up to scalp him or something. Still, the challenge in those eyes . . . A sexual challenge? One like this could get him off without . . .

"I'm Westergard's campaign manager," he said.

Her thigh was almost touching his. She laid a peanut on her flattened palm, the chipmunk took it.

She said caressingly, "That must make you real important."

"Important enough," he admitted, preening.

Her knee touched his. Her eyes were direct. Her voice was soft. " Tell me about it."

To his surprise, Jarvis found himself doing so. At length.


Nicole had to detour around a uniformed janitor mopping the floor by the gift shop. He moved with the hesitant gait of a lamed dog, head down. Lamed, like her dad.

She thrust guilt away. The shop was long and narrow, with a number of upright floor displays at

354

the far end. The glass wall cases featured pottery and sculpture by the tribes in and around the Grand Canyon—Hopi, Navajo, Havasupai, Paiute, Hualapai. The Story Tellers, seated figures with little children perched all over them, made her homesick, suddenly, for the kids. They were also stunningly expensive, far out of her reach.

Other cases displayed silver-and-turquoise jewelry, most of it Hopi but with some exceedingly fine inlaid Zuni wrist bands, necklaces, brooches. Again, well outside her price range.

Not everything was Native American. One floor display at the far end of the shop featured original foot-high Duncan Royale sculptures of key figures in the Santa Claus legend. The fourth-century St. Nicholas of Bari, original St. Nick as well as the patron saint of Russia, dressed in his episcopal robes and holding three bags of gold. Father Christmas, a much sterner figure than Germany's dough-faced Kris Kringle or the conventional Night Before Christmas Santa.

Who transfixed Nicole, however, was Black Peter, St. Nick's opposite number, who carried a black leather-strapped volume open to youths who had transgressed against their parents' wishes. He wore black elbow-length gloves, black leather cavalier boots with black pantaloons tucked into them, a black singlet with brass buttons, over it all a flowing black cape. Obviously a Satan figure: thrusting up from his head were twin black horns wreathed with twisted ivy vines.

But it was the face, framed by thick black hair, that held her. Ruddy outdoor cheeks, strong nose, eyes deep-set, brown, hypnotic, almost fanatic under furrowed heavy brows. Except for an almost

Manchurian mustache and a jutting beard, the resemblance to her father's face was eerie, almost frightening.

She raised her eyes and was looking into Fletcher's living face from three feet away.

David stopped as if hitting a wall. *Fletcher! Here!* To kill him.

Overmastered by terror worse than his worst nightmare, he ran, letting the gift-shop door swing silently shut behind him. If he thought of Nicole at all in that terrible moment, it was to hope that she would stall Fletcher enough so *he* could escape. He took the stairs two at a time: the .357 Magnum was in his suitcase in their room.

"Why, Nicole? Why did you . . .?"

Unexpectedly, she was terrified. In the weeks since she had seen him, he somehow had become an almost satanic figure, like Black Peter. Or was that just guilt? There was hurt in his voice, but anger too, and suddenly she *knew* why. Just like that.

"Because alone he wouldn't stand a chance against you."

You could have just told me you wanted me to . . . stop."

"Would you have?"

"I almost did a couple of times—*then*. But now . . ."

She took a step toward him, finally seeing hurt as well as hate in him. "He . . . A weak man, can't you see that? He thought . . . this was his chance at the brass ring. He was afraid of losing me, afraid of . . . losing. Of being . . . nobody."

Jarvis said, "And after the second debate we'll be going to this place outside Palm Springs overnight, a resort where Al Capone used to relax and make it with the broads. Not even the press is gonna know where we are. But—"

"You like to make it with the broads?" she asked softly.

Jesus, with this one he could get it up, he knew he could, without any rough stuff. He turned her toward him.

"How about tonight? Come to my room, we can—"

But her head came up suddenly as if she heard the baying of distant hounds. She slapped his hand away and sprang to her feet in one lithe movement.

"Hey, goddammit, wait—"

She was gone, running swiftly and silently across the grass, angling toward the public parking lot behind Hopi House. She ran like a warrior, knees high and arms pumping, heavy shining braid jouncing and popping against the small of her back.

"Goddamn bitch, wait a . . ."

Oh, the bitch, the whore, the goddamn *whore!* He ever got his hands on her, he'd make her hurt, he'd make her scream, he'd wipe that contempt off her face, that defiance from those eyes.

"Who are you to say that love isn't good enough?" Nicole demanded. She was frightened but finally angry. "What sort of love did you ever really give Mom?"

"Not enough, and I've paid for it ever since she died. So you love him, you still didn't have to protect him from me." A sneer entered his voice for the first time.

Hell, he's got good old Gary for that."

"Gary doesn't know! Not about anything."

"Don't lie any more to me, Nicole. He's the one who—"

"All he ever said was that you knew something that could stop him from being president. He was just thinking aloud, he didn't want anyone to actually hurt you."

"So Ross did this to me all on his own."

"I told you he was weak!" she cried, almost wringing her hands. "Weak men get brave at the wrong moments, they do the inappropriate thing they most fear being done to them."

Fletcher's anger was swelling; his eyes flashed. "Well, he's right this time. I'm going to kill the son of a bitch."

"No, no, you mustn't . . ." The corner of her eye caught one of the hotel's uniformed guards outside the shop. In final betrayal she screamed as loud as she could, *"Help! Security!"*

He spun away from her out the door, smashed the heel of a hand into the face of the guard fumbling at his holster flap, was across the lobby in his wounded-wolf lope before the guard's butt even hit the floor. Nicole had never seen anyone move so fast.

A beat-up 4x4 smoking around the circle of driveway made Jarvis jump it. The squaw was behind the wheel, face set and eyes flat. She hit the brakes to slow for the crippled maintenance man to throw himself headfirst in the open door, then gunned it. Just like Bonnie and Clyde. Too late, one of the Secret Service men ran down the steps with a gun in his hand.

"You get the license?"

When Jarvis shook his head, the agent thrust his gun away and jerked the walkie-talkie off his belt. Jarvis picked up the fugitive's fallen cap. No license number, and he didn't know what the hell had happened inside, but Jarvis had gotten one thing: a look at the running man's face. He was Hal Fletcher. Nicole's father.


Nicole was finally free of the security people. Some crazy man had accosted her in the gift shop with a rambling tale like the Ancient Mariner — she had been sure to make the literary allusion — that had gotten so scary she'd finally screamed.

Nothing about any threat to Westergard.

Nothing about him being her father.

David was sitting hunched on the foot of the bed with his face in his hands. On the spread beside him was that gun of his, broken open to load but with the bullets still scattered across the bedspread. His face was red-eyed and puffy from crying.

"I saw him there with you and I ran."

"It's okay, honey," she said softly.

"You don't understand. I didn't even try to save you. I just ran. He scared me too much."

She took his head in her arms and pressed his face to her bosom. "He scared me too, honey." After a long pause, in a voice like a sigh, she said. "He wants to kill you, David."

359

"Oh, God." His body had stiffened at her words. A long shudder ran through him. "Oh, God, what are we going to do?"

"It all depends whether they got the license plate."

Maria had swung the 4x4 off the road into the thin pine forest as soon as they passed the turnoff to the clinic so they could bypass the ranger station at the south entrance of the park. Fletcher said nothing. She eased down into a shallow arroyo, started up the far side with the engine whining.

"You saw your daughter?"

Instead of answering, he demanded, "How did you know to be there at the right time?"

"I just knew you were getting into trouble."

"She's dead to me," he said. "I'm dead to her." After a long moment he added, "I told her I was going to kill him."

They reached level ground again. With four-wheel they could run cross-country under the trees until dark, then drift east to pick up U.S. 180 toward Flagstaff.

He said, as if to an objection, "You ought to understand that, maybe better than I do. I know Old Charlie would have."

"Eating the heart of the enemy to get his bravery."

He drew a deep breath; she did understand. Pine boughs scraped along the side of the pickup.

"This is where we part company. Before it was talk. Now it's real."

She shook her head. "You can't do it without me."

"I'm going to have to."

"No." She cast a triumphant look at him. "I know where they'll be after the next debate."

# 43

Two nights before the second debate, The Candidate found out it had been Fletcher at the Grand Canyon. He was in a motel suite on I-5's motel row overlooking the Stockton Deep Water Channel, and Edith was dedicating a hospital in Carmel, because Della Weinberg had stuck the new mayor of San Francisco with the check: a record city-budget deficit of $172.4 million. With Weinberg on the ticket, suddenly California was on the line.

"Mayor of the Year!" Westergard fumed to Kent Jarvis. "I should have gone with Jackie Jefferson for veep."

"You really think this country is ready for a black left-wing Chicago preacher a heartbeat away from the presidency?"

"He wouldn't have lost me California."

"Della hasn't either yet."

Nicole was the most sensitive yet dynamic — also *creative* — member on staff, but in terms of continuous service Kent went back further than anyone; Westergard, old-shoe-comfortable with him, leaned back against the couch and massaged his eyelids with his fingertips. California could be the election tie-breaker, but so could a good showing in the next debate. He was juggling both imperatives and it was wearing him out.

"Give me the schedule for tomorrow again, Kent."

"Staff breakfast at eight A.M. in a private room off the motel coffee shop. Noon, a rally and speech at the Pacific Memorial Stadium. We're estimating a crowd of—"

"The water-conservation speech, right? Northern wetlands versus agricultural irrigation here in the Valley and—"

"That's the one." Jarvis, who had maneuvered hard to get this time alone with the guv, was about to put his move on him. "Not a very good speech, but . . ."

Westergard sat up quickly, his eyes popping open.

"What's wrong with it?"

"You can't really blame Nicole and David, not after that terrible scene at El Tovar with her father. I think—"

"That was her *father* at El Tovar? *Hal Fletcher?*"

Jarvis managed to look confused. "Didn't she tell you? I thought . . ." He gave an artful shrug. "It wouldn't be good for the campaign if it got out to the media, but I thought you . . ."

Westergard was already on the phone, an ominously self-righteous look in his eye.


"How could you *do* this to me, Nicole?"

Westergard was striding up and down the room, more angry than Nicole could remember him ever being, lips compressed to a white line, fisted right hand slamming repeatedly into his left. It was just the three of them in the suite, because she had refused to discuss anything if Jarvis was present.

"I didn't tell you because it was something between my father and me. I didn't think—"

"You've been lying to me all along, you're lying to me now. Your lies are damaging this campaign." Westergard stopped to point a finger at her as if it were loaded. "I need the truth."

This was it, then, the moment she had dreaded and had hoped she would never have to face; for that instant she hated her father. Through the window she could see the running lights of a freighter in the turning basin by the grain terminal on the south side of the channel.

"The truth is—" and David interrupted.

"The truth is, Governor, that I tried to kill Hal Fletcher after that April meeting last year when you said he was a danger to your campaign for President of the United States."

"Are you *crazy?*"

"No. I'm not." There was no puppy dog in him, no pleading. "Maybe I was then, a little, but—"

"You're out, both of you," snapped Westergard; he had found his proper stance. "Whoever puts his personal affairs ahead of this campaign has no place in it. You've both done that. You've acted recklessly and lied to me and endangered my chances for the presidency and I want no more to do with you."

Nicole was back on her feet, eye dangerous. "My father has sworn to kill David. He needs protection until—"

"Then go to the police. Of course, when they find out David is guilty of attempted murder—"

"Do you want them to find that out?" demanded Nicole icily.

Ross put his arm around his wife's shoulders. "Nicole is saying that helping us now won't endanger the campaign any further, and might help it." There was suddenly a surprising strength in the man. "An honorable man would help us out, it's the decent—"

"*Honorable! Decent!* You have the gall to talk about—"

"Tell me you wouldn't be happier if Fletcher was dead."

"Yes, Gary," said Nicole, "tell us you want the police questioning my father. Tell us you want the media in on this."

Westergard made a weary gesture. "Two days before the debate, you do this to me. All right, you'll have your

364

answer in the morning. Now get out of my sight."

Kent Jarvis was a rough-cut diamond, that was true, but he was Westergard's diamond. Not like Nicole. She'd shown her true colors tonight. No concern for him and the campaign, only for her own problems. Through her recklessness and careless disregard the campaign had been compromised and endangered.

To think he'd been considering her for a cabinet post!

Jarvis said, "On the surface, of course, Guv, I'd tend to agree with you. Cast 'em out, let 'em fend for themselves. But . . . if they *should* go to the police for protection . . ." He took a turn around the room himself, pausing momentarily to look out at the shipping in the channel just as Nicole had done. "That could screw you pretty good."

"But I didn't suggest to Ross that he do . . . *anything*. You were there that day, you didn't rush out and buy a gun. I merely overstated a vagrant concern and Ross took it as—"

"Anyway," said Jarvis, "I think I see a way out."

Westergard sat down suddenly, as if all of his bones had turned to rubber. "Thank God. What do we do, Kent?"

"We disappear 'em."

"Disap—"

"Hide 'em where he can't find 'em. The debate's in two days, the election's two weeks after that. Hide them for now, with the understanding that after the election they're on their own with your blessing."

He wanted desperately for it to make sense, so he could concentrate on the great, the only real issue: the presidency.

"Where would we—"

"I'll handle everything, Governor. Leave it all to me."

Westergard solemnly shook his hand. "God bless you, Kent. You're my good right arm. I won't forget this."

Jarvis went down the hall to his own room feeling as if he could walk on water. *Yeah!* Goddamn right Westy wouldn't forget it. Jarvis wouldn't let him. Now he could even whisper the height of his own ambition to himself.

Secretary of State.

Because Nicole and her wimp husband would be gone from between him and the light. *He* would be running the rest of the campaign—along the lines she had laid out, of course, she did have a brilliant political mind, but she'd be paddling around out among the fucking lily pads. Literally. He was going to stash them in the delta. Hundreds of miles of waterways out there, sloughs, canals, bays, rivers, channels—all interconnected. On a houseboat they could hide out forever. By the time they were back in circulation, Kent Jarvis would be in Washington sewing his gown for the Inaugural Ball.

He stopped abruptly in the corridor outside his room, key in hand, two words colliding in his mind like bowling balls.

*Utilize. Discard.*

Nicole was a very smart woman, she might someday make a comeback. But here was her wild-eyed old man running around like a loose cannon, wanting to kill her husband, and here was Kent Jarvis, the only man who would know where to find that husband. Could he somehow bring those explosive elements together? At least he'd keep the old eyes and ears open.

He keyed the lock and went into his room.

Shaking hands with Arbor in the Walnut Street Theater a few blocks from Philadelphia's Independence Hall, Westergard thought: Ninety minutes equals four years. That was the equation they both faced.

George Arbor, a stern-faced humorless man in a tie to be buried in and one of those indestructible suits seemingly cut out with a blowtorch, looked like a retired high-school principal. But as ex-director of the FBI and current VP, he knew where a lot of political bodies were buried.

"The first question is for Governor Westergard," said Jane Pauley, the moderator, in her no-nonsense midwest voice.

"Governor," said a network newsman, "the vice-president has charged that you favor unilateral disarmament and oppose Star Wars. Could you state your position on these issues for us?"

Feeling the moment-of-attack power surge that had earned him the campaign nickname of Chesty Westy, he began, "The vice-president's inaccuracy of language is equaled only by the vice-president's imprecision of thought . . ."

There was laughter along the crowded bar in Lyons Steakhouse in Palm Springs. Fletcher sipped his beer.

"I believe it is in our best interests to stay alive, but I have never opposed Star Wars. Until the Soviets quit seeing negotiators as sissies, I believe the best way to do that is to walk soft and carry a big stick—a big *nuclear* stick."

"Hey, he's fun!" exclaimed the woman on the next stool. "That Arbor puts me to sleep."

"All you think about is the bedroom," said her companion.

"Fletcher, table for two," said the P.A. system.

He and Maria were here because she had ferreted out which fancy resort had once been owned by Al Capone. They had finished their rare roast beef and were on coffee and dessert by the time the debate ended.

As two men in parrot-bright sport shirts walked past their table, one said, "So who do you think won?"

"The Dodgers," said the other, and they both laughed.

# 44

It was literally a houseboat, a house on a barge with a living room, kitchen, head, shower, and a bedroom with bunk-style double beds one above the other. On their first night in the delta they tied up after dark to a tree out over the water, in the morning awoke crammed up against the bulkhead under the window by the canting of the boat. The tide had gone out as the fog had come in, grounding them.

The next night they listened to the debate on the radio and decided that Westergard had won going away. David had his .357 in the waistband of his trousers with his shirt out to hide it.

Nicole said, "If that thing goes off on its own we'll never be more than roommates again." He quit wearing the pistol.

The next night they made love for the first time aboard the gently rocking boat. Sort of like doing it on a waterbed.

The next morning they moved on, Nicole at the wheel looking out the picture windshield at each turn of Disappointment Slough—which never disappointed: a flock of pintails, a storage shed sagging halfway into the water, three little girls diving off a dock wearing only their white-blond hair.

David said, "Jarvis sure did get us out here where God couldn't find us."

"While he's there angling for a cabinet post when the time comes for Gary to divvy up the goodies."

But Jarvis really had surprised her. Hastings Crandall would have had David in the gas chamber by sundown, but Jarvis had been only efficient, lining up the houseboat and supplies and blankets and bedding and fuel.

"The Guv wants to keep in touch in case the situation changes, so I'll call you at specified times on the boat-refueling dock pay phone at Terminous."

Which had meant nothing at the time, but now David, studying the waterways chart that had come with the houseboat, said, "At a fork up here a mile or so, we want to go left."

"Port," said Nicole. With the engine going ka-thunk ka-thunk behind her, she was Mark Twain piloting the *Delta Queen.*

"White's Slough. By the chart, it takes us to Terminous. Which apparently is a little country-store-type place under the drawbridge where Cal Twelve crosses over the Mokelumne River."

"Aye, aye, Captain." She gave him a lascivious wink. "Does this feel like a second honeymoon to you, or what?"

David grabbed the wheel to turn them in at a tiny dead-end slough where they could toss the anchor out on the mudbank and lock the doors. It was very romantic, making love on your way to Terminous. In broad daylight yet.

Terminous. End of a journey. For them, anyway, at least until after the election. Then . . .

Worry about it then.


It was hard to worry about anything at the Desert Palms Resort and Spa. This was Westergard's last moment of relaxation before two nonstop weeks of hard stumping, ending with a final shot at California, and he was making the most of it. Lying on a king-size bed in the rock-hewn Capone Suite, he watched Edith through half-closed eyes as she removed her makeup.

"What will you wear for the Inauguration?" he asked lazily.

She smiled at his reflection in the mirror of the ornate rosewood vanity. All of the furniture was antique, the decor art deco.

"Isn't that bad luck? Talking about it?"

"Losing the election, *that* would be bad luck."

She would make a grand first lady. Better than . . .

As if reading his thoughts, she asked gently, "Do you miss having Nicole to advise you, Gary?"

"No." He unfolded his arms from behind his head and sat up. He spoke with unexpected fervor. "She betrayed me; she and that husband of hers almost poisoned the well for all of us."

"I've never understood what it is that Fletcher knows."

"*Thinks* he knows," said Westergard quickly, masking the tension in his voice. "I've never figured it out myself."

There was an uneasy pause; had someone told her his incautious comment at that fateful April staff meeting eighteen months ago? But she said only, "Are you coming to bed, darling?"

"One more soak in the hot pool first."

He went into the bathroom to get into his still-damp trunks. Tonight he just wanted to be with himself. The thing with Nicole had brought a lot of the past rushing in. That drunken night kept thrusting up into his consciousness like . . .

No. He forced his mind away from memory. That day's boy was not father to this day's man, not now, not ever.

When he came out with one of the big woolly towels tossed over his shoulder, Edith was already in bed with

371

Tuchman's *Distant Mirror*; she folded it shut around a finger and smiled gently at him. He bent and kissed her on the forehead.

"My love, sleep tight."

She giggled sleepily. "And don't let the bedbugs bite."

Maria had dropped Fletcher half a mile south of the lighted and guarded gate of Desert Palms Resort just after sunset, when the shimmering light hid movement. They had bought the old car in Phoenix in her name; the pickup had been sold to a second-hand dealer in Flagstaff the day after their escape from El Tovar.

"I still think I should come with you."

"We've been over all this. It's a one-man job."

"Hell," she said, "I thought *I* was the red Indian."

Going over the adobe wall, he slipped into a Korean night-patrol mind-set with alarming ease. Alarming, not surprising: apart from the prey, it was little different from Old Charlie's recently rehoned nighttime stalking skills. In the next hour he could have taken out three Secret Service agents: one in the tamarisk grove down by the picnic area; a second in a patch of rare clumpy California grasses near the tennis court; the third in the ornate teaberry bushes flanking the exercise pool.

He also saw Jarvis talking to two pretty girls at the front desk. Secret Service men changing shifts on the rooftop of the Capone Suite as the mobster's bodyguards once had done. Pete Quarles stepping on a rock by a "sun bin" designed for solo nude sunbathing and hopping around naked on one foot, swearing.

But no Nicole. No Ross.

The gambling casino of Capone's day had been converted to the Casino Restaurant. Plush tapestries, a huge fireplace, a great chunky refectory table that would have graced a medieval monastery. A convenient tree branch

372

showed him people eating harlequin salads and salmon aphrodite and orange ruffi muscovite and veal gandolf and chicken gabriel and tournedos savoy and cheesecake with strawberries and pecan pie with whipped cream.

He didn't see Nicole or Ross.

Much later, Gary Westergard came out of the Capone Suite in swim trunks, exchanged a word with the Secret Service agent on guard beside the inset entrance, then went up the walkway toward the pool. Fletcher followed. Silently.

Like all else at Desert Palms, the hot natural-mineral-water pool was artfully conceived and beautifully executed. A blue smooth-bottomed concrete cup, ranging in depth from one foot to five feet, set within decorative rock and shrubbery and surrounded by Polynesian-hut dressing areas. The natural mineral waterfall boiled up from the earth's recesses at regular intervals to spill down a manmade cliff into the pool. The closer to this overflow, the hotter the water.

Westergard drifted in a faintly steaming one hundred degrees, letting it soak into his pores. He had the pool to himself tonight, a blessing indeed: the past possessed him. He missed Nicole despite her betrayals. His mind leapt like a flea to another consideration. How the devil had Fletcher so easily breached the security of El Tovar? She'd always said her father was like a ghost in any kind of cover; now he believed her.

The flea hopped again. If the media should ever get hold of Fletcher . . . or of what Ross had done to trigger Fletcher . . . or worst of all, what he himself had said to trigger *Ross* . . .

"Hello, Gary."

His head was jerked around by the never-forgotten voice.

373

Fletcher was hip-deep in the water just a few feet from him, his nude body glistening in the soft light of the foliage-masked lights around the pool. Physically he was little changed from that drunken night they had busted Old Charlie out of the poor farm—except for a long white scar along his rib cage where Ross's bullet had struck. But his face was dark, ungiving.

"I want Ross."

The Candidate felt stirrings of anger. "He's not here. They've left the campaign entirely."

This was not the hero of his youth. This was Mr. Nobody, a wreck of a man who was nothing, had nothing except the gall to threaten Westergard's great dream of presidency.

"I could call for help, you know. The Secret Service—"

"And you could be dead by the time they got here."

Anger washed over him. Anger over the years of sleepless nights, the years of guilts and self-repugnance and self-doubts that winning the presidency would surely still forever.

"Are you threatening me? Do you dare threaten—"

"For Chrissake, Gary, we're two guys talking." Fletcher's face looked faintly amazed in the dimness. "You aren't Galahad of the Grail and I'm not the Black Kni—"

But that's exactly who each of them was. With an inarticulate cry of rage, Gary Westergard threw himself on his erstwhile idol, his fingers scrabbling at that throat to

He was drowning. Oh God, drowning! His head underwater, hands with an awful strength holding him threshing there. Water in his eyes, his mouth, sucking up his nose to . . .

He came up gasping and choking to the confused shouts and running feet of the Secret Service men. The geyser erupted—splashing, steaming, hiding, confusing. Powerful flashlights slashed the darkness, found The Candidate hunched and coughing, leapt across the pool area, danced to pierce the banks of foliage.

In vain. They found wet fading footprints on the rocks beyond the waterfall, but by then Fletcher was back into his clothes and over the wall and away.

# 45

It was well after midnight and they were eating Maria's favorite, steak chicken-fried in axle-grease, in an all-night café halfway between Palm Springs and L.A. Two hours earlier he'd been in the Desert Palms compound.

Maria leaned forward to deliver an opinion, putting her sleeve in her gravy as she did. She'd done some drinking while waiting for Fletcher to either show up or not show up.

"If you quit now, you're never going to . . ." She threw up her hands. "Eat the heart of your enemy! Bullshit!"

"They weren't there at Desert Palms, I would have seen them. Gary didn't know where—"

"Why didn't you drown *him* instead? He's the one who started it all."

Fletcher waved a hand in dismissal. "All he did was think out loud about something. Ross did the rest."

"Ross and your Nicole," she said waspishly.

"I've told you that you're more daughter to me than—"

She burst out, turning heads, "I don't want to be your fucking daughter! I want . . ." She glanced around and stopped. "A piece of that gooey stuff for dessert.

Apple crisp."

Fletcher laughed. He couldn't help it with her.

Back at the motel she made them a pair of very dark drinks with ice and Seven-Up from the dispenser outside. He slugged it and felt it immediately, loosening inhibitions, showing truths.

"So you're just going to give up. Just like that."

He shrugged and finished his drink. "What else can I do except quit?"

"If it's money, I can always make money—"

"Not that way. Not while you're with me."

Seeing the look in his eyes, she dropped it. "Anyway, somebody knows where they are."

"Nobody we can get to."

"I got to Jarvis, that's how we knew about Desert Palms." She drank, nodded wisely. "He's the kind of guy makes sure he knows everything."

Fletcher got up and made them both another drink. Others followed. An hour passed. It was very hot in the motel room; they started shedding clothes, as had become the casual fact of their unthought journey together. For years he had drunk almost nothing; now, after the dramatic shift in his life, he was reverting to the habits of his youth. Bookending his life with drinking the same way he had bookended it with hunting.

He demanded abruptly, "Don't wanna be my daughter, who *do* you wanna be?"

She threw herself on him, pinning him to the bed, giggling but taking the opportunity to seriously writhe against him. He rolled her off.

"Maria, you're less than half my age. And I told you—ever since Terry I can't . . ."

"Lighten up, man." She went abruptly serious also. "But I can't live forever not getting laid."

"Maria, if I could . . ."

377

"Yeah, yeah, I know." She was in bra and panties, he in his shorts. Looking at her lithe beauty, he suddenly wished he could still feel the heat of passion. But even tussling with her had left him inert.

He fell asleep, woke later with Maria asleep against him, her face shoved up into the hollow of his neck. She felt him come awake and drew back enough to focus on his face.

"If you knew where he was, you'd go and kill him, wouldn't you?" she asked in a sleepy but almost pleading voice.

His head throbbed, his tongue was thick, he had trouble focusing his eyes. "Why does it matter so much to you?"

"You gotta do something or you'll never be . . . never get over . . ."

She shut her eyes and was silent again. Her breathing evened out. Then a single tear rolled out from under her closed lid and ran down her cheek. He drifted off into sleep again.

When he came up to half-consciousness again, Maria was crouched over him, naked, her breasts ripe pods, her buttocks warm melons inviting his hands in the night. So beautiful, so woman.

Belatedly his sluggish brain realized she was kneading his penis with one hand, gently but skillfully cupping his scrotum with the other. To his amazement, almost his horror, she already had made him half-hard, half-erect. Which couldn't be. It just wasn't there for him, his mind screamed silently. No! No, he couldn't be unfaithful to Terry. . . .

*I love you. Fletch.*

No! It must not be. It was a tenet of his existence that with Terry had died his sexuality, his maleness, his *right* to sexual release. He tried to rear up, buck her off,

378

but the body refused a befuddled mind's orders. The body knew better.

*Fletch, I have to, I love . . .*

She was working him with both hands, he could feel his testicles swell with unspent seed. So could she. She swung herself around between his splayed legs and took him in her mouth.

*You can't stop me now, I love . . .*

Oh, God, no one had ever before . . . Yes. Once. Unknown girl that night they'd rescued Old Charlie . . .

She was kneading his balls, wanting what they held.

Here it comes. His body jerked and bucked galvanically. Oh, ohohoh, he spent, again, spurting

He burst out crying.

And yet again he spent, Gary's mouth frantic around

*No*, unknown girl's not

*No.* Maria . . .

as Gary tore himself from between Fletch's legs, face contorted with the horror of what he had just done, fleeing to the bathroom, Fletch drunk, only vaguely aware, block it out, must have been one of the girls, block it out, didn't really even know what was going on, block it out

the sounds of retching into the toilet, pass out

pass out


Fletcher woke with a shattering headache, alone in a sweatstained bed in a cheap motel room made momentarily golden by dawn light through cheap lowered roller shades.

Had it happened? Had it

Yes. Both times. Now, Maria, then

Jesus Christ, look at it, say it. Then, Gary.

Small wonder the subconscious Gary had found a way

379

to send Ross out with a gun in his hand to wipe Fletcher from the earth, not even knowing he had. How long had that knowledge festered in him? A lifetime, made acute by reporters' probings into every incident of a candidate's life.

How long, now that it had broken through into his own consciousness, would it fester in Fletcher?

Couldn't think it now. Maybe never. Now, Maria.

Maria, giving him . . . wanting him to have . . .

He rolled out of bed, sat up on the edge, head in hands, groaning. Why had he merited such a gift of . . .

Of life.

Why? She was wiser than he.

He staggered to his feet, crossed to the closet, knowing but having to be sure. Yes. Backpack gone. Reeled to the bathroom. Yes. Toothbrush, toilet articles. Gone.

Gone.

Maria.

Easy for her to hook a ride with a trucker to Vegas. L.A.?

If Vegas, gone for good. She would have made her choice. If L.A., he had something he could do. He had a name in L.A. May Martínez. Her sister. He had to believe L.A.

She had given him back to life, then had left him with only his quest for stolen selfhood. The questing beast. God, his head hurt.

Except Maria was now his quest. He seemed unable to search alone. First Nicole. When she had withdrawn, he had drifted until Maria. Without her goad he would drift again.

He sat down heavily on the edge of the bed again. For the second time in as many hours, he cried.

\* \* \*

"Guv, I hate to say it, but you're blowing it," said Jarvis in Louisville, Kentucky. It was the lousy end of a lousy day spent stumping across the East through Buffalo, Baltimore, Atlanta, and finally Louisville.

"I don't know what you mean," said Westergard stiffly. "I thought the City Hall rally went extremely well. Four thousand people—"

"Yeah, the Louisville Slugger," said Jarvis dryly. "But that thing you said about taxes—"

"Nobody caught it."

"Yet."

The patrician in Westergard recoiled from Kent's familiarity while knowing he had opened the door to this himself when he had let Kent handle the problem of Nicole and Ross.

"A night's rest, that's all I need."

"I hope you're right, Guv. See you in the morning."

Riding up to his suite in the elevator, blessedly alone for a few moments, he knew, despite his denial, that Kent was right. Five days before the election, California and forty-seven vital electoral votes at stake, here he was with his mind wandering when he should be white-hot and focused.

Fletcher was the trouble. Coming to him and demanding information, forcing the memory of that night into his consciousness after all the years. God, how he hated that man!

And he couldn't talk to anyone about it. Edith would never understand such a moment of weakness. Jarvis? The mind boggled at the thought. He wished he could just blot it out as Fletcher obviously had done. Fletcher, to blame for it all. He'd been an idealistic youth, hero-worshiping the older teenager, had been gotten drunk by him, had been aroused by the drama of Old Charlie,

381

then the drunken Fletcher had sprawled nude and passed out on the bed after the girls had flounced out. Gary there alone with him, aching to be like him, to *be* him . . .

God, how he hated that man! If Fletcher were dead, his own shame would be dead also.

He realized suddenly that he had seduced Fletcher's daughter after she had come to work for him because some hidden subconscious part of him hoped the seduction would reduce Fletcher, make him ridiculous in the same way a cuckolded husband is ridiculous. A ridiculous Fletcher he could erase from the mind, burn from the soul. But not the whole Fletcher, not the Fletcher of his shame.

For a while the affair with Nicole had worked, Fletcher had receded, had been nothing to him. But then in turn he had been seduced into seeing Nicole only as herself.

Finally, a promising poll, a few too many drinks and, with suddenly a great deal to lose, out of his mouth had popped his subconscious fear, and ambitious Ross had seized upon it and . . .

The elevator stopped; he got out and went down the hall to their suite with a Secret Service agent standing in front of it looking like someone who yawned a lot. Compose your mind, your face, as you had to compose your life, your rampaging self.

His whole life had been built on discipline; discipline was what would save him now. Save the campaign. The presidency.


Every morning Fletcher drove the battered, rusted-out old Chevy from his cheap motel in downtown L.A. to the cool wide quiet streets of Beverly in search of a yardman named Martínez who had a wife named May. His third day found him on Loma Vista, a street above Sunset so steep that the downhill run was plastered with signs warning USE LOWEST GEAR and 25 MPH. There even was a sand-filled runaway-truck turnout near the foot where it dead-ended in Doheny.

He was here because a yardman on Beverly had said he used to work with a "dude, man" named Izzy Martínez who "did" three places on Loma Vista.

Fletcher parked in the street below an old pickup full of mowers and blowers, ropes and a ladder and plastic bags of grass clippings, a pruning saw with a snaggle-tooth grin. A Latino wearing work gloves was muscling one of the mowers out of the truck. He was very handsome, with liquid eyes and sleek black hair in fifties pompadour. He straightened up and nodded shyly when Fletcher approached.

"Señor."

"Habla inglés?"

"Sí." He grinned. "Sure."

"Izzy Martínez?"

The smile went away. The face closed up.

Fletcher said, "My name is Fletcher."

He waited. After an eternity, the Latino said, "She talked about you a lot, man, but I dunno where she is. May either. She came, stayed a day, two days, y'know, then she saw something in the newspaper an' she was gone. Two days ago."

Only then did Fletcher realize how large Maria had become in his life. She had released him from self-defeating memories and guilts, forced him back to the land of the living, refused to let him quit.

"Did she give any hint at all? Anything?"

Izzy shrugged expressively. "Said she'd call, thass it. A good chick but a little *loca*, y'know?"

Fletcher left his number for May to give Maria if she called.

Something in the papers. It could only have been something about Westergard's election campaign. What was she planning?

# 46

Tomorrow was election eve. The last preelection Gallup was giving Arbor a one-point lead. Harris was giving the guv a one-point lead.

"Shit, neither one means anything," Jarvis said to Hastings Crandall. They were in the situation room set up on the fifteenth floor of the unbelievably elegant Beverly Hills Marquis.

"I believe 'not statistically significant' is the phrase they used," said Crandall.

Across the room a television set was blaring. Jarvis sat down with a felt-tip pen and a yellow legal pad to try to figure some scenarios for tomorrow's magic number, 270 electoral votes, but his head wouldn't work right. He was too nervous, too tense. The final moments after half a million campaign miles.

At least the Guv was back on track. Sharp and hard and tight, as if he had turned the voltage way up. He was up in Northern California, the Mendocino Coast somewhere, talking about unemployment and knocking the latest federal proposals for offshore oil drilling. This afternoon, San Francisco. Tomorrow night, a final live broadcast to the nation from Burbank.

He'd finally told Jarvis about Fletcher at Palm Springs. You almost had to admire the guy. Balls as big as watermelons, probably gave the Guv a shot about whatever it was from the past—though the Guv hadn't admitted that.

He stood up to leave—forty-five minutes to the check-in call to Ross and Nicole—and one of the phones started ringing. He reached for it, then saw that Crandall had gotten it.

Waiting to see if it was for him, he thought: Once the election was over, the public eye turned elsewhere . . . Maybe an Indian woman, maybe one like Fletcher's whore at the Grand Canyon. She'd had him really going there for a while.

Crandall hung up and swiveled his chair around to face him. He felt no slightest premonition.

"Some volunteer down in the lobby asking for you. Says she has a bunch of fliers you wanted. I can send—"

"I'll go. I'm going nuts sitting around here anyway."

He was mildly intrigued: he knew he had left no order for any fliers. Maybe some enterprising newswoman trying to come up with a clever human-interest angle?

A short woman with long black hair was waiting by the check-in desk, her back to him. She wore a mini and hose with a seam up the back of the legs. Dynamite legs.

"I'm Kent Jarvis—"

She turned. She was the squaw from El Tovar. *Fletcher's* squaw. His mind was racing. What was she doing here?

"Something to do with fliers?" He smiled, stalling.

"I just said that to get you down here."

He saw the whole thing with breathtaking clarity. She didn't know he had recognized Fletcher at the Grand Canyon or seen her driving the pickup. So Fletcher was sending her in to con Ross's whereabouts out of him. It was a crude play; but then, survivors like Fletcher didn't have to be subtle. They just had to survive.

What if he just went ahead and gave him Ross? He could have two days to decide whether he wanted to set a trap—or just let them fight it out. Whoever won, wouldn't the Guv be ahead? But it had to be subtle or the predator would scent the trap. He took the squaw's arm as if she were made of emeralds.

"Hey, it's really great to see you again! Why don't you come up to my room in about fifteen minutes, okay? Nineteen-twenty-two. We can get a little privacy up there."


They had found privacy about a mile from Terminous in a little stub of a slough north of the drawbridge. There was a little island they could anchor behind and this time of year get almost total isolation.

It was limbo time. Read books and watch animals and birds. Lots of waterfowl, more coming in every day, driven south along the Pacific Flyway by the winter squalls starting to swirl down out of Canada. Her favorites were the coots; at the first hint of danger they would take off across the water, squawking and running on the surface like plump matrons caught in their underwear. When their stubby wings finally got them airborne, they would immediately go into their landing glides, splashing down again fifty yards from where they had started.

There also was a colony of muskrats with a messy dumped-off-the-back-of-a-truck house over along the rushes on the northeastern shore. On this great heap of interwoven rushes and twigs, at dawn and at dusk, a fat-bodied little sentinel got up to sit and strip the bark off tender twigs and chitter at the rare vehicles passing along the stone levee raising Glassrock Road above flood-stage.

They had discussed cutting loose, but here at least they had a lifeline—the calls from Jarvis—and they certainly couldn't go home to the kids with Fletcher rampaging around somewhere below the horizon. Couldn't seek police protection either, because of the unanswerable question of *why* Fletcher would want to threaten them.

Stuck. For the moment, stuck.

Meanwhile, it was check-in time, which meant thunk-thunk-thunking out of their retreat toward Terminous. David was outside on the front deck cleaning the coals from last night's supper out of the barbecue.

"What happens after the election?" called Nicole.

He came to lean in the open doorway, one hand on the frame. This adversity had brought them together in ways she wouldn't have thought possible even a month ago.

"I'd better ask Jarvis about that today on the phone."

She spun the wheel hard aport; with slow majesty the boxy craft swung under the drawbridge into the channel that would take them to Terminous.

"I will," she said. "It's my turn."

As the Terminous dock hove into view around the turn in the channel, he said, "Okay, I'll go fuel up while you do."

The whole game board was laid out in his mind like a chess match with Karpov. That's why he had told her fifteen minutes. He needed time to set up the props.

The bell rang. She wore a fake black leather jacket over the miniskirt. She tried not to show it but was obviously awed by Jarvis' room. The basket of exceptional fruit on the coffee table, the heated towel racks in the bathroom, the plush bath towels and scented soap, the rich carpet, the complimentary robes and slippers in the closet—everything bearing the hotel's monogram.

She finally broke down and asked, "What does a room like this cost?" She seemed smaller, more vulnerable here than she had in her element in the wild canyon rim out in Arizona. That vulnerability beckoned to him now, aroused him.

He chuckled. "If you have to ask, you can't afford it."

But she turned those hawk eyes on him. Nothing vulnerable in them. "You're not paying for it anyway, are you?"

"No," he said flatly.

But you'll pay for that, bitch, he thought. Somehow I'll make you pay for that.

What he hoped would impress her even more than the room was the notebook lying open beside the phone. In the minutes before she had come up, he had written on it the word TERMINOUS, underlined twice, under that "Mokelumne River" and "CA-12 (by Stockton)," with an artistic-looking circle slashed around them. Finally were the name ROSS and the number of the pay phone on the Terminous dock.

That ought to be enough unless she was a total idiot. He started by her toward the bathroom, paused to say, "There's some Godiva chocolates by the phone."

He would have loved to see if she went for the notebook, but any woman with that predator's face would be too wary not to sense a door being left ajar. He gave her five minutes, brushing his teeth and washing his hands and flushing the toilet and running water. When he went back into the bedroom she was sitting on the bed with the last of the Godivas disappearing down her throat. The notebook looked undisturbed.

"God, are those good!" she exclaimed.

He was nonplussed. Was she just a greedy little teen-age whore after all, without a thought in her head except pigging down chocolates?

"I'll make one more phone call, then we'll go."

He took the notebook to the other phone, across the room by the window. God damn her! He didn't know how to react. He had her here for one purpose, one alone—to pass something on to Fletcher. But she was just a cunt, not playing a devious game.

Which somehow made him want to take her right

here, hard and dirty, and damn the danger. Because this one he could get it up with, hell, he was halfway there already. But he couldn't touch her. She still might be a pipeline to Fletcher—and this was campaign headquarters. Cool it, for Chrissake!

He dialed the area code and the Terminous number. Nicole today. She answered on the first ring.

"Yes," said Jarvis. "Everything all right, Nicole?" He used her name deliberately so the Indian girl would hear it.

Nicole said yes, then asked, "How soon after the election can we have a face-to-face with the governor?"

"A face-to-face?" She was out of the power equation; he wanted to keep her out. "The Guv isn't going to want to do that."

"Well, I want to do that, all right?"

"Okay, Nicole," he said dubiously. "I'll check with him and let you know day after tomorrow. Election Day. Noon sharp."

"Noon it is."

He hung up and looked over at the Indian girl. She was still sitting on the bed staring straight ahead, a vacant look on her face. Not a thought in her head. No pipeline to Fletcher at all. Probably just came up to put the make on him, now wasn't even doing that.

*You'll pay for that, bitch.*

Before he even thought, he stepped across the room and doubled up his fist and knocked her off the bed. Then used his foot so she couldn't start screaming. He stopped himself in time but just barely. He couldn't stop everything; he ejaculated on her unconscious body before somehow dragging her unseen to the fire door and out into the stairwell. He left her there, propped up against the wall in a sitting position.

She looked pretty bad, but hell, someone would find her soon. Just a fucking whore. Who'd believe anything

390

he said anyway?

Going down in the elevator to the situation room, he realized that he hadn't wanted to stop at all. Which should have been pretty goddamn scary, but . . .

# 47

Fletcher, following the MEDICAL WING signs, passed other visitors, doctors, nurses, patients in their blank-eyed shuffle with the bottoms of their pajama legs under the heels of their slippers, and saw none of them. He walked as if he wanted to smash his fists into walls.

His fault. All his fault. He should have known she would go to Westergard's convention headquarters and try to get the information he needed. Should have gone there himself to . . .

Maria Horseman was in M-Seven. It was a four-person room, Maria on the right by the window. He pulled the white curtain closed around them on its half-moon of metal ceiling track.

One of her arms was in a cast and her body was swathed in bandages under the hospital gown. What little of her face could be seen was purple, almost black. The one visible eye was too puffed to tell whether she could open it or not. He felt tears swimming in his own eyes.

When he took her undamaged hand gently in his, something gleamed between the puff-paste lids.

"Fletch?"

He nodded, then realized she might not be able to see him. He squeezed her hand and said, "Yes."

Something happened in her eggplant face and he realized she was trying to smile. Her lips were split and puffy. "In my jacket pocket . . . piece of paper . . ."

"It doesn't matter right now, Maria, I—"

"Yes it does. That's where they are. Phone number and everything. He'll be at the phone at noon on . . . Election Day. They're on . . . a houseboat . . ."

Ignoring what she said, he asked, "This . . . who?"

"Jarvis."

He made himself keep his voice down. "Why?"

"He likes it." Long pause. "Kinky. Gets . . . off on it. I . . . played so dumb he . . . believed it . . ."

He stayed until they asked him to leave. He had Ross on a silver platter. But what did he want to do with him? It didn't seem important anymore. Later for him. Now, Jarvis.

Dawn of Election Day. The Indian girl must have been found by the hotel, Jarvis thought, and spirited out to some nearby hospital. She must not have talked; obviously hadn't been sent by Fletcher after all. Status quo all around.

Gary Westergard, too, thought fleetingly of Fletcher before there were any significant vote totals over which to cast the I Ching or read the cards or peer into the crystal ball about. Just trivia and tedium as the first returns began dribbling in.

So the mind seized anything it could, and his seized on Fletcher briefly. Then he tried to feel the rush of destiny's wings within him, but nothing came. Destiny's child, or a man overreaching himself? No. Not that. He was meant to be president. And when he was, Fletcher's leverage would disappear. No need then to keep holding a safety net for the betrayers. Then, if something happened to Ross, well, it happened. Not really his concern, then.

393

Fletcher spent the morning sitting with Maria, working off some of his guilt at having not been there for Terry all the times she had needed him. Then talked to the doctor in the hall.

Feet and fists, the doctor told him. Luckily, nothing fancy like clubs, knives, or soda bottles. Just your good old-fashioned brutal beating. Casts on her broken arm and collarbone, a cracked shin, a permanent metal pin in one wrist, which would probably give her trouble with arthritis when she was older. Two cracked ribs. Spleen bruised but not ruptured.

"One or two harder blows, she wouldn't have made it. One of these days, he keeps on, he's going to kill somebody."

"Unless somebody kills him first."

The doctor looked at him with sharp distaste. "Tough guy, huh?"

"No. Just an angry one."

Maria fell asleep again just before noon, so he went down to the ground-floor bank of pay phones. He'd spent the night thinking it through. David was finally and forever safe from him. He was going to use the information Maria had paid so dearly for in a way she wouldn't approve, but it had to stop.

After five years of self-pity and exaggerated guilt about Terry, he was quite literally out of the woods. Ross had taken hunting from him, true, and he would miss it; but there had to be other ways to live besides killing things.

So he was calling Ross to tell him . . . What? Good-bye and Godspeed? He seemed to be getting transparent to Fletcher, insignificant. He belonged to Nicole; she had done the right thing to stand by him. Because she too was becoming transparent. Fading back to the distant spaces she had always occupied in his life, except for the few brief weeks when they had been looking together for his killer.

Nicole wandered around the little general store that was Terminous as David went out on the dock to the pay phone to wait for Jarvis' call. You had to love a place with plastic fishing worms displayed next to the Tootsie Rolls.

She could feel it all winding down. Pretty soon she'd be seeing the kids again. They'd called them a couple of times, but it was hard to say anything important on a phone.

As she thought it, through the window she saw David out on the dock suddenly reach for the receiver.

"You're late, Jarvis," he said into it.

"This is Fletcher. I just wanted to let you know—"

With a wild cry, Ross slammed up the phone. He spun in a circle like a man under attack by a swarm of bees. Nicole was running toward him from the store. She put her arms around him, he almost collapsed against her chest.

"David! What's wrong?"

"It's him." He made indecipherable gestures. "Him. Your father. On the phone." He grabbed her arm, tried to drag her toward their houseboat. "We have to—"

"David!" She jerked free. "Stop! You're panicked. That was his warning. He's not going to attack us in broad daylight."

"Yes, you're right, you're right." His eyes were feverish, his actions jerky and febrile, but his voice had returned to something like normal. "I'm . . . better now. It was just hearing his voice like that . . ."

Nicole was turning to the phone. "To hell with Kent,

395

I'm going to call Gary."

"How . . .? What are you going to ask him to do?"

"Whatever's necessary to stop my father."

# 48

The phone call to the situation room caught Westergard totally by surprise. How did she dare call him on Election Day when, like some Venetian doge, he had banished her and her husband from his kingdom?

He demanded of her, "*Who* called?"

"My father, damn you. He's going to come here and kill David unless—"

"All right, all right, calm down."

"I won't be put off, Gary."

By God, he couldn't deal with this! His eyes were on the TV monitors as he was talking; meaningful results were starting to come in, it had taken her two hours to get him, it was late afternoon back east. Someone was to blame for this; the call never should have been put through. The thought made him huffy.

"Nicole, I'm not going to stand for—"

"Neither am I." Her voice was flat and deadly. "I don't care what you have to do, I want protection for my husband."

He sighed. "Stay by the phone, Kent will get back to you."

Fletcher drove north in the rusted-out old Chevy even though there was no need to go. It would do David's soul good to stew a little longer, but not too long; he had heard the man's anguished cry as he slammed down the receiver. Nicole had to be stewing too. She had chosen husband over father and would stand by that — *Because alone he wouldn't stand a chance against you.*

He felt lighter than he had at any time since he had been shot. Something in him had cried "freedom" when he had hung up the phone from David. He now only had to make it permanent, like spraying fixative on a charcoal drawing.

Driving, he let his mind go back to that night nearly forty years ago. Now, freed of hangover and able to be objective, he could see how it had happened.

Gary, young, impressionable, from a sheltered upbringing, wanting to be a man among men. An equal. Wanting to belong.

And roughneck Fletch, older, full of adventures, seemingly out from under the parental thumb — the perfect hero to worship. Too strong an identification, so he mistook attraction to, and admiration of, as love for. Both of them drunk and Fletcher passed out naked . . . Which didn't make it any easier to accept.

The irony was how their paths had diverged since.

For Fletcher, those days had been the apex. Young, tough, reveling in both qualities. Since then, a steady withdrawal from life. Choosing always to turn away. Always the overseas jobs, giving his wife and child only his money, not his presence. When Terry died, turning away completely. Embracing a past way of life, becoming a semiparasite existing by arcane skills no longer relevant to the world.

But for Gary, a rising curve on the graph. Attorney, teacher, politician, governor, possibly president — according to the radio, the race was neck-and-neck. But win or lose, he had made his solid commitment to life. So, let the past be dead.

Maybe he owed Gary a sign-off too. After talking with Nicole and Ross, maybe he should try to see him and tell him . . . Tell him what? Congratulations? Good-bye? Good luck?


Jarvis couldn't believe it. The squaw had been Fletcher's woman after all. Now the events he had set in motion had boomeranged. The one thing he had never expected: fucking Fletcher calling them up and *telling them he was on his way.*

Hold still, Ross, I want to murder you.

How did he keep the Guv from finding out about what he had done to the Indian girl?

Go on the offensive. There was no other way. Get the men he needed, fly up to the Delta. Beat Fletcher to the houseboat. Be there ready to do what had to be done.

But first he had to convince the governor of the necessity of it all.


Westergard was jumpy and impatient. While his life was being decided on the TV screens in the suite below, he was up here in the disused ballroom on the roof, where they could not possibly be overheard. Sitting in a straight chair face-to-face with Kent, knees almost touching his, trying desperately to keep the sole shoddy incident of his life from taking away what was rightfully his. Talking of such deeds as Shakespeare had said were without a name.

"We have to decide fast," said Jarvis. "Fletcher is

probably already on his way there."

Westergard said, "But good God, Kent, what if I lose the election anyway?"

"If we don't act, it'll probably get out and people will believe you ordered Ross to kill Fletcher. That's what will destroy you, Governor—not whatever happened in the past."

He said helplessly, "Where can you find men who—"

"There's someone in Chicago I can call who'll know others."

"He couldn't ever know that I—"

"He wouldn't. None of them would. I take the heat if anything goes wrong."

Westergard gave a long sigh. "You'd be willing to . . . to do this, Kent? For me?"

"And for the country." And to be Secretary of State.

So it all came down to this, Westergard thought: what was an individual human life worth?

He knew—*knew*—that he could be the greatest American president of the twentieth century. So much to give! So many ideas! But could he ever be truly effective if he had to be always looking over his shoulder?

So . . . individual death versus the greater good. Seen that way, what was any individual against the welfare of millions? Billions, if he could stop the proliferation of nuclear arms.

He released a long sad sigh of decision. "Make your phone call, Kent."

Jarvis saw no need of saying that he had already called Sharkey, who had given him names of a couple of local pimps willing to be . . . *involved*. For a price, of course.


So, she had conjured up the assassins of her own father. So be it. But still . . .

As if by telepathy, David said, "We could still cut and run on our own, honey."

"To what? He would catch up sometime. He's obsessed."

"Maybe he'll become unobsessed."

"I won't let you take that chance," she said fiercely.

With last light they had run the houseboat up against the stone levee and hooked their anchor around one of the rocks so it would hold even through the changing of the tides. Jarvis had insisted he be able to come aboard directly from the levee.

The fog was in, oddly muffling and at the same time amplifying every sound from outside. The curtains were drawn, the Coleman lantern pumped and hissing its cheery pale light. The radio murmured election news sadly immaterial to them now. It all hinged on the Big Eight: New York, New Jersey, Illinois, Pennsylvania, Ohio, Michigan, Texas, California. All around the country it was still too close to call.

She thought impatiently: What is that against a muskrat swimming past the boat in dawn light? Or a white heron against a fading pink sunset?

Or the life and death face-off with her father?

David said, "It's funny, but now I keep having these feelings that I want to see him again to tell him I'm sorry. Yet at the same time I'm terrified."

Oh God, if one of them has to die, husband or father, let it be my father. On my head be it.

By common assent they were on their feet, clinging to each other. She held him, eyes closed, their bodies swaying gently in unison. She could say it now to herself: she loved him.

That's when someone jumped aboard the boat from the levee with a thud, rocking it slightly with his sudden weight.

Ross jerked the .357 Magnum off his belt and thrust Nicole behind him in one unthought movement, himself between her and the danger beyond the door. Now, in this ultimate moment, it was all so simple. He must defend this woman with his life. Yes, how simple! How sublime! How profound!

A heavy fist pounded on the door. As he cocked the Magnum, a line from *Macbeth* ran crazily through his mind:

> Hear it not, Duncan; for it is a knell
> That summons thee to heaven or to hell.

Then Jarvis' equally heavy voice bellowed, "It's me. Kent. For Chrissake let me in. It's cold as hell out here."

He felt weak with relief and anticlimax even as he went to the door and threw back the bolt. "The cavalry has arrived," he said to Nicole in a silly voice. Jarvis stepped in quickly and closed the door again.

Jarvis looked like they felt: hyper, frazzled, almost feverish. "Jesus," he said, "am I glad we beat him here."

"Us too," said Ross. He was delighted.

But Nicole was almost angry. "What happened? We've been dying here, we expected you hours ago."

"The goddamn fog." His teeth were almost chattering, his eyes seemed to bulge with pent excitement. "We had to pay the pilot extra just to land the plane. Pea soup."

"Where are the others? You alone against my father—"

He gestured. "Out there—watching. Waiting." Then

402

he saw the still-cocked revolver forgotten in Ross's hand. "For Chrissake, gimme that thing before it goes off."

With a rather sheepish grin, Ross reversed the Magnum and put it butt-first into Jarvis' gloved hand.

# 49

The dense tule fog had caused a seven-car crash on I-5
north of Stockton, holding traffic up all the way back to
Manteca. No one killed, but it took the HP three hours
to clear the jackknifed big-rig that had started it all. It
was past three A.M. when Fletcher parked in the Terminous lot and walked out onto the deserted dock in the
fog. The air was cold and wet with mist, but clean: after
L.A., a benison. No houseboats moored conveniently
along the dock, but there was the pay phone on which he
had spoken with David.

David, where are you?

He went back to the car. Might as well drive around,
look for houseboats moored in the sloughs. If he saw
one, this time of year it would probably be theirs. Once
he found them, he would wait for first light to hail them:
he didn't want a jumpy Ross shooting him before he
could tell them it was over.


It was over very quickly.

3:28 A.M.: CBS declared Hawaii for Westergard.

3:30 A.M.: NBC awarded Mississippi to Westergard.

3:31 A.M.: The same network flashed it on the screen:
WESTERGARD ELECTED. From the suite, the governor could
hear the cheers and shouts down the hall in the situation
room.

3:33 A.M.: ABC did the same.

3:37 A.M.: CBS followed suit.

All the years, the work, the miles, the money, all of it had paid off. Westergard hugged his wife in the middle of a throng of leaping, yelling aides and friends. Only Jarvis wasn't there to share in the victory, and only Westergard really missed him. But then, Westergard had a lot riding on the endeavors of his new Secretary of State.

With first dawn, Jarvis started to feel better. He could begin to savor the experience rather than just feel nauseous at the abyss opened beneath his feet. So this was the way it felt. Now he knew.

"There he is!" he exclaimed.

From this grassy hillock the binoculars gave him a good view of the houseboat a quarter-mile away, and of the old blue Chevy that had just rolled to a stop on the levee a hundred yards beyond it. The door of the car opened and Fletcher got out into the uncertain light.

Jarvis put down the glasses and picked up the receiver of the car's modular phone. The two L.A. pimps recommended by Sharkey in Chicago opened their rear doors and got out, taking their guns from under their arms. Their stylish black ankle-length Jimmy'Z topcoats made them unreal in the wild marshland.

"Time to do it, babe," said the taller one. A knife scar from the corner of an eye back to an ear gave him the slight distortion of a clay sculpture left too long in the kiln.

The pretty one nodded, a coquette sipping champagne. "Time to earn our bread," he agreed in a voice just short of a lisp.

"This is Kent Jarvis, chief of staff for President-elect Garrett Westergard," said Jarvis into the car phone. "I need to be connected to the state police

405

immediately. . . ."

Fletcher stood on the road staring through the rising dawn at the houseboat. No sign of movement, but his hackles had risen. He sniffed the air. Nothing. Only marsh and wet. A fish broke water with a muffled, lazy splash out in the middle of the slough. Three mallards whistled by, angling up sharply as his tall unconcealed figure began moving again, slowly, precisely, in his slightly uneven way.

Eyes busy in all directions. Danger. Something wrong. He stopped on the levee directly above the boat, looking down.

"Nicole!"

No answer.

"Nicole! David! It's me. Fletcher."

No answer. No movement.

"I'm unarmed. I want to come aboard."

No answer. No flick of drape at window. No slight lapping of wave out away from the boat to show nervous movement by someone waiting tensely inside.

Bullet hole in the big windshield across the front of the cabin where the helm would be. Fired from inside.

Terribly wrong.

Fletcher moved. In a sudden unexpected burst he sprang with great agility from rock to rock to the deck of the houseboat. Over the past year he had learned to compensate for the shortened tendons in his left knee.

Another bullet through the door, the splinters also on the outside. Here he could smell the death.

He opened the door and went in. He feared no ambush. Nothing lived on this craft.

Ross was lying on his back in the middle of the room in the classic death pose, arms out and legs slightly splayed. He had been shot once in the chest. Heavy-caliber weapon. Stench of loosened bowels and bladder.

Fletcher couldn't let himself look at Nicole directly, not yet — only obliquely, as across the lens of an eyeglass one is polishing. Instead he went to one knee beside David's corpse and pressed two fingers into the inside of the wrist. Still the faintest hint of body heat. A few hours ago. He stood.

A Python .357 Magnum was lying on the floor near the body. Fletcher stopped, sniffed without touching. Cordite. He knelt again, peered. All chambers emptied.

Only then could he straighten up and bring himself to look at his daughter. Dear God. Sweet Jesus. He fell on his forearms and knees beside the corpse. The beautiful wood duck had been destroyed, its bright plumage soaked in blood and urine.

Nicole had been pounded backward up against the bulkhead beside the couch, had died in the same lax sprawl as her husband. Fingernails broken, what looked like dermis under two of them. Had tried to fight, unsuccessfully. Head over at an angle, eyes open and already glazing, tongue out one corner of her mouth.

The doe's head was wedged up against the bole of a burr oak and her eyes already were glazing. The protruding tongue was flecked with blood.

She had taken all the rest of the rounds. Stomach, with powder burns around it. Both breasts. Mons veneris. None of them necessary after the belly shot that had killed her.

Hatred. So much hatred, directed at her specifically.

The horror of her death thickened his throat and stifled his breathing. His own gunshot wounds ached intolerably. For a moment he was almost sick. He didn't touch her. He couldn't.

*Nicole.* Flesh of his flesh, blood of his blood. The last

remnant of the love he and Terry had shared, gone from this earth. The cold wind blew through him, the cold wind by which he lived while others died. Freezing things inside him, bringing other things to life. Icy coal beginning to burn in his gut, pity and remorse dying in his brain.

Look. Absorb. Feel.

This is your fault, Fletcher. They were pawns to one man's ambition and delusion, another man's hatred and envy, but you, Fletcher, you set it all in gear. You destroyed them by coming after them. See it. Know it. Absorb it. But never forget:

It was Westergard who gave the orders.

*Are you threatening me? Do you dare threaten*

It was Jarvis who carried them out.

*One of these days, he keeps going, he's going to kill someone.*

Jarvis had masturbated on her body after she was dead.

After she was dead, to then

Revulsion again gagged him. Time scraped by him. Man was neither fallen angel *nor* risen ape. *Fallen* ape.

He began to come out of it, his mind began to work again.

*Dead why?* And David, *why* — apart from the thrill of it?

Because their deaths in this place at this time could be used to set up Fletcher. Fletcher, legendary survivor. Fletcher, very hard to kill. But Nicole and David — they were easy to kill. And their deaths could be blamed on Fletcher. *Would* be blamed on Fletcher. And then . . .

Then kill Fletcher too. In a shoot-out. End of story. Everyone who knew about Gary Westergard's shame would be dead except for Jarvis — too compromised himself to ever be a threat, Jarvis could be his confidant without ever knowing what the President had done that drunken night so long ago to set things

The *President!*

408

And if, by some unimaginable chance, Fletcher should elude death at their hands, he then merely would be wolf's head for every shoot-first lawman in the country. Would be gunned down with no chance to speak . . .

The first shot splintered the bulkhead behind him.

Fletcher went flat on his belly, on elbows and knees snaked his way down the passageway toward the stern as the fusillade of slugs ricocheted above him. Distant police sirens. He reached up, unlocked the back door, shoved it open, eeled his way out onto the deck without even checking for danger.

Had to make his move *now* or not at all. Headfirst off the stern of the vessel like an otter sliding into a stream. Icy water closing over his head. He already knew where he was going.

Shit, trickier now, thought Jarvis. They'd planned to kill him just before the cops got there. Neat: three corpses, one gun. One killer, two victims.

He shot them, officers, then opened fire on us. We returned fire. He was hit and went down just before you got here. Yes, his own daughter. He had threatened her, threatened her husband. A year ago in northern Minnesota, some deer hunter shot him up pretty badly and he fixated on the idea it was his son-in-law in collusion with his daughter. Hopeless paranoia.

It would still work, but he had to make sure Fletcher was killed in this face-off with the police.

The uniformed deputy beside him used his bullhorn.

"WE KNOW YOU'RE IN THERE! COME OUT WITH YOUR HANDS UP! YOU HAVE THIRTY SECONDS!"

Twelve minutes later, after tear gas, they moved in.

Nobody here but us corpses.

"Over the stern and into the water, slick as an eel," reported one of the deputies.

"He's got to be bottled up in the slough," said another.

"Call for more men," said Jarvis. "Bring in helicopters. Two of the President-elect's staff have been murdered, and this has Mr. Westergard's highest priority."

Just at dusk, the sentry muskrat came out on top of his house to scold the last of the searchers. Two of them, mud-caked and weary, chased him off by sitting down on his home for a smoke before it was too dark to see a hand in front of your face.

Well sir, most likely he cramped up and drowned in the icy water. Or, less likely, was still somehow holed up on the little island or in the long rushes — but two dozen searchers had combed everything a dozen times. Or — not likely at all, with the helicopters patrolling all day the way they'd done — he'd made it to the main channel and away.

No sir, those scuba guys would find his body tomorrow.

One of them had a boom box; as they talked of Fletcher, it murmured its election litany. Nicole's political wisdom lived after her: go for the 270 electoral votes, not the 400-vote landslide. Westergard had taken 297. Arbor, 241.

In the popular vote, a bare plurality: 50.1 percent to 48.0 percent. Not a mandate, but a win.

A fragment of the winner's ebullient acceptance speech: "A small win, but our own. During the next four years we'll grow on you, America."

In an allied story, darkness interrupted the hunt for . . .

The searchers snuffed their butts in the mud and heaved themselves wearily to their feet for home and wives and dried-out dinners too long in the oven. During this evening's news, they had for a clock-tick been history.

Fletcher, buried up to his eyes and nose in the mud floor of the muskrat house, heard it all three feet above his head. He had swum directly here from the houseboat, mostly underwater, to dive down and ram and wriggle himself headfirst up through the glutinous mud and water to the air inside the house.

Then he had retreated within himself, had ceased to project his presence, as Old Charlie had taught him as a youth. Through the numbing hours of his vigil he made himself first into a fish, then a coot, then the muskrats themselves. He had become the loping gray wolf he had always longed to be, the wolf who had accompanied him up the burn — or through his hallucination — on that snowy Minnesota night a year ago.

Since he was no longer there, the muskrats returned. One sat with its tail curled unwittingly around his nose. He mouth-breathed until it moved. They were his protectors; the seasoned trackers brought in after midday ignored the muskrat house because its denizens were in residence — as they obviously would not be with an intruder present.

The searchers were gone. The light was gone. His protectors fled with his human return. Twenty minutes of tensing and untensing each muscle in turn finally let his body move from the icy mud encasing it. He came up beside the house, spent and blowing in the dark. His teeth chattered with the cold, but he knew the water would feel warmer than the air.

His car would have been impounded, of course. But some moored rowboat somewhere around would break loose and drift off through the night. Drift him miles from here.

Those scuba guys would come up empty tomorrow.

He could contact no one that he knew, ever. Nicole and David were gone. Victor would continue to thrive in his little clinic in Cochrane. Maria Horseman would emerge from the hospital and reshape her life. Admitting she was Daughter-of-Horseman instead of Maria Amore had been the first giant step.

As Fletcher finally had admitted who *he* was.

A hunter after all. A hunter pure and simple. With the hunt of a lifetime before him.

# 50

January 20. Inaugural day. In D.C., twenty degrees under milky skies. Wind chill, five above. It would be frigid on the football-size stage set up on the East Steps of the Capitol.

Not as frigid, however, as the heart of the President-elect. When he overrode security opposition to his plan for an open car, the Secret Service gave him the telegram just before the motorcade set out. The telegram had been sent from Idaho—but as they hastened to point out, there were planes from Idaho to the east coast every few hours. He went in a closed car.

The telegram read: CONGRATULATIONS TO A DEAD PRESIDENT.

It was signed simply, FLETCHER.

## FOR THE BEST OF THE WEST—
## DAN PARKINSON

**A MAN CALLED WOLF**                          (2794, $3.95)
Somewhere in the scorched southwestern frontier where civilization was just a step away from the dark ages, an army of hired guns was restoring the blood cult of an ancient empire. Only one man could stop them: John Thomas Wolf.

**THE WAY TO WYOMING**                          (2411, $3.95)
Matt Hazlewood and Big Jim Tyson had fought side by side wearing the gray ten years before. Now, with a bloody range war closing in fast behind and killers up ahead, they'd join up to ride and fight again in an untamed land where there was just the plains, the dust, and the heat— and the law of the gun!

**GUNPOWDER WIND**                          (2456, $3.95)
by Dan Parkinson and David Hicks
War was brewing between the Anglo homesteaders and the town's loco Mexican commander Colonel Piedras. Figuring to keep the settlers occupied with a little Indian trouble, Piedras had Cherokee warrior Utsada gunned down in cold blood. Now it was up to young Cooper Willoughby to find him before the Cherokees hit the warpath!

**THE WESTERING**                          (2559, $3.95)
There were laws against settin' a blood bounty on an innocent man, but Frank Kingston did it anyway, and Zack Frost found himself hightailin' it out of Indiana with a price on his head and a pack of bloodthirsty bounty hunters hot on his trail!

*Available wherever paperbacks are sold, or order direct from the Publisher. Send cover price plus 50¢ per copy for mailing and handling to Zebra Books, Dept. 3095, 475 Park Avenue South, New York, N.Y. 10016. Residents of New York, New Jersey and Pennsylvania must include sales tax. DO NOT SEND CASH.*

## MASTERWORKS OF MYSTERY
## BY MARY ROBERTS RINEHART!

**THE YELLOW ROOM** (2262, $3.50)

The somewhat charred corpse unceremoniously stored in the linen closet of Carol Spencer's Maine summer home set the plucky amateur sleuth on the trail of a killer. But each step closer to a solution led Carol closer to her own imminent demise!

**THE CASE OF JENNIE BRICE** (2193, $2.95)

The bloodstained rope, the broken knife—plus the disappearance of lovely Jennie Brice—were enough to convince Mrs. Pittman that murder had been committed in her boarding house. And if the police couldn't see what was in front of their noses, then the inquisitive landlady would just have to take matters into her own hands!

**THE GREAT MISTAKE** (2122, $3.50)

Patricia Abbott never planned to fall in love with wealthy Tony Wainwright, especially after she found out about the wife he'd never bothered to mention. But suddenly she was trapped in an extra-marital affair that was shadowed by unspoken fear and shrouded in cold, calculating murder!

**THE RED LAMP** (2017, $3.50)

The ghost of Uncle Horace was getting frisky—turning on lamps, putting in shadowy appearances in photographs. But the mysterious nightly slaughter of local sheep seemed to indicate that either Uncle Horace had developed a bizarre taste for lamb chops . . . or someone was manipulating appearances with a deadly sinister purpose!

**A LIGHT IN THE WINDOW** (1952, $3.50)

Ricky Wayne felt uncomfortable about moving in with her new husband's well-heeled family while he was overseas fighting the Germans. But she never imagined the depths of her in-laws' hatred—or the murderous lengths to which they would go to break up her marriage!